I0763266

The Magical Inventors

The Magical Inventors

Liz Kingett

This is a work of fiction. All names, characters, places and events are a product of the author's imagination. Any resemblance to real people, alive or dead, or to businesses, companies, events, institutions, or locations is purely coincidental.

First published in Australia in 2025

ISBN 978 0 646 71589 6

www.lizkingettstudios.com

In memory of Diana Wynne Jones,
whose stories inspired me to try writing my own

1

Hunting an Invention

Rose crept over the grass, her bare toes damp from the recent rain. The moon broke through the clouds as the wind picked up, illuminating the tops of the trees before ducking out of sight. Rose glanced around her, searching for a place to hide, and came to a halt beside the trunk of a sprawling elm.

To her left, a garden shed stood partly hidden between two tall shrubs and the hanging branches of a gum tree. She made directly for it, pulling the rusty door open just enough to squeeze inside and wincing at the groan of the metal as she heaved it shut. She hesitated, hoping the sound hadn't given her away, but all was quiet except for the chirping of the crickets in the bushland that enveloped the grounds, and she relaxed a little, turning to the space behind her.

Breathing in the scent of damp earth and mildew, she waited for her eyes to adjust to the darkness. Cobwebs hung from the roof, trailing between the silhouette of a lawn mower and a bulky object covered in an old, yellowed sheet.

She stepped over the gardening tools that littered the floor and the workbench beside her, working her way toward the opposite wall. A small window let in enough of the fading light outside to illuminate the layer of dust that had collected over everything. Tiny particles flew into the air as she passed through the room, catching the light as they slowly settled.

Deciding that this was as good a hiding place as any, she crouched behind the sheet and waited, watching the light on the back of the door waver. A sudden gust of wind sent the branches of the overhanging tree tossing and swaying, scratching against the roof of the shed and casting wild shadows on the walls.

It wasn't long before the unmistakable sound of footsteps could be heard approaching her hiding place. The door creaked open and a shadowy figure stepped inside, closing the door hastily behind them and throwing the room back into darkness.

Rose sank further down behind the old sheet, accidentally stepping on it as she retreated, disturbing the dust. It swirled into the air, tickling her nose. Holding her breath, she waited for it to settle, but it was no good.

She sneezed, burying her face in her hands to stifle the noise, and then cringed, not daring to move. The trees had fallen still, the eucalyptus boughs hanging limp in the night air. Even the crickets seemed to have stopped chirping.

A scuffling sound broke the silence and Rose tensed, looking over her shoulder as a shape loomed out of the darkness. A hand grabbed her arm and a voice rang out.

"Gotcha!"

Rose jumped up, startled, and then relaxed, brushing

the dust off her clothes and cursing her own clumsiness.

"All right, you found me."

She went to the door and stepped out onto the grass with the shadowy form of her younger sister behind her. Mary grinned at Rose triumphantly.

"You were lucky, that's all," Rose told her, shoving the shed door shut.

"Looks like I was lucky twice in a row, then," Mary teased.

"Have you found Matt already?"

Mary nodded, looking pleased with herself.

"He was hiding up a tree, but he fell out, so he was easy enough to find."

"Is he OK?" Rose asked with a frown.

Mary shrugged.

"Yeah, he's fine. He went straight back up into the tree." She looked over at the house, outlined against the sky. "What's the time?"

"It's half past eight," said Rose, checking the phone in her pocket. "We'll have to go inside soon."

A gust of wind blew her hair back from her face, fresh drops of rain striking her skin as she looked up at the dark sky. She searched the trees for her brother and found him climbing in the towering elm that grew in the middle of the yard. Working his way up into the tree house, he perched in the centre of the spreading branches, grinning down at them.

"Hey, come up here!"

Rose and Mary ran across the lawn towards the tree as thunder rolled in the distance. The yard was a green expanse, dotted with gum trees. It sloped gently for half an acre, gradually blending with the bushland that surrounded them.

Their German Shepherd bounded over and Rose rubbed his ears fondly before climbing the rope ladder up to the tree house. Mary did the same and the dog whined, looking up at them from the base of the tree.

"Sorry, Cocoa," Mary called down. "You know you can't come up here."

Cocoa paced around the tree for a moment before going to dig in the garden bed beside the house instead. Rose pulled a bean bag over from the corner and settled herself down on it comfortably, listening to the soft pattering of the rain on the leaves around her.

The tree house was spacious and boasted several other rooms higher up, which could be entered by climbing the rope ladders that wound up the thick, twisting branches. Their parents had made the tree house for them years ago, using magic to keep it warm, dry and protected from the wind.

She breathed in the fresh, clean scent of the rain, watching Cocoa tear up Mum's favourite flowers as Mary began to talk at top speed, reciting everything that had happened at school that day. Rose's insides squirmed uncomfortably. It had been a bad day, even by her standards, and she didn't feel much like reliving it. She half-listened to Mary's chattering as she pulled an assortment of objects used for making magical inventions out of her pocket.

She'd gone through her parents' box of spare parts

earlier, looking for anything she might be able to use, picking out a collection of glass fragments that shone from within, a handful of grey lumps that appeared to be solid metal, but could be fashioned into different shapes like putty, and a tiny bottle of clear liquid with a shimmering, pearly sheen, which bestowed a deep sense of peace and contentment on anyone who handled it.

After some thought, she'd decided to add most of the parts from her latest invention to the collection, too, hoping she could find another use for them. She arranged them on the floor in front of her and let her imagination wander, waiting for inspiration while her sister prattled on beside her.

"Are you making something?" said Mary, pausing to draw breath. She pointed at the familiar pieces and her face fell. "Aren't they from the Diviner you just finished? Why'd you take it apart? I liked that one. Mum and Dad said it was the best invention you've made so far."

Rose sighed and pressed the metallic putty between her fingers.

"It didn't turn out right. I want to make something better this time, but I haven't decided what yet."

Matt gave her a look of stunned disbelief.

"You're joking, right? There was nothing wrong with it! You're just letting those kids at school make you feel like rubbish because they hate magic!"

Rose opened her mouth to protest at this, but Matt continued, his expression changing to one of exasperation.

"That was an awesome invention! And now you've

ruined it! It could see people's real thoughts and intentions, couldn't it? You should've used it on the kids at school!"

"It's got nothing to do with the other kids!" Rose lied, heat spreading across her cheeks.

"Well then, stop pulling apart all your best work and be happy with what you've made for once."

Rose glared at him and he rolled his eyes.

"You care too much what other people think."

"I wish I had your confidence," she shot back.

Mary gave Matt a quelling look and picked up a glass piece.

"This is pretty. You know, if you're not sure what to make, maybe you should look in the library? I bet there's something fun in one of the spell books."

"Yeah, I think I will," replied Rose, grateful for the change of subject. "If Mum and Dad will let me near the library, that is."

She gathered up her invention pieces and returned them to her pocket. Bending her head down, she peered through the branches of the tree, trying to see into the library where her parents were working.

"I wonder what they're doing? They've been in there all day."

"I heard them talking about Grandpa's new project in the kitchen yesterday," said Mary. "Mum was on the phone and I think she said she'd check something for him. I didn't hear what. So they could be helping him with whatever he's working on."

"Must be," agreed Matt, brushing an ant off his arm.

"But that's not how Grandpa usually works," countered Rose. "He likes to do all of the research for a new project himself."

She stared distractedly out of the window and wound a lock of her long blonde hair around a finger, her mind going over the events of the last few weeks.

"It's weird. Mum and Dad keep saying they're not making anything, even though they're acting like they are. But if they were helping Grandpa, they'd be at his house or working in the invention room, wouldn't they? They never work in the library."

"I know," replied Mary. "I wish they'd just tell us what they're doing. We could help!"

Rose nodded, but Matt still seemed unsure.

"I think it's something official, so we might not be allowed to," he said after a pause. "I've heard them talking, too. Those men who came to see Mum and Dad the other day said they worked for the government. They must want help with something magical. Mum and Dad's project might have nothing to do with Grandpa at all."

Rose stared out at the rain as she thought about this, feeling put out by her parents' refusal to allow herself or her siblings to help with their work, and hating how distant her parents had become since Grandpa had begun his latest creation.

"It could be some kind of protective invention," she said eventually. "And that's probably why they can't tell us anything. They have to keep it secret."

Matt bent down to peek into the library, too.

"All I can see are stacks of books."

Rose moved over to get a better view. The rain made it difficult to see, but she could just make out a cluttered room filled with pile after towering pile of books and papers. Dad sat at the desk in the middle, partially obscured by boxes of documents.

Rose watched as he put his book down and yawned, running his fingers through his blond hair. Mum stood in front of a bookshelf, sorting through a handful of loose pages. With a scowl, Matt leaned against the wall of the tree house and folded his arms across his chest.

"I get that they can't tell just anyone what they're doing, but I don't see why they have to hide it from us! Even if we can't help, it's not like we'd tell anyone anything. We're not stupid!"

He glanced at Rose and bit his lip, his expression sheepish.

"I hid behind one of the shelves in the library yesterday so I could listen to what they were saying, but Mum caught me when my watch started beeping."

Rose and Mary laughed.

"I thought she'd get mad, but she just pushed me out into the hall," he admitted with a grin. "I asked her what they were looking for, but she told me to go downstairs and get ready for school."

"Have you gotten anything out of them yet?" Mary asked Rose. Rose shook her head.

"No. They keep telling me it's nothing to worry about."

Soon lights came on in the house, glowing brightly

in the gloom. Rose joined in with Matt and Mary as they made wild guesses about what Grandpa's invention could be, the rain drumming on the roof and almost drowning out their voices. Their theories gradually became more and more far-fetched until the library window was thrown open and Mum stuck her head outside.

"I want you all inside, please!"

"But it's not even late yet!" Matt protested.

"Inside!" Mum shouted over the rain, closing the window with a snap.

Grumbling, they made their way down the rope ladder and over to the house, splashing through the puddles that had formed all over the yard and shivering as the rain drenched their clothes.

Cocoa shook himself off under the veranda and Matt followed suit, making Rose and Mary throw their arms up in front of their faces. Rose dried herself off with a spell and they all trooped into the dining room.

The two-storey house was old and slightly shabby, with worn steps and a weather-beaten façade, but it was comfortable, clean, and tidy, and it had everything they needed. A veranda ran along the back of the house, lined with colourful garden beds, and the trees overhanging the gravel driveway made a high green archway. It stood back from the road in the Australian countryside, out of sight of the nearest houses but still close enough to the city of Armidale to have only a short, ten-minute drive to its centre.

When Rose had been very young, she and her

parents had settled in a crowded, busy street in Sydney. Everyone had been happy until Rose began learning how to use a travel spell on small objects, and the neighbours became tired of balls, toys and anything else she could get her hands on appearing unexpectedly in their letterboxes and backyards, on their doorsteps, and occasionally in their dinner.

Rose soon discovered that she was different from everyone else when she started school, and she quickly grew used to being alone. It had been a relief to hear that they were moving to the Northern Tablelands, away from the noise and pollution. She loved the open spaces and never got tired of looking out of her bedroom window to see bushland stretching away into the distance. Nearly ten years had gone by, and still she didn't regret leaving the bustle of her old home.

Gazing around the house appreciatively, Rose walked through the kitchen and living room with Matt, Mary and Cocoa trailing after her. She ran up the narrow, creaking stairs and down the hall, where rows of family photos and snapshots of places they'd visited on holiday filled every available space on the walls.

She opened the door at the end of the hall and entered the library to find both of her parents at the desk, immersed in books, letters and reports. They glanced up as Mary shut the door behind her. Rose stepped carefully between the tottering piles, reading the titles of some of the volumes as she passed. She glanced around the room, taking in the uncharacteristic mess.

Along each wall, the bookshelves that were usually

filled to bursting point were almost empty in places, leaving the room looking strangely bare. The documents, normally stacked in boxes on the floor when there was no space left on the shelves, had been replaced by a jumbled mass of papers that had spilled over, taking up a large portion of the available floor space.

Rose stared for a second, wondering what piece of magic could be so important or so complex that her parents had been forced to tear apart the entire library for information.

Mum pushed back her light brown curls and closed her book, yawning and rubbing her eyes, and Rose suddenly noticed how pale and stressed her parents looked.

"You've been up here all day," she said after a moment, hoping for a useful answer.

Matt gave her the thumbs up, but Mum said nothing, putting her book back on the shelf and pulling out a report instead. Rose tried again.

"What are you looking for?"

She turned to the nearest stack of books and journals. One of the largest volumes was titled *Most Notable Magical People and Inventions of the Century* in bright red lettering. She thumbed through it while Matt and Mary looked at their parents eagerly.

"Just something we've been asked to help with, that's all," said Dad, opening yet another book and scanning the first page before tossing it aside. "It's not something you three need to worry about."

Mary's face fell into a pout and Matt groaned.

"Can't you just tell us what you're doing?" he pleaded. "I'm fourteen and Rose is sixteen! Whatever it is, I'm sure we can handle it!"

"We've been through this already," said Mum. "We're not allowed to tell anyone. It's part of the contract we signed."

Matt gave Rose a meaningful look at this.

"And besides," Mum continued, "Mary's only nine, and it wouldn't be fair if we told you and not her."

Matt groaned again and Mum looked stern as she began putting books back onto the shelves.

"That's all I'm telling you."

Matt opened his mouth to protest, but Dad interrupted him.

"That's enough, now. We'll tell you what's going on when we can, but we're not saying anything until then."

Matt glowered.

"Come on, let's go downstairs," said Mum with a smile. "You can help me get dinner ready."

Disappointed but not discouraged, Rose, Matt and Mary followed her back down to the kitchen, which also served as the dining room on one side. It was Rose's job to clear the table while Matt and Mary set the plates and cutlery out. Mum emerged from the kitchen half an hour later, her arms full of dishes.

"Would one of you mind running up to the library and telling your dad to come down?"

"I'll do it," offered Rose, keen for another chance to inspect the books her parents had been reading.

She turned into the living room and had begun to

climb the stairs when a sharp knock sounded on the door behind her. She went to the door instead and opened it to find a tall man with black hair and a thin face standing in the doorway, his plain but well-tailored clothes dry despite the rain.

"Hi, Rose. Are your parents free? I've got news for them."

"Sure." Rose stood back to let him in. "Mum's in the kitchen and I'm just on my way upstairs to get Dad now. I'll tell him you're here."

"Thanks," said the man, hanging up his jacket.

Rose climbed the stairs two at a time and went back down the hall to where Dad was now poring over an old newspaper clipping.

"Dinner's ready, Dad. And Dave's here to see you. He says he's got news."

"OK," said Dad, scratching the stubble on his chin. His blue eyes were puffy and red-rimmed with tiredness. "Where is he?"

"In the living room."

"All right, I'll be down in a minute."

Dad examined the newspaper clipping for another moment and then tucked it into a book, placing it on top of the nearest pile. He stood up and stretched, looking ruefully around the room before following Rose downstairs.

Rose tried to ignore the anxious knot that had formed in the pit of her stomach. Dave didn't visit often, but whenever he did, the atmosphere was tense. Mum and Dad would shut themselves away for hours, speaking in hushed voices, and when they emerged, their faces were always stern and worried.

"Hi, Dave," said Dad, shaking the man's hand. "Rose said you've got news for us. I hope it's good?"

Dave shook his head as Dad led him into the living room.

"I'm afraid not. There seems to have been a problem." He stopped and glanced at Rose, who was still standing at the foot of the stairs, listening.

"Sorry," she said, tiptoeing into the kitchen to get her mother.

"Hi, Charlotte," said Dave as Mum appeared, carrying a bowl of mashed potatoes.

"Has something happened?" asked Mum warily.

Dave nodded. Mum turned around to find Rose, Matt and Mary gathered in the kitchen doorway, all listening intently. She handed Rose the mashed potatoes.

"We're just going upstairs for a moment. Stay down here and eat dinner, please."

She watched with an amused expression as they sat down at the table and started eating mutinously. Giving them one last warning look, she headed for the stairs, speaking to Dave in an undertone. Rose waited until their footsteps had disappeared down the hall and a soft click announced the closing of a door.

She glanced across the table at her brother and sister and put her knife and fork down with a clatter, pushing her chair back and running across the living room and up the stairs with the others at her heels. Racing down the hall on tiptoe, they squeezed and pushed until each of them could hear Dave's voice through the library door.

"Well, she's definitely up to something," he was saying quietly. "We saw her hanging around his room in the Archives, but she disappeared before we could get at her. As far as we know, she didn't get inside, but I'd feel better if we knew for sure."

"Well, we thought she'd try something like that," Rose heard her father say. "And she didn't take anything? Nothing's missing?"

"We went through everything in the room and checked all the records," said Dave. "Nothing's gone, but that doesn't mean she didn't get in. I've got people watching the area in case she comes back. They'll message me if they see her."

"Good," said Mum in a satisfied tone. "Have you found out who she is yet?"

"She's one of the junior Archivists. I can't say I'm surprised."

"Yes, if she works there, she'll be one of the first people to know when Dad finishes the Fragmenter and registers it," Mum continued. "At least that explains how she seems to know about everything he does, as soon as he does it."

"But is she doing this on her own, or is someone else helping her?" asked Dad. "What about Miranda and the other Archivists?"

"Well, we've been wondering about that, too," said Dave, "and it seems like she's in it alone. There are only two junior employees in the Archives at the moment and she's one of them …"

"What does she do there?"

"She regulates the registration and documentation of magical objects. But she's also responsible for destroying inventions that are unsafe or illegal, so she'll have access to all the information she wants, whenever she wants it. She seems to have been using the excuse that she's just checking Peter's progress reports to make sure the Fragmenter complies with the regulations. It makes it easy for her to interfere. All she has to do is find some little detail Peter's missed somewhere in his documentation and then claim he's broken the rules and confiscate the invention. So he'll have to be careful."

"I'll make sure he's got all the paperwork right," replied Mum. "It's the invention itself I'm most worried about. Dad loves pushing the boundaries, but even he doesn't like taking them this far."

"How's the Fragmenter going? It would help us a lot if it was finished soon."

"It's been a few days since we've heard from him," said Mum. "We'll probably check on him tonight, but the last time I spoke to him he said he was almost done. He was just doing some final tests. There were a couple of unexpected things that showed up in the invention's reactions, so he was adjusting the parameters. It's slowed things down a bit, but it can't be long now, I'm sure."

"He was hoping to have it finished about midday tomorrow," added Dad.

"Well, he should have set up some protection by

now, then. What has he done?" asked Dave. "And what else can we do to help him that won't get in the way of his tests?"

"We gave him our Shield. It should be more than enough on its own, but we gave him a few other things, too. Just in case."

"Good."

The room was silent for a moment, and Rose waited as the clock downstairs chimed. Mum's voice was quiet when she finally spoke.

"The sooner this is over, the better. I hate the suspense."

"It won't be long now," said Dave. "Just keep to the plan and everything should be fine. It nearly always works out, but it's best to be prepared, so we'll give you as much protection as we've got. Remember that she could be targeting you, too, not just your dad. Have you told your kids anything?"

"Not yet. It's been hard keeping all of this from them," said Mum, a smile in her voice. "They still haven't given up asking us about what we're doing. I've caught them sneaking in here and going through the books when they think we're not looking."

Dave laughed.

"I don't blame them! I'd be curious too."

There was the buzzing sound of a phone and a pause.

"Sorry," muttered Dave. "I'd better check this."

Rose pressed her ear harder to the door.

"It's one of the guys at the Archives," Dave said, his

voice tense. "He's just seen her heading for your dad's room again. If we're quick, we might be able to catch her this time!"

A chair was pushed back.

"What can we do to help?" said Dad in a rush.

"Don't worry about that. You just concentrate on helping Peter get the Fragmenter finished."

"But there must be something we can do," insisted Mum. "We could at least track her and find out what she's up to?"

"Well, if you really want to help, I suppose it would make things easier for us …"

There was a short moment of silence before Dave spoke again.

"Watch to see if she gets in; if she does, do what you can to stop her. I'd better get down there. I'll see you tomorrow at Peter's place."

Two more chairs were pushed back and the voices came closer to the door. Rose, Matt and Mary scrambled to get out of the way, hurrying back down to the dining room and trying not to make a sound. Rose's thoughts were uneasy. What was Grandpa making? She'd never had any doubts about this project of his before, but now she felt unsure.

She threw herself into her chair and began shovelling down mashed potato and peas. Dad said goodbye to Dave and closed the door against the rain.

"What's going on?" Matt asked innocently as Mum and Dad entered the room, their expressions troubled.

"Just sorting something out, that's all," said Mum,

glancing back at the front door in a preoccupied kind of way. "But I do think we should talk to you all later tonight."

She looked at Dad, who nodded. Rose dropped her fork.

"We're not telling you about the invention yet!" Mum added, seeing their eager expressions.

Rose tried to act as though she hadn't overheard the conversation in the library.

"So you *are* working on an invention, then! I knew it!"

Mum let out a sigh of frustration, realising she'd let something slip.

"*We're* not working on anything, like I keep telling you. The invention isn't ours." She sat down and thought for a moment, clearly trying to find a way of explaining without giving anything else away.

"We just need to go through what we should all do tomorrow if somebody turns up," she said slowly.

Mary stuck out her chin. "Why?"

"We've got to get back to work," said Dad, a note of urgency in his voice. "You kids finish dinner, please."

Rose suppressed a grin as her parents left the room.

"Ha! Told you it had something to do with an invention!" said Mary jubilantly as soon as they were alone. Matt rolled his eyes and speared a piece of carrot on the end of his fork.

"Well, what else would it be? That's our job. We invent things."

"You didn't seem so sure when we were in the tree

h-," began Mary defensively.

"Shh!" Rose flapped her hand at the other two as Dad reappeared on the stairs, carrying a handful of small objects Rose recognised as inventions.

"Does anyone know where the Tracker is? I can't find it upstairs," he said, leaning around the doorframe.

"I've got it," said Rose, rummaging in her other pocket.

The Tracker was small and diamond-shaped, with a heavy, gold-plated base and slender loops on either side. Inside each loop was a tiny peg, wrapped with delicate white and gold threads that followed the inside rim of the invention and framed a metal slider that ran from left to right along its centre.

"Do you mind if I borrow it for a while?" Dad asked. "You were studying the spells on it, weren't you?"

Rose shrugged and held it out to him.

"I've finished with it. I was hoping to get some new ideas, but I haven't come up with anything I'm happy with."

"Sometimes it takes a while to think of new designs," said Dad encouragingly, taking the Tracker.

Rose stood in the doorway to watch as he settled himself in front of the coffee table. He moved Rose's half-finished maths homework to one side and set the inventions out on the other. Placing the Tracker in front of him, he moved the slider to the correct position and began the difficult task of tuning the threads to the frequency that matched what he was tracking, turning the tiny pegs until the invention began to hum.

Dad stared at it blankly, guiding it and concentrating on whatever it was showing him while Mum rushed down the stairs, her feet clattering on the steps.

"We need to know exactly what she's up to or we won't be able to do anything about her," she said, turning into the living room.

Dad nodded at the Tracker. Comprehension dawned on Mum's face and she sat on the edge of the sofa, waiting patiently.

"She found a way in this time," Dad muttered, still staring at the little invention. Mum made a sound of irritation.

"I thought she might. What's she doing?"

"She's looking through the files," said Dad, blinking several times as though coming out of a trance. He searched for something on the table. "We're going to need your old Breaker in case she tries to block us. You didn't bring it downstairs, did you?"

"We gave it to Dad, remember?"

"Oh, that's right." He shifted the other inventions around on the table uncertainly. "But this won't work without it. She's bound to try and stop us."

"If we go to get it, we might miss her. Maybe we should just try to make do without it."

"I don't think we can," replied Dad. "And this will probably be the last chance we get to catch her before they all try to get at your dad. It would help if we could get her out of the way."

Mum bit her lip uneasily.

"It might work if we go get it and then come straight

back. The others are already on their way, too, I suppose, and we need to check on Dad anyway. He should have almost finished his tests by now."

Rose stood up straighter at these words, and hope flared in her chest for the first time since Grandpa had closeted himself away to work on his mysterious invention. Mary, who had been following her parents' conversation from the dining room, sprang up from her chair and rushed into the living room.

"We're coming, too!" she insisted, coming to stand beside Dad. "We haven't seen Grandpa in ages!"

"Darling, it's not safe for you there at the moment," said Mum, as she and Dad got ready to use a travel spell. "We're only going to be gone a few minutes. We can go and see him together when all of this is over and everything's back to normal."

Mary sat back down, looking close to tears.

"Please, can we come? We'll all be good, I promise!"

"We haven't got time to argue about this," said Mum. She turned to Dad. "If we don't go now, we'll miss our chance."

"Stay inside the house and you'll be safe," Dad instructed. "We'll be back in a minute."

Their forms blurred and then faded like wisps of smoke until they were gone, leaving Rose, Matt and Mary staring at each other across the empty living room. Rose sighed, feeling strangely isolated.

"I'm going, too," declared Matt, beginning a travel spell of his own. Rose's hand darted out to take hold of him before he could disappear.

"Matt, no! Wait! I think we should stay here."

"Come on, Rose!" protested Matt, pulling free from her grip. "Grandpa's bound to tell us something!"

"Mum and Dad'll be angry," Mary warned him.

"They said it wasn't safe at Grandpa's, and you know they wouldn't say that if it wasn't true," urged Rose. "Didn't you hear anything they said in the library?"

Matt rolled his eyes and took a step back, out of Rose's reach.

"You always worry too much! How bad can it be?"

"But what if it really is dangerous? Matt, don't -"

But Matt wasn't listening. He finished the spell and disappeared before Rose could stop him. She let her hand fall, muttering an oath under her breath.

"I'd better go and get him before Mum and Dad explode," she told Mary.

She closed her eyes and held the spell in her mind, wrapping it around her like an invisible blanket. It took her longer to appear and disappear than it did her parents, but several seconds later she opened her eyes to find her grandfather's gravel driveway coming into focus.

Matt was already marching up to the small, white house between the bushes and garden beds. It was dark and silent. There was a crunching sound of feet landing on gravel and she turned to see Mary slowly appearing behind her.

"Hey, no fair! I'm not staying home if you're all going!" she said, hurrying to catch up.

Rose threw her hands up in frustration and turned back, watching helplessly as Matt strode past the garage.

Rose caught up with her brother as he reached the garden, and she took hold of him once more, attempting to stop him before they came into view of the front steps, but it was too late. Dad stretched out a hand to open the front door and then glanced back to see all three children approaching the house.

"What are you doing?" he demanded. "We told you to stay at home! It's not safe for you here!"

Rose stopped grappling with Matt and he took off up the driveway. Feeling guilty now, Rose hung her head, seeing that Mum was starting to get her stressed look again.

"I just wanted to see -" began Matt, but Dad cut across him, looking angrier than Rose had ever seen him.

"No, go back! You know we're not allowed to show you anything!"

"We'll meet you all back at home," repeated Mum.

Rose waited for her parents to open the front door and step inside before beginning a travel spell back home. Her surroundings began to fade, and her eyes lingered on the house briefly before coming to a stop on Mum and Dad, standing transfixed in the doorway.

Something was wrong. The door swung shut with a crash, and she saw that the curtains over the front window were torn and hanging in shreds. Rose cancelled her spell hastily. Matt and Mary reached the door at the same time and threw it open. They, too, stopped just inside the room, and Rose ran the rest of the way, leaping up the shallow stone steps in front of the house as dread washed over her.

She opened the door for a third time and fell over something solid on the doorstep, landing on her hands and knees, sprawled over the shadowy remains of a half-demolished armchair. Her heart sank as she stared around at the rest of the room. There was nothing but debris everywhere she looked.

2

A Narrow Escape

Rose got to her feet, unable to believe her eyes. Everything in the room had been destroyed. Light from the street flooded into the room, illuminating the wreckage, and Rose's horrified eyes travelled from the smashed television to the antique clock that had fallen from the wall, finally settling on the demolished sofa oozing stuffing from several long gashes.

"No!"

Mum grasped the doorframe for support, the colour draining from her face. She rushed into the dark hallway without another word. Dad ran after her, leaping over what was left of a side table and calling her back.

Leaving Matt and Mary standing shocked and silent by the door, Rose scrambled up and hurried after her parents, attempting to stifle the panic rising up inside her. She stepped over the fallen photos that had once lined the walls, searching wildly in every room she passed, but the house was quiet except for the occasional crunch of glass and wood beneath her feet.

Both bedrooms were empty, the bedclothes thrown over the floor. The dresser and cupboards were open, too, the drawers pulled out and their contents strewn over the room as though someone had been searching for something. The only thing still intact was a plain wooden door at the end of the hall.

It was dented and heavily scratched. Mum put her hand on the doorknob and turned it, but the door remained firmly shut. She stepped back and removed the spells guarding it. This time it swung open, allowing Mum to enter.

Rose edged in after her, her heart hammering in her chest. It was the only room in the house that hadn't been demolished. Shelves crowded with inventions covered all of the available space on the walls. A bookshelf beside the window displayed a collection of aged, leather-bound books, and a sturdy oak workbench stood in the centre of the room, littered with tools and materials.

Sobbing, Mum whirled around and began to search the house a second time. Rose stumbled her way back down the hall to the living room where Matt and Mary still stood, looking dumbfounded. Mum reappeared minutes later, tears streaming down her face.

"I can't believe it! They've taken him!"

She collapsed onto the ruined sofa. Rose hesitated, not knowing what to say. She went over to her mother and wrapped her arms around her in silence. Mum continued to sob, her head in her hands.

"How could this happen? He had the Shield! And all of the extra protection everyone's put over the house! How can it be possible?"

Dad appeared in the hall a second later, ashen-faced and carrying a twisted lump of metal and broken glass that Rose recognised as the Shield. She stared at the invention. What could have damaged it so badly? Dad turned the broken invention over in his hand.

"It would've taken strong magic to kill this. Something must have gone wrong while Peter was testing the Fragmenter. It's missing, too."

They gazed around the devastated room in silence until Mum got to her feet and headed for the hall again. She wiped her eyes with a trembling hand.

"We can't leave his other inventions here. People might try to steal them. If we take them with us, they'll be safe."

"If the person who took Grandpa couldn't get past the invention room door, I don't think anyone else will," said Rose faintly. "It looks like they had a good try."

"All it would take is for them to find out what spells he has over it and it wouldn't stop them getting in anymore," said Mum, as they helped her gather up the inventions.

Rose took as many as she could hold. A glint of metal caught her eye as she returned to the living room and she glanced down to see something golden peeking out of the debris on the floor.

"Grandpa's pocket watch!"

Rearranging the inventions in her arms, she stretched out a hand awkwardly to pick it up. The gold case was bent and the glass over the face was cracked as though it had been trodden on. She brushed the dust off the old watch and slipped it into her jacket pocket.

A much smaller object brushed her fingers as she

searched the floor for anything else that might be valuable, and she picked it up with curiosity. It was ornate, vaguely butterfly-shaped and appeared to be solid silver, but it reflected subtle glimmers of yellow, green, blue and pink as she held it up to the lamplight.

"What's that?" asked Matt, coming over for a closer look. Rose could only shake her head.

"I don't know. It doesn't look much like an invention, but I'll keep it safe anyway."

Using another travel spell, she reappeared in her own living room and placed the inventions on the coffee table. Her parents materialised behind her seconds later with Matt and Mary and deposited the rest of Grandpa's creations onto the pile. Mum cleared her throat and picked up her phone.

"We need to tell Dave what's happened. He's with the police, he needs to know."

"I'll call him," said Dad, pulling out his own phone and dialling.

Rose hesitated, unsure what to do with herself. Tears streamed down Mary's face and her shoulders shook as she set the last of the inventions onto the table. Matt wrapped an arm around her, shock and confusion still etched on his face.

Rose couldn't bring herself to listen to her parents' anxious voices as they spoke to Dave on the phone, describing the scene they'd just left. Deciding she wanted some time alone, she ran upstairs to her bedroom and closed the door before anyone could call her back.

Sitting down on the end of the bed, she stared at her knees unseeingly. Soon she heard the crunch of gravel as a car pulled up in the driveway, and she stuck her head out of the window in time to see two policemen entering the house.

She gazed out over the treetops, her mind racing. Who could have done this to Grandpa? She wished she knew more about what he was making and the people who wanted it.

Her fingers grasped the old watch in her jacket pocket and she pulled it out, tears welling up in her eyes again as she looked at the familiar object. Running her thumb over the glass, it took her a second to realise that the hands were moving in the wrong direction, drifting aimlessly back and forth around the clock face.

"That's weird," she muttered. She had never seen the watch do that before …

She fixed her gaze on the broken glass and the pieces rearranged themselves, melting back together seamlessly and erasing the scratches. The case bent back into shape and fitted itself over the watch. Then she turned her attention to the hands.

Trying all of the usual repairing spells, she pictured in her mind what she wanted to happen, using all of her willpower to make the magic work, but the hands seemed to want to keep moving the wrong way. Nonplussed, she placed the watch back in her jacket and hung it over her chair, deciding she'd have another go at fixing it in the morning.

It was getting late when she became aware of her

surroundings. The room was dark and she could hear her parents calling her from downstairs. Taking a tissue from her desk drawer, she hastily wiped her eyes and descended to the kitchen, where Mum handed her a mug of hot chocolate.

Rose breathed in the comforting scent, wrapping her hands around the mug despite the heat. Mum gave her a small smile and they joined the others in the living room, where Matt and Mary sat huddled together on the sofa, staring miserably at the television.

Rose curled up beside them with a book, hoping to distract herself for an hour or two. Several pages in, however, her mind began to wander, and she sighed, putting the book back down.

"What are we going to do about Sunday?" said Mum from one of the armchairs, her face still pale and drawn.

"Sunday?"

Rose looked at her mother, confused.

"The Magicked Masterclass," Mum reminded her. "Magical people from across the state are going to be here to talk to your grandpa about his work."

Rose groaned. She'd forgotten about the masterclass. Dad stirred his tea, looking troubled.

"Dave wants it to go ahead if possible. We know most of the details about what your dad was working on and we'll need help figuring out where to go from here, so I guess we'll have to do what we can."

Rose grimaced, picking at the tattered cover of her book. She attempted to watch the late-night news with the others, but she couldn't keep her mind from wandering back to Grandpa's ruined house, reliving the scene over and over again. Discontented, she gave up and decided she might as well go to bed.

She had just stretched out a hand to turn her bedroom light off when an idea struck her. Wondering why she hadn't thought of it sooner, she raced down to the now dark and empty living room and snatched up three of the inventions Mum and Dad had used earlier.

The first was the Tracker. The second was a Connector, an adaptor-like invention with thick grey cords protruding from each end, and the third was a tarnished brass object called a Scope. Greatly resembling a metronome, the Scope was used to find things.

The spells for locating and tracking were very different, which meant that the Tracker was only useful once you knew where a person was. It contained no locating spells, so it needed a starting point to work from before it could follow someone.

The Scope was the opposite. As long as you knew what you were looking for it could find it, but it was unable to track a person or object unless you used it continuously. However, if she were to link the two inventions, she would be able to both find and follow whatever she wanted.

She activated all three and made sure the Connector was in contact with the other two. Doing her best to tune the Tracker to the right frequency, she closed her eyes and allowed a picture of Grandpa to form in her mind, waiting impatiently as the Scope began to search, ticking in the darkness like a clock.

Both inventions had been working for only a moment or so when they stopped and fell silent. Surprised that it had taken so little time, Rose waited expectantly to be shown where Grandpa was. She sat bolt upright, drumming her fingers on her knee, but no picture or scene formed in her mind.

She placed a fingertip on the Scope instead, hoping the contact might help. A surge of energy rippled through the invention as she touched it, and she pulled her hand away with a yelp, feeling like she'd stuck her finger into an electrical socket.

"That felt like a blocking spell," she muttered. "A strong one, too."

Perplexed, she disconnected the inventions and leaned back into the sofa. Wondering what would happen if she used her own magic to find Grandpa instead of relying on the Scope, she closed her eyes and let her mind wander. When she was calm again, she concentrated on her grandfather, mentally reaching out for him. A house in ruins presented itself to her mind's eye, but when she attempted to push further the image dissolved. A vagueness crept over her and she found it increasingly difficult to concentrate.

Confident now that a blocking spell was to blame, she opened her eyes and deactivated the Scope, feeling both exhausted and disappointed. Someone had gone to a lot of effort to make sure that she and her family were unable to use magic to find Grandpa …

But Mum and Dad had always told her that even the strongest spells could be broken if you went about it the right way. She knew what kind of invention she wanted to make now. Tired but determined, she went back to bed and turned off her lamp, promising herself that she'd start work tomorrow. Grandpa would be back home again soon.

Rose dragged herself out of bed early the next day. She put on jeans and a T-shirt and brushed through her hair impatiently, taking her jacket off the back of her chair and pulling it on before opening her window onto a stormy, overcast day.

Stepping out into the hall, she found the library door open and her parents hard at work again. She sighed and made her way down to the dining room, where Matt and Mary were already eating breakfast. Rose watched them from the kitchen while she decided what she wanted.

Mary was unusually quiet. Her wavy, caramel-brown hair was unbrushed and tangled like a tumbleweed, and her hazel eyes were red-rimmed and puffy. Matt was still in his pyjamas, slouched morosely over his toast, his thin face pale and his blond hair unkempt.

Rose poured some milk and cereal into a bowl and sat opposite her sister.

"Mum and Dad are in the library again," Mary informed her.

Rose picked up her spoon and poked at her food, not feeling remotely hungry.

"I know. I reckon we should help them this time. To find Grandpa, I mean."

Mary scowled over her porridge.

"They'll say no."

Rose knew that her parents were unlikely to let them help, but she also thought that Grandpa's disappearance might have made them more willing to open up about what was going on.

"I think that's different," she said eventually. "When they said no last time, they were talking about this new invention. The Fragmenter, or whatever it is they're researching. They haven't said we can't help find Grandpa, so maybe we should ask them."

"Wait! What about the Scope?" said Mary, her eyes lighting up. But Rose shook her head.

"I tried it when I went to bed. It didn't work."

"Why not?" said Matt, finally looking up. "It's always worked before."

"I think blocking spells are interfering with it," said Rose dully.

She took a mouthful of cereal, creating a mental outline of how she was going to make her invention. Summoning her sketchbook and a pencil, she began to make notes, only to jump, startled, as someone hammered on the front door. She got up to answer it, but Dad came charging down the stairs and reached it first.

He opened the door and Dave stepped inside, followed by a stranger. Their faces were grave. Wolfing down the rest of her breakfast, Rose waited for them to go upstairs before picking up the Scope. Matt and Mary watched as she activated the invention.

Placing a finger on the metal, she waited as the Scope began to work. It came to a halt seconds later, just as it had last night, and Rose took her hand away as another surge of energy rushed through it.

Feeling a little let down, she shoved the Scope unceremoniously into her jacket pocket with Grandpa's watch as Mum appeared on the stairs.

"What are you all going to do today?" she asked, leaning on the banister so that she could peer down at them.

Matt suggested their usual Saturday morning activity: a trip to the arcade to wander and eat as much junk food as they could handle. Mum decided against this, however.

"I'd rather have you here at home, please. I'll feel better if I know where you all are."

Rose shrugged, reminding herself of the small mountain of schoolwork she still hadn't completed. Desperate to make a start on her invention, she told herself she'd begin once her homework was complete, and with a sigh, she sat cross-legged on the floor in front of the coffee table and pulled her maths books towards her instead.

Matt settled himself on the sofa restlessly, apparently unsure what to do with himself, while Mary picked up a book on beginner's magic, practising the spells on a tennis ball.

Mum drifted back upstairs and silence descended except for the scratching of Rose's pen. She worked half-heartedly until midday, trying in vain to remember the details of trigonometry.

"I wonder what they're going to do about Grandpa's invention now?" said Matt, glancing over at the stairs to check they were still alone. "It seems like whoever kidnapped him took the Fragmenter, too."

Rose paused and scrutinised her work, the corners of her mouth pulled down into a frown.

"I'm not so sure they did. I think if they had it, they wouldn't have needed Grandpa, too."

"Maybe they don't know how to use it," said Mary.

"Anyone capable of kidnapping Grandpa is probably smart enough to figure out how to work it on their own," said Rose darkly. "Grandpa might be old, but his magic is as strong as ever. Judging from what we heard Dave telling Mum and Dad yesterday, it could have been that woman from the Archives who kidnapped him, and if she really does work there she'll already know how to use his invention from his reports."

Mary rubbed her eyes and turned a page of her book.

"Oh, yeah. I forgot about that."

Her face scrunched up with effort as she aimed a spell at her tennis ball, only to drop it with a gasp as it swelled to twice its normal size. It burst with a loud *pop*, sending bits of it all over the room. Rose picked several pieces off her homework and Mary repaired the ball sheepishly.

"So you reckon it was her, then?" said Matt, as though nothing had happened.

"Well, we know the person who took him wants the invention he's been working on, right?" said Rose. "So they must know about what he's been making, and as Mum, Dad and Grandpa haven't even told *us* about it, the only way I can see anyone getting that kind of information is if they were going into his files. By the sound of it, even the people coming to the masterclass tomorrow don't really know what Grandpa's been working on, and you heard what Dave said. Every time Grandpa submits a report on his invention, *she* gets it, and if she has his reports, it wouldn't be hard to figure out how to use it without his help. It all makes sense!"

Rose put down her pen, admitting to herself that she probably wasn't going to get any more homework done. She stared out of the window, lost in thought and hardly noticing the rain that had begun to fall.

"What else did Dave say about her?"

"He said she was outside Grandpa's room in the Archives," Mary reminded her. "And they tried to catch her but she got away."

"So she's definitely up to something," muttered Rose. "But if she doesn't have the Fragmenter, where is it? And why wasn't Grandpa doing the testing in his invention room? If he'd been working in there, it would've been safe. He should've locked himself in there with it."

They lapsed into silence. Rose's gaze swept over the driveway and down towards the road, and she blinked, realising that the gate was swinging open. She got up and pressed her face to the glass, trying to see into the yard.

"Where's Cocoa?"

"He's out the back, isn't he?" said Matt, not looking up.

"Not anymore."

The sound of a dog barking and whining reached her

ears as she spoke.

"But how'd he get out?" asked Mary as the noise grew louder. "Mum and Dad put spells all around the yard to keep him in."

"It sounds like something's hurting him," fretted Rose.

Matt and Mary joined her at the window and they all peered through the thick avenue of trees lining the driveway. A man stood a short way down the street, advancing on Cocoa, who was growling fiercely at him. Rose groaned.

"Uh oh. I'd better get out there quick."

"You can't!" said Mary. "Mum said not to go outside!"

Rose rolled her eyes as she slipped her sandals on.

"I'll only be going to the end of the driveway."

She went to the door and threw it open as a deafening clap of thunder rolled overhead. Cocoa yelped in fright and Rose looked up. Storm clouds filled the sky above and flashes of lightning lit up the horizon. The rain became heavier as she reached the gate, quickly forming puddles on the gravel. Rose called to the dog, beckoning him over to her.

"Here, Cocoa!"

Cocoa remained where he was, growling loudly, and Rose took hold of his collar after a short struggle, pulling him away from the man in the street. He was short, with a stocky build, and he wore shabby, worn-out clothes that were soaked through. Rose surveyed him suspiciously, wondering why he was standing in the road.

"I'm so sorry!" she yelled over the rain. "Did he hurt you?"

The man didn't answer. He stared at her reproachfully as she held Cocoa with one hand and wiped her dripping hair out of her face with the other. Matt and Mary caught up with her and she asked the stranger again if he was injured, but another loud roll of thunder drowned her voice. Terrified, Cocoa pulled himself free from Rose's grip and took off down the road. Rose groaned and started after him.

As she ran, she noticed another man leaning against a tree, only a short distance from the first. He, too, was drenched from standing in the rain, his dark hair and clothes dripping. Rose stared at them both as she passed, wondering why they didn't go stand under cover. As she watched them, they both turned and sauntered off toward the narrow stretch of bushland that enveloped the road into town.

She reached the corner a moment later and peered through the tangled mass of gum leaves and pine needles. The road curved to the left and ran straight ahead for some way before it swerved and disappeared once more. Rose followed it with her eyes as far as she could see before the rain made everything hazy, but Cocoa had disappeared.

"Can you see him?" asked Matt, coming up behind Rose.

"No, he must have run into the bush."

Mary stepped forward into the trees, but Rose held her back.

"No, let him go. Standing in the driveway is one thing, but I'm pretty sure Mum and Dad wouldn't be so happy about us running around in the bush. Cocoa can find us. He'll find his own way back."

She turned and started walking towards the house. They were within sight of the garden fence when barking and growling broke out once more. Rose stopped.

"Scratch that. I'm going in. You two go back home, and if Mum and Dad ask where I am, tell them I've gone to get Cocoa."

She dove into the trees, following the dog's howls. Matt and Mary ran after her, not bothering to argue. The howling became louder as they went further from the road. The scent of damp earth met Rose's nose as she leapt over fallen branches and skidded on dead leaves. After running for several minutes, Rose thought she could see the rest of the city on the other side of the pines. The rain began to let up as she emerged onto a grassy slope, splashing through muddy puddles until she reached the pavement.

The traffic made it impossible to hear Cocoa, so Rose pulled the Scope out of her pocket and set it up in her hand. It ticked for a moment and then stopped. She paused, concentrating on what the Scope was showing her before crossing the road with Matt and Mary, heading towards the centre of town.

"Now it works!" said Rose in frustration, shoving the Scope back into her jacket.

They turned the last corner and Rose spotted Cocoa

wandering around the park, exactly where the Scope had shown her. He saw them coming and ran to meet them, crying and licking Rose's hands. She took hold of his collar, sighing with relief. He whimpered as she pulled at him to come with her.

"What was all that about?" she asked him, patting his head.

He whined again and she rubbed his ears soothingly. Cocoa attempted to pull away from her grip, crying softly, and Rose glanced at Matt, nonplussed. She checked Cocoa's collar and found drops of blood on it. Moving the collar aside, she saw a long, bruise-like mark on the dog's neck. It looked like someone had tried to cut him, only to decide that it would be easier to strangle him.

Feeling afraid now, she glanced around furtively, scanning the streets, but of course, there was no sign of the men who'd been standing in the rain.

"It doesn't make sense," murmured Matt. "Why would someone do that to Cocoa? He's a pushover. He's never hurt anyone in his life."

"I don't know," replied Rose in a low voice. "But now we really do need to get back home."

They left the park and headed for the trees. As they entered the main street, Rose glanced around her again and soon recognised a group of teenagers she knew from school, keeping dry under the shelter beside the arcade. They were only a short way away, and Rose tried desperately to blend into the background.

"No! Not now!"

She cringed and walked faster. Matt and Mary spun around to look, too, and immediately turned back, glowering.

"Can't we get away from them for even one day?" Matt muttered.

"They might not see us if we go this way," said Rose, ducking into the adjoining street. A few moments passed before she heard the sound of raucous laughter behind her. "No such luck," she said. "They've seen us."

She tried to act as though they hadn't, walking straight ahead and adjusting her grip on Cocoa's collar as the teenagers followed them.

"Hey, Stephensen!" one of them yelled. "I saw your grandpa on the news this morning. What did he blow up this time?"

They all laughed hysterically, making Rose bristle with fury.

"Ignore them," she said through gritted teeth.

"You say that every time and it never helps," snapped Matt.

"Well, at least it doesn't make things worse!" retorted Rose. "Starting a fight with them isn't going to make them stop!"

"It will if I put a few of my favourite spells on them," said Matt, his eyes narrowed menacingly.

Rose ignored him, too. She reached out her free hand to Mary, who had started to cry, and the laughter behind them grew louder as Mary wiped away her tears with the back of her hand. Rose, sensing that Matt was about to hit someone, dropped Cocoa's collar and took hold of the back of Matt's shirt instead as he tried to turn around.

"Use a travel spell and take Mary home," she told him. "I'll take Cocoa and meet you there. You know he hates the travel spell."

Matt stood in silence for a moment, fuming, before taking Mary's hand and disappearing. Rose exhaled in a rush, picked up Cocoa's collar and crossed into another street, trying hard not to listen to the jeering voices. Cocoa padded along beside her as she walked through town quickly, almost running until the voices faded into the distance.

Breathing easier now, she took a different path home than usual, hoping to avoid another encounter with her classmates. She checked her phone. They'd barely been gone twenty minutes, but she quickened her pace anyway, wanting to get back before Mum and Dad noticed she was missing and began to worry.

Cocoa pressed himself close against Rose's legs as they stepped off the road, and without knowing why, Rose felt a trickle of fear run down her spine. Shafts of weak sunlight lit up the pavement before being chased away by more clouds, throwing everything into semi-darkness.

She crossed an empty car park and stopped beside a bus shelter. A second later, a shadow appeared at the opposite end of the street, walking silently towards her. Rose hastily turned around and chose another route. After a moment she glanced back and, seeing no one, began to relax. She took another deep breath and hurried on.

The stretch of trees concealing the road home was close now. The familiar outline of the pines rose up behind the last row of houses, dark against the overcast sky. A cold wind began to blow, and she shivered in the rain-washed street. Hesitating for a fraction of a second before hurrying across the road, she continued down the lamplit street, wondering if she was being paranoid. She shook her head, trying to calm herself. Losing her head wouldn't help anything. She turned a corner and, to her immense relief, saw the entrance to the forest. Cocoa whined.

"Shh, Cocoa, it's OK." Rose stroked his head as she walked, noticing as she spoke how small her voice sounded. "We'll be home soon."

As a final check, she changed her route once more, looking behind her as she went. The shadow appeared on the pavement almost at once, this time accompanied by two others. Rose gulped.

Panicking in earnest now, she started to run, diving into an alleyway and taking off along it at full speed. She was halfway through when she saw one of the figures enter from the other side. Horrified, she skidded to a halt. How could the man have caught up to her so quickly? He couldn't have run that fast …

Confused, she grabbed one of the rubbish bins lining the alley wall and threw it between herself and her pursuer, hoping it would slow him down at least a little. It began to rain again as she whirled around and retraced her steps, the droplets falling so thickly that it was difficult to see.

The footsteps behind her broke into a run as she raced back out into the road. The men were quickly closing the distance between them. Trembling, she threw herself into another side street and attempted to calm her mind enough to disappear. But it was no use, the spell wouldn't come. With a gasp of fear, she darted back out into the street and kept running, her eyes fixed on the narrow stretch of bushland.

The trees loomed up in front of her. She had almost reached the winding road home when two figures appeared out of nowhere, blocking her path. They closed in, and Rose gave a panicked cry, looking for a way out. Another clap of thunder rolled overhead and a thin mist began to develop around the trees.

One of the men dove at her, grabbing her tightly by the arm, pulling her back. She felt someone searching in her pockets for something, and without bothering to use any of the spells she'd been taught for self defence, she lashed out like a wildcat, scratching, biting and kicking hard at the figure holding her, while Cocoa snapped at the others.

"Get off me!" snarled Rose, sending a spell Dad had once shown her at the man gripping her arm.

He cried out in pain and let go, his skin erupting in angry red blisters. As she fought with the other man, she tried to get a clear look at his face, but it was strangely obscured by the rain and mist surrounding them. Suddenly it dawned on her that this was not a natural storm. The men were using magic. They'd created the rain and mist to hide themselves.

Hackles raised, Cocoa launched himself at the man searching Rose's pockets, sinking his teeth into the man's leg. The man let out a yell of pain and kicked Cocoa with his free leg, while the first figure wrapped his blistered hands around the dog's neck, forcing him to let go, whining and gagging.

"No!" gasped Rose, horrified. "Leave him alone!"

She ducked under the hand reaching for her and snatched up Cocoa's collar again, pulling him away towards the trees. But there was still one more person waiting, barring her way, and she pelted straight into him, almost knocking him off his feet.

He stumbled backwards but kept his balance, and once again Rose was held fast by an iron grip. With a cry of fury, she squirmed and beat at him, using her burning spell until he let go.

Free at last, she took off along the road with all three chasing behind her. Glancing over her shoulder, she concentrated hard on the pavement in front of the man leading the chase. The edge of the paver heaved up, tripping him up before he could reach the road. His friends leapt over him and charged after Rose.

Trying to ignore the stitch in her side, she sprinted the last few paces, diving into the tangle of trees and hoping they would keep her hidden. Soon there was nothing but the sound of her footsteps crashing through the underbrush, and she stopped and hid behind a tree to regain her breath and attempt another travel spell.

She stood motionless, gasping and listening to the

gentle sound of rain on the forest floor. She tried to keep Cocoa still while she quieted her mind and wrapped the spell around them both. One of the men appeared with a rustling sound, only a short way off among the trees.

Rose resisted the urge to keep running and closed her eyes, concentrating on the spell and picturing the warm, safe house in her mind. A yell told her that the man had seen her, but she forced herself to stay put. Relief washed over her as she felt herself and Cocoa begin to fade. The seconds trickled by and her eyes flew open as she realised something was wrong.

Instead of disappearing, the trees had come back into focus. Confused and slightly disoriented, Rose stumbled into a run. All three men were in the bush and hurtling towards her, but now she could see the house through the thinning trees.

Willing her screaming muscles to keep going, she neared the edge of the forest and saw Dave and his friend leaving the house. Dave's companion turned into the driveway and disappeared, but Dave continued further down the drive, looking preoccupied. Rose waved her arms over her head to get his attention.

"Dave!"

Emerging from the trees, she sprinted down the road to the house, Cocoa snarling as he bounded along beside her.

Dave saw her and stopped. His jaw dropped as he took in the three men tearing after her.

"Hey! Help!"

He broke into a run and Rose's pursuers made one last attempt to catch her, sending her to the ground with a dizzying spell before running back towards the edge of the bushland for cover. She crawled forward, desperate to reach the house. The protection of the newly repaired Shield washed over her as she touched the garden fence.

Dave reached her and attempted to help her up, but his hand slipped in the rain, and Rose finally hoisted herself up using the fence, scrambling clumsily over it with her head still spinning. Cocoa cleared the fence in one great leap and disappeared behind the house.

Rose stumbled down the driveway, out of breath and weak with shock. She hopped over the garden beds, not bothering to keep to the path, reaching the back door as the rain turned into hailstones. Lightning stabbed through the sky, followed by more peals of thunder that shook the windows in their frames.

She removed the dizzying spell and peered between the trees while Cocoa shook himself dry beside her. Seeing no one, she opened the door and let Cocoa slink inside, his tail between his legs. Rose followed him in and slammed the door shut behind her. Then she locked it.

Leaning on the wall, she took a moment to catch her breath, numb with horror at what had just happened. She jumped in fright as someone knocked on the door. She let Dave in quickly, after peering through the peephole.

"Close call," he said, giving her a grim smile.

"Thanks!" she gasped, straightening up.

"No problem. But I think we'd better tell your parents what happened. They're not going to be happy."

Rose thought this was an understatement, but she said nothing as Dave turned and disappeared upstairs. She waited until she had recovered a little before peeking through the peephole again. A face loomed out of the darkness by the fence. Two more figures appeared seconds later, standing at the edge of the trees, their faces obscured by the hail.

They turned their backs on the house as she watched them, melting into the shadows. Rose shuddered and backed away, tottering up the hallway and into the living room as the clock over the mantelpiece chimed a quarter to one.

Matt and Mary were watching television, flicking absent-mindedly through channels. It was brightly lit and warm inside the house, and it seemed slightly unreal to Rose that she had just been chased through the streets. Matt looked up as she entered the room, taking in her haggard appearance.

"What happened to *you*?"

Rose flung herself down onto the sofa beside Mary. Cocoa lay down in his usual spot in front of the empty fireplace and blinked up at her dolefully.

"Three men chased me from the city all the way here," she said in a hollow voice.

Matt and Mary's mouths fell open in unison.

"What?! Are you OK?" Matt asked.

"Go and tell Mum and Dad!" Mary commanded.

"If you tell them you were chased home, we'll never

be allowed out of the house again," warned Matt.

"It's better than being followed all over town," retorted Rose. "I'd rather not go through that again. Mum and Dad are in the library, are they?"

Matt nodded, his eyes wide.

"They'd just finished talking to Dave when you came in."

Rose got up wearily and made her way to the stairs.

"I'd better go and tell them what happened. They're bound to want all the details."

The others trailed after her as she trudged up the stairs and along the hall to the library. Placing a hand on the doorknob, she hesitated for a second before opening the door. One look at her parents told her that they were furious.

"You were chased home?!" Mum gasped, clutching the desk for support. "We told you to stay inside the house! Are you hurt?"

She rushed to Rose's side and began checking her for injuries. She fixed her gaze on Rose's hands and the tiny cuts covering them slowly healed. Dave stood by the window, looking out silently in the direction of the forest.

"I know, I'm sorry," pleaded Rose.

"Did they hurt you?" Dad pressed, surveying her with anxious eyes. "How many of them were there?"

"There were three of them. I'm fine, but Cocoa got hurt. I went out to stop him from attacking a man in the street. Actually, I think he was attacking Cocoa. I'm pretty sure he was one of the men that chased us, but I can't be completely sure. They were just standing there, out in the storm, and they used the rain to cover their faces. I don't know what they did to Cocoa, but he got cut pretty badly. Look!"

She showed them the marks around Cocoa's neck. Dave turned around to inspect the cuts, too. Mum ran her fingers over them gently and they shrank away, replaced by healthy skin. Rose went to the desk and sat down. She brushed her hands and knees off on her clothes, dislodging some of the mud from the road.

"You should have come straight here with a travel spell," said Mum weakly, tears sparkling in her eyes. Cocoa put his head on Rose's lap and she scratched behind his ears.

"I tried to, but I couldn't. I don't know how, but it's like they pulled me back or something. One minute the trees were starting to fade, and then they were coming back into focus. And the men searched my pockets."

"Did they take anything?" Dave asked urgently.

"No. But all I have on me is the Scope and this."

She held up the pocket watch. Mum, Dad and Dave stared at it in surprise. Dad took it and examined it closely, then handed it to Dave.

"Cocoa protected me, though," said Rose.

She patted his head and he licked her hand. Mum and Dad waited as Dave studied the watch, turning it over and opening the lid. Dad turned to Rose, Matt and Mary, his gaze stern.

"OK, I don't want any of you leaving the house anymore except for school," he declared. Matt groaned loudly. "And if you have to go out, your mother and I will go with you. There'll be no more wandering around on your own, do you understand?"

"But we won't be alone if all three of us are together," said Matt in a persuasive tone.

"I don't care. That's not going to stop anyone from attacking you."

"See, I told you," Matt said to Rose.

Rose rolled her eyes and went to the window. She looked out towards the winding road, but the men had vanished into the rain and mist.

3

The Magicked Masterclass

"Well, I'd better get going."

Dave gave the watch another long look as Rose returned it to her pocket.

"Thanks again," said Mum, following him to the door.

Matt looked at Dad pleadingly as Dave left the room. "We don't really have to stay in the house, do we?"

Dad folded his arms across his chest and frowned. "Yes, you do."

Matt's face fell, and he turned to Rose for backup. Knowing it was pointless to argue, Rose left him to it. She went down the hall to her bedroom and changed into clean, dry clothes, her hands still shaking a little as she buttoned up her blouse.

Sitting at her desk, she opened the bottom drawer and lifted out the carved wooden box containing her small collection of jewellery. Setting the Scope aside, she placed Grandpa's watch beside the delicate silver necklace her parents had given her for her birthday. Locking the box with magic, she hid the key on a hook holding up a picture of her family at the beach.

Like Dave, she was beginning to wonder about the watch. The men who'd followed her couldn't have been interested in the Scope, so it had to be the watch they were after. But why did they want it? It was just an old watch that had been trodden on, after all …

Placing the wooden box back in the drawer, she picked up her sketchbook and a pencil and headed out into the hall. She opened the library door, expecting to find her parents hard at work again, but for the first time since Grandpa had disappeared, the room was empty. Surprised, she went downstairs and found everyone in the living room.

The atmosphere was tense. Mum was flicking through a magazine without reading it, her eyes slightly unfocused as she stared down at the pages. Dad sat in his armchair, fixing the lid back onto Mary's pink ballerina music box, absent-mindedly winding it up again and again.

Lunch, which was normally a noisy affair, was strangely quiet. Even Mary, who could chatter endlessly when she wanted to, was silent. Rose settled herself in one of the armchairs and spent the rest of the day sketching possible designs for her invention while she watched Matt and Mary play games on their ancient Nintendo 64, occasionally acting as judge to stop Matt from cheating.

Night fell around them, and at ten o'clock Rose went upstairs to bed, yawning and rubbing the bruises that were rapidly forming on her knees, but pleased to have made a start on her project.

It seemed like she'd only been asleep for a moment or two when a loud wailing jolted her awake. Sitting upright, she peered through the darkness and found her mother standing beside her. Rose eyed the screaming black object in her mother's hand, her body tensing with fear as Cocoa howled somewhere downstairs.

"What's going on?"

"Shh!" Mum moved towards the hall and beckoned to Rose. "The men have come back again. Keep quiet and follow me."

She pressed a small white button on the side of the Shield which muted it, making it flash instead of scream, and then tiptoed down the hall to Mary's bedroom. Rose hurried over to her window and moved the curtains aside a fraction to peek outside. Street lights lit up the road almost to the forest, but there was nobody in sight.

She ran to catch up with Mum. The house was now dark and silent. Mary was bleary-eyed with sleep when they woke her and did not appreciate being dragged out of bed.

"Everything sounds normal to me," she grumbled as they continued down the hall. They emerged onto the landing and found Dad waiting with Matt at the foot of the stairs.

"What's going on?" Matt called.

"We're going into the basement," whispered Mum, leading them through the living room, into the kitchen and over to the laundry, where Cocoa was pacing up and down.

Mum opened the door of what appeared to be an ordinary cupboard, revealing shelves full of bottles, scrubbing brushes and sponges. She tapped the top shelf four times and the disguise disappeared. A narrow staircase took its place, leading down to a basement. One corner of the room had been converted into a tiny kitchen area, and another into a bathroom.

As a small child, Rose had thought it a bit excessive to have the space set up like this, but she'd soon learned that there was good reason for it. She could remember several times in her life when someone had attempted to break into the house and steal their inventions. Some intruders were armed and some weren't. It was rare, but it happened.

Rose crept down the shallow, rickety steps after her brother and sister, and Mum closed the door behind them with a snap. Dad turned the light on and Rose watched the back of the door take on the appearance of the cupboard once more. Yawning, Mary sat down on the tiny, collapsed sofa pushed up against the back wall.

"Are we going to stay in here for long?"

Mum's eyes lingered briefly on the back of the door, her expression uneasy.

"At least for tonight, I think."

Mary nodded in resignation and Rose sank down beside her, wondering if there was any point in asking her parents what the men had come back for. Matt seemed to be thinking the same thing, but he merely shrugged his shoulders and tried to soothe Cocoa, who had curled up, bristling, in the corner by the small electric heater.

Now and then he would lift his head off the floor and let out a low growl, but all Rose could hear was the steady dripping of water from the makeshift kitchen tap.

Dad placed spells around the room to make sure any sounds from the basement could not be heard outside before turning the Shield's alarm back on. It sat silently in his palm, resembling a rounded, twisted hourglass, glittering darkly in the dim light.

"They must have run for it when they heard the noise," he murmured, as the roiling, black fluid inside the Shield slowed to a gentle swirling movement.

Rose's stomach unclenched slowly and she went to the cupboard to help Mum drag the spare mattresses out. The basement was cold, and they spent the rest of the night huddled under thick blankets until they fell asleep, listening for sounds in the house above.

The room was still dark when Rose opened her eyes. Mary was snoring gently beside her, and her parents' whispering voices were barely audible from across the room.

"But we don't know if it's going to be safe to go upstairs tomorrow," said Mum. "They might come back when it's light. They're not going to give up that easily. Not for the Fragmenter."

"I don't think they'll try to get in during the day," whispered Dad. "It'd be stupid. Dave will be here, as well as almost every other magical person in the area. This place is going to be packed."

"That could just make it easier for them. It's easy to lose someone in a crowd."

"We'll have the Shield running," said Dad with his

usual optimism. "That'll tell us if they come anywhere near here and stop them from getting inside the house if they do."

"I'd still feel better if we held off until things settle down."

"I'm not sure they're going to settle down."

Silence descended for a moment, and then Mum gave a gentle sigh. "At least we know they haven't found the Fragmenter yet. If they had, they wouldn't be snooping around here. So we still have a chance, at least."

Rose lay still, listening intently and staring at the floor in front of her, hoping that Mum and Dad would keep talking. She closed her eyes and waited, but the silence stretched on and she drifted into a troubled sleep.

She awoke the next morning tangled in a mess of blankets and sheets. She'd been dreaming that she was being stalked by a horrible creature she couldn't put a name to, that changed shape and gave her the feeling that it was watching her somehow, even when it was out of sight.

Still a little unsettled, she concentrated on disentangling herself from the bedlinen and tried to forget about the dream. She sat up, realising her father wasn't in the room. Mary grinned at her from the sofa, where she was watching cartoons on the spare television while Matt fed Cocoa in the kitchen and Mum stood by the door, looking like she'd hardly slept at all last night.

"Where's Dad?" Rose asked.

Mum glanced up.

"Good morning, sweetheart. He's gone to check if it's safe for us to go up, that's all."

"Oh! OK, then. I hope he took the Shield with him?"

Mum nodded and Rose got up to join Mary. It wasn't long before Dad edged back into the room with the Shield tucked under one arm.

"Everything's fine."

He smiled and Mum relaxed, relief flooding her face. Mary jumped up and raced for the stairs.

"Awesome! Let's go, then!"

Rose bundled up the blankets and helped Dad pack away the mattresses before heading upstairs into the kitchen. The house was quiet, and as Dad had reported, everything seemed normal. The sky was clear, and rays of bright light streamed in through the windows.

"Time for something to eat, I think." Mum turned to Rose, Matt and Mary. "Your dad and I have a lot to do for the masterclass today, and we're going to need you three to help us get things ready."

Matt hung his head and Mary pouted, but they did as they were told and went upstairs to put on their best clothes while Mum made scrambled eggs and toast for breakfast. The weather was still unusually cool, so Rose put on a knee-length denim skirt, tights and a long-sleeved shirt.

Stepping out into the hall, she found her mother in the library yet again, shoving books and reports back onto the shelves. A long table had replaced the desk. Magic had been used on the room so that it stretched to accommodate the number of people who would be attending, and Rose stared at the strange sight of the elongated window, which was now letting in much more light than usual.

"This will have to do for a meeting room," said Mum, pushing chairs around it. "Could you ask Matt and Mary to set the table outside, please? Tell them to use the good plates. Then you can help me make some snacks."

Rose nodded and went back downstairs to the kitchen as Matt and Mary came in from helping Dad tidy up the yard. A large canopy had been erected on the grass over a long table, and the gum boots and dog toys that were normally scattered about the place had been packed away. Rose stood back to let her brother and sister wash their hands at the kitchen sink.

"Mum wants you to set up outside," she told them, pointing to the gold-rimmed plates and the cutlery stacked on the countertop.

She opened the kitchen window and turned on the radio just as the morning news started. Deciding she'd make some of her favourite vegetable pies for lunch, she took some onions from the pantry and placed them on the cutting board, where they peeled and diced themselves. She was slicing the tops off the carrots when Matt ran up to the window and stuck his head inside.

"All done."

He reached inside and turned up the volume on the radio. Rose leaned over the kitchen sink to get a clear view of Matt's handiwork. She shook her head and nodded at the white cloth folded neatly on one of the dining room chairs.

"That's great, but what about the tablecloth?"

She passed it to him through the window and he mumbled something under his breath as he jogged back. His voice echoed as he called to her across the expanse of grass.

"Hey, Rose! Watch this!"

Rose bit her lip as he levitated all of the plates and glasses several feet above the table. Looking pleased with himself, he spread the tablecloth out underneath the hovering dishes. The newswoman on the radio began the next story as Matt finished tugging the cloth into place.

"A local eighty-one-year-old man was reported missing on Friday night after his family discovered his house partially destroyed. Authorities have confirmed that there were signs of a struggle at the premises. Anyone with information is urged to contact the police."

A loud crash sounded outside and Rose jumped, narrowly avoiding cutting herself with the knife in her hand. Cocoa leapt up with a yelp. All of the plates and glasses had come crashing back down onto the table. Matt and Mary hastily threw up shield spells as shards of glass and china flew through the air.

One piece shot through the kitchen window and struck the wall, clattering onto the tiles. Rose cursed and ran out into the yard, hurrying to beat the footsteps she could hear racing downstairs. The broken pieces came back together and reassembled themselves as she repaired them and directed them back onto the tabletop.

Matt gave her an apologetic look and cancelled his Shield spell.

"Whoops."

The three of them spun around as the back door flew open and Mum stumbled out looking pale.

"What happened?"

Rose, Matt and Mary stood in front of the table, trying not to look guilty.

"Nothing," said Rose quickly. "Everything's fine."

Mum glanced at the table suspiciously but let it pass, turning back inside. Matt flopped down onto one of the chairs and grinned at Rose.

"Thanks. She'd have grounded me for a month if she'd seen I'd broken the plates."

He fixed his gaze on the radio and it fell silent. Rose went back into the kitchen to finish her pies while Mum bustled around her, tidying up the house. She held out a crimson, cube-shaped contraption with slots on each side, and with a whooshing sound, it sucked up all of the dust and dirt like a magnet. Removing one side, she emptied the contents into the bin as the clock in the hall struck half past eight. There was a knock on the door, and Mum put the Cube back together again.

"Could you take this upstairs, please?"

She held the invention out to Rose, who took it and made her way up the stairs to the invention room, looking over her shoulder at the small crowd of people Mum had just greeted. All of them were strangers except for Dave, who looked much more cheerful than usual.

Finding the door to the invention room already open, she went inside and discovered Dad standing in front of a black cabinet she hadn't seen before, hidden in the corner between the workbench and the table that held most of their finished inventions. He placed a heap of loose pages and what looked like a report inside it, then began rearranging something further inside. Wondering what it could be, she peered around him.

The invention room was one of the largest rooms in the house. It held a battered workbench along the far wall under a wide window and a scrubbed wooden table that stood against the adjoining wall, which bore a variety of inventions that were mostly used around the house and yard. The third wall was taken up entirely with hooks and racks of tools, many of them highly specialised and strange-looking, even to Rose. Opposite the table was a collection of bookshelves, pushed higgledy-piggledy against the wall.

Setting the Cube back in its place on the table, she turned towards the door, watching her father over her shoulder, and glimpsed a flash of green, like metal glinting in the light. Unable to see what was creating it, she loitered in the doorway until Dad ordered her out and locked the cabinet door with protective spells.

Grinning, Rose obediently left the room and marched back down the hall. Voices carried upstairs and she wondered how many people would be coming to the masterclass. By the time she'd arrived in the living room, more than a dozen people had gathered there, all talking in whispers together as though they were at a funeral.

Mary, suddenly shy, crept over to Rose and attempted to hide behind her. The room was starting to become full when Mum ushered everyone upstairs.

"Do you think we'll be able to hear anything?" whispered Matt from beside Rose, watching everyone go past.

"I doubt it," replied Rose. "They'll make sure we can't. I think I'll just go and tidy my room up a bit and start working on my invention."

She waited until the crowd was settled in the library before heading upstairs herself, closing her bedroom door and gazing around at the mess in front of her. The room was bright and comfortable, but also small and a little cramped. A desk with a lamp and shelves stood on one side of the window, and a dresser on the other, adorned with trinkets and photos.

More pictures covered the pale blue walls above her bed, which stood in the corner beside the door, littered with homework sheets and textbooks. A wooden shelf ran along the wall between the photos, displaying all of her childhood inventions, along with some of her later ones, including her first Shield and an invention designed to predict the weather. On the other side of the door stood an old wardrobe, its doors plastered with notes and reminders about school events.

Deciding to tackle the desk first, she collected the books scattered over the bed and placed them back onto the shelves. Throwing all of the rubbish and scrunched up pieces of paper into the bin under the desk, she put the clothes piled up on her chair back into the wardrobe and dresser.

After a while, she decided that the room was tidy enough and took out her sketchbook again. Picking up her pencil, she turned to a fresh page and listed everything she wanted her invention to do, scanning the list with a critical eye.

What she needed was something that possessed the seeking abilities of the Scope, the tracing skills of the Tracker, the spell-destroying traits of a Breaker, and the amplifying effects of a Booster.

This last invention could be particularly useful to her if Grandpa's kidnapper was powerfully magical, because it allowed the user to layer one spell on top of others of the same type, making the overall effect stronger. But Boosters were rare and difficult to make because of the way spells had to be fused. It would require her to use magic well beyond her current abilities, meaning she would have to wait much longer to get the finished invention right.

She leaned back in her chair. It was going to be quite a challenge to combine the properties of all four inventions into a single working piece. Wondering if she could persuade Mum or Dad to give her some magic lessons when they weren't in the library, she returned to her sketchbook and thought about what kind of design she wanted.

After filling up eight pages with designs of various shapes and sizes, she stopped and considered her work. Not happy with any of them, she tossed her pencil down in frustration.

"Think," she muttered to herself. "You're making an invention to find Grandpa. So, what finds things? What do location spells do?"

She gazed around the room for inspiration. A thought struck her as she caught sight of her reflection in the small mirror on top of her dresser, and she snatched her pencil up once more.

"They see things, like eyes do. Maybe I should make the invention eye-shaped?"

Excitement took hold of her and she wrote this idea down, deciding that she'd look through the box of spare parts again later to check if any of them would work for an eye shape.

She stared at the paper in front of her, lost in thought until she was suddenly brought back to her senses with a jolt. She blinked in surprise, wondering what had disturbed her, and noticed a strange sensation stealing over her. The hairs on the back of her neck stood up and she sat up straighter, feeling as though invisible eyes were watching her.

Startled, she surveyed the room, but nothing unusual presented itself. Then, when the sensation only intensified, she crossed to the window. The yard below was empty except for Cocoa, chewing contentedly on his favourite tennis ball under the climbing tree.

You're just imagining it, Rose told herself, sitting back down at her desk. *You were thinking about eyes and got carried away, that's all…*

Someone rapped on her door and Rose jumped, startled. She glanced over her shoulder uneasily, only to let out a sigh of relief when Mum stepped inside. People were walking past the doorway towards the stairs. The presentation must have ended.

"Can you help me in the kitchen, please?" asked Mum.

Rose put down her pencil and pushed her chair away from the desk. Mum picked up the sketchbook, looking at the sketches with curiosity.

"What are you working on?"

Rose hesitated, wondering if Mum would approve of her getting involved in the search for Grandpa. Mum gave the book back and Rose hastily shoved it into a drawer.

"Oh, nothing much. I'm trying to make a new kind of Scope. I'm not happy with the one we've got."

Mum's expression softened.

"It didn't work when you tried to find your grandpa?"

Rose shook her head, trying to swallow the lump that had formed in her throat. Mum sighed and sat down on the end of the bed, tugging Rose down beside her and wrapping a comforting arm around her.

"I'm not surprised. The people who took him weren't going to make it that easy for us, were they?"

"I guess not."

Rose looked down at her knees, her face burning, and added, "But it's not just that. The inventions you and Dad make are loads better than mine. I want to be able to make things like that, too."

Mum blinked in surprise.

"Darling, you already do make wonderful inventions.

And besides, your dad and I have been doing this for decades now. You're only sixteen. It's not fair on yourself to think like that."

Rose hung her head, avoiding her mother's eyes.

"Yeah, I know. But everything I've made so far is really just kids' stuff. I feel like I should be able to do better than that now."

Mum shook her head disbelievingly and pulled Rose into a hug.

"You will. But you need to give yourself time. You're a perfectionist, you know that. If it makes you feel better, how about when the school holidays start, we take a look at the work you've done so far on your new Scope? I'll give you some lessons on a couple of spells that might help. It'll still be all your own work. I'll just teach you some more advanced magic."

"OK," said Rose, feeling more cheerful. "Thanks, Mum."

Mum's expression was thoughtful as she stood up.

"I guess, if you've tried the old Scope and you're not getting any results with the one finding spell, you could always blend a few different ones together ..."

Rose hesitated.

"I've never tried to blend spells before," she said uncertainly. "It's supposed to be difficult, isn't it?"

"It is a bit tricky, but you'll use blended spells a lot when you make advanced inventions, so it's worth learning."

Rose pondered this as they made their way downstairs.

"Come to think of it, do you need to find your grandpa with an invention?" said Mum, entering the kitchen. "It might work best if you used your magic by itself and didn't worry about channelling it through an object that might create problems?"

But Rose sighed and shook her head.

"I tried that, too. It still didn't work. And besides, I can make the magic stronger if I use it in an invention because I can layer lots of spells on top of each other, or blend them, like you said. If I can manage the spells, that is. The people who took Grandpa are bound to be a lot better at magic than me, so I probably have more of a chance that way."

"Hmm. Maybe we should start with removing blocking spells, then. That could be the problem."

"I think you might be right," said Rose, remembering the surge of energy that had rushed through the Scope when she'd used it.

"They're not uncommon," said Mum mildly. "Wait a few more weeks and I'll start teaching you."

Rose beamed and threw her arms around her mother. Feeling hopeful again, she picked up a bowl of salad and took it out to the yard, where people were standing about in small groups, talking in hushed voices. They all stopped abruptly when she walked past with Matt and Mary. Matt had clearly noticed, too. He trailed behind Rose, carrying a platter of her pies and looking irritable.

"All this secret stuff is driving me mad!" he grumbled. "What do they think we'll do if we hear something? Start blabbing to everyone we see?"

He put the platter down on the table and glared around at the party. Rose put her bowl down and gave her brother a sympathetic pat on the shoulder before wandering through the crowd to the barbecue, where Dad was talking to Dave.

"Your dad's just been saying that you've got a talent for repairing inventions," Dave said to Rose as she stared around at the guests, feeling increasingly uncomfortable among all the grim faces.

"I'm OK, I guess," she said, thinking of Grandpa's pocket watch, which remained broken in her jewellery box. Her latest attempts to fix it had been entirely unsuccessful. But Dad protested, giving her a proud smile.

"She's better than OK. I don't think there's ever been an invention she couldn't sort out. She's already reconstructed our old Spell Breaker, even though the magic we used on it was almost twice her level at the time."

Dave looked impressed.

"You should consider getting a job in the Archives when you've finished school."

A thrill of excitement ran through her at the mention of the Archives.

"I thought the Archivists only catalogued and stored inventions and journals," said Rose eagerly.

"Oh no, a large part of their job is maintaining and repairing the older inventions, too, and they're always looking for more employees. It's a tough job and not many people are up to it. Most of the apprentices are gone within a year. But they're always on the lookout for promising people."

"I will consider it, then," said Rose politely.

She thought about this as she moved towards the table to make herself a sandwich. She'd always loved old things and had enjoyed the rare trips she'd made to the Archives with her parents when she was a small child. The seemingly endless rows of documents and mysterious inventions intrigued her. She wondered what they all did and who had created them.

Some of the inventions were ancient, stored for centuries after the death of their maker, and now only the Archivists knew what they did and how to work them. It was even said that there were secret sections in the deepest part of the Archives, where the public was forbidden to go, and where the most dangerous and delicate inventions were kept.

She took a bite of her sandwich, trying to guess what kinds of inventions would most likely be in the secret sections when she heard her name spoken. She glanced up without thinking and felt her mouth go dry.

Mum was introducing Matt and Mary to some of the guests. Rose guessed Mum must have pointed her out to them, too, but it wasn't this that held her attention.

Behind them, edging around the house and only visible for a second, was the man she'd spoken to yesterday, standing in the road, out in the rain. Mum moved towards the platter of pies and Rose rushed to meet her, taking hold of her hand and wheeling her around to face the house.

"Mum, something's wrong! I swear I just saw one of the men who attacked me sneaking around the side of the house!"

Mum gasped and towed her over to where Dad was now talking to some of the guests. He was about to take a bite of his sandwich when Mum drew him away from the others.

"They're here," she hissed. "Rose saw one of them by the house."

"It was the man Cocoa almost bit," explained Rose.

"What does he look like?" asked Dad in an undertone.

"Short, with a stocky build and old, worn-out clothes."

"I didn't see him at the masterclass, did you?" Dad turned to Mum, his face full of concern.

"No. He must have got in after it started. But the gate's open. It would've been easy to sneak into the yard while we were all inside." She gazed up at the house. "Not that a locked gate would have stopped them," she added darkly.

"But why didn't the Shield go off? It protects the grounds as well as the house ..."

Anxiety clouded Mum's face and her eyes swept over the people gathered in the garden. Rose stood in silence as she listened to her parents' whispers, feeling like nowhere was safe anymore. Whoever this man was, he'd not only returned, he'd also managed to slip past the Shield.

"Find Matt and Mary and go down into the

basement," Mum commanded.

"But he's probably already gone," said Rose. "I think he saw me looking at him. I doubt he'd hang around if he knew we'd seen him."

"You can't be sure," insisted Dad. "We'll tell you when it's safe to come out."

Rose sighed and began searching for her brother and sister. She found Matt by the table with a sandwich in his hands, interrogating a tall man with red hair who was regarding him with a mixture of exasperation and amusement. Rose approached them awkwardly and gave Matt a meaningful look.

"Sorry to interrupt, but I need you to come with me."

"Why? What's wrong?" He frowned as Rose took hold of his arm and pulled.

"I'll tell you in a moment," she said, dragging him away. He seemed thoroughly put out as they headed for the back door.

"You know, I haven't been able to get a single thing out of anyone here," he complained. "They're all as unwilling to talk as Mum and Dad. Every time I ask someone what they know about Grandpa's invention they just laugh and tell me it's none of my business."

"Never mind that," said Rose when they were out of earshot. "One of the men who followed me has come back again."

Matt stopped and stared suspiciously at the people around him, but Rose shook her head and pulled him forward.

"No, he disappeared out the front a moment ago.

We need to find Mary. Where is she?"

"I haven't seen her. I thought she was with you?"

They pushed their way through the crowd, searching and calling for her, but there was no answer.

"Maybe she went into the house," suggested Rose. She threw the back door open and charged inside, fear prickling in her chest. "Mary!"

Still there was no reply. Rose went over to the stairs and was about to climb them when Mary came hurrying down, looking unsettled.

"I think there's something in the house," she said haltingly.

"A man? Yeah, I saw him outside. Come on, Mum and Dad said to go down into the basement."

But Mary hung back, glancing back towards the hall.

"No, it's something else."

"What do you mean?" said Rose, confused. "What is it, then?"

"I don't know. Something weird. Come and see!"

She led them up the stairs to the library before turning and signalling for them to be quiet, pointing at the door.

"What?" whispered Rose after a several minutes of hearing and seeing nothing. "Mary, there's nothing there."

Mary pointed again, indicating the gap underneath the door, and this time Rose saw it. Something strange was moving about, making the air appear blurred in a single spot. The thing was barely visible, flowing through the air like water. The bookcases and the legs of the table and chairs appeared vague and out of focus until the blurred spot moved on, changing shape as it went.

Rose jumped back in alarm. The room was completely silent, and she thought she could feel the strange presence better than she could see it. It was as though a mild current had travelled over her skin, making the hairs on her arms and the back of her neck stand up. The air around her crackled with electricity, reminding her of the pressure before a storm, and the feeling of being watched by something or some-one swooped down on her again, intensifying until the blur disappeared, leaving no trace of it having been there.

Unnerved, Rose tiptoed to the invention room and found the Shield. Taking it down to the laundry, she ushered Matt and Mary into the basement and closed the door behind them. She flopped down on the sofa with the Shield on her lap.

"I see what you mean. What *was* that thing?"

"Your guess is as good as mine," said Matt, looking shaken.

"Why didn't the Shield pick it up?" said Mary breathlessly. "Or the man creeping around the house? We've had it for ages and no one's ever got past it before."

Rose turned the Shield over and her eyes widened. It had been deactivated.

"But it was working just hours ago!" she cried. "You know what this means, don't you? Someone's been inside our invention room! The Shield's been in there all day, no one took it out. We'd have noticed if they had!"

She stopped, staring down at the dark liquid moving

thickly inside the Shield.

"But then, how would someone get into the room without triggering the Shield if it was working?"

She turned to her brother and sister, perplexed.

"You probably just *thought* it was running," said Matt, with a wave of his hand. But his expression was uneasy despite the confidence in his voice. Rose folded her arms across her chest.

"I know what I saw."

Rose looked down at the Shield, feeling truly afraid now. She reactivated it and placed it by her feet, thinking of all the unusual things that had occurred over the last several weeks.

"It's weird," she said slowly. "Mum, Dad and Grandpa have been making inventions for ages and they've always been able to handle things. But everything's been going wrong since Grandpa started this last invention. I don't know what it is, but I wish he'd never made it. Then we wouldn't have to keep hiding down here all the time and we'd have Grandpa back."

She fidgeted in her seat, tired of not knowing what was going on and frustrated that she could do nothing to help. She put her chin in her hand and fell silent, waiting for her parents to come down. Hours passed before the lock on the door clicked and Mum and Dad appeared, looking stressed and exhausted.

"It's safe to go up now. Everyone's gone and we've checked the house," said Mum.

Rose stood up at once.

"Please, can't you just tell us what's happening?

Something weird is going on with this." She held out the Shield. "It's been turned off since this morning and we found something in the library that wasn't like anything I've ever seen before."

Mum gave her a startled look. "But how could that happen? What kind of thing did you see?"

"I don't know how to describe it," said Rose slowly. "It was a sort of blurry shape in the air. It moved around a bit and then it disappeared."

Mum and Dad hesitated, glancing at each other apprehensively. Dad took the Shield and looked down at it, avoiding their eyes.

"Oh, that. It won't hurt you if you don't do anything to disturb it."

"You know what that thing is?" pressed Matt, his eyebrows raised.

"We know what it is, yes." Dad paused again, searching for the right words. "I suppose you could say it's a kind of magical defence mechanism, but it's strange even for magic. It's made of energy, like all magic, but somehow it can behave almost like a person sometimes."

"But what is it guarding?" asked Matt. "Did you make it?"

"Not exactly, no," said Dad.

"Grandpa made it, didn't he?" guessed Rose. "It's something to do with his invention, isn't it?"

Rose knew she was right even before Mum sighed and nodded.

"I don't like having it in the house, but we don't have much choice."

"What kind of invention needs its own defence mechanism?" asked Matt in amazement.

"It's supposed to stop people misusing it," Dad explained. "Only the people who know how to control it can go near it. It's quite an old-fashioned idea, really, but lots of inventions still have them."

"I've never seen one," remarked Mary.

"Well, you wouldn't have," replied Dad with a wry smile. "We only ever make things that will help people, not attack them. Most of the ones that do have defence systems are in the Archives for safekeeping. The Archivists are trained to deal with them."

"Can't you just tell us what Grandpa's invention is?" said Mary, looking up at her parents imploringly.

"We want to tell you, we truly do," replied Mum wearily. "But we can't yet. We're not allowed. Not until this is all sorted out. Then we'll tell you everything. We promise."

Dad held out the Shield, his expression thoughtful.

"You know, that's probably why this stopped working."

Mum's eyes widened. "Of course!"

Rose didn't understand any of this, but she didn't bother asking her parents about it. Mum ran her hands through her hair, looking exhausted. Several locks had escaped the elegant knot she'd made at the base of her neck.

"Come on, let's go up."

Rose followed her mother out of the basement for the second time that day and ran up to her room to think. As she sat at her desk, scribbling distractedly in her sketchbook, she found her thoughts returning to her grandfather. It already felt like he'd been gone for months, and she couldn't help but worry that he might be suffering, wherever he was being kept.

Lifting out her jewellery box, she opened it and reached for the pocket watch, wanting to hold something that Grandpa had held. But her hand met only wood and felt. She stared down at the box in disbelief. The watch had disappeared.

4

Grandpa's Invention

"Hurry up!" Mum called from the foot of the stairs. "It's almost half past eight. You're going to be late again."

Rose grimaced as she went down the hall to her room after breakfast and dragged her school uniform out of her wardrobe. She pulled on her blue and white checked dress, thinking longingly of the summer holiday. The unseasonal cold had disappeared as quickly as it had arrived, and she threw the window open to let the breeze float in.

Crossing off another day on her calendar, she began the hunt for her school bag, collecting her shoes, books and timetable from all over the room as she searched, finally using a travel spell downstairs to gather her homework up from the coffee table.

She raced upstairs again to pack and then back down to the kitchen, where she slapped together two cheese sandwiches, shoving one into her bag covered in a tangle of plastic wrap and passing the other to Mary, along with an apple. Matt skidded over to the pantry and tossed a jar of peanut butter and a spoon into his bag as Mum entered the room, carrying a wash basket filled with forgotten school things.

"Can't we stay here and help you look for Grandpa?"

Matt asked for the second time. Mary nodded frantically, turning pleading eyes on her mother.

"Yeah, we've only got two weeks until the holidays, anyway, and we never do anything at the end of the year."

"Don't be silly," chided Mum. "Two more weeks won't hurt you."

"It might," said Matt darkly, swinging his bag onto his back. "They're making us sing at assembly."

"What if those men come after us again?" said Mary, trying a different tactic. Rose couldn't help but laugh as she collected her textbooks from Mum's basket.

"I don't think they will," she said. "It's broad daylight and we're going to be surrounded by people all day."

Matt gave her an offended look.

"Do you want to stay home or not?"

Mum hurried them along, zipping up Mary's bag and pressing a pencil case into Matt's hands. Her expression was tense as she readjusted the jumbled knot that was Matt's tie.

"Come on, you've only got ten minutes until school starts and you can't be late again."

She gave them all a quick hug before handing out lunch money and following them out into the driveway. Matt stopped, catching sight of the car waiting for them.

"Why're we taking the car?"

"Because sometimes it's nice to act like we're normal," answered Rose, climbing into the old Holden Commodore. "And because Dad just likes cars."

She returned her father's grin and pushed her bag down by her feet.

"I *like* not being normal," countered Matt, getting into the front seat. Rose let out a splutter of indignation as she fastened her seat belt.

"Speak for yourself! I'd rather be like everyone else and fit in with the rest of the world, than magical and an outcast."

Matt shook his head in disbelief and Dad frowned at Rose in the rear-view mirror.

"Magic is a rare gift these days, that's all. It doesn't mean there's something wrong with you."

Rose didn't entirely agree with this, but she didn't want to argue, so she shrugged and attempted to tie her shoelaces as Dad reversed down the driveway. The trip into town was quick, even with the morning traffic, and ten minutes later they clambered out of the car, waving goodbye to Dad.

"I'll meet you under the tree at lunch," Rose called to the other two, running for her English classroom as the bell rang.

All eyes seemed to be on Rose as she chose a desk at the back of the room. She ducked her head, trying her best to ignore the whispering and muttering that had broken out around her. The day trickled by in a dull blur, and she became more and more annoyed by the staring of the other students.

Don't they have anything else to do? she thought irritably, turning away from the latest set of curious eyes with a scowl. By the time the lunch bell rang, she was eager to make a quick getaway.

Packing up her things hastily, she got to her feet,

noticing a girl with long, dark hair and tanned skin looking at her keenly from the other side of the aisle. She took a tentative step forward.

"Er, you're Rose, aren't you?"

Rose nodded, wondering why this girl was speaking to her. Nobody usually did.

"I'm Natalie," said the girl, misinterpreting the blank expression on Rose's face. "I'm sorry about your grandpa. I hope the police find him soon."

"Thanks," said Rose awkwardly.

"Are they getting anywhere with the investigation?"

Rose shook her head and walked with Natalie out to the grounds.

"Not really, but it's only been a few days since he disappeared."

"They said on the news this morning that they'd found a suspect," prompted Natalie.

Rose stopped in her tracks.

"I didn't hear anything about that!"

"It was on the radio about half an hour ago." Natalie held out the phone and earbuds she'd been using during class. "I bet the police have already told your parents."

"Did they say who the suspect was?" asked Rose urgently.

"Yeah, a woman called Alison Maxwell. I think they said she's an Archivist or something?"

Her tone suggested that she had no idea what this meant, but Rose immediately felt her chest tighten. She thanked Natalie and ran to find her brother and sister. She was out of breath by the time she reached the crooked pine tree in the far corner of the grounds. Matt and Mary were already sitting beneath it, waiting for her.

"Did you hear?" Rose shrugged off her bag and settled herself cross-legged in the shade.

"Yep," said Matt. "Everyone's saying someone called Alison Maxwell did it."

He pulled out his jar of peanut butter and scooped out a spoonful. A strange mixture of agitation and hopefulness coursed through Rose as she stared around at the other students.

"I bet you anything it's the same woman we heard Dave talking about in the library," she said. "It has to be!"

She dug her sandwich out of her bag and bit off a mouthful, trying to remember everything Dave had said about the woman. Mary cocked her head to one side thoughtfully.

"Now we know her name we could find out where she lives! We could go and have a look at her house."

Matt snorted. "Yeah, right! What are you going to find? If she did kidnap Grandpa, she's not going to put a sign out the front saying he's in there. She'll have made sure there's nothing lying around that could give her away."

Mary rolled her eyes.

"I know that. I just want to help, that's all."

"If the police think she kidnapped him, I bet they'll have gone through her house already," said Rose.

"So far, they've only said she's a suspect," Matt reminded them, throwing his half-empty jar back into his bag. "They don't know for sure that she did it."

Mary shrugged, looking unconvinced.

"Yeah, I guess."

"Dave *did* talk about an Archivist," continued Rose.

Matt rested his back against the trunk of the tree. Rose could tell from the fear in his eyes that he was as concerned about Grandpa's well-being as she was. He plucked at the grass beside his feet, his voice tight when he spoke.

"Yeah, it probably is her, but we don't know for sure. If the police are after her, I don't think there's anything we can do to help. We'll just have to see what happens."

They remained under the tree until the bell rang. Rose heaved a great sigh and got to her feet, dreading the rest of her classes. She waved to the other two and trudged off to her next lesson.

"See you at the gate."

History, which she usually liked, was strangely boring to her that afternoon. She fidgeted in her chair, staring at the whiteboard until movement caught her eye in the doorway. Mum was there, waving at her. The teacher, Mrs Wilkes, stopped mid-sentence and stared.

"I've come to take Rose home," said Mum casually.

Rose bristled with fury as several of the students looked at Mum with scornful laughter, but Mum seemed indifferent to all of the attention and simply waited by the door. Mrs Wilkes nodded at Rose and continued her lecture as though nothing had happened. Stifling her anger, Rose hurried out of the classroom, throwing her school things back into her bag as she went.

"What's up?" said Rose, the moment they were

alone in the corridor. Mum avoided her eyes and headed for the exit.

"Nothing. I just decided that I'd feel better if you were at home, that's all. Let's go and get Matt."

Rose raised an eyebrow but said nothing. She swung her bag onto her back and walked with her mother over to the two-storey brick building on the other side of the quadrangle.

"Did you listen to the radio this morning?" Rose asked tentatively.

"Yes, I did." Mum frowned as she opened the door and led the way into the building. Rose followed in silence, surprised by Mum's reaction to this discovery.

"Do you think they've got the wrong person?"

"I don't know," replied Mum. "Maybe."

Rose thought about this as they continued down the corridor. People peered out at them as they passed by, finally stopping outside a small room with faded green carpet and a collection of shabby desks arranged in rows.

They waved at Matt, who, like Rose, was sitting alone at the back of the room, scribbling on a sheet of paper with his feet up on the chair beside him. He glanced up in surprise, and Rose couldn't help but feel a stab of envy as he sailed out of the classroom without a backward glance, as unaffected by the whispering and staring as Mum had been.

"Why're we leaving now?" he asked, but Mum merely shrugged and gave him the same answer she'd given Rose.

Matt looked questioningly at Rose, but all she could

do was hold up her hands to show she had no more information than he did. They headed for the school car park and met up with Dad and Mary. Mary ran for the gate.

"Yeah! Early holidays!" she cried ecstatically. Rose laughed and decided to try her father instead.

"What's happened?"

"Oh, nothing." Dad gave her a reassuring smile and climbed back into the car. "Your mum spent the whole morning imagining all of the ways someone could attack you at school, so we decided it would be better to have you where we can see you. And seeing as there are only a couple of weeks left …"

He trailed off as he started the engine. Matt flung his bag into the boot and settled himself on the back seat between his sisters.

"Well, I'm not complaining."

He stretched out his legs, lounging in his seat.

Rose arrived downstairs after depositing her school things in her bedroom to find him relaxing on the sofa in front of the television.

"This is awesome," he said blissfully.

Mum gave him a disapproving look.

"We didn't bring you home early just so you could sit on the couch and watch TV. Why don't you go and do something constructive?"

"Like what?" said Matt, turning the television off.

"You can help your father and I put defensive spells around the house if you want."

"Why're you putting spells around the house?" asked

Mary. "We've already got the Shield."

"Because someone still managed to break into my room and take Grandpa's watch the other day?" guessed Rose.

"Right," said Mum.

Matt stood up, looking interested.

"OK. What do you want us to do?"

"You can do anything you want," said Mum. "Be creative. Start with your bedrooms and then you can help with the rest of the house and the yard. Your dad and I will start down here and come up to check what you've done later."

"Sounds like fun," said Rose, grinning at Matt on her way to the stairs.

She closed her bedroom door and put some music on, standing back to survey the room. The window struck her as a reasonable place to start, so she got to work, singing along with the music as she cast all of the best defensive spells she knew.

Placing magical barriers around the room, she then bewitched the window so that it would slam shut on anyone attempting to climb through it. If that failed, the curtains would wrap themselves around the intruder, holding them there, and the rug would roll itself around the person's legs.

As a final touch, she placed a spell on the doorknob so that the door would seal itself shut if a stranger touched it. Satisfied with her efforts, she went down the hall to see what the others had done.

She wasn't surprised to see that Matt had transformed his room into a war zone. Mary came to watch, too, as Matt explained how the electrical cord powering his desk fan would bind the hands and feet of any trespassers, and then pointed out the spell hidden around the doorframe, which, he declared with pride, would cause intruders to become disoriented and forget why they were there.

Five minutes later, Mum and Dad came in to add their own protection. Dad gazed around the room with an amused expression before going to the window and looking down at the gravel driveway, a floor below them.

"Matt, we want to *catch* anyone who gets inside, not *kill* them," he said, removing a spell for paralysis, which had been placed along the windowsill.

When the upper floor was so completely covered in spells that anyone attempting to sneak into the house would barely be able to move without being held captive by furniture or becoming so confused that they were unable to recognise where they were, Dad enchanted the staircase so that an intruder's feet would stick to the stairs if they tried to reach the upper rooms.

Rose and Mary stood beside him, giggling, as he completed the mix with a complicated protective spell that wrapped around the entire house. When they'd finished casting spells, they got to work in the invention room, sorting through all of the inventions and throwing the broken and outdated ones into a plastic tub. By six o'clock, everyone was exhausted and Dad pulled leftover pasta out of the fridge for dinner.

Too tired to do any more work on her project, Rose

picked up a book and settled down beside Mum on the sofa, reading and watching Dad, who had brought the tub of old inventions downstairs and was now pulling them apart for useful pieces, adding them to the box of spare parts.

After an hour or so, Rose drifted off to bed, yawning. She changed into her pyjamas and got into bed, feeling a little stiff from running up and down the stairs for most of the day. She'd barely fallen asleep when her door opened with a creak.

Half-awake, she sat up quickly, startled and thinking that it was a good thing she'd put defensive spells on the doorknob when she noticed the silhouettes of her brother and sister standing beside her bed. The rest of the house was quiet except for the sound of Dad snoring down the hall. Rose's eyes narrowed.

"What's going on?"

"We're going into the invention room to see what's in that black cabinet," whispered Mary with excitement. "I bet you anything Grandpa's invention is in there!"

"Are you coming?" Matt's grin was visible even in the darkness.

"What?! No!" gasped Rose, a little too loudly.

"Shh!" implored Matt and Mary, anxiously peering over their shoulders towards the hall. Rose crept out of bed and closed the door before whirling around to face the other two.

"Mum and Dad will have put spells on it so you can't touch whatever's in there! And even if you *do* get your hands on it, you don't know what it does! It could do all kinds of horrible things! Do you really think they would've gone to so much trouble to keep it away from us if it wasn't dangerous?"

Matt threw his hands up in frustration.

"I can't believe it! After everything we've heard, don't you want to know what Grandpa's been making?"

"Of course I do," snapped Rose. "But I'm not going to get myself cursed for it or something!"

Matt rolled his eyes. "Are you coming or not?"

"No, I'm not, and you shouldn't be going in there, either."

"Fine. We'll go on our own, then."

And with a haughty look, he turned and marched out of the room with Mary. Rose got back into bed and pulled the sheets up under her chin. She stared up at the ceiling, trying to forget about the black cabinet and its contents, but the thought of Matt and Mary creeping around in the invention room alone kept her wide awake. What if they found a way to open the cabinet and got hurt?

She tossed and turned, unable to get comfortable. She already had a bad feeling about Grandpa's invention, if that was what Mum and Dad were keeping in there, and she certainly didn't want to play with it before she knew just how bad it was.

Maybe I should go after them and make sure they don't do anything stupid, she thought.

She hesitated, arguing with herself until the anxiety and curiosity became too much for her to bear. Flinging back her sheets, she raced down the hall to the invention room. The protective spells on the door had already been removed, and she eased it open.

Matt and Mary were bending over the black cabinet. They glanced up as she closed the door behind her.

"I knew you wouldn't be able to help yourself," Matt chuckled.

He turned his attention back to the cabinet and Rose tiptoed across the room, passing the table of inventions. They shone faintly in the moonlight, some of them twirling, humming or ticking like a clock, while others glowed with pulsing or shimmering lights, casting moving gold and blue patterns on the walls.

Labels here and there along the table marked the various categories of inventions, including cleaning, repairs and other useful tasks. At the very end of the table sat the inventions ready to be sold to individuals and businesses. She stopped here, close to the small group of protective inventions, and looked down at the black cabinet she'd seen Dad piling reports and papers into before the masterclass.

It was well hidden in the shadows. She considered the cabinet for a moment, feeling the energy around it. As she'd suspected, the spells guarding it were strong.

Something about the cabinet seemed to repel her, as though it was silently commanding her to back out of the room and lock the door behind her. She had to stop herself from pushing Matt's hand away as he reached out to open it. There was no lock, but the door remained closed despite Matt pulling hard on the handle.

"I reckon a strong breaking spell should do the trick,"

he murmured, his voice almost lost among the gentle sounds of the inventions around them. "Let's see …"

He knelt in front of the cabinet. As he worked, he gripped the handle and tugged with all his might, but the door remained in place as firmly as though it had been welded shut.

"Maybe if we all tried together?"

Matt looked up at Rose hopefully before making a sound of annoyance at his sister's hesitant expression.

"Come *on*, Rose, we need you to help! On the count of three. One, two, three!"

Rose reluctantly fixed her eyes on the cabinet, and each of them used their strongest breaking spells, directing them at the door. She could feel the force of their combined effort pushing and straining at the protective spells, but they refused to break.

Matt gave up and leaned against the table beside him, panting.

"There has to be something in here that can open this for us."

He began to search the room for useful inventions, and Rose's eyes immediately jumped to the Shield. It hummed gently, the glittering black liquid inside it swirling thickly. Snatching it up, she checked that it was running at full power, resisting the urge to run from the room holding it over her head.

"Matt, I don't like this," she said, setting it back in its proper place on the table. "Don't you think we should go back to bed?"

But he was too busy trying to pry open the door to

hear her. After a second of silence, Mary let out a loud gasp.

"Hey, I know! What about the Spell Breaker in the box downstairs? Mum and Dad would've made it using their strongest magic, so it should be able to get through the spells on the cabinet, even if they're strong, too. Everyone can undo their own spells."

"Good idea," breathed Matt. "You keep trying and I'll go get it."

He checked that their parents were still asleep before hurrying down the hall, returning several minutes later with a plain wooden box tucked under his arm.

"And Mum and Dad were about to take this apart," he said with a mischievous grin, setting the Breaker on the workbench.

As he lifted the lid, a series of circular mirrors folded out, connected by a tough iron frame. He tilted each one until the cabinet was reflected squarely in the centre of the glass, forming a semicircle of mirrors around it, and Rose waited as they gradually turned colour, detecting the spells over the cabinet.

"Well, here goes."

Matt flicked a switch to activate the Breaker and then backed away. They waited in silence as heat enveloped the invention. Soon the cabinet glowed with blue light, and Rose had to shield her face from the blazing heat radiating from it. Its surface appeared to ripple, and just when it seemed that the cabinet would burst into flames, the heat began to die down and the blue light faded, leaving both the Breaker and the cabinet smoking, but cool to the touch.

Mary tried the door once again while the smoke haze cleared. Grasping the handle once more, she pulled until her knuckles turned white, but still it refused to open. Rose exhaled with relief, but Matt let out a growl of exasperation and sank to the floor in front of it.

"If the spells are that strong, I think we should leave it alone," insisted Rose, but Matt shook his head, more determined than ever.

"No, let's try one more time! And we'll all do breaking spells to help it." He reset the Breaker and activated it a second time. "On the count of three … one, two, three."

Rose hesitated, wondering if she should leave Matt and Mary to it, but Matt's jaw was set and Mary continued to tug on the door stubbornly. Rose knew that they wouldn't give up, even if it took them all night to unlock the cabinet, so she sighed and pushed at the door with her mind, willing it to open.

Even with the Breaker's help, Rose felt like she was trying to beat her way through a brick wall with her mind alone. She was about to give in when the protective spells began to weaken, caving under the combined pressure.

"It's working!" said Mary through clenched teeth, her hands balled up into fists with effort.

They pushed harder until the cabinet door clicked and swung open. Rose cancelled her spell gratefully, feeling drained. They'd hardly bent their heads down to peer into the cabinet when all of the protective inventions in the room wavered and died.

The Shield deactivated without a sound, the glittering liquid inside it falling still. Alarmed, Rose straightened up and, almost without thinking, reached out to slam the cabinet door shut again.

"What are you doing?" Matt protested, taking hold of her wrist. "Leave it open!"

"Matt, this is a really bad sign. You saw how much energy it took for the Breaker to destroy the spells on that door! Whatever's in there just took out every protective spell in the room in an instant! We need to leave it alone and go back to bed."

Ignoring her, Matt swung the cabinet door all the way open.

"You worry too much, Rose. There's nothing in here except papers! Look!"

Rose bent her head down and saw a pile of books, pages and reports crammed inside the cabinet. Confused, she eyed the papers suspiciously as Matt opened the book on top of the pile. He flipped through the pages and put it back, looking disappointed.

"None of this makes any sense."

"I'm not surprised," replied Rose, reading the complicated instructions and descriptions over his shoulder. Matt gathered up the documents and returned them to the cabinet.

"Wait a moment," he said, peering further in. "There's something else here." He reached in all the way to the back and lifted out a green object that had been hidden in the shadows. "This is more like it!"

Rose gasped in wonder as he held it up to the light. The invention was slightly larger than Matt's hand, with a decorative casing that formed the shape of a flower bud, blossoming out wider near the bottom before curving gracefully to a point. A single band of metal formed the base of the invention, shaped to look like it had been braided.

Rose stared, captivated by the magic radiating from it. Her eyes travelled to the centre of the invention, where a cluster of long, jagged glass pieces protruded into the air, mimicking the stamens on a flower. They seemed to grow out of the braided metal base, and they glistened in the light, looking painfully sharp. Matt noticed them, too, and immediately handled the bud more carefully, making sure none of his fingers slipped through the casing.

A faint white light emanated from the flower bud, illuminating Matt's face as he weighed it in his hand. Rose felt strangely drawn to it, and she repressed the urge to reach out and touch it with difficulty.

"I didn't think it'd be so pretty," said Mary in a hushed voice. Matt held the invention closer, staring at the bud with wide eyes.

"This has to be Grandpa's invention. Why else would Mum and Dad have hidden it in here with such strong spells to protect it?"

"But I thought they didn't know where it was?" whispered Rose.

"I guess they must have found it," replied Matt. "I wonder how you activate it …"

He turned the invention over, searching for a way to open it.

"I don't think that's a good idea," said Rose quickly, waking up to herself. "You wanted to see it and now you have, so let's put it back."

But Matt shook his head.

"Don't be stupid!" he said, holding the invention out of her reach. "We can't get this far and not even try to open it up!"

"Yeah, I want to see how it works!" said Mary.

She and Matt began aiming spells at the bud.

"Don't do that!" said Rose, horrified. She cancelled their spells with a wave of her hand. "You don't know what that thing does! And Mum and Dad are always telling us it's dangerous. Put it back!"

She lunged for the invention and caught hold of it, but Matt wouldn't let go. He pulled at it, and Rose pulled back.

"This is stupid!" she cried. "You're going to get us all into trouble! Let go!"

But the metal casing had already begun to unravel from its decorative pattern, shrinking back down into the base of the bud. Rose gasped and let go, backing away as the pieces moved like snakes, stopping about halfway down the invention and fanning out at the ends, exposing the glass shards. Matt held the bud in his palm nervously as the glass pieces began to glow. Rose eyed the bud warily.

"How did you activate it?"

"I don't know … I must've done it by accident,"

Matt said, his voice wavering. "But it's not doing much, anyway. See, it's not so bad!"

"Just because you can't see anything happening, doesn't mean it's not doing anything," snapped Rose, thinking of something Mum had once told her.

There were three types of inventions: ones that affected a person physically, ones that affected the mind, and ones that influenced both. Rose surveyed her brother and sister. They both appeared normal. This invention must be doing something they couldn't see or feel.

The hairs on the back of her neck stood up suddenly. She peered over her shoulder, expecting to see someone standing behind her, but the room was empty except for the three of them.

"Whatever you did, Matt, you'd better undo it quick!" growled Rose as the feeling intensified.

Matt and Mary must have felt it, too. They exchanged looks of alarm. With a flash, the metal casing of the flower bud glowed red hot and Matt dropped it with a cry of pain, his hand covered in blisters.

The invention hit the floor with a clang. The white light glowed brighter, gathering at the tips of the glass pieces before travelling down into the centre of the bud. Rose concentrated on the invention with all the strength she had left, willing it to deactivate, but nothing she did made the slightest difference.

"How do we stop it?" Mary's face was desperate as she looked down at the angry burns covering Matt's hand. "We don't know how to turn it off!"

"Go and get Mum and Dad," ordered Rose, who was now wondering how she could have been so stupid as to go near the cabinet in the first place.

The room lurched as she spoke, sending her reeling into the table, and the air around her became distorted, just as it had in the library after the masterclass. Matt and Mary both staggered and toppled over, and Mary narrowly avoided cracking her head on the corner of the workbench. Rose caught herself on the table, gripping the sides with trembling fingers.

"It's making me dizzy!" cried Mary, struggling to get to her feet.

Rose attempted to steady herself as the room spun, and she took several deep breaths, hoping she wasn't going to throw up. She'd get to Mum and Dad even if she had to crawl.

She hadn't gone more than a step when she noticed a new sensation stealing over her. Her energy seemed to be draining away, leaving her ice cold, weak and shaking all over. Matt blinked furiously, clutching his head as though trying to clear it.

"Go and get Mum and Dad!" Rose screeched again.

Mary scrambled across the floor to the hall as Rose searched the room for something that could help them. Matt was now slumped against the leg of the workbench, his eyelids drooping and his burnt hand twitching.

Rose stared up at the rows of inventions on the table, fighting the impulse to curl up on the floor and sink into unconsciousness. Her eyes found the Shield and she stretched out her hand.

"The protective spells in this will help," she mumbled, hoping Matt could still hear her.

The glow from the bud was so bright that it hurt her eyes. She clutched the Shield tightly, her fingers fumbling over the switch. The invention flickered to life with a whirl of glittering fluid, only to explode seconds later, sending pieces of glass and metal flying through the room, splattering dark liquid over the walls.

Horrified, she grabbed another protective invention and activated it, flinching as it, too, exploded. Too weak to continue, Rose sank onto the floor alongside Matt, barely conscious. She turned her head in time to see the door fly open. It struck the wall with a crash as Mum and Dad charged in. Mary peered into the room from behind them, her face pale with shock.

Dad did something to the flower bud and waited as the green covering grew back up over the glass pieces, interlocking and curling at the tip. The glow from inside it died away, leaving the room looking dim as he put the bud back into the cabinet with the papers and placed the protective spells back over the door.

Rose felt her strength returning the moment the invention was locked away. She looked up at her parents' furious faces and waited for them to start yelling.

"Go downstairs." Mum's voice was quiet but firm as she stared around at the broken pieces littering the room. "We'll come down when we've cleaned this up."

Rose, Matt and Mary obeyed in silence, scurrying down to the dark living room and sitting on the sofa. The minutes trickled by agonisingly slowly, but Rose didn't dare move. It was well after midnight when her parents finally reappeared.

Mum glanced at the bulb above their heads and light filled the room. Then she sat down in an armchair and fixed her gaze on each of them. Matt's burnt hand and the cuts that covered Rose from the broken inventions slowly healed. Rose bowed her head, unable to talk due to the lump that had formed in her throat.

"We know it's been hard having all of this going on around you, and that you're frustrated at not being able to get involved," said Dad, standing beside the stairs. "It's fine to be curious, but going into the invention room and playing with something you don't know anything about by yourselves is just plain dangerous. You know that."

Rose sat in silence and let her parents rage on. She kept her eyes fixed on the carpet, feeling more and more guilty. Mum spoke quietly, her voice carrying in the still night air.

"Now that you've had a taste of what that invention does, I hope we can trust you not to go near it again. If we weren't forced to keep it, I'd make sure it was destroyed. It might be only a prototype, but it's still close enough to the real thing for it to be dangerous."

"So that's not the real one?" said Rose, finally finding her voice.

"No. It's the test version your grandfather made when he started designing the real invention. The real one is much worse."

Rose blinked, not expecting such a straightforward

answer.

"But if it's that bad, why is it *here*?" asked Matt.

Mum sighed and explained in a weary tone.

"When your grandpa went missing his invention disappeared with him, and he kept a lot of what he did to make it a secret. So we've been asked to keep the prototype and study it in case we can't find the real thing or it's been destroyed. Now that he's gone, we're the only ones who know enough about it to control it, so we're the best people to keep it safe."

Rose felt guiltier than ever.

"I want all three of you to promise me you'll leave it alone from now on," said Mum.

Rose, Matt and Mary answered in unison.

"I promise."

"OK, then." Mum's face softened as she looked at each of them. "Get back into bed, please."

They stood up without a word and left the room.

"You were right, Rose," said Mary once they were in the hall. "We shouldn't have opened the cabinet."

But Matt shook his head, his grin back in place.

"It was worth it. Now we know what everyone's been fussing over."

5

Frustration

Rose sat outside with Matt and Mary the following morning. The three of them had risen early, eager to discuss their encounter with the strange invention, and they sat on the wooden bench, whispering among themselves until their parents appeared.

It was another clear day and the scent of eucalyptus filled the air as the sun warmed the leaves of the trees above them. Mum had remembered her promise to teach Rose some advanced spells for her project, and after declaring that the weather was too fine for sitting indoors, they had decided to take their work out into the yard.

"You're going to need more than finding spells on these if you want to break through strong blocking spells," she said, picking through the pieces Rose had chosen for her invention.

Rose made a sound of agreement, thinking of her failed attempts to find Grandpa with the Scope.

"What if I use breaking spells too? That would work, wouldn't it?"

Mum nodded. "You could try that, yes. But you might have to experiment a bit. Spells that cancel magic come in three different groups. In the first, the effects of the blocking spell are counteracted, and in the second, they're broken apart by force, like breaking a piece of glass. Breaking spells are in that group, so they can't be used for everything."

Mum picked up the cushion she'd brought with her.

"The third group of spells will undo the block bit by bit. These spells are called compound spells because they're almost always used alongside other magic. The one I'm going to teach you now is called a dissolution spell, and because it's a compound spell, if you do it right, it'll blend with whatever else you decide to use."

Mum placed the cushion on the table and contemplated the mix of invention pieces on the table.

"You know, you might want to consider making at least some of these blue. It sounds strange, but over the years I've noticed that dissolution spells work even better when at least one part of the invention is blue. I'm not sure why."

Rose raised her eyebrows in surprise.

"I didn't know the colour was important!"

"It makes quite a bit of difference," replied Mum. "There are people who study those kinds of influences on magic. It's very interesting, really, but let's concentrate on breaking spells for now. They might be all you need."

Mum's cushion rose up into the air, hovering above the tabletop.

"Let's see if you can break my levitation spell."

Rose fixed her gaze on the cushion, willing it to fall, and seconds later it obeyed, bouncing off the table.

Mum caught it before it hit the ground, looking pleased.

"Very good. Let's try something harder, then. Do you want to try the dissolution spell?"

"All right," said Rose, shifting in her seat a little apprehensively. Mum levitated the cushion again.

"This time, instead of concentrating on breaking the spell, try to feel like you're undoing it. Imagine my spell's like a cloth, made up of lots of little threads. Instead of trying to cut through it, or tear it, you're trying to pull the threads apart."

Rose concentrated on the cushion again, staring hard at the fabric until it began to unravel. She yelped and cancelled her spell, but Mum nodded encouragingly.

"Yes, that's the effect you want. You're thinking the right way." She repaired the cushion and sent it back up into the air. "Now try to focus on my spell, rather than the cushion itself."

Rose tried again, staring at the cushion and waiting for something to happen. When it remained in the air, she took a deep breath and pushed at the spell until her hands were balled up into fists. Reaching out with her mind, she tried to pick at the edges of Mum's spell, but they held tight. She might as well have been attempting to prise them apart with her bare hands.

After several minutes of directing all of her energy at the spell without any success, Rose let her breath out in a rush. She reached out and pulled the cushion down. Mum laughed, but Rose poked the fabric moodily with a finger as all of her doubts returned.

"I think this spell is too advanced. I can't do it."

"You'll get it, don't worry," said Mum reassuringly. "You need to practise, that's all. You've only just started learning it. How about I go and get my old textbook? It used to be my mother's, but she gave it to me when I was your age and it taught me how to do compound spells, so it might help you, too."

Rose sent the cushion into the air again while Mum went back into the house. She thought about what Mum had told her, focusing her attention on the levitation spell. When this had no effect at all, she pulled the cushion down again and rested her head on it comfortably, watching Dad give Matt and Mary a lesson on invention-making at the other end of the table. He picked up the box of spare parts and set it in front of him.

"Mary, I think you know enough magic now to start making some serious inventions. How about we start you out with a basic shield or something like that?"

Mary nodded frantically, her face shining with excitement as Dad turned to Matt.

"Matt, show me what you've been working on."

Matt held up something that looked a bit like a metal centipede except for the flexible and stretchy wire that ran through the centre. It bore an assortment of tiny attachments that had been fixed at certain points along its length in place of legs.

"It's a kind of Hook," he explained, holding it out for inspection. "It can reach into any hole or gap and grab hold of things. I got the idea from the time Mary dropped your keys down the storm water drain."

Mary rolled her eyes and Rose snorted with laughter.

"I like it," said Dad with a chuckle. "Keep going with it for a minute while I help Mary make her Shield and I'll get back to you."

Matt pulled some more attachments out of his pocket and began adding them to his Hook.

"Now, the first thing you have to do when you make an invention is decide what you want it to do, in as much detail as you can," Dad told Mary. "Then you need to think about *how* it'll do what you want. The function of the invention will give you some ideas about how to make it, what shape it should be, and things like that. Its build has to allow the spells you use to work freely. It's also a good idea to make finished piece light up or move in some way. If people can't tell an invention is working, they can get impatient, or they might think there's something wrong with it, so that's another thing to remember. But for now, let's start at the beginning and see what we can come up with."

He helped Mary choose some pieces and they got to work. Mum returned and offered Rose a plain, scruffy-looking book titled *A Guide to Advanced Magic: Compound Spells and Spell Deconstruction.*

Rose flicked through the pages. They were yellowed and folded over in several places, but to Rose's immense relief, they contained detailed and helpful descriptions and explanations. Even better, she saw full lessons on boosting and tracking spells, which would form two of the key components of her invention. Handwritten notes filled the margins here and there, and Rose read them eagerly, thrilled to be holding something that had once been her grandmother's.

When their lessons were over, Rose took her sketchbook, invention pieces and new textbook up into the tree house and began to use some of the magic she'd just learned. Matt and Mary followed, bringing their own work.

"Look at this!" Mary trilled, waving the beginnings of her Shield in Rose's face. Rose admired it with a grin while her sister launched into a full description of the spells and method she'd used to make it.

"That's great, Mary. Which pieces did you use?"

"I took some parts from Mum and Dad's Scales," said Mary, placing her Shield on the floorboards in front of her, where everyone could see it. Matt sat down on a bean bag and jerked his chin at Rose's sketchbook.

"How's your invention coming along?"

Rose's shoulders slumped and she turned the pages of her textbook a little despairingly.

"It's going all right, I suppose. But I think I'll have to change my idea again. The invention will have to work in a completely different way than I'd planned."

Setting her textbook aside, she opened her sketchbook and rifled through the pages, searching for a blank page. She still liked the idea of an eye-shaped invention, but she would have to modify her original design now that she had new spells to accommodate, so she picked up her pencil and began sketching.

After an hour or so of hard work, she sighed and scratched out all of her ideas, frustrated with her efforts.

She shook her head and started again, grumbling.

"I don't know. None of these are right. I've got parts of four different inventions and I can't seem to get them to fit together. I'll be lucky to find Grandpa before next Christmas at this rate."

"You'll figure it out," said Mary, peering down at Rose's sketches. "You always do."

Rose grinned at her sister, grateful for the confidence in her voice.

"Try thinking about something else for a while," suggested Matt. "Sometimes taking a break helps you come up with ideas."

"Yeah, I guess."

Starting to feel truly baffled, Rose leaned against the wall of the tree house, enjoying the warmth of the sun on her face as she watched an ant crawl along the windowsill. She rubbed her eyes and yawned, thinking about last night. She hadn't been able to stop herself replaying everything that had happened in the invention room over and over again in her mind, seeing the ornate covering of the flower bud begin to move, and remembering the horrible, weak feeling that had stolen over her.

Now that she'd seen the invention, she was keener than ever to know more about it. She was curious to know what it would have done to them if their parents hadn't reached them in time, but remained convinced, somehow, that it wasn't simply putting them to sleep. All she knew for sure, however, was that she never wanted to go near the thing again. She was more than happy to learn what she could about it from a safe distance.

They sat in silence, Mary admiring her Shield and Matt staring out of the window until Rose spoke.

"You know, I thought we'd had it for sure last night. When we were in the invention room, I mean."

"Yeah, so did I," admitted Matt. His gaze was distant, as though he, too, was reliving the night before. "I can't believe we got off that easily. We don't usually. Last time I did something like that they grounded me for six months. Remember when I was eight and accidentally demolished part of the house?"

Mary's mouth fell open and Rose cringed, the memory still fresh in her mind. Matt looked at his younger sister sheepishly.

"I was trying to destroy an invention like they do in the Archives, but I didn't know what I was doing." He bit his lip, shamefaced. "The invention threw my spell back at me and it hit the house instead."

Rose shook her head, trying to dispel the image in her mind's eye.

"You were lucky you weren't hurt. Mum and Dad were so angry! But I think they let us off last night because they feel bad about keeping us in the dark for so long."

Mary tucked her knees up under her chin, looking guilty.

"Yeah, that's probably it. But at least we know what Grandpa's invention is now."

"Well, kind of," said Matt, his eyes bright with

excitement. "We know what it looks like. But it's a start, isn't it?"

"They said it was a test version," continued Rose. "A prototype. And that the real one is still missing. I wonder where it is and why Grandpa needed to make a tester? People don't usually, do they?"

Matt shrugged. "Mum and Dad don't, but I guess it's like they said last night. It must have seriously complicated magic on it and Grandpa wanted to see if the spells he planned to use would work without risking his better materials. I wonder what it was doing to us? The brighter the light got, the weaker I felt. Did it make you feel like that, too?"

"Yeah. It felt like it was sucking the energy out of me or something. But I think it affected you more than me. I was further away from it. By the time Mum and Dad got there, you were almost unconscious."

Rose shuddered, feeling cold despite the sunlight. Mary hung her head and picked up her Shield, fiddling idly with it.

"Mum and Dad looked really scared when I told them what was happening. I've never seen them that scared before."

Rose's insides squirmed as a fresh wave of guilt engulfed her. They lapsed into thoughtful silence again, the only sound the steady droning of a cicada somewhere in the tree above their heads.

"We should have done as they said," murmured Rose eventually. "We shouldn't have gone anywhere near that cabinet."

"It was so pretty, though," said Mary. "I wonder what was making the white light? It was so bright."

But Rose could only shrug her shoulders.

"I don't know. I've never seen anything like it before."

"Why would anyone make an invention that sucked the energy out of you?" said Matt, after a pause. "Isn't that kind of magic illegal?"

Rose frowned. She hadn't thought of it that way before. Their parents had always warned them that the invention was something bad, but it had never occurred to her that it could have illegal magic in it. She closed her sketchbook with more force than she'd meant to, sending her pencil skittering across the floor.

"That can't be what it's doing."

She caught the pencil before it rolled out of the tree house and twirled it between her fingers distractedly, searching for another explanation.

"What if it makes you feel weak but it doesn't hurt you? I've heard of inventions that create illusions ..."

"Yeah, I bet that's it," agreed Matt, a hint of relief in his voice.

"Grandpa wouldn't do anything bad," declared Mary. "He hates stuff like that. And the Archivists wouldn't have let him make the bud if he hadn't got it approved and everything, would they?"

Rose's frown deepened.

"No, they wouldn't. He'd have to get permission. But he must have, seeing as he made the invention."

Matt's expression darkened and his eyebrows knitted

together in confusion. "That's another thing. He shouldn't have been able to get permission for something like that, so why did he? If the invention is doing what we think it is, someone must have broken a lot of laws to approve it."

Rose was now wishing she hadn't brought up the subject of Grandpa's invention. She made a half-hearted sound of agreement and tried to think of something else, but Mary chattered on relentlessly beside her, her voice low and urgent.

"Didn't Dave say that the woman from the Archives was going through Grandpa's reports?"

Rose sighed and nodded.

"He did. It could have been her who approved it."

"Either way, it looks like someone wants that flower bud pretty badly," said Matt. "I wonder what they want it for?"

"I'm not sure I want to know," replied Rose fervently.

"If Alison wanted Grandpa's invention, why didn't she didn't just make it herself?" wondered Mary. "It'd be better than stealing it."

This, at least, seemed obvious to Rose. Grandpa had been inventing for decades and knew things that could only be learned from a lifetime of experience. It made perfect sense that he would be commissioned to make an invention like the green bud.

"You're not going to find anyone better than Grandpa when it comes to making complicated inventions," she said. "You know, I think I'm beginning to see why everyone wants this kept so quiet. Mum and Dad did say they've been sworn to secrecy."

She clutched her pencil tightly in her hands as silence descended once more.

They ate lunch together in the tree house, enjoying the fine weather, and then ran around in the yard, tossing a stick for Cocoa to fetch until they'd forgotten all about the mysterious invention.

Thirsty now, Rose ran into the kitchen through the back door and stopped, hearing an unfamiliar voice in the living room. Intrigued, she, Matt and Mary stepped into the kitchen, and all three of them stuck their heads around the door. Mum saw them and immediately tensed.

"Oh, here they are."

Rose noted the anxiety in Mum's voice as she beckoned to them, and the guarded expression on Dad's face as they entered the room. Rose sat down beside her mother and smiled at the woman opposite her. She was wearing smart clothes and her hands were twisted nervously in her lap. She sat bolt upright in her chair, looking quite as awkward as Rose's parents.

Her dark brown curls brushed her shoulders and her deep blue eyes searched Rose's face in an almost desperate way. She was slender, and while she seemed healthy, Rose thought she had a slightly frail look about her.

"Er, this is Kate," said Mum falteringly.

"Hi," said Rose, waving at the woman.

"This is Rose, Matthew and Mary," said Mum,

indicating each of her children.

"It's good to meet you," said Kate, shifting in her chair. She opened her mouth to speak, met Rose's eyes and then stopped, seeming unsure of what to say. Confused, Rose gave the young woman a look that she hoped was friendly and reassuring.

"Have you got something to do with Grandpa's invention, too?" asked Mary, peeking out from behind Mum's shoulder.

"Yes, you could say that," said Kate hesitantly.

Dad turned to Rose, apparently sensing danger.

"Kate is from the Archives."

Rose blinked in surprise. "Are you really?"

Kate nodded, looking grateful for the change of subject.

"Your parents said that you're thinking about working there when you finish school."

"Only if I get good enough grades," replied Rose. "I've heard they only take the best."

"Well, we'd love to have you, I'm sure," said Kate. "We don't have anywhere near enough staff. There's only myself and one other person working there, so it's a bit of a job to get things done on time. What level of magic and invention are you doing this year?"

"I'm about to finish grade seven in magic and grade five in invention," recited Rose.

"Already?" Kate looked impressed. "You must be talented."

Rose blushed and glanced down at her knees. "I started early."

Mum began to ask Kate about an old friend who had once worked at the Archives, and Rose, getting the feeling that all was not as it seemed, watched the young woman carefully, wondering why she had come to visit. Had the Archives perhaps sent her to explain the situation with the other Archivist, Alison Maxwell?

She could tell that her parents were wary, but also keen to get to know the woman, making Rose even more curious. Mum and Dad were as used to isolation as she was herself, having been shunned by most of society all their lives. It was unusual for them to open up to a stranger these days, even if that person was magical.

When Kate got up to leave, thanking Mum and Dad for seeing her, Rose got up, too, and watched her parents walk with Kate to the door, listening silently as Mum invited Kate to visit again whenever she wanted. Rose exchanged puzzled looks with Matt and Mary. She turned to her parents as soon as they had closed the door and Kate had vanished from view.

"What was that about?"

Mum gave her a wide-eyed look of surprise. "What was what about?"

"What did Kate want to see you about? Was it Grandpa's invention?"

Mum said nothing as she walked over to the sofa and began straightening the cushions.

"Not his invention, no."

"Does she know Grandpa, then?" piped up Mary.

"Why was she dressed so smart if she just wanted to see *us*?" added Matt before Mum could answer.

"And why was she so nervous about meeting us?" asked Rose.

Dad smiled and shook his head.

"You'll find out soon enough, but not today, I'm afraid."

Rose caught the pained expression on her brother's face and couldn't help but laugh.

She was on her way upstairs after breakfast the next morning when she heard a hurried knocking on the front door. Turning back, she opened it to find Kate on the doorstep, looking elated and a little windswept, like she'd just run a race.

"Hi, Rose," said Kate breathlessly. "Sorry to visit so early, but there's something I need to talk to your parents about. I'll only keep them for a minute."

"It's OK, come in."

Rose stood back to let her inside and called for her parents. Mum appeared on the landing and led Kate into the living room while Rose went upstairs to continue work on her project.

Sitting at her desk, she pulled her sketchbook and invention pieces towards her, only to realise that she'd left her grandmother's textbook on compound spells on the coffee table. She tiptoed down towards the living room and was about to announce her presence when Kate handed Mum something small and golden.

Rose stopped in the doorway and then backed away, her interest piqued. Mum took the object with a word of thanks, turning it over in her hand before moving it out of sight.

Rose waited, but neither Mum nor Kate mentioned the golden object again. They spoke in voices too low for her to hear for several minutes until Kate stood up to leave. Rose retreated upstairs, not daring to venture back down to the living room until she heard the dull thud of the front door being closed.

Life inside the house became busier than usual over the next few days, as Mum gave Rose, Matt and Mary a list of things to do around the house. Christmas was approaching fast and it was Rose's job to help with the cleaning and put up the decorations.

Mary came running downstairs the moment Rose had conjured the two heavy boxes into the living room. With a squeal of excitement, she opened the nearest box and began pulling out containers of baubles and tinsel. Rose threw out an arm to stop her from upending the box all over the floor.

"Help me set up the tree before you unpack everything else!"

With a pout, Mary acquiesced, and for the next several hours, they had fun setting up the Christmas tree and covering the house in icicles and silver lights. Dad entered the room to check their progress, and at Mary's request, placed her favourite spells over the tree, so that tiny stars flashed and sparkled all over it, constantly changing colour. Once they'd finished, Rose used the leftover tinsel to decorate her bedroom before heading into the kitchen for lunch.

Both of her parents were in the invention room for a change, working on new creations of their own. Rose had noticed a definite change in their behaviour over the last week or so. Judging by their restlessness, their work in the library had not gone to plan. Instead of poring over books, they'd taken to roaming around the house at all hours, and adjusting the protective spells on it almost obsessively.

"I think all this drama with Grandpa is starting to drive them mad," remarked Rose in an undertone as she sat down at the table.

Matt stopped with his fork halfway to his mouth as Dad entered the room and stared around as though searching for something before disappearing into the laundry without a word. Matt grinned.

"I know. I don't think I've ever seen them this preoccupied."

"Dad forgot to give me another magic lesson this morning," said Mary from the other side of the table. "I don't think he even realised I was talking to him when I reminded him. He just ran back upstairs saying he had to check on something."

Rose swallowed a mouthful of salad and watched in silence as Mum drifted into the living room and dropped an enormous spell book onto the coffee table with a crash. She summoned another book from the library, barely glancing at the first page before tossing it aside, too. Heaving a heavy sigh, she wandered back upstairs with Cocoa at her heels.

"Well, at least they're telling us some of what's going

on now," said Rose in a cheerful tone. "That's something."

Since she'd gone into the invention room with Matt and Mary and discovered the metal flower bud, Mum and Dad had not bothered to disguise the fact that they were searching for Grandpa's real invention, and while this was a definite improvement, Rose still wished that she could help her parents in some way.

Deciding it was best not to ask, she and Mary headed out into the backyard to play with Cocoa after lunch. Just as they had the previous day, Mum and Dad opened the back door to join them outside.

"We're going out to search for your grandpa again, and maybe see if we can find out what he did with that invention of his, too," Mum told them. "It should've been in his invention room, but we cleaned it out thoroughly yesterday and it's not there. And we're sure no one else has found it, so we're going out to look for it."

"It shouldn't be too hard to find," added Dad with his usual confidence. "He must have hidden it somewhere else in the house."

"I thought people had been searching for it for a while now?" said Rose. "If it was that easy to find, wouldn't they have found it already?"

Mum gave her a small smile.

"Yes, but the people who have been looking don't know about most of his hiding places, and I do, so we might have more luck."

"All right, then," said Rose peaceably, glad to know

what was going on.

"I don't think we'll be gone long, but I've asked Kate to come over and keep you company. Is that OK?"

"Sure," said Rose, keen to have another opportunity to find out more about Kate, and perhaps the golden object she'd given Mum.

"We still want you to stay inside the house," Dad reminded them, hugging each of them goodbye.

"We won't go anywhere."

She took the chewed-up tennis ball Cocoa brought to her as her parents opened the back gate, waiting by the front of the house for Kate to arrive. There was the crunch of footsteps on gravel and Rose turned to see Kate walking up the driveway. She stopped to speak to Mum and Dad for a moment before heading for the backyard, waving at the two girls.

"Hi!" she said, making her way over to where they were playing in the shade. "I hope you don't mind me staying for a while."

"Of course not," replied Rose, following Kate and Mary inside.

They found Matt in the living room, engrossed in his video games, and Mary rushed to join in, begging Kate to play, too. Kate agreed with a laugh and they all settled themselves cross-legged on the living room floor. The hours crept by and darkness descended around them, the glare of the television screen illuminating their faces and throwing deep shadows on the walls behind them.

They talked as they played and Rose soon decided that she liked Kate. After an hour or so, Rose grew tired of video games and asked Kate what it was like to work in the Archives. Kate gave the game controller to Mary for her turn and entertained them with stories about the most unusual and exciting inventions she'd worked on during her time there, as well as her travels and meetings with magical people in other countries.

Rose was fascinated and forgot to question her about the mysterious golden object. Rose had never been outside of Australia, and although she knew there were magical people overseas, she knew very little about them.

"At the start of my apprenticeship they sent me to Germany to study the ways medieval Europeans used magic," said Kate with a reminiscent smile. "All of the apprentices have to learn how to put inventions together the way makers did before modern materials and spells were invented, so that they can restore the old inventions using the right methods."

Matt and Mary gazed up at Kate, their eyes wide with curiosity, and Rose asked, "Do you ever make your own?"

Kate shook her head.

"I put them back together quite a bit for work, but I never make anything from scratch. I'm actually repairing some inventions at the moment. What about you three? It must be great having parents that are inventors."

"It is pretty cool," agreed Rose as Matt defeated the final boss and cheered while Mary began a victory dance around the living room. "We all started inventing at a young age because of it. Watching them made us want to try it, too. Matt's been making inventions since he was six and Mary's already made her first real Shield." She grinned at her sister proudly. "And inventing with Grandpa is fun because he knows even more than Mum and Dad."

Kate looked down at her hands.

"It must be hard. To lose him, I mean. Especially when you're not allowed to know what's going on."

Rose nodded, biting her lip.

"Yeah, it is. We've been trying to find out what everyone's up to for a while now, but Mum and Dad say they're not allowed to talk about it. I suppose you can't tell us anything, either?"

Rose tried to keep the disappointment out of her voice, certain that Kate would say no.

"Actually, I wasn't forbidden to talk about it."

Mary gasped and Matt dropped the controller.

"But if your parents can't tell you anything, then I'm not sure I should," Kate added, chuckling at the eagerness on their faces.

"Are you sure?" said Matt wheedlingly. "Not even one tiny detail?"

"I'd better not. Not unless your mum and dad say it's OK."

Mary seemed to deflate at these words and Matt gave a sigh of resignation, turning back to his game. Rose changed the subject, knowing full well what her parents would say if she asked them.

"So, what do you have to do to work in the Archives?"

"You'll start an apprenticeship, which lasts for three years," said Kate. "Once you've finished the training you can choose to specialise in one particular area. And they teach you how to recognise the spells and specifications that different inventions have."

She pointed to Rose's collection of invention pieces, scattered over the coffee table, where Rose had been working on them before abandoning them in frustration.

"For example, judging from the spells on those pieces, I can see that the finished invention will have an infinite range and will be made of aluminium and glass. Glass is perfect for inventions that need to be able to cut through other spells because it amplifies the effects of the spells and clarifies the response. It will have compound finding and dissolution spells on it, and it'll be made in the classic design style."

Rose's jaw dropped.

"You got all that just from looking at the pieces?"

"They make everyone learn that kind of thing before they send you off to one of the sectors," shrugged Kate.

"Did you have any accidents when you were learning?" asked Matt with a grin.

"All the time," said Kate. "Sometimes it's funny when things go wrong, but other times it can be dangerous. One invention grew razor-sharp, three-inch fangs when we tried to dismantle it and we couldn't figure out how to control it. It was like a wild animal or something. It terrorised us for days before suddenly hiding somewhere. It took us a week to find it."

Unsure whether she should laugh at this or not,

Rose made a sound halfway between a snort of laughter and a gasp of horror.

"Did you catch it?"

"Eventually, yeah," replied Kate. "One of the other apprentices, Ben, found it hiding underneath the sofa in the staff room. We were all too afraid to go near the thing, so our supervisor had to grab it. I felt really sorry for him. He came back from a job somewhere else to find us all standing on the tables and chairs."

"What happened to the supervisor?" said Rose, picturing the scene in her mind's eye and fighting back a giggle.

"He was fine, but Ben tried to help and got bitten quite badly. He needed loads of stitches and he nearly lost a finger. The doctors at the hospital didn't believe him when he told them an invention had done it. He made a full recovery, but he still likes to joke that his hand's never been the same since."

Kate rolled her eyes.

"But like I said, you can specialise in one particular area, so you don't have to deal with dangerous inventions if you don't want to. Mind you, they're so short on employees that we all end up doing a bit of everything these days, regardless."

Rose stared at the television screen, lost in thought.

"It'd be great to work in the Archives, but I just can't decide whether I want to be an Archivist or an inventor like Mum and Dad."

"When the time comes to choose, you'll know which one is right for you," Kate assured her. "Working in the

Archives can be hard because so few people are accepted, and there are thousands of inventions and records to maintain. It can be a lonely job, too. That's definitely worth considering."

Rose dismissed this with a wave of her hand.

"That wouldn't bother me. I'm used to being on my own. Whenever I'm not with Matt and Mary, I'm usually up in my room doing my own thing anyway."

Kate looked like she understood.

"I don't suppose it would help, living in an isolated place like this. But at least you have your brother and sister. I was the only magical person in my entire school and I didn't have any siblings."

"It must have been a lot harder for you than it is for me, then," Rose admitted.

"I couldn't wait to graduate and get away from school, I was so sick of being alone and picked on all the time," groaned Kate. "But I suppose it wasn't all that bad. I used to hide in the library at lunch every day, studying and doing my homework, so at least I got good grades. And it gets a little easier when you're older. Most people like us get a job working for the government, controlling how magic is used, so they get to meet other people like themselves."

Mum and Dad materialised by the front door as Kate spoke, their faces drawn and pale. Mum stepped into the living room and turned the overhead light on with a glance.

"No luck," said Dad, in response to Rose's questioning look. "There doesn't seem to be any trace of the Fragmenter anywhere, but it can't just disappear!"

He threw himself down on the sofa, yawning widely while Mum kicked her shoes off, looking exasperated.

"He must have made a new hiding place! But I don't see why he'd keep it a secret from *us*. I guess we'll just have to keep looking."

Kate straightened up from helping Matt pack away the games.

"Can I help? It's possible he might have hidden it somewhere in his room at the Archives …"

"Yes, he might have." Mum's expression was pensive as she shrugged off her bag and placed it on the table. "He's never used the room much before, but I suppose this time is different, isn't it?"

"I think I've had enough of inventions for today," declared Dad, getting up and going into the kitchen. "It's time for dinner."

Rose tuned out of the conversation as Mum thanked Kate for babysitting, wondering why Grandpa would hide his invention somewhere without telling her parents. She turned to ask Matt what he thought, but he and Mary were busy bundling up the controllers and weren't paying attention to the adults, so she went into the kitchen to help her father get dinner ready instead.

Mum and Dad continued to search for Grandpa's invention over the next several weeks, leaving them under Kate's supervision. They returned home looking more and more disappointed each time, and Rose began to think that the invention might have been destroyed when Grandpa's house had been torn apart. She voiced this concern to her mother one night while they were packing the dishes away, but Mum was quick to reassure her.

"I don't think so. We've cleaned the place up and checked everything. There's no sign of it in the house. The only place I can think of that we haven't searched is the Archives."

Rose dried off a stack of cutlery and began sorting it into a drawer.

"But Grandpa usually keeps his inventions in his room at home. He would've told us if he'd put it somewhere else, wouldn't he?"

"Yes, he would have, unless he thought we'd be safer not knowing," replied Mum. "He does occasionally use his room in the Archives, so I guess it's possible he could have put it in there."

She pursed her lips, staring out of the kitchen window.

"We'll find it, sooner or later. It can't stay hidden forever. And we'll find your grandpa. Everything will be back to normal soon, don't worry."

She pulled Rose into a hug and then turned away to stack the plates, but Rose only managed a weak smile as all of her anxious thoughts returned in a rush.

6

Betrayal

Christmas finally arrived, bringing a scorching heat wave with it. Rose sat hunched at her desk, pressing a bottle of icy water against one side of her face and feeling both happy and sad at the same time. She'd never had a Christmas without Grandpa before and despite Mum's assurances that they would soon find him, they were no closer to it now than when he'd first gone missing.

But her parents had persuaded Kate to spend the day with them, as she had no family of her own to celebrate with, and Rose cheered up a little at the thought of seeing her new friend again. Mum got an album of carols playing while Mary raced at full speed down the stairs to the tree and began sorting gifts into piles.

"Merry Christmas," said Rose, hugging her parents and extracting two clumsily wrapped parcels from under the tree.

She, Matt and Mary had pooled their pocket money to buy Dad a set of his favourite books, and Mum a bottle of perfume. Ten minutes later, the room was covered in shreds of wrapping paper and Mary managed to part company with her new magically-locked diary long enough to admire Matt's new video game and then dump a present onto Rose's lap.

"Open it!" she trilled. "I want to see what you've got!"

Rose picked up the parcel and unwrapped it to find a small roll of fabric inside. Mum and Dad smiled but said nothing as she untied the knot at the front and unfurled the cloth, revealing a set of tools specially designed for miniature inventions.

She brushed a finger over them. They would be perfect for her new project. With a gasp of delight, she jumped up and gave each of her parents a tight hug.

Their guest arrived soon after, bearing a bottle of wine and several parcels tucked under her arm. Rose ran to the door to let her in and beckoned her into the living room, where the family was gathered. Matt and Mary smiled and waved in greeting while Mum and Dad offered Kate food, and Kate accepted a small pastry with thanks before distributing her gifts.

Mary looked down at the sky blue invention in her hands, watching the six delicate, paper thin extensions that fluttered like a butterfly's wings. Kate explained that it would give its owner a good night's sleep as she gave Matt a small, inky-black object made of thin, black threads of a silky material that could conceal things.

To Rose she gave a sparkling, red-gold invention the size of a large marble. It was heavy for its size and shaped like a twelve-pointed star with soft, rounded edges. Rose held it in her palm and felt a warm, soothing sensation steal over her, like standing in the sun on a cold day.

"It's a Calming Stone," said Kate, smiling as Rose flipped the star over in her hand, watching golden spots of light shimmer over its surface. "I thought you'd like it. It's good for when you're feeling upset about something, or in a stressful situation like before an exam. It helps you to relax and lifts your mood."

"This is beautiful! Thanks!" said Rose, placing it in her pocket.

Lunch was noisy as usual. Rose showed Kate the set of tools her parents had given her and asked about the damaged inventions Kate was repairing for the Archives.

"I'm still trying to source new pieces for them," said Kate, inspecting the tool set. "The ones I've tried so far haven't been quite right, but at least I've managed to figure out the pattern of spells on the Curse Breaker. The other invention is a Booster and it's going to need a lot more work. If you wanted to, you, Matt and Mary could help me with them. If your Mum and Dad don't mind, that is."

Matt pulled a cracker with Mary and glanced up from searching through the shreds of paper for the toy inside.

"Are we allowed to help with stuff from the Archives?"

"Yeah, it'll be fine as long as I'm supervising you," replied Kate. "The inventions aren't dangerous."

Rose looked at her mother eagerly and Mum laughed.

"All right, you can help. I suppose it will be good for you to get out of the house for a while."

Brimming with excitement, Rose whirled around to

face Kate.

"When can we start?"

"Well, I still need to buy the new parts for them, but if you visit on Wednesday, I should have everything ready."

Kate grinned at Rose as she picked up a dish of roast potatoes, and Rose turned back to her plate, hardly able to believe her luck.

They drove to Kate's house early on Wednesday, curious to see the old, damaged inventions. The house was well out of town and Rose stared out of the window as the countryside became wilder. Twenty minutes later, Dad stopped outside a neat brick house with a small veranda and Mum turned around in the front seat.

"Now, I want all three of you to remember this place. Your dad and I are going out to look for Grandpa again. If anything happens to us, I want you all to come straight here to Kate, OK? She'll take care of you."

Rose's mouth opened in surprise. She tore her attention away from the landscape to look at her mother.

"Mum, nothing's going to happen to you or Dad!"

Rose's feelings of confusion only intensified when Mum didn't respond, and Rose added in a suspicious tone, "You're telling us this as a precaution, right?"

"Of course." Mum turned away quickly to search for something in her bag. "I just want you to know you can come here for help if you ever need to. I'll keep my mobile on, so all you have to do is call me if you need us for anything."

Rose caught Matt's eye as she climbed out of the car, hoping that Mum was worrying for no reason. Matt seemed as perplexed as Rose. His expression was tense as the three of them walked up the garden path and knocked on the door. Kate appeared a moment later, beaming at them.

"I'm glad you found the place all right." She waved to Mum and Dad, and Dad rolled down his window to call back to them.

"Do you want to use a travel spell back home, or do you want us to pick you up?"

Rose shook her head, checking that her own phone was tucked into her back pocket.

"That's OK, we'll use a travel spell."

"Have fun and be good!" said Mum as they drove off.

Rose waved and waited until they were obscured by the trees lining the road before turning to the house, still feeling uneasy. Kate stood back to let them inside.

"Come on in. I've got everything ready for you. I found some good parts in the supplies store. There are a few I've never used before, so it'll be fun to try them out and see how they do."

Rose took a step inside and stopped, reacting to the thick layer of protective magic enveloping the building. It was almost as though she had run into an invisible wall, and she had to push herself forward for several steps before she could move freely once more. She glanced over her shoulder to see Matt and Mary stepping forcefully over the threshold. Kate gave them an apologetic look.

"Sorry about that. It's only there as a safeguard. You won't even know it's there after a moment or so."

"That's OK," said Rose amicably.

Kate closed the door behind them and led them into a small, simply-furnished living room, littered with books and invention-making equipment.

"This is a nice house," said Mary, peeking through the nearest window, which looked out onto a small courtyard.

The place had a strong cottage feel to it, with cream coloured walls and soft, thick carpet that contrasted with the dark exposed beams, making Rose think of warmth and comfort.

"Yeah, it is," replied Kate. "It's not mine, though. I'm only staying here for a while. My friend owns it."

Rose remained where she was, allowing herself to become acclimatised to the atmosphere. She was used to the feeling of her parents' Shield wrapping around her like a warm blanket, but these spells felt entirely different.

"Why does your friend need such strong protection?"

"Oh, he doesn't," said Kate casually. "But he specialised in defensive magic when he finished his apprenticeship at the Archives and he likes to use his training whenever he can. This is probably one of the safest houses in the country. Anyway, how about I show you around and then we can get started?"

She led them through the rest of the house and then back to the living room where two partly-finished and very complicated-looking objects lay on the coffee table. Rose pointed to the collection of brand new parts beside them.

"Those pieces are interesting."

She bent down to get a closer look. The first invention had been opened up to reveal a spiral shape on the inside, rather like a seashell. Rose could see hundreds of tiny colourful pieces arranged inside it in patterns.

The flexible casing was blackened and charred as though it had been in a fire, and many of the tiny internal parts had fallen out, chipped and cracked. But as intriguing as this invention was, she couldn't help but turn to the object beside it.

She recognised it at once as the Booster. Made of ebony, its carved cylindrical casing lay open so that she could see the large spring inside, wrapped in several thick, metal wires bound with spells.

Clusters of metal spikes protruded from the inside of the casing at regular intervals, where they would make contact with the spring at certain points, and symbols representing spells were carved underneath them, layered and grouped together in a way that amplified the abilities of each individual piece of magic.

Rose inspected it gingerly with a fingertip. It was so old that the metal spring was dull and rusted, and many of the spikes were bent and broken in places. Several of the symbols etched into the wood had worn away, destroying much of the invention's effectiveness.

"I've never worked on anything like this before," breathed Rose, suddenly feeling very unskilled. "Are you sure we can help?"

Kate gave her an encouraging smile.

"I'll show you how to do everything. You'll be fine, don't worry."

They gathered around the table as Kate pulled the first invention towards her.

"So this one's the Curse Breaker?" asked Mary, her eyes bright with enthusiasm. "There are loads of breaking spells on it, but they feel different to the ones Mum and Dad taught us."

"Yes, you're right. These spells are a bit unusual." Kate moved the invention so that Mary could see clearly. "It's going to be a fair bit of work to put it right, but it's put together in a predictable pattern and part of it is still intact, so we just need to fill in the rest. It will be time consuming rather than difficult." She pointed to the Booster. "This is going to be a bit harder to restore because of its age."

Rose glanced at the overflowing pile of new parts.

"What do you want us to do?"

"First we have to take the casing off the Booster," said Kate. "Then I'll get you to replace the teeth that are broken or missing." She showed Rose how to detach the casing and gave her a handful of new pieces. "Play around with these and see what works best. If none of them are right, I've got some others you can try."

Rose nodded and got to work, keen to pick up tips for her own project. Deciding she'd start with the wooden pieces first, as they would be the easiest to remove, she slotted one of them out of the base, admiring the pattern carved into its surface. It crumbled as she handled it, and she brushed splinters off onto the table ruefully.

Matt and Mary sorted through the tiny colourful pieces, making piles of the ones Kate wanted and arranging them into a copy of the pattern inside the Curse Breaker. By mid-morning, Rose had managed to clean off the dirt and grime that had accumulated on the Booster's casing and replace all of the broken and bent teeth.

She had begun to adjust the ones that had shifted out of place when her tweezers slipped and jabbed the ebony casing. It snapped shut angrily on her hand, clamping down like a vise. Rose yelped and attempted to pry it off, but it clung on tight. Kate surged to her feet at once, sending invention pieces everywhere.

"Are you OK? It must have defensive spells on it."

She struck the invention with her free hand and it deactivated, opening up slowly like a clam. Rose pulled her hand free with relief and flexed her fingers to get the blood flowing again.

"I'm fine," she said with a laugh. "It's so old that most of its parts are pretty soft anyway."

She finished adjusting the teeth, careful not to do anything that the Booster could consider a threat, and turned her attention to the markings carved into the wood.

Some of these were familiar. Her parents had shown her the basic symbols used to describe magic, but some inventions bore complicated inscriptions and she wasn't surprised to see that many of the marks on the Booster were new to her.

Looking more carefully, she discovered that the interior contained long passages in the magical language. Much of it had faded, however, worn away from use, and Rose was forced to consult the reference book on the table to decipher the missing sections. Soon they were carved fresh using a gouging spell, and with her paintbrush, Rose brushed any remaining bits of loose wood from the casing.

Removing any debris from the exterior, she buffed it with polish until the wood gleamed in the morning light before rotating a piece at the end to test if the new pieces worked well together. The spring twisted tighter, building up pressure until the topmost teeth connected with the wires, activating the first layer of spells. She rotated the end piece again, making it tighter still, and felt the second layer activate.

She repeated the process until the spring was wound as tight as it could go, and the force of the combined spells radiated out from the invention. With a satisfied nod, she pressed a button on the opposite end of the casing and held it down, waiting for the energy to dissipate before releasing it.

The only thing left to do was to replace the crooked hinges. She eyed them warily, wondering how best to go about this. Deciding it would be easiest if the casing was clamped shut to stop it from snapping at her, she placed a thick rubber band around the invention before searching the table for the tools she'd need.

"Hmm. Kate, is it OK if I borrow a screwdriver? I think I'm going to have to replace these hinges and I don't dare use magic to do it if the Booster's got defensive spells."

"Sure," Kate murmured, immersed in arranging the tiny metal pieces inside the Curse Breaker. "There should be a whole set in the chest of drawers in the spare room. Try the top drawer."

Rose unburied herself from a mess of spare parts and splinters of old wood and went into the room at the back of the house. Finding the chest of drawers in a corner by the window, she opened the top drawer and found only invention pieces, divided into categories.

She closed it and opened another. Still nothing. She pulled open the last drawer and finally found what she was looking for, buried underneath a jumble of other tools and completed inventions wrapped in strips of soft fabric.

She moved aside a heavy tool and glimpsed a flash of gold. Her finger had disturbed a fine chain. Lifting it carefully from the drawer, recognition shot through her as the cloth fell away from a golden pocket watch.

Opening it with trembling fingers, she saw that the hands were moving backwards and forwards randomly, roaming around the clock face. Disbelief kept her rooted to the spot, her hand grasping the watch with enough force to turn her knuckles white. Grandpa's watch had been stolen from her bedroom the day of the masterclass, and there was only one way it could have ended up here.

She peered down the hall. Kate was still arranging tiny pieces, her back to the doorway. Rose glanced down at the watch again, her heart beating fast as she debated what to do.

Telling herself that there could well be an innocent explanation, she considered shoving the watch in Kate's face and demanding to know how it had come to be in a drawer full of her possessions. But caution won out against anger and she thought better of it.

If Kate wasn't their friend, waving the watch she had stolen in front of her face and forcing her to come clean might not be the best idea. Between the three of them, Rose, Matt and Mary outnumbered her, but Kate was an Archivist ...

Mary appeared in the hallway as Rose was coming to a decision, and Rose took hold of her sister as she walked past the door.

"What's up?" Mary said a little too loudly, frowning at the expression on Rose's face.

"Shh!" Rose hissed. "Not now. I'll tell you when Matt's here."

She stuck her head around the door and called to her brother.

"Matt, I need you for a moment."

Matt was sitting cross-legged on the floor, playing with the new hinges of the Booster.

"Why?"

Rose beckoned to him, hoping the movement would catch his eye, but he didn't look up.

"I need to talk to you about something, that's all."

"I'm busy," he complained.

Rose stifled a growl of frustration with difficulty. "Will you just come here, please?"

"OK, fine, I'm coming." He sighed and got to his feet, dawdling down the hall. "What is it?"

Rose held the watch up in front of his face.

"Recognise this?"

Matt and Mary stared at the watch in astonishment.

"Where did you find that?" asked Matt, his voice carrying down the hall.

"Shh!" said Rose again, pulling him further away from the door. "It was here, in this drawer with all of Kate's stuff."

She pointed at the chest of drawers.

"It can't be what it looks like," said Matt uneasily. "Maybe Mum and Dad let her borrow it or something."

Rose raised an eyebrow.

"Without telling us? I locked that watch in my jewellery case, and Mum and Dad thought it was stolen too, remember? If Kate was our friend she would've asked us for the watch instead of sneaking in and stealing it, wouldn't she?"

"I suppose so," said Matt slowly.

"What do we do, then?" asked Mary.

Rose hesitated, wondering what her parents would do in a situation like this.

"Maybe we should ask her about it," she suggested. "What do you think, Matt?"

But before Matt could answer, Kate entered the room herself.

"Did you find the screwdrivers?"

She stopped, her eyes travelling to the watch in Rose's hand. She took a small step back and her eyes met Rose's for a second before flickering down to the floor. The guilty expression on her face was enough for Rose to make up her mind and run to the living room, gathering up her things as she went. Kate hurried after her, twisting her hands anxiously.

"Wait!" she cried. "Let me explain! You don't understand!"

Rose snatched her phone up from the floor beside the Booster and grasped Matt and Mary's arms. The last thing she saw before the travel spell whisked them away was Kate, attempting to grab hold of them. But her hand met only air, and they appeared in their own driveway a second later, looking up at the dark and silent house.

Rose wrenched open the front door and followed the other two inside. Numb with shock and anger, she stood at the foot of the stairs, trying to calm her nerves and squash the sense of betrayal that had taken root inside her.

"I can't believe it! I can't believe Kate stole the watch!"

"Yeah, I know," said Mary, looking crestfallen. "She always seemed so nice. I wonder what she wanted the watch for?"

"Who knows," said Matt weakly. "Maybe she took it for Alison Maxwell. She works at the Archives, too, so they must know each other. I bet they're both after Grandpa's invention." He looked shaken. "I wonder if

Mum and Dad are back yet?"

He stared up at the ceiling as though he could see through it to the rooms above. Rose listened for any sounds of movement, but the sound of Cocoa barking loudly in the backyard made it impossible. She stuck her head into the living room. It was deserted.

"Huh. Looks like we beat them here. If they were home, they would've let Cocoa inside to shut him up."

"Well, they can't be too much longer," said Matt. "They said they'd be back by twelve and it's already half past. I'm getting something to eat. I'm starving."

"How can you think about food after what just happened?" cried Rose incredulously.

Matt shrugged his shoulders and strode into the kitchen. Mary went out into the yard to check on Cocoa, who was now pacing up and down the veranda.

"I think I'll go put this in the invention room," muttered Rose, holding up the pocket watch. "I wonder what Mum and Dad will say when we tell them where we found it?"

She ran up the stairs, listening to the sounds of Matt raiding the fridge. Rose tossed her phone onto her bed and continued down the hall to the invention room. She took the protective spells off the door and stopped, her hand outstretched.

A rustling sound reached her ears from the direction of the library. Was it her imagination, or was there something moving around down the hall? She took a step closer and heard it again: a scuffling sound, like the pages of a book being turned.

For a fraction of a second, Rose thought her parents must be home after all, but something about the sound put her on her guard. She thought of the strange disturbance she'd seen in the air after the masterclass and her eyes darted to the gap beneath the library door, her breathing coming faster.

Reminding herself that the blur had been totally silent, she pressed her ear to the door and waited. There was another rustling sound and then a low murmur. She stepped back. She knew what must have happened. Wanting to be sure, she took hold of the knob and turned it, opening the door a crack.

She could see a sliver of the desk and one of the bookshelves behind it. Someone had been searching through the pile of books and papers Dad had stacked on the desktop, scattering them all over the place. The deep voice spoke again, closer to the door than Rose had been expecting, and she jumped in fright.

"I thought they said they didn't know anything about a compass?"

"They've been hiding a lot of things," said a second, rougher voice.

The speaker moved in front of the desk and Rose saw a short, thickset man with curly brown hair and worn-out clothes reading a report. He rifled through the pages before moving out of sight again.

There was a soft thud, and Rose guessed that the man had tossed the book back onto the desk. Again, she wondered how the men could have got past the Shield. Her eyes found the invention room and she backed away quietly. Matt called to her from the kitchen, telling her to come and get something to eat, and Rose stopped, silently willing him to be quiet.

"What was that?" asked the man with the deep voice.

"It's probably that wretched dog of theirs again," said the other.

Rose took a deep breath and continued creeping towards the invention room.

"Hang on, I didn't leave the door open …"

Rose blanched as the library door flew open. Silence filled the hall for a moment as Rose and the short man stared at each other. He seemed as stunned to see her as she had been to see him.

Recovering himself, he cursed and lunged for her. He managed to move a few steps down the hall towards the invention room before his feet stuck to the carpet. He overbalanced and fell face down, and Rose watched with amusement as the carpet took hold of him, giving Rose time to run. At least some of their spells had held.

The second man came charging out of the library, and Rose glimpsed a tall man in dark clothes before she turned and dove towards the invention room. He leapt over his friend, moving too fast for the carpet to attach itself to him.

Rose pulled the door open and burst inside, slamming the door shut on the man's foot, wedged between the door and the frame. Rose aimed burning spells at the foot and the man howled in pain as a hole appeared in his boot. Rose could see his skin blistering before he wrenched it free.

She forced the door shut and placed the protective spells back over it. A loud tearing sound issued from the hall and Rose guessed that the man must have pulled his friend free. She collapsed with relief against the table, only to think of Matt and Mary downstairs.

Leaping up again, she whirled around, searching the table for the Shield, and snatching it up, she used a travel spell into the kitchen. Matt and Mary were sitting on the counter eating corn chips when Rose appeared beside them.

"What's up with you?" said Matt, noticing her agitated expression as she stared up at the ceiling.

"Be quiet!" Rose hissed, clapping a hand over his mouth. He squirmed out of her reach but obediently stopped talking. Rose listened for movement upstairs, but the house was silent.

"We need to go into the basement right now!"

Comprehension dawned on Matt and Mary's faces as Rose led the way to the laundry, checking the Shield as she went.

"Wait a moment! It's been turned off again!"

Rose checked the invention for signs of damage, but everything appeared to be in order.

"Now's not the time, Rose," said Matt, pushing her along.

He took the Shield and activated it, pressing the white button to shut off the alarm. It immediately began to flash, having detected the two men upstairs.

Mary gave a small gasp and Rose looked up to see the short man materialising in front of the basement door, cutting them off. The sound of footsteps thundering down the stairs told her that the other man was coming up behind them.

She spun around as he came into sight, barring the way into the living room. Dressed all in black, he was more than a head taller than his friend. His face was bony and his hair was a mud-coloured brown, but his eyes were an icy, cruel blue that made Rose want to back away in fear. He glared at Rose, one of his boots still smoking.

"You might as well turn that off," he said after a pause, his eyes flicking down to the Shield with distaste. "It won't help you. The prototype upstairs has already removed most of the protective spells you've put on this place. How do you think we got in here?"

"What prototype?" snarled Rose, refusing to play along.

"The invention your grandfather was kind enough to make for us, of course."

"What!?" demanded Matt. "Grandpa didn't make it for you!"

The shorter man began to laugh.

"What have you done with him? Is he OK?" said Rose, her voice full of desperation.

"You know, I'm surprised you haven't heard anything from Alison yet," he said, ignoring her question.

Rose wasn't sure what he meant by this, but her eyes widened at the sound of that name. The man's grin grew wider.

"Oh, yeah, we know Alison. She was always very

curious about your grandpa's invention."

"Is he OK?" Rose repeated.

"Don't worry, he's fine," said the taller man dismissively. "But you don't have to take our word for it. You'll be seeing him soon enough. I'm sure he'll tell you everything. Just turn that Shield off and we won't hurt you."

"Nice try," said Rose in a wavering voice, "but it's staying on."

The man seemed to consider them for a moment, before heaving a disappointed sigh. Eyeing the Shield warily, he aimed a curse at them in a half-hearted kind of way. The Shield deflected the curse at once, pushing it over Rose's head towards the ceiling, leaving a black mark across it.

The man blinked in surprise, and Rose suppressed a grin as he glanced at his friend. He sent a much stronger curse this time and Rose winced as the Shield deflected it with a sizzling sound. Struck with a sudden idea, Rose fixed her gaze on the shorter man and shoved the spell towards him like an invisible spear, forcing him to hop out of the way, muttering an oath under his breath.

Mary giggled at the sight and Rose began to feel more confident. She shot a spell at the shorter man, temporarily blinding him, and then pulled him into the kitchen so that he blocked his friend's path. As he blundered around in circles, Rose ran to the laundry and yanked the cupboard door open, tapping the top shelf and waiting impatiently for the basement stairs to appear.

"Come on!" groaned Mary, beating at the shelves as

the man in black shoved his friend aside, his expression livid.

The stairs appeared and Rose hurried Matt and Mary onto them, gripping the door in one hand, ready to slam it shut. But before she could retreat into the safety of the basement, the Shield's gentle hum fell silent. She stared down at it in dismay as the feeling of being watched by someone or something unseen descended on her without warning. The man in black removed the spell on his friend and both of them stopped and turned as if they, too, expected to see a figure lurking behind them.

Rose tensed as dread settled over her. She waited for something to happen, her parents' warnings about the prototype replaying in her mind. The energy in the room continued to build until the air crackled with electricity, and Rose flinched as currents of energy buzzed against her skin.

The sensation grew steadily stronger, and everyone stood in silence, not daring to move. Cocoa ran up onto the porch behind the sliding door, barking frantically and scratching at the glass.

The two men's faces filled with uncertainty and Rose realised with satisfaction that they knew little more about Grandpa's invention than she did. The energy slowly began to dissipate, and Rose's fear eased a little. It was bad enough that they had to deal with intruders. She didn't fancy trying to fight Grandpa's prototype at the same time.

But her relief was short-lived. Both men turned their attention back to Rose, Matt and Mary, sending a rain of spells at the basement door, and without thinking, Rose flipped the Shield's switch back on. To her surprise, it sprang to life. A crash sounded from somewhere upstairs, followed by the heavy thud of something hitting the ground. The air rippled and seethed before Rose's eyes, and she backed away, clutching the Shield tightly in both hands.

Guessing what was about to happen, she retreated further down the basement steps just as the Shield and Grandpa's prototype, triggered by the men's curses, began to fight. Rose stared in shock as the magic of the invention upstairs hurled the men's spells back at them, twisting and altering them in bizarre ways so that they were unrecognisable.

Her eyes widened as a curse for weakness was tossed back at the shorter man as a vanishing spell which struck the kitchen table and most of the chairs, missing the man himself by inches. Shield spells were returned with enough force to shatter the windows and punch holes through the walls into the living room and out into the yard, where poor Cocoa was howling with fright.

Soon the two men were fighting for their lives to avoid the barrage of magic being aimed at them.

"Stop fighting with it!" Rose screeched. "You're just provoking it!"

But neither of the men listened. The man in black held the remaining kitchen chair in front of himself for protection, and Matt uttered a sound of disbelief and shock as it was ripped apart with brutal strength. The man threw himself behind a side table instead, clutching it tightly with pale fingers, only to let go with a cry of pain as it, too, was torn apart, sending splinters of wood into his face.

Both men were out of breath now, and Rose could feel their spells getting weaker. But the prototype's attack was relentless, and the man in black finally dove behind the kitchen counter, dragging his friend across the floor with him.

They had barely a second to catch their breath before it exploded. Rose and Mary shrieked and threw their arms up over their heads as cupboards collapsed and the door to the basement was ripped off its hinges. Rose could feel the protective spells of the Shield wrapping around her, attempting to protect her from the effects of the other invention, but it was outmatched by the brute strength of the green bud, and the protective bubble around her trembled and faded.

Cocoa yelped and ran for cover as the sliding door shattered, spilling onto the veranda as though a giant foot had gone through it, and as the glass flew out onto the lawn, both men seemed to realise they were fighting a losing battle. They glanced at each other briefly before running out into the yard at full speed, disappearing between the trees. Rose turned around, deciding she'd seen enough.

"Run!" she cried, shepherding Matt and Mary further down the stairs, away from the line of fire.

She deactivated the Shield, hoping to stop the fight, but the fluid inside the invention continued to roil, protesting at the presence of the bud upstairs. Sounds of destruction filled Rose's ears as the prototype itself continued to demolish the house, and she stood perfectly still, cringing until a ringing silence descended.

Shaking and lost for words, Rose waited for what felt like hours before finally mustering the courage to creep to the top of the stairs and peek out at the wreckage of the kitchen, trembling from head to toe and suddenly reminded of the state they'd found Grandpa's house in when they'd discovered he was missing. She'd never seen such a violent reaction from an invention before.

She repaired the basement door and was about to close it when she remembered Cocoa, who was now cowering on the veranda, terrified. She brought him into the room with a travel spell and then slammed the door shut, sealing it with her strongest magic.

It wouldn't be enough to protect them from the prototype, but it was the best she could do. Matt and Mary stood huddled together, their faces white with shock. Matt stared up at the door as though transfixed.

"That was too close!" he said in a hoarse whisper. "If it wasn't for Grandpa's invention, we'd be toast by now. It just took out those guys for us!"

"Yeah, along with the kitchen and the veranda," grumbled Rose.

Cocoa whimpered and pressed himself against Mary's legs, quivering all over. Mary bent down and stroked his head soothingly.

"Well, I'm happy as long as it doesn't come for us, too," she said.

Rose took a deep breath and nodded.

"If we don't do anything to set it off like those men did, I think we'll be OK. That's what Dad said, anyway."

"D'you think we're really safe down here?" asked Mary tremulously.

The corners of Matt's mouth twitched.

"After what just happened out there, I don't think those guys are going to come back any time soon."

"But we'll get the Shield working again, just in case they do," added Rose. "Mum and Dad have had it running even with the prototype in the house, so if we're careful not to do any magic that upsets either of them, the Shield should still be able to protect us."

She lowered herself onto the collapsed sofa and balanced the invention on her knee. When she was sure that the invention had settled down, she flicked the Shield on experimentally. It hummed back to life.

"So it's the bud upstairs that keeps turning this off," Rose mused. "Both inventions must see each other as a threat and try to disable the other, and that's why they started fighting. The bud definitely has enough dangerous magic on it to trigger the Shield."

"Your guess is as good as mine," said Matt with a shrug. "Why did the Shield explode when you tried to use it that night we were in the invention room, and only turn off now?"

"I think when Mum and Dad repaired it they must have done something to stop it reacting like that," said Rose with a shrug.

They sat in silence until Mary voiced something else

that had been weighing on Rose's mind.

"What d'you think has happened to Mum and Dad? What if they've been taken now, too?"

"Well, they should've been home ages ago."

The fear etched in Matt's features as he said these words betrayed the calm of his voice. He turned away to stare up at the basement door, hiding his face from view. Tears welled up in Mary's eyes.

"What if they *are* gone?" she sniffled. "They've never left us like this. They always tell us where they are. What're we going to do? We can't stay down here forever!"

Rose pulled her into a tight hug.

"They'll be back," she said, trying to convince herself as well as Mary. "Those men out there didn't mention Mum and Dad. They talked about Grandpa."

She gave Matt what she hoped was an encouraging kind of look, but he avoided her eyes.

"Sure, maybe they're late or something," he mumbled.

"And no one's been into the invention room, so we've still got a whole room full of inventions to protect us," continued Rose. "We'll be safe, don't worry."

Mary nodded but her eyes still shone with tears. Rose searched the room for a distraction and her eyes found the game console in the corner. Rose grinned at her sister.

"We can play video games if you want."

She jerked her chin towards the games and Mary smiled reluctantly.

"Now you're talking," said Matt, with the air of someone who'd just been saved from drowning. He pulled out the controllers and settled down on the sofa with Mary.

Rose fidgeted, trying hard to ignore the queasy, anxious knot in the pit of her stomach as Matt and Mary took it in turns to play their favourite games. She waited, tense and restless as darkness descended around them and the clock in the living room chimed.

Unable to contain herself any longer, she summoned her phone into the basement and dialled her mother's mobile, hoping Mum would pick up. She wandered over to the door, where she would be most likely to get reception, but there was no answer. She refrained from pacing around the room with difficulty and marched over to the cupboard instead.

"I think we'd better stay in here from now on. Just in case. At least until Mum and Dad come back, and we know for sure that it's safe to go upstairs."

She tucked her phone into the back pocket of her jeans and hauled out the mattresses and blankets. At half past ten, they packed the games away and climbed into their makeshift beds. Rose set the Shield beside her pillow, checking that it was still running before turning the lights off.

"When you wake up in the morning, Mum and Dad will be here and everything will be OK, you'll see," Rose told Mary, trying to sound reassuring.

"But what if they're *not* back by then?" Mary fretted, becoming tearful again.

Rose did her best to smile naturally.

"They'll be back, I know it. We'll be OK, no matter what."

Matt remained quiet as Rose wrapped the blankets around her sister and then huddled down beside her. She closed her eyes, telling herself that her parents would be back, trying to make herself believe it. But as she lay curled up under her sheets, she thought of her grandfather and couldn't help but fear that Mary was right.

She glanced at the Shield, humming quietly in the dark, and sighed, privately agreeing with her sister that if Mum and Dad were OK, they would have contacted their children somehow to say that they were running late and there was no reason to worry.

Trying hard to stay calm, she stared up at the dark ceiling, listening for sounds in the house above until she drifted into a troubled sleep.

7

A Secret Uncovered

It took Rose a second to remember why she felt so miserable when she opened her eyes the next morning. Sitting up, she glanced around the room, but it was empty except for Matt and Mary's sleeping forms and Cocoa, draped over Matt's legs. Rose's spirits fell even further.

She heaved a heavy sigh and checked the Shield. To her relief, it was running at full power, humming quietly on the floor beside her. The men must have stayed away. Perching on the edge of the sofa, she ran her fingers through her unkempt hair and tried Mum's mobile once more, letting it ring until it reached voicemail. Tossing the phone aside, she settled into the sofa cushions, fighting back tears.

She closed her eyes, wondering what they were going to do, still struggling to believe that Kate had taken the watch. It seemed that Matt was right. Alison Maxwell was not the only one after Grandpa's things. But why was the watch so important? And those men said they knew her …

Rose opened her eyes and summoned the pocket watch, wondering if it was safe to trust anyone anymore. She lifted the golden lid, looking for any tiny detail that might explain why, or if, it was so special. Apart from its habit of ticking backwards, it appeared to be an ordinary watch. Nonetheless, she couldn't deny that there was something strange about it. She placed it on the sofa cushion beside her as her brother and sister stirred.

"Morning," Matt said with a yawn, rolling over onto his front and disturbing Cocoa.

He glanced around the room and saw that their parents hadn't come home. His face fell, and Rose knew that he was feeling the same empty feeling that she was. And, just as Rose had, he turned his attention to the watch to distract himself. He gave it a dark look.

"I wonder why everyone is so interested in that?"

"I've been wondering the same thing." Rose stood up, rubbing her eyes. "I can't feel any spells on it. If there *are* any, they're well hidden. But maybe everyone's wrong and it isn't important at all."

She scooped the Shield up off the floor as Mary stretched and pushed her hair out of her face.

"You might be right," said Matt, flinging his blankets back and getting to his feet. "If it was important, Grandpa would have put it in his invention room instead of leaving it lying around. It was on the floor with all the debris, wasn't it?"

Rose nodded, thinking that Matt might have a point.

"I mean, if it had something to do with his invention, he would have hidden it, too, wouldn't he?" Matt continued musingly.

"I guess so."

Rose stifled a yawn with one hand and they lapsed

into thoughtful silence. Mary sat up and looked around the room. Tears welled up in her eyes and she sobbed as Matt drew her into a hug.

"They really are gone!" she gasped, burying her face in his shirt. Matt gave her a consoling pat on the back.

"We'll be OK, I promise."

His eyes met Rose's and he squared his shoulders.

"Mum and Dad can take care of themselves, and so can we."

He went over to the foot of the stairs. Mary followed him, wiping her eyes on her sleeve, and all three of them gazed up at the basement door. Matt took a tentative step forward.

"What do we do now, then? I suppose it's safe to go up?"

Rose looked down at the invention in her hands.

"It must be, or the Shield would be flashing." She climbed the stairs and pressed her ear to the door. "I can't hear anything."

She removed her spells and opened the door a crack, peering out into the rooms beyond. The laundry and kitchen were a mess, but they were deserted. Cocoa brushed past her without hesitation and squeezed himself through the gap. Reassured, they followed him out into the laundry, staring around at the devastation Grandpa's prototype had created.

Matt gave a low whistle, looking impressed.

"Wow! It's like the invention threw a gigantic tantrum."

"Er, I think we should clean this up before we do

anything else," said Rose, her eyes travelling from the shattered windows to the overhead cabinets, which had collapsed onto the floorboards.

Standing in the doorway, she began the same spell she'd used to repair Mum's plates. Glass flew back into the windows and the sliding door, the cabinets reattached themselves to the wall and the scattered planks of wood from the veranda slotted into their proper places. She waited for the last pieces of the flooring to settle before entering the kitchen.

"All right, then, let's make some breakfast. We can decide what to do after that."

Matt looked at the newly repaired stove with a hint of uncertainty.

"OK, but I don't really know how to cook."

He and Mary turned to Rose expectantly and Rose rolled her eyes.

"Well, it's about time you learned then, isn't it?" She opened the fridge and scanned its contents. "Don't worry, I know the basics. How about we make scrambled eggs and toast? That's easy enough."

"If you say so," said Matt.

Mary fed Cocoa as Rose took out the ingredients and showed Matt what to do, and together they cooked breakfast with the Shield sitting on top of the kitchen counter. Rose had no idea how to bring the table and chairs back into being, so they sat on the sofa to eat, which was something they never did when their parents were home.

While she ate, Rose thought about what they should

do now that their parents were missing, too. When Mary had finished her toast, Rose turned to her brother and sister to see what they thought of her plan.

"I think we should figure out what we're going to do now, before anyone comes back and tries to get inside the house again," she said. "We need to be prepared."

"All right," said Matt, putting his empty plate on the coffee table. "What are we going to do?"

He and Mary looked at Rose again.

"Well," said Rose after a pause, "I don't think we have any choice but to stay here for now. We don't have anywhere else to go, do we? And we can't stay with Kate."

Matt and Mary scowled.

"What about Dave?" suggested Matt. "We could ask him for help. He's from the police and he's been helping Mum and Dad ever since Grandpa started his invention, so he knows what's been going on."

"That's true," said Rose, thinking the idea over. "But we don't know his phone number. Or where he lives. We don't even know his last name, or we could look him up. Mum and Dad never told you the names of any of the other people they were working with, did they?"

Matt and Mary shook their heads.

"I kind of got the feeling they didn't want us talking to any of them," said Mary. "I wonder why?"

"I guess they knew someone was after Grandpa's invention and they couldn't be sure who to trust," said Matt with a shrug.

"Well, we *do* need to tell the police," said Rose,

picking up her phone again. "They need to know they're not just looking for Grandpa now."

"No, wait!" Matt snatched the phone out of her hand, his expression suddenly desperate. "If you tell them Mum and Dad have gone missing, too, they'll tell us to leave it all to them! It's been ages now since Grandpa disappeared and they still haven't found him. This time no one's going to stop me from helping!"

"That's the stupidest thing I've ever heard!" Rose protested. "Our parents have disappeared and you don't even want to tell the police? You can't seriously think we can sort this out on our own? Mum and Dad didn't have any luck finding Grandpa, either, remember, and they know him better than anyone."

She yanked her phone out of Matt's resisting hand. He opened his mouth again to argue, but Rose cut across him.

"No, I don't care what you say. As soon as we've got the house secured, we're going to go down to the station and tell them everything."

She gave Matt a scornful look and he folded his arms across his chest, glaring at her.

"Fine, do what you want," he muttered to the floor. "But don't blame me if we're not allowed to do anything to help."

Rose ignored him.

"If Dave doesn't see Mum or Dad for a while he might come to check what's going on," said Mary, in an obvious attempt to change the subject.

"Yeah, maybe," said Rose dismissively. "But we

can't count on him just happening to show up."

"I can't believe Mum and Dad didn't give us any phone numbers or addresses in case something happened to them," raged Matt. "Usually we can't even go to the cinema without them telling us what to do or where to go if we get into trouble. Why is it so different this time? The one time we're actually in trouble?"

"But they *did* tell us what to do," Rose reminded him. "When they dropped us off at Kate's friend's place. They told us to go and stay with her. Obviously, they didn't know she's not our friend."

"I wish they'd just come home!" said Mary miserably. "I bet those guys who broke in yesterday know we're here on our own!"

"They might not want to come back again after the prototype almost killed them," suggested Matt, his voice becoming hopeful. But Rose shook her head.

"I doubt it. They'll come back, and sooner rather than later. If they got in last time by waiting until the Shield stopped working, we're going to have to figure out some way of keeping it running."

Matt made a sound of scepticism before casting a dark look in the direction of the invention room, where the green bud lay undisturbed.

"How're we going to manage that? If it *is* Grandpa's prototype that keeps deactivating it, we'd have to change the way it works to stop it shutting off the Shield."

Rose considered this for a moment. The mere thought of going near the flower bud again made her break out in a cold sweat, and she shuddered at the idea of trying to alter its spells.

"Well, we'll just have to make do, then. You're right. We don't know enough about the prototype to change it and I don't dare touch it again, not after what it did to us last time. I think it's best if we stay away from it and try to keep it docile."

Matt and Mary nodded, apparently all too happy to keep their distance from the invention.

"We'll go around the house and check if any of our protective spells are still working, filling in the gaps where they've been destroyed," said Rose, coming to a decision. "But make sure they're protective rather than aggressive, or we might set the bud off again. Other than that, all we can do is try and keep the Shield going as best we can until the police sort something out."

Matt and Mary agreed, and they spent most of the morning repairing the layer of magic around the house. Rose offered to check the yard while Matt and Mary took care of the house, and she took Cocoa outside with her so that he could stretch his legs.

She noticed as she repaired a cluster of spells over the gate that they had been destroyed in a patchy, unpredictable sort of way. Some were partially removed or scrambled somehow, while others in the same area remained untouched. Rose scratched her head, wondering how this could be.

Calling Cocoa to her, she moved towards the driveway, where she'd sensed a large gap in their protection. Feeling exposed and uneasy out in the open, she darted a glance over her shoulder, peering through the trees and down the gravel drive, but the road was clear.

When she was confident that she'd done everything possible to make sure no one found a way inside, Rose hurried through the back door with Cocoa, slamming it behind her and locking it. Taking a deep, steadying breath, she went into the living room, where Matt and Mary were putting the finishing touches on the interior.

"Well, I think that's as safe as we're going to make it," she said, her skin tingling in response to all of the magic around her. "Maybe we can leave now without coming home to unwanted visitors. Let's go talk to the police."

Matt groaned loudly, hanging back.

"Come on," said Rose, her voice firm. "We'll use a travel spell."

Rose took hold of Matt and Mary's hands and focused her mind to begin the spell, but Mary gasped and pulled away, pointing out of the living room window.

"Hey, what are they doing out there?"

Rose and Matt turned to see what was the matter. There were four men outside, standing here and there in the street, watching the house. Rose went to the front door and peered through the narrow pane of glass beside it, and to her horror, saw more figures stationed along the fence, all the way to the stretch of bushland separating them from their nearest neighbours.

"They're making sure we can't go anywhere!" she cried.

Mary joined her at the door, bending down for a

clearer view underneath Rose's elbow.

"We can still use a travel spell."

"Maybe not," replied Rose. "If they're using magic to stop us, too."

Mary's eyes widened.

"They can't do that, can they? Not with all the protection we've put around the house."

Rose straightened up again.

"I'll use a travel spell and see what happens. I'll try to go upstairs."

Matt and Mary watched in silence as Rose closed her eyes and wrapped the spell around her, concentrating on the upstairs landing. She opened her eyes. The living room began to fade as it normally would, but within seconds it had come back into focus as some invisible barrier blocked her spell. Panic squeezed at her insides, making it hard for her to breathe.

"Not again! How are they doing this? We can't even go to get help or food without going past those guys out there!"

"What're we going to do?" moaned Mary. "No one even knows what's happened!"

Rose snatched up her phone.

"We'll call the police instead."

She dialled the number and waited, her heart hammering in her chest. There was no answer. She sat down on the sofa and stared at the rug, feeling truly defeated.

"We'll keep trying," she said after a moment, refusing to be put off. "They're bound to pick up sooner or later."

Rose spent the rest of the morning alternately calling her mother's mobile and the police.

"Something weird is going on here," she declared, her eyebrows coming together into a worried line. "Stopping us from using a travel spell is one thing, but how can they stop us from calling someone?"

"If you're good enough at magic, Rose, you can do pretty much anything you want," said Matt matter-of-factly. He looked more cheerful than he had all morning. Rose scowled at him.

"I know you wanted to go to the police, but at least this way we can stay here instead of going to live with someone we don't even know," he said with a consoling kind of look.

"Hmm," said Rose, her eyes narrowing. "I suppose that's true."

It was now well past midday and they were all starting to get hungry.

"Oh, let's just order some pizzas or something."

Rose reached for her laptop, wondering if the men outside had stopped that from working, too. Matt snorted with laughter.

"I hope they let the delivery driver through."

But the figures simply retreated into the cover of the forest when the car arrived, though Rose felt certain they hadn't gone far. Sure enough, as they sat by the living room window, looking out at the road, no fewer than eleven people came slinking back into sight, arranging themselves around the house once more.

Feeling increasingly uneasy, Rose spent the rest of the day in the living room, trying to decide what to do now that she was trapped inside the house. She could see no alternative but to do as Mary suggested and wait until Dave or someone else who knew about Grandpa and his invention came to visit Mum and Dad.

"And if that doesn't work, we'll just have to sneak out of the house and try to make a run for it, I suppose," she said, staring out of the window miserably.

The day drifted away with no calls or visitors, and she eventually went upstairs, unsure what to do with herself.

It was mild and clear when she got up the next day. Wispy white clouds stretched across the sky and a cool breeze wafted in through her window, making her think of the lessons her parents had given her under the trees before Christmas.

With a pang of worry and regret, Rose turned her back on the scene and went to the kitchen for some breakfast. Much to her surprise, she found that Matt had made scrambled eggs for the three of them to demonstrate his newfound cooking skills.

Mary gave him an appreciative pat on the back, and they ate at top speed before making their way to the library, having decided to go through all of the books and reports they'd seen their parents poring over. Rose hoped that the books might give them a clue as to what her family had been doing, but she also worried that, if they did happen to discover something useful, it was likely to be very advanced and complicated, and therefore useless to them. However, it was the only thing left for them to do, so they trooped upstairs and made piles of everything that might be significant.

"Maybe we should take these down to the living room?" suggested Rose, looking at the tiny desk. "It'll be more comfortable there."

"Good idea," said Matt approvingly.

He bewitched the books so that they flew out of the room before following behind them. Mary sat on the sofa and Rose curled up in an armchair, pulling the nearest stack of books toward her. Choosing a thick, leather-bound volume titled *Advanced Spell Construction*, she settled down and began to read. By one o'clock, they had worked their way through more than half of their piles, and Rose was beginning to form some strange ideas about what her family had been doing for the last six weeks.

"Well, it looks to me like Mum and Dad were researching some kind of new spell or method of using magic," concluded Rose, putting down *Magic in the Twenty-first Century* with a yawn. "But most of these explanations are way too complicated for me to understand. Have either of you found anything yet?"

Matt and Mary shook their heads, looking baffled.

"These are all reports written by inventors who made really unusual things," Matt informed her, holding up the book in his hands. "This one here describes an invention that was used as a sort of trial for binding spells, back when they'd only just been discovered. I think you must've been right all along, Mary. I bet Grandpa's invention uses new or rare magic and Mum and Dad were doing research for him."

Mary scratched her chin, letting her book fall flat.

"Knowing what they were reading about doesn't help us find them, though, does it?" she replied.

"No, it doesn't." Rose turned a page and gawked at the long strings of magical symbols covering the paper from top to bottom. "But people from the government came to talk to them ages ago, before Grandpa was taken. They must be the ones who commissioned the invention. If we could find their names, we could ask them for help."

"How are we going to contact them?" asked Matt.

Rose sighed and picked up the next book.

"Let's take one problem at a time."

Mary tossed her volume aside and stretched.

"I'm bored. Let's do something else for a while."

Stiff from sitting still for so long, Rose hoisted herself up from the armchair and Matt unburied himself from the floor where he'd spread out in front of the empty fireplace. They took a short break and played with Cocoa, who was unhappy about being confined to the house now that they knew there were people stationed outside.

When he'd tired of chasing his ball around the living room, Rose gave him a treat and they went back to their reading. It was getting dark when Rose finally closed the last book, none the wiser about the details of what had happened to her family.

"At least we kind of know what they were doing now," said Mary. "We know they were reading about new spells, anyway."

"Yeah, that's something I guess," said Matt in a low voice. He stared at a hole in the carpet for a moment, and then said, "You haven't managed to put your invention together yet, have you, Rose?"

Rose shook her head and Matt's face fell as he stacked his books beside him on the floor.

"I'm starting to think it might be the only way to find them after all."

Rose privately agreed and, not wanting to let her brother and sister down, she sat at her desk in her bedroom the next morning, attempting to work on her invention. It was now New Year's Eve, and she was having difficulty concentrating on her work. The reference books in the library had failed her and she wasn't sure what to try next.

As a last resort, she took the box of spare invention pieces into her room and spent several hours picking out the extra parts she needed to make the eye shape she'd chosen. Laying them all out on her desk, she arranged and rearranged them until she found something she liked, but no sooner had she pieced them together than she discovered a problem with the way they worked as a whole and had to take them all apart again.

Frustrated, she roamed the rest of the house instead, searching for any scraps of information about Grandpa's work that they might have missed. Finally, in desperation, Rose decided to check the invention room.

She opened the door with caution, remembering the loud bang that had carried down the stairs when the prototype had attacked the two men, and immediately saw what had made the noise. The door to the black cabinet had been blown off. It lay underneath the workbench, twisted and dented. The loose pages and report book had also been tossed out onto the floor at the foot of the bench.

Edging over to them warily, she snatched them up. A flash of green metal caught her eye as she bent down. Her attention was drawn to the bud almost irresistibly, and she found herself crouching down to peer into the cabinet before she could stop herself. Reminding herself why she was there, she snatched up the papers and hurried out of the room, leaving the bud untouched.

She brought them downstairs to the living room and took a seat beside Mary. The papers were the same ones Matt had removed from the cabinet before activating the bud, but he hadn't read them thoroughly and Rose wanted a closer look. Matt and Mary recognised them at once.

"Grandpa's report! I can't believe we forgot about that!" exclaimed Matt. "It'll tell us everything we want to know about his invention in detail! And there should be loads of other useful things in there, like who Grandpa was working for!"

Matt vaulted over the armrest of the sofa, settling down on Rose's other side as she opened the report and began to read. But the hope that had sprung up at the sight of the book soon faded. Most of the pages contained confusing and very detailed diagrams and descriptions of magic that none of them had ever heard of. Worse still, whole chapters were written entirely in the strange symbols used to describe and identify spells, and the contacts page was suspiciously incomplete.

"In order to separate the two forces, magic must first be converted into its purest form," Mary read aloud. "Its purest form? What does that mean?"

Matt blinked, looking perplexed.

"No idea. I never knew magic had any other forms."

Rose rifled through the rest of the pages, but all she found were more lengthy descriptions of complicated pieces of magic. Disappointed, she placed the report on the table with the other books.

"Well, I'm all out of ideas," said Matt dully.

With nothing else to do and no other leads to follow, Mary positioned herself by the living room window, where she watched the comings and goings of the men outside. They showed no sign of leaving and kept close watch over the house at all times. Rose sighed and joined her, thinking over everything she'd read and trying to ignore the anxiety bubbling up inside her.

She sat moodily at her desk that afternoon, staring out of her window. A strong wind had developed, howling around the house and making the gum trees bend and sway violently. They'd had no calls or visitors in days and Rose was beginning to feel cut off from the rest of the world. She glared at the invention lying in pieces in front of her. In the last few hours alone, she'd assembled it and then pulled it apart five times, trying countless arrangements of the components without success.

She'd brought her work down to the living room around midday so that she could keep working during lunch, and had just taken the invention apart yet again, insisting that the arrangement of the pieces was the key, when Matt had entered the room and accused her of being obsessed. Annoyed and increasingly desperate, she had gathered up all of her pieces once more and stormed off in a huff to continue her work in her room without distraction.

With no other spare parts left to try, she'd decided to alter the best pieces so that they fit together the way she wanted. Her latest attempt at remodelling had been a partial success. When she'd tested the invention, instructing it to search for her family, she'd experienced a curious sensation of almost-understanding, as though the answer to her problem was just out of reach. But it had vanished as quickly as it had come, and she was left feeling confused and let down yet again.

She sighed and rested her head on the desk, wondering what she was doing wrong and trying to forget Matt's accusations. It was true that she'd spent the majority of her time lately working on her invention, testing it and trying new pieces, but this was only because she, like Matt, was now sure that making a powerful finding invention was the only way to rescue their family.

As she sat slumped in her chair, she admitted to herself that she probably *was* a little obsessed, but this did nothing to improve her mood. Grumbling, she put the pieces down.

"Think," she told herself out loud. "Why isn't it working?"

She returned to the invention room, racking her brain for inspiration. She had almost reached the end of the table when a small invention that her parents sometimes used to isolate problem spells caught her attention.

Two of the curved metal pieces would, when put together, create an eye shape. Hoping her parents wouldn't mind her taking the invention apart, she took it back to her room and began to dismantle it.

When she had the parts she wanted, she set them flat on the desk and carefully used a spell to reshape them. Reshaping pieces was one of the things she enjoyed most about invention-making, and she had fun stretching the metal until it more closely resembled an eye. Once she was happy, she melted the ends of the two pieces, fusing them.

Choosing a metal ring about the size of a bangle, she placed it inside the eye to represent the iris and reshaped four other pieces to make two smaller eyes. Her creativity flowing fast now, she took the eyes and arranged them one on top of the other, forming a cross.

Remembering Mum's advice about making part of the invention blue, she turned one eye a deep, midnight blue and the other a light, sky blue. Putting her best finding and boosting spells for non-living things on the dark blue eye, and her strongest spells for living things on the light blue eye, she then fused the two pieces together.

Once the metal had cooled, she placed the smaller eyes inside the metal ring and used the tools her parents had given her for Christmas, along with some fancy assembling spells, to fasten them in a way that allowed them to spin from side to side, but also rotate up and down.

As a final touch, she picked through the remainder of her spare parts and chose a blue piece of glass for the centre of the invention, where the pupil would be. This would act as a magical filter and be where the invention would show her a small but clear picture of whatever she was searching for. She fixed the little piece of glass into the frame and then set it down on her desk, looking for things she might have missed.

Fixing dissolution spells to the outer pieces, she held the finished invention in both hands. She prodded the smaller eyes with a finger, checking their movement. Satisfied with her design, she sat back and admired her work. The invention was about the size of her hand and would fit easily in her pocket, making it lightweight and easy to carry.

Deciding it was time to test it, she rotated the centre so that the dark blue eye was horizontal, thinking of her science textbook. Holding the invention in both hands, she pictured the book clearly in her mind. The small eyes began to spin, gathering speed before coming to a stop seconds later, displaying a tiny but clear picture in the glass pupil, showing her the book on top of her dresser.

She glanced behind her. The book was there! It had worked! Time to try it on something living. She rotated the centre so that the pale blue eye was level instead, thinking of her brother and sister. Letting the eyes spin, she waited patiently as they whirled around several times and stopped.

Rose gazed into the pupil, grinning at the perfect picture of Matt and Mary downstairs in the laundry, attempting to load the washing machine. She watched with a mixture of amusement and exasperation as Mary threw clothes into the machine at random and then poured in too much powder.

Thrilled with her success, she focused on her parents this time. Hope and excitement coursed through her as the invention began to spin. It came to an abrupt stop, almost as though the moving pieces had hit an invisible barrier. Her heart sinking, she waited, her eyes fixed on the pupil. She peered into the glass and saw nothing but her own reflection staring back at her.

She lifted the invention up to her eyes, telling herself she wasn't looking carefully enough, but the glass remained clear, and the familiar rush of almost-understanding coursed through her again. She let out a wordless grump of rage and folded the invention flat on the desk, glaring at it.

Footsteps approached her bedroom door and she glanced up as Mary entered the room with Cocoa trailing behind her. She gave Rose a sympathetic look and sat on the end of the bed as Rose threw her hands up in defeat.

"I give up! It's not possible!"

"It's still not working?"

Rose grimaced in answer. She turned around to talk to Mary and caught her sister hastily rearranging her features to hide her disappointment. Like Matt and Rose, Mary was convinced that the invention was the only way to find their family now that the books and reports, not to mention the police, had failed them.

"I've tried everything I can think of," moaned Rose, tossing her notebook of ideas into a drawer.

Mary stared down at her hands, her expression distant as Cocoa settled himself on top of Rose's feet. Rose scratched behind his ears and took a deep breath, trying to forget about her invention.

"I wish the police would answer us," Mary said, her voice wavering. "I keep imagining all of the horrible things someone might be doing to Mum, Dad and Grandpa."

She avoided Rose's eyes, but the devastation on her face was plain to see. Suddenly all of Rose's anger seemed to melt away. She pulled her feet out from underneath Cocoa and sat down beside her sister, pulling her into a tight hug.

"Me too," she said. "But we *will* find them. Or the police will, anyway. They'll find something soon, I'm sure of it."

She tried to smile encouragingly, but Mary looked unconvinced.

"Come on, let's go and see what Matt thinks of my invention." Rose stood up and headed for the hall. "He might be able to figure out what I'm doing wrong."

They went downstairs and Rose placed her invention on the table in front of him so that he could examine it, trying her best to describe the strange almost-knowing that came over her whenever she tried to find her family.

"Well, I'm not exactly an expert," said Matt, watching the invention spin, "but I can feel finding, tracking, dissolution and boosting spells on this. That's a lot to combine in one invention. There might be too many spells competing with each other."

"Yeah, it's possible," said Rose with another pang of frustration. "But I've seen other inventions with a lot more magic on them than this and they work fine."

"Maybe the design isn't letting the spells do what you want them to do, then."

He held the invention closer to his face, watching the eyes spin.

"Hang on … is it me, or are these pins making the moving parts catch now and then?"

He pointed to where the eyes connected to the outer ring.

"If they sat right, the eyes would be able to glide over them through this groove in the ring here, but they seem pretty old to me. I reckon they've been recycled too many times."

Rose leaned in to inspect the pins for herself. He was right. She clapped a hand to her forehead.

"How did I miss that for so long?"

"I haven't been obsessively staring at the invention all day, every day," Matt replied with a wide grin. "It helps to look with fresh eyes."

"I guess so," laughed Rose, taking the invention back.

"Other than the pins, everything looks fine as far as I can tell. I'm guessing that either your dissolution spells aren't strong enough to break through the blocks yet, or the spells aren't working together."

Rose nodded in a resigned kind of way. "You're probably right. At least the pins shouldn't be hard to fix. If I could just go out and buy new ones …"

She glowered at the men outside, still standing guard.

"I know! Let's give it a name!" said Mary, calling Rose's attention back. "Every invention has to have a name. You could call it a Scope, like Mum and Dad's invention!"

"No, let's give it a fancy name like the ones in the library books!" said Matt with a teasing grin. Rose shook her head.

"No, I think I'll just call it a Viewer. It has a wider range of spells than the Scope, and besides, I like names that are simple and self-explanatory."

Deciding that she needed a break from inventing, she stowed the Viewer in her pocket and stretched out in Dad's armchair, watching the crowd of people outside come and go. Matt helped her make tacos for dinner that night after they'd rummaged through the pantry for what little food they had left.

As they always did whenever she was busy these days, Rose's thoughts soon turned to her family. It had now been four days since Mum and Dad had disappeared and she still wasn't sure what to do next.

She grimaced, wondering what would happen if the men who'd broken in came back again. She didn't think it would be long before they did.

Later that night, after Mary had gone to bed, Rose searched the drawers in her mother's bedside table and found the address book Mum kept there. She read through it frantically, but the phone numbers and addresses were all for distant family long since dead, or for one or two of Mum's old school friends. Disappointed, she went back downstairs and cleaned up the kitchen.

She gazed out of the window as she washed the dishes by hand for something to do, watching the moon rise above the treetops. The gale outside had blown itself out, so she sat up late with Matt to watch the midnight fireworks from the library window. They were distant, coming from the centre of town, but high enough to be clearly visible.

Rose stood by the window in silence as brilliant colours lit up the night sky, glittering and twinkling in the air before falling like rain. She waited for the last of the embers to die away before closing the library door and going down the hall to her room. Saying goodnight to Matt, she got into bed feeling strangely hollow. She sighed and rolled over, falling asleep to the sounds of distant firecrackers and loud music as the rest of the city celebrated.

Rose woke late the next morning, having had bad dreams again. Stumbling out of bed with a grumble, she got dressed, wondering if there was any point in working on her invention again when someone hammered on the front door. She froze. Nobody had come near them for almost a week, and Rose's first wild thought was of the strangers outside. But she shook herself mentally, reminding herself that intruders would hardly knock on the door.

She stuck her head out into the hall and found Matt racing towards the stairs. Mary burst out of her own room a second later, looking flustered as Matt greeted whoever was at the door. She followed Rose out onto the landing and they peered down into the living room. It was Dave. He waved up at them.

"Hi. What's going on? You've got a whole guard outside and your parents were supposed to meet me this morning."

"They're gone," explained Matt in a flat tone. "They disappeared just like Grandpa, about five days ago."

Dave stared at him for a moment, stunned.

"They went out to search for Grandpa while we were helping Kate," added Rose, "but they never came back, and when we got home there were people in the library, going through our stuff."

Dave glanced up at her in shock before gazing around the room at the scattered piles of books and reports. He lowered himself onto the sofa as Rose and Mary hurried downstairs.

"Grandpa's prototype scared them off for us, though," continued Mary, "so we've been trying to find everyone on our own."

"On your own?" repeated Dave faintly. "Didn't you

tell anyone what had happened?"

Rose shifted uncomfortably.

"We tried to, but we can't go outside and every time I call the police they don't answer. I think the people out there must be using magic to stop us." She jerked her chin towards the road.

"But the police haven't been much help yet, anyway," said Matt with a dismissive wave of his hand. "We would've told you about it earlier, but -"

The colour returned to Dave's face in a rush.

"You can't stay here by yourselves! If the people who're after your grandpa's invention got in here once, they'll find a way in again. How have you been managing all on your own?"

"Well, we've still got the Shield," said Matt a little defensively, "and Grandpa's invention helped us last time they broke in."

Dave gave him a quelling look.

"That's not good enough. The Shield didn't help your grandfather much, did it? And the Fragmenter is what destroyed the Shield and made it possible for him to be kidnapped in the first place."

Rose gave a splutter of indignation. She opened her mouth to protest, but Dave seemed to guess what she was about to say. He ran a hand through his dark hair, frowning.

"Yes, I know the Shield has protected you in the past, but this time is different. You have no idea what these people are capable of! And if the Shield let you down once, it'll do it again. You need to be somewhere safe. Somewhere we can protect you properly."

In answer, Matt threw himself into an armchair and folded his arms across his chest.

"I'm not going anywhere. We've been fine here for almost a week already. We'll survive."

"But it could take months to find your family!" said Dave with exasperation. "Or longer!"

"Even if it does, I'm staying here."

"Me, too," said Mary, her voice full of determination as she folded herself into the other armchair.

Dave made a sound of disbelief and looked around at Rose. Rose hesitated, twisting the end of her braid with anxious fingers.

"I'd like to stay here, too, Matt, but you have to admit we couldn't stay here alone for months," she said in a hurry before her brother could argue. "It's been ages since Grandpa disappeared and no one's found him. We're already running out of food, and we don't have that much money left …"

Matt shifted in his chair uneasily, but after a tense moment of silence, his face became set once more.

"We'll find a way to make it work." He fixed his gaze firmly on the wall behind Dave's head. "We always do."

Dave regarded Matt for a moment before seeming to recognise defeat. His shoulders slumped as he conjured a scrap of paper and a pen with a sigh.

"Look, I can't force you to leave, but soon you're going to find it difficult to stay here by yourselves."

He scribbled something on the paper and pushed it

across the coffee table towards Matt and Mary.

"If you need anything, or if you get into trouble, my number's there, and my address, so give me a call or come by my house if you change your mind. I'll make sure those guys outside can't stop you. I've got to go and start the search for your parents."

He stood up, and with a regretful look, strode to the door. Rose followed him.

"I'll come back and check up on you all in a couple of days if I haven't heard from you. Just in case."

"Thanks," said Rose, trying to manage a smile.

Dave walked a few paces down the driveway and then disappeared. Glancing towards the road, she noticed that the dark figures in the street had retreated again. She closed the door and went back to the living room. Everyone was silent. Matt showed no sign of wanting to leave his chair ever again.

"I think I'll go and test out my Viewer some more," said Rose finally, heading for the stairs.

Matt nodded but said nothing. Rose sat at her desk, staring out of the window. How on earth were they going to support themselves until their parents were found? Matt and Mary might be happy to stay here indefinitely, but Rose felt far from safe with the prototype deactivating the Shield all the time.

Maybe they'll change their minds once the food has run out and we're all starving, she thought, pulling out her Viewer and twirling it in her hand.

But at least someone knew what had happened now. Their situation was at least better than it had been this time yesterday. Rose prodded her invention with an irritable finger. Why couldn't she get it right? She'd never had this much trouble with a project before, but then again, she'd never made anything that had to break through such strong magic.

She put the Viewer back on the desk and stared out at the distant hills, somehow feeling more alone than ever.

Rose settled herself in Dad's chair again later that night, listening to the television rather than watching it as she flicked through Grandpa's report. Darkness descended slowly around her and she stifled a yawn with one hand. She no longer expected to make sense of the passages or diagrams, but she found herself reading and re-reading sections of the book anyway, as though the explanations would become clear if she stared at them long enough.

Matt was on the floor playing tug-of-war with Cocoa, while Mary sat slumped in the other armchair, watching the late-night movie. The clock over the mantelpiece chimed ten o'clock and she stood up, stretching.

"I'm off to bed," she mumbled, trudging to the stairs. "See you in the morning."

Rose turned over a page and squinted down at the dark, flowing handwriting. Soon Matt drifted off to bed, too, and Rose was left alone. She glanced at the lamp across the room and it flickered to life, filling the room with warm, bright light. Settling down more comfortably, she turned the volume down on the television and scanned the final page of the report.

It was the last thing Grandpa had written before he'd disappeared, and it looked like he'd been in a hurry. His handwriting became more untidy as she read. Her eyes moved across the first line, which turned out to be quite as baffling as the previous ones, and decided to give up for the night.

She closed the report and placed it on top of the nearest pile. Rising from her chair, her eyes found the report once more and she stopped, staring. The back cover bore scribbles in a different hand. Bending closer to the book, she immediately recognised the writing as her mother's. Holding the page up to the light, she read reminders to check some fact or other, a scrawled phone number that she now knew was Dave's, and a note about the meeting her parents should have gone to that morning. Underneath this, however, was an address Rose didn't know.

Curious, she summoned her laptop from her bedroom and typed in the address. Expecting it to belong to someone she'd never heard of, she was taken by surprise at the name that appeared on the screen. Rose sat up straight, her heart hammering. Why would Mum have written Alison Maxwell's address on the back of Grandpa's report? As far as she was aware, her parents had never had any contact with her.

Thinking back over the last several months, Rose was sure that they had never mentioned speaking to the woman, or even meeting her. She was about to rush upstairs to see what Matt and Mary thought about this discovery when she stopped, deciding she'd let them sleep. They couldn't do anything about it until morning, anyway.

She put the report back on the pile and went upstairs to bed, too tired to make sense of this new piece of information. She would try to decipher it in the morning.

"Alison Maxwell?" gasped Matt, as the three of them sat around the kitchen counter for breakfast the next morning.

"Yep," said Rose, pouring the last of the cereal into a bowl. "And I know Mum and Dad never mentioned seeing her or talking to her, so I wonder why they wrote down her address?"

Matt's eyes lit up with excitement.

"We could go and find out! Let's go and ask her!"

"If she kidnapped Mum, Dad and Grandpa, walking up to her house and knocking on the front door might not be such a good idea," Rose told him.

Exasperation replaced the eagerness on Matt's face with almost comical speed, and Rose fought to keep her face straight as she added, "But I've been thinking about it and I don't know what else we can do. I mean, we've read every bit of information in the house and we haven't got anything else to go off, and Dave and the police don't seem to be having any luck, either."

Matt's expression cleared.

"OK, let's go this morning, then!"

He forced down the rest of his toast and stood up, ready to leave. Rose, however, was not so willing to approach the Archivist accused of kidnapping her family without a plan, especially after what had happened with Kate. She picked at a frayed section of the tablecloth.

"We'll have to be careful about this. She's had a lot more magical training than we have. We can't just march up to her and demand answers, or we'll probably disappear, too."

"At least we'd be back with Mum and Dad," said Mary with longing, poking at her cornflakes with her spoon.

"D'you think we should make up a cover story?" asked Matt. "Say we're lost and need her help or something? Once we're inside the house we could do some investigating. Or should we be honest and say we want to hear her side of the story?"

"Well, if we do go, I think honesty is the better idea, and I want to take the Shield with us, just in case," said Rose.

"We can't rely on the Shield all the time," Matt reminded her. "Dave said so himself."

"I know, but it still works most of the time, and I'll feel better about this if we have it with us."

Matt shrugged his shoulders and ran for the stairs. "All right."

They finished breakfast and dressed hastily. Much to Rose's interest, the men who'd surrounded the house had not returned after Dave's visit yesterday, making things much easier. She wondered what he'd done to get rid of them.

Soon they were ready to go and Matt handed Rose the Shield. Checking that it was running at full power, she stowed it in a small backpack before standing in the middle of the living room, already nervous and wondering if they were doing the right thing.

Mary bit her lip and fiddled with the drawstring on her jacket, but Matt seemed perfectly at ease. Rose checked the address on the back of the report one last time.

"Thirty-eight Rockvale Close. I've never been there before. I hope we find it OK."

She slung her bag onto her back and took Mary's hand, remembering that her sister still found it difficult to find unfamiliar places with the travel spell. Rose took a deep breath, struggling to find her own confidence.

"If we get into trouble, we'll come straight back here, all right?"

The other two nodded and Rose closed her eyes, ready to begin the travel spell.

8

Alison Maxwell

She opened her eyes and felt her spirits drop. They stood in a narrow, tree-lined street in the outskirts of town. She swept her gaze over the derelict, weather-beaten houses and down a grassy lane which led to an empty field overrun with weeds. There was no one in sight. Under a bleak grey sky, it all seemed dreary and depressing.

"This isn't very encouraging," remarked Mary, staring up at the nearest house. It looked like it had been deserted for decades.

"Let's keep moving," said Rose in an undertone, stepping onto the footpath and trying to ignore her growing sense of unease. She pointed to the sign beside them.

"Well, this says Rockvale Close, so we've come to the right place. Let's find number thirty-eight."

It was a long road, lined with flowering shrubs and terminating in a dead end. Rose walked quickly, feeling exposed and unwelcome. They'd almost reached the end of the street when Mary called out, pointing across the road.

"There it is! Next to the old house with the peeling white paint."

Rose turned and saw a thick, green hedge of trees and bushes, hiding the house behind it from view. She glanced up and down the street once more before hurrying over to the gate. The number thirty-eight was painted on the letterbox beside it, and Rose looked down the path winding through the greenery with apprehension.

"Well, here goes nothing."

She swung the gate open and stepped inside. Matt and Mary kept close behind her, their eyes widening in surprise as they stared around.

It couldn't have been more different from the neglected houses and overgrown gardens on either side. Rose walked up the path, drinking everything in. It was exactly the kind of old-fashioned cottage garden her mother had always wanted, with jasmine and ivy rambling along the fence and up onto a trellis over the gate. Roses and daisies were planted around the yard and a gentle breeze created ripples on the surface of a small pond.

A single-storey brick house came into view as they wended their way through the flowerbeds. A veranda ran across its front and pots of colourful flowers were placed on either side of a wooden chair.

She led the way up the stairs and rang the doorbell nervously. Soon the sound of footsteps could be heard coming up the hall, and Rose told herself it was too late to back out now.

The door swung open and she gasped, staring in horror at the person standing before her. Without saying a word, she turned on her heels and raced back down the veranda steps.

"I can't believe it!" she exclaimed in outrage, as Matt and Mary scrambled to keep up.

"No, wait!" Kate ran after them, looking miserable. "Please don't go! You don't understand! If you'd just let me explain -"

"I understand things fine already, thank you very much, Kate. Or should I say *Alison*," snapped Rose, glaring at the woman over her shoulder as she continued along the path. "Why should we listen to anything you say? It's because of you that Grandpa's gone, and you stole his watch. As far as I'm concerned you're just a thief and a liar!"

She slowed from a run to a fast walk to avoid running into the thorny rose bushes, and Alison hurried after her, twisting her hands in agitation.

"Hear me out, OK? I swear I didn't steal the watch and it's definitely not my fault your grandpa was kid-napped!"

Matt and Mary remained silent, their expressions livid, and Rose continued walking, ignoring Alison's pleas for her to stop. Matt whirled around to face Alison, his eyes narrowing.

"Why did we find the watch in your drawer, then? I suppose it just materialised there from Rose's jewellery box?"

"It *was* taken, yes, but not by *me*," retorted Alison. "I had it because your parents thought it had something to do with your grandpa's invention. They asked me to take a look at it, so I kept it to study it. That's all, I promise."

"Yeah, that's a likely story," snarled Rose, stomping up to the gate.

Alison threw her hands up in the air, glaring at the three of them.

"You don't have a clue what's really been going on! You're just assuming you do, even though all you've done is listen through doors a few times! I saw on the news this morning that your parents have disappeared now, too," she said, her expression softening, "and I understand why you want to join the search for them, but how far do you think you're going to get on your own?"

Rose stopped and turned around, bristling.

"I don't believe you. We know a lot more than you think! Just leave us alone, Alison."

Alison took a deep breath before continuing in a tone of forced calm.

"If you leave now, you'll be fighting Hunter and his gang all by yourselves. Who else is going to help you? You've got nowhere to go, and you're not going to find your family unless you know how things really are. Come inside and sit down so we can talk about this without being disturbed. It's not safe out in the open."

She glanced around the garden and over the gate as though she expected someone to be listening, but Rose was too angry to care. She flipped the catch on the gate and tugged at it, but it wouldn't budge.

"Stop it!" she said, scowling at Alison. Deciding

she'd use magic instead, she wrapped a travel spell around herself, Matt and Mary and concentrated hard, but that didn't seem to work, either. "You're blocking me, aren't you?"

She put one foot on the gate and started to climb over it, but Matt sighed and took hold of her wrist to stop her.

"No, she's right, Rose," he said. "We've been trying to find useful information for days now and where has it got us? We still don't know anything."

"I suppose it can't hurt to hear what she's got to say, can it?" added Mary, looking up at Rose beseechingly.

Rose hesitated, fuming. She knew Matt and Mary were right, but she was so angry with Alison that all she felt like doing was getting as far away from her as possible.

"You could have just told us who you were!" she burst out. "You didn't have to lie!"

Alison shifted from one foot to another and glanced down at her hands.

"I know, it was a stupid idea. But I thought if I told you who I was you'd have hated me before you even got to know me, and you really do need my help!"

Rose chewed her lip, trying to think of something else to argue about, but Alison was already retreating towards the house.

"Come inside and we can talk."

"Come on," said Mary bracingly, taking Rose's hand and carting her back up the path.

Rose made an angry sound and shot Alison another

mutinous look, but allowed her sister to pull her up the veranda steps. Alison held the front door open for them and Matt and Mary went inside, dragging Rose along behind them.

The inside of the house was light and airy. Rose glanced around with curiosity in spite of herself as Alison led them down a hallway and into a living room painted a pale sage green.

The room was small, but the windows looked out over the garden and the sheer curtains allowed the sunlight to stream in, giving the room an open, pleasant feel. Rose crossed the room and sat sandwiched between Matt and Mary on the sofa.

"Why are you living here now?" she asked accusingly, removing her backpack and placing it on her lap. "I thought you were staying at your friend's place."

Alison hovered by the fireplace for a moment, her eyes lingering on the empty grate.

"I was. But everything I need is here and I was only supposed to be at my friend's house until I'd put enough protection around this place. I decided I wasn't going to let anyone chase me out of my own home. So, I'm back here now."

Rose folded her arms across her chest and eyed Alison doubtfully.

"All right, then, tell us what's going on. Start at the beginning and don't leave anything out."

Alison nodded and sat down in an armchair, looking tired but also relieved. "How much do you know about the magical groups in the government?"

Rose glanced at Matt and Mary's blank faces.

"Not much. We've never had any contact with them because we're not old enough to sell inventions yet."

"Well, there are magical organisations that work with the government," Alison explained, "and as I'm sure you can guess, their job is to represent magical people, although they're getting rarer these days. Anyway, about three months ago, people from one of those organisations approached your grandpa. I'm not sure if you already know, but there's been a lot of trouble over the last year or so with someone called Lawrence Hunter."

Rose blinked. "Never heard of him."

She hadn't watched the news since Grandpa had disappeared and she hadn't listened to the radio in weeks.

"Well, nobody knows all that much about him," Alison continued. "He's a bit of a recluse, so he's managed to keep lots of things about himself and his past quiet, but about a year ago it got out that he and his friends have been doing all kinds of questionable things with magic, like misusing prohibited magical substances and materials for their own gains. The police have never caught Hunter himself, but whenever they lock away his friends they always manage to escape somehow. It's becoming a real problem.

"Not too long ago, I went into his room in the Archives and found out that he's been making and collecting loads of things that were never approved by the Archives. It's been a nightmare trying to sort everything out," she groaned.

"But how could they get out of prison?" Matt

exchanged a look of scepticism with Rose before turning back to Alison. "They have special cells for magical people, don't they? And there are spells on the building so that people can't use magic to escape."

Alison put her chin in her hand, her expression troubled. She gave Rose a fleeting smile, but Rose saw how tense her posture was as she picked at the upholstery in a distracted kind of way. This Hunter person had clearly been causing her a lot of trouble.

"That's the problem," Alison said, her voice becoming bitter. "All of the usual spells that are used to control magical people don't work on any of Hunter's friends, which means they're effectively free to go around doing whatever they like."

Matt seemed intrigued. "Why don't the spells work on them?"

"We don't know for sure. But they must have come up with something that can undo the magic keeping them in. It's probably one of Hunter's new creations."

Mary's face puckered like she'd just bitten into a lemon.

"Why would people like that have anything to do with us?"

"Well, because of Hunter and his friends, a lot of people in government have been talking about more radical methods of controlling magical criminals."

Alison hesitated, looking uneasy.

"They've decided that if they can't be controlled in any of the usual ways, and they're using their abilities to do the wrong thing, they should have their magic taken away from them."

Matt and Mary made noises of outrage at this and Rose's mouth fell open with shock, her nails digging into the palms of her hands. Another part of her, however, thought of her family, kidnapped and held somewhere against their will, and couldn't help but feel that perhaps removing a person's abilities might be appropriate in some circumstances.

"I didn't think it was possible to take away someone's magic," she whispered.

Alison's face darkened.

"It's not. At least, it wasn't until your grandpa made the Fragmenter. It wasn't even legal until a few months ago, but a law was passed in September that changed all of that. Now any magical person who breaks the rules will face having their magic stripped if a judge decides their crime is severe enough. The whole law enforcement system is being rewritten to accommodate it. Magical people have never been popular anyway, because there's always been too much suspicion about how they might be using their abilities, and Hunter has made it all worse.

"It seems that when the government approached your grandpa about it, Hunter decided he'd steal the invention. I can see the idea of taking away other people's magic appealing to him. It fits with everything I've heard about him, anyway. It'd be an effective way to threaten someone. He's been waiting quite a while for your grandpa to finish his work on the Fragmenter so he could walk in and take it."

"And that's what Grandpa's been making all this time?" asked Rose, mortified. "No wonder it's been kept so secret!"

Alison ducked her head apologetically.

"From what I can gather, government representatives told him what they wanted him to do and asked if he'd be willing to make the invention for them. But his reaction was the same as yours. He refused to make it when they described what they had planned in detail," she insisted. "When I spoke to him, he was adamant that imprisonment should be the goal for these people, rather than permanently harming them. I'm not sure what the government said to change his mind, but they must have said or done something because he agreed to make it in the end. But he wasn't happy about it.

"I was working in the documentation area of the Archives when I started getting his reports. I couldn't believe my eyes when I saw what he was doing. I had to check all of the information carefully because of what the Fragmenter was being made to do. That's how I met your grandpa. There were so many dangerous and barely legal things involved in making the invention that I had to go and talk to him about it, to make sure he was aware of all the rules and what the implications would be if something went wrong. I couldn't believe the law had even been passed."

"It shouldn't have been!" said Matt, his voice shaking with anger. "There must be other ways of controlling people!"

"It is a bit extreme," agreed Alison. "But you must

admit that if a magical person is using their skills to hurt others and they can't be controlled any other way, removing those abilities would be the next logical step."

Mary opened her mouth to protest at this, but stopped, evidently realising Alison had a point.

"Normally, when something like this happens, I have to report the maker to the police and confiscate the invention so it can be destroyed," said Alison. "I told your grandpa that, even though the new law made his invention legal, he'd still have to be careful about how he made it, who would use it and why. All of the usual stuff I have to go through. But then he disappeared, and the Fragmenter vanished, too, just when he'd finished working on it."

"And Mum and Dad got stuck with it," intoned Rose gloomily. Alison nodded again.

"They didn't want to get involved. They'd only been given the barest details about what your grandpa was making and were looking up general information about experimental magic that might be useful, to help him get the job done faster. But when they were given all of the information about the invention, they were angry at the government and upset that Peter had been pushed into making it.

"They decided they weren't going to have anything to do with it, and told the government representatives they'd have to find it themselves if they wanted it. But in the end, they didn't have a choice, either. They told me that they started getting anonymous threats when they chose not to look for the invention. But I don't think it's hard to figure out who was behind it. We all knew Hunter wanted the invention and we were all sure it must have been him."

A stunned silence met these words and Rose shook her head in disbelief.

"Wait, Mum and Dad were being threatened? I had no idea!"

Her mind went back to the last day of school, when her parents had arrived to take them home early, and she realised what must have happened. She exchanged horrified looks with Matt and Mary. Alison edged forward in her seat, her face full of concern.

"They said nothing because they didn't want you to worry. They were forced to become more involved and had to keep going with the project. They looked for the Fragmenter, but they couldn't find it. Your grandpa must have hidden it before he was taken, to stop Hunter from getting his hands on it. Your family and the government both knew Hunter would try to take it once Peter's work was done, so they all put defensive magic around your grandpa's house. But Hunter managed to get past it all, when everyone thought it was safe."

She gave Rose a sympathetic look and Rose gulped, fighting back tears of anger and guilt.

"But why can't the government make its own inventions if it's so clever?" asked Mary, her voice wavering. "Wouldn't it be easier?"

Alison seemed to consider this for a moment. The clock on the mantelpiece chimed and she waited for it to fall silent before answering.

"I guess some might see it that way. But your family has always been very good at inventing. Your grandpa's been creating magical inventions professionally for more than sixty years now, so he's got a lot of experience. He knows the craft inside and out, and if you're going to make a dangerous and experimental object like the Fragmenter, you need someone who knows what they're doing or things can go very wrong. Even Hunter decided to let your grandpa handle the making of the Fragmenter. Hunter's smart, but I doubt he knows anywhere near as much about how to make an invention as your grandpa does."

A sound of annoyance escaped Rose's lips and she brushed away a tear with an impatient hand. It sounded like her family had been unwittingly aiding this Lawrence Hunter person all along. Alison seemed to guess how Rose was feeling. She stood up and began to pace restlessly around the room.

"I promise you, your family didn't want to help Hunter. It was the government they agreed to work with. By the looks of it, a lot of the people at the Magicked Masterclass were pressured into helping, too, dealing with the legal side of it all. Hunter's played a big part in this whole affair."

Matt's fists were clenched and he was biting his lip. He looked very much like he wanted to hit something.

"I can't believe it's been so easy for him to get what he wants," he raged. "I mean, he goes around making trouble so that people start talking about removing people's magic, then all he has to do is keep provoking them until it's made legal, wait for the government to have the invention made, and steal it! We're all doing what he wants, aren't we? It's stupid!"

Rose could feel the frustration coming off him as though it was tangible, and her own jaw clenched in response, her mind going back to all the times her parents had been forced to go out searching for an invention they wanted nothing to do with, just so Hunter could take it from them.

"But why does he want to take away people's magic in the first place?" asked Mary.

"Yeah, what good does it do him if a few less people can do magic?" demanded Matt. "And if he wanted the Fragmenter made and couldn't do it himself, why didn't he come and force us to make it straight off? Why did he wait for the government to make it legal and everything? It would've taken longer that way …"

"If he removes enough people's magic he won't have much competition anymore, and there won't be anyone powerful enough left to stop him from doing whatever he likes," replied Rose, suddenly sounding as bitter as Alison. "He's going to use the invention made to control *him* to control *us* instead.

"And as for why he waited for it to be made legal, I guess it makes things a lot easier for him. It's like you said before, Matt, he doesn't have to do much except sit and wait for the invention to be finished. That way, it's all organised by someone else. It's the government's responsibility and he can't be blamed for making an invention like that himself."

She scowled again and turned to Alison.

"One thing I don't understand, though, is why he kidnapped Grandpa. He was after the Fragmenter, wasn't he? Did he realise it was gone and kidnap Grandpa to find out what he'd done with it? And maybe Mum and Dad found out where it was hidden, and he attacked them, too, to force them to tell him where it was? Or to stop them telling someone else?"

Alison shrugged.

"Your guess is as good as mine." But she caught the look on Rose's face and said, "Even if Hunter used force to make them talk, there's no guarantee he'd get what he wants. I don't think he's hurting them, wherever he's keeping them. It doesn't appear to be his style. From what I can gather, he's more interested in exploring the nature of magic and seems to have a real need to contribute. He just goes about it the wrong way."

Rose squirmed uncomfortably, her own feelings of inadequacy suddenly surging to the surface. She understood the need to contribute all too well, the desire to prove one's worthiness, but she pushed her feelings back down, refusing to acknowledge any kind of common ground with the man who had kidnapped her family.

"Apparently he was a member of the Guild at one time, but he hated the restrictions they placed on him, so he left," Alison continued, her gaze distant as she stared out of the window. "I think your family will be safe as long as we stop him from using the Fragmenter on them. That's the real danger."

Rose shuddered at the thought of this and turned the conversation to something else.

"Where do you come into all of this?" she asked, looking at Alison. The young woman blinked.

"I told you. I was working in the Archives."

"Yeah, but you came to our house that time, a few days after the masterclass, and later everyone was saying that you were the one who kidnapped Grandpa. And when we got home from your friend's place after Christmas, two men were searching our library. They said they knew you and that they were surprised we hadn't heard from you. I wasn't sure what they meant by that."

Alison thought for a moment, seeming genuinely confused.

"I suppose they must have guessed I'd go to meet your parents and tell them everything I'd seen and suspected about what had happened to Peter, but they didn't realise that you three didn't know anything. They thought I'd told you who I was and who Hunter was …" She trailed off, looking guilty. "And they probably thought that if they said they knew me, you'd be more suspicious of me."

Mary glanced from Rose to Alison, looking perplexed.

"But why would they want that?"

"Because I know too much," replied Alison with a small smile. "It helps Hunter a lot if everyone is after me instead of him. When I went to see your grandpa about the Fragmenter and he told me he wouldn't stop making it, I got curious. I started going into his reports to find out more about it. In the end, I found out that Hunter was interested in the invention, too, and I couldn't help but wonder if your grandpa was being pressured to make it."

"So the first time you came to see Mum and Dad, you were trying to convince them you were innocent?" guessed Rose, remembering how uncomfortable Alison had been, not to mention her parents, who must have hated lying to their children about Alison's identity.

"Yes. I came because I couldn't stand the thought of you all thinking I was the one who'd kidnapped your grandpa. The police wouldn't listen to me because Hunter had done everything he could to make sure it looked like I was guilty. But they couldn't prove that I'd done anything, so they couldn't lock me up. I just wanted to explain to you all what had really happened. I thought if I gave you all the facts and the evidence to back it up, you'd believe me."

She turned to Rose imploringly and Rose reluctantly met her gaze. She hesitated for a fraction of a second before giving Alison a stiff nod to show that she believed her. Alison's posture relaxed.

"Your parents told me that one of Hunter's friends had taken your grandpa's pocket watch when you were all outside after the masterclass," she went on, "and that the Fragmenter prototype had stopped your Shield from working. I guessed that Hunter had put the watch in his room in the Archives, so to prove that I wasn't lying I broke into his room and got it back. It took me a while to figure out where he'd put his things. He keeps it all hidden away, where the Archivists can't find it, but I found a way in and the watch was there, lying on a shelf. Maybe he thought it was useless after all.

"When I gave it to your parents, they told me about how you'd tried to repair it, Rose, but couldn't. They thought it was strange that Hunter would be interested in it at all, so they asked me to take a look at it, to make sure it really was just a pocket watch."

"And is it?"

Matt and Mary leaned forward eagerly, waiting for the verdict.

"I don't think so, no," said Alison. "It's not acting like a normal watch, anyway."

"Ha!" cried Rose, clapping a hand to her knee triumphantly. "I knew there was something weird about that watch! It's the only thing my repairing spell hasn't worked on!"

"Yes, I don't think it's broken exactly, but it's not responding to any of my tests either." Alison began pacing back and forth again. "If it's an invention, like your parents suspected, Peter did a good job of hiding it, and I'd like to know why he went to so much trouble."

Rose turned to Matt and Mary questioningly and they both nodded, apparently satisfied that Alison was telling the truth. Alison completed another circuit of the room, looking more cheerful now that she'd unburdened herself.

"Does that answer all of your questions?" she asked.

"I guess so," said Mary, who had been sitting with

her knees tucked under her chin, unusually quiet.

"So now we know it's Hunter who has our family." Matt stood up abruptly, squaring his shoulders. "Where do we find him?"

Alison stopped pacing to stare at him.

"Don't be silly! You can't just go storming up to him, or wherever he has them hidden. If Hunter gets to the Fragmenter before we do, he'll almost certainly use it on your family, and they'll lose their magic forever! No, we need to concentrate on finding the invention before we do anything else."

Matt gasped and took a step back as though Alison had dealt him a physical blow.

"What?! You can't seriously think we care about the invention more than our family?"

"Yeah, we don't care about the stupid Fragmenter," snapped Mary, glaring at Alison. But Alison glared straight back at her.

"Do you know what happens to someone when their magic is torn away from them permanently?" she challenged, her tone icy.

Rose shook her head, not sure if she wanted to know.

"They could go into shock and die!" said Alison. "People aren't meant to have their magic stripped. The body finds it hard to cope."

Rose felt the colour drain from her face. "They could die?"

Matt sat back down, his eyes suddenly bright with unshed tears.

"What are we going to do, then? Everyone's been looking for Grandpa's invention for ages now and no one's found it. How are *we* supposed to do it?"

"That's why you're going to need help," said Alison with a tight smile. "The only way we're going to find it before Hunter does is if we all work as a team."

Rose looked helplessly at Alison, feeling out of her depth. It seemed like she was asking them to do the impossible.

"Let's try not to freak out too soon," said Alison, seeing the fear on their faces. "First, we should sort out where you're going to stay. If you don't mind, I think you'd be safer here with me, where we can stick together."

Rose, Matt and Mary nodded in unison.

"Good," said Alison, looking pleased. "We'll use a travel spell back to your place and you can pack what you want to take with you."

They all surged to their feet. Rose wrapped herself in the spell and opened her eyes a second later in her own living room. Matt was already upstairs, and Mary appeared beside Rose as she rushed to the door.

Not being a member of the family, Alison was unable to enter the Shield's sphere of influence without direct permission, and Rose opened the door to find her waiting on the doorstep.

"Thanks."

Alison grinned and stepped inside. Rose closed the door and the protective spells sealed the house behind them. Alison ran upstairs with Mary and called out so that Matt could hear her.

"Just pack some clothes and the things you really need. We won't be able to take everything."

Mary disappeared down the hall while Rose hurried out into the yard. She called for Cocoa, checking all of his favourite hiding places. After several minutes of searching, she found him underneath the house, chewing on his tennis ball, and she got down on the ground to coax him out. She held out some dog biscuits and he lifted his head.

"Come on, Cocoa. We've got to hurry. You can't stay here all by yourself."

He sniffed at the treats and started to wriggle his way towards her. She gave him a biscuit as soon as he was out and then led him inside.

"I'm taking Cocoa over now," she called out.

Alison stuck her head over the stairs and peered down.

"OK, I've got a space in the yard I think he might like."

Rose gripped Cocoa's collar in one hand and arrived seconds later in Alison's backyard. Cocoa shook himself, his fur standing on end. Rose stroked his head to soothe him.

"Yeah, I know you hate the travel spell."

She gave him some more biscuits and reappeared in her bedroom this time. Taking her camping bag down from the top of her wardrobe, she brushed off the dust and contemplated her belongings, trying to decide what to leave behind. She went to her dresser and began tossing in clothes at random before gathering up her Viewer and notebook of ideas.

She put them in the bag, along with the set of tools her parents had given her, threw in her bag of toiletries and paused with a hand on the pile of books she'd taken from the library on finding spells. Deciding that they hadn't been of much use, she left them where they were, zipping up her bag and placing it in the hall.

Matt had made a haphazard pile of his possessions outside his bedroom door and was now in the library with Alison, sorting through the reports and books.

"We'd better take your grandpa's report, too," Alison said, reaching for the book. "We can't risk it falling into the wrong hands."

"Hunter wouldn't need it if he has Grandpa, would he?" said Matt.

"Maybe not, but we'll take it anyway," replied Alison. "We can't leave it lying around, and besides, we might find a use for it ourselves."

Rose went down the hall to help Mary pack. Her sister had crammed so much into her bag that she was struggling to close it. Rose picked through the tangled mess of clothes, books and invention pieces and couldn't help but chuckle.

"Are you sure you need all of this?"

Mary gave her an offended look as she forced another jacket into the bag, making it strain at the seams.

"Yeah, I do! We don't know how long it's going to take to find Grandpa and his Fragmenter. We could be gone for ages!"

Rose held her hands up in surrender.

"All right, then."

She carried the heavy bag into the hall for her and waited for the other two to be finished in the library. By the time everyone was standing at the top of the stairs, laden with all of their luggage and ready to go, it was past lunchtime, and Rose could hear Matt's stomach rumbling.

"OK, have you got everything?" said Alison, rearranging the books in her arms. "There's not much I can do about your invention room right now, but it's already well protected, so it should be OK. I'll have to do some preparation before I can safely destroy the Fragmenter prototype, but I'll come back for it later. All right, let's go!"

They reappeared in Alison's living room and Rose put her baggage down gratefully.

"I'll show you around the house and then we can have some lunch," said Alison briskly.

She led them down the hall and into a small room with the same sage green walls as the rest of the house, but with a window looking out into the backyard.

"This room can be yours, Matt. It's not too big, I'm afraid, but it'll have to do."

She showed them into the room next door, which was somewhat bigger and contained a large wooden dresser in one corner.

"I've only got two spare rooms, so you and Mary will have to share," she said to Rose apologetically.

"That's OK, I don't mind," said Rose. She went to

the window to find a sprawling tree outside, filtering the dappled light streaming into the room. "This is great. Thanks!"

Alison smiled and Matt's stomach groaned again.

"Time for lunch, I think," said Alison with a laugh.

Later that night, as they were getting ready for bed, Rose found Alison cleaning the kitchen. She helped stack the dishes in a cupboard and tidy up, and they chatted for a while until Rose cleared her throat, trying to summon the courage to speak aloud the thoughts that had been running through her mind.

"Er, thanks for letting us stay here, and for telling us everything this morning," she mumbled.

Alison smiled and handed her another plate to put away.

"No problem. You do have the right to know why your family's gone missing."

"It's just that no one else has told us anything, so I wasn't sure you would. It's nice to know the truth finally, that's all."

"Fair enough," said Alison with a shrug. "I'm glad you believed me. Not many people have done that so far, either." Alison grinned and Rose gave her a shy smile.

"And … and I'm sorry I called you a thief and a liar," Rose added after a moment, blushing magenta and concentrating on the dish in her hands. Alison turned away to wipe down the countertop.

"Don't worry about it. I've been called worse."

Relieved that Alison wasn't upset, Rose finished putting away the cutlery and went to brush her teeth. As she climbed into one of the two single beds in her room, Rose thought about everything Alison had told them and hoped that she, Matt and Mary were right to trust her. They'd made mistakes before, after all, and they only had her word that what she'd said was true.

Rose stared at the moonlit tree outside, her mind wandering back to the night the prototype had attacked them in the invention room. It dawned on her suddenly that she and Matt had been risking losing their magic.

Finally understanding why her parents had been so desperate to keep them away from the invention, she tried to imagine what it would be like, after using magic her entire life, to live without it. It dawned on her that this was the fate of Lawrence Hunter and his friends if they were caught, and she wondered if anyone truly deserved such a punishment. But if they were hurting other people, that made it different, didn't it?

She sighed, thinking that if she, Matt and Mary stayed with Alison, they would at least have a chance of finding the Fragmenter before Hunter did, whether she was their friend or not. And besides, everything she'd said made sense.

Exhausted now, Rose pulled her blankets up and rolled over onto her side, yawning and trying not to let her mind linger on Lawrence Hunter or the Fragmenter. There would be plenty of time for that later …

9

The Fragmenter's Curse

Rose sat at the table during breakfast the next morning, nibbling on a piece of toast while she went over the plan in her head. Alison had decided the night before that it was time to destroy the Fragmenter prototype, claiming that it was too risky to leave it unsupervised and that it would be better to dismantle it now, before Hunter could steal it. Rose, Matt and Mary had immediately offered to help, but Alison had refused to let them near the invention.

"Your parents wanted me to keep you safe," she'd told them with a stern look. "They'd be devastated if you lost your magic."

However, this merely resulted in a chorus of begging and pleading from Matt and Mary, and the argument had gone on for nearly an hour before Alison finally relented, insisting that they could accompany her on the condition that they follow any instructions she might give them.

Rose wound a strand of her hair around a finger as she ate, her thoughts racing. Despite wanting to help, she was uneasy at the thought of going near the prototype again. She glanced at Alison, who was now flipping through a slightly tattered and dog-eared book at the opposite end of the table. She turned a page, seeming perfectly unconcerned at the prospect of destroying the bud.

"Is that Grandpa's report?" Rose asked, taking a sip of juice to soothe her dry throat.

Alison nodded.

"It's a good idea to know as much as possible about an invention before you try to destroy it, especially if you're dealing with a dangerous one like the Fragmenter. That way, you know its strengths and weaknesses and you can predict how it will react when you attack it. It won't be easy getting rid of this one."

Mary looked up from her cereal, her mouth open as though she'd just remembered something.

"What does 'magic in its purest form' mean? We read it somewhere in the report, but I didn't get what it meant."

"It's a bit hard to explain." Alison turned another page and stared down at a detailed diagram of the Fragmenter. "When some kinds of spells are bound to an object, they change it permanently. In a way, they become part of it. You can't destroy one without destroying the other. Your grandpa said the Fragmenter has defensive spells made of magic in its purest form. That means they're separate from it, instead of being built into it."

Matt blinked, his face going blank. "Why is that so important?"

"It just means that the bud itself is the weakest part of the invention," said Alison with a shrug. "Magic is energy. When people do magic they're using that energy, and the strength of their spell depends on how strong and skilled the person is mentally. When a spell is bound to an invention, it's the strength of the object that decides how strong the spell can be. There's no use binding strong magic to weak materials that can't survive the amount of energy going through them.

"But because the Fragmenter's defensive spells are separate from it, they're free from those kinds of limitations. The materials will still have to be sturdy because powerful spells are running through them, but the spells aren't built into them, they're not a part of them, so your grandpa could make them as strong as he liked. That's why the Fragmenter's going to be so difficult to deal with. It's protected by the strongest kind of magic there is." She drained the last of her tea and set her cup aside. "But on the bright side, it makes it just as hard for people like Hunter to get near it."

Rose took another sip of juice, trying to make sense of this.

"So that means we don't have to destroy the defensive spells to kill the invention?"

"That's right," said Alison, looking pleased. "We can kill it by destroying the bud. It will be much easier than trying to overpower its magic. Once the invention is destroyed, the defensive spells will stop attacking because the connection will be lost. And that reminds me, if you're going to help me, you'll need to be able to protect yourselves. Have you been taught any magical self defence?"

Rose stifled a grin, her thoughts going back to her

childhood. She'd just turned nine when Dad had marched her downstairs into the living room alongside Matt for their first defence lesson. Mary, who had only been three years old at the time, had sat on the sofa laughing as she watched the others take turns sending hexes and curses at one another.

After several hours of this, Dad had stopped them and looked ruefully around the devastated room, from the torn curtains to the ruined picture over the mantelpiece, and vowed to never practise defensive magic inside the house again.

"I can make barriers and deflect curses and stuff like that," said Rose, her thoughts returning to the present. "I've started learning dissolution spells, too, but they don't always work." She blushed and picked at her toast, but Alison nodded, looking pleased.

"That's good." She turned to Matt and Mary. "OK, what about you two?"

Each of them demonstrated their best spells and Alison seemed satisfied. She closed the report and placed it with the sheaf of loose pages they'd removed from the black cabinet.

"I think these have told me everything they can. Are you ready to go?"

Rose swallowed the last of her breakfast and got to her feet, pushing her chair back with a clammy hand.

"As ready as I'll ever be," she murmured, standing beside Alison.

Matt and Mary hurried over, both of them pale with nerves. Rose began a travel spell and opened her eyes a second later to find herself back at home. She ran downstairs to let Alison in, and they all gathered around the invention room door.

"Remember what I told you," said Alison, in a tone that suggested she was steeling herself for something unpleasant. "If it gets too dangerous, go straight back to my place. I'll meet you there when I'm done. I don't want you to be stuck in the room with the invention."

They nodded and Rose took the protective spells off the room. Alison led the way inside and they huddled around the cabinet. Crumpled and dented, its door still lay beneath the workbench, where it had fallen. A faint green glow emanated from the cabinet and Rose bit her lip as Alison reached in and drew out the bud.

Rose couldn't help but stare at it, entranced as soon as her eyes met the familiar, shining metal. Matt and Mary gazed at it avidly, as though nothing else in the room existed. Only Alison seemed unaffected by the bud's allure.

She began to inspect it at once, holding it up to the light and peering at it closely as she turned it this way and that, examining every tiny detail like a gem expert searching for imperfections in a diamond.

"Wow."

She ran her fingers over the casing, tapping it here and there and listening to the sounds it made.

"This has so much defensive magic on it! I'm not surprised the real Fragmenter did so much damage to your Shield! I'm amazed your parents could even work on this without it going haywire."

She weighed the invention in her hand.

"The spells on this particular version seem to be a little different to the ones on the real thing. This bud will only react if someone performs aggressive or destructive magic around it, or if anyone makes an obvious attempt to force it open in some way."

"That sounds about right." Rose shuddered, her thoughts straying to the bud's reaction when Matt and Mary had attempted to open it. "It's always been very sensitive."

"The real one is even more sensitive," replied Alison. "Your grandpa disappeared before he could add the finer details to his report, so there are still a lot of things I don't know about the Fragmenter's reactions, but with the number of defensive spells on this prototype, I'm certain it will do something to protect itself."

She took a heavy mallet from the rack of tools beside the door and cleared a space on the workbench. She lay the invention on its side and struck it with the mallet. Rose flinched as a burst of energy shot through the room and Alison jumped back. The glass pieces inside the casing flashed threateningly, but the invention remained inactive and unharmed.

"Looks like it's not going to be easy to kill it without magic, either," said Rose in a small voice.

"No, I never really thought it would be." Alison sighed and rolled up her sleeves. "OK, then. Stay close to the door, in case you need to run."

Rose backed away, holding her breath. Alison

approached the bench once more and aimed her first spell at the bud.

It was as though a switch had been flicked. Energy surged through the room for a second time, making the hairs on Rose's arms stand up, and the green tendrils of the casing began to unwind out of their decorative shape.

She could feel Alison working on the invention as the glass pieces began to glow, gathering light at the tips. Rose tensed, waiting for Alison's signal. The bud's casing curled back and fell still like a flower's petals unfurling and Alison glanced over her shoulder at them.

"Now!"

Rose, Matt and Mary each sent their best magic at the invention and Rose braced herself for retaliation. But the bud began to shrivel the moment their combined spells touched it, and Matt and Mary cheered as the glass pieces cracked and the green casing turned an earthy brown. Whatever Alison had done seemed to have worked. Rose let her breath out in a rush, surprised that it had been so easy to defeat the bud and chiding herself for having spent most of the morning worrying for nothing.

These thoughts had barely crossed her mind, however, when she turned back to the workbench and gasped. The braided base of the invention had begun to move, unravelling to create root-like green shoots that grew across the surface of the workbench and wound their way down towards the floor at an alarming speed.

Alison took a hasty step back and, using a spell Rose didn't know, managed to slow the roots' growth a little, but they continued to creep forward relentlessly, and Rose stared in shock as two of them reached for the table beside the bench and curled themselves around the nearest inventions.

Some were stripped of their magic but left physically intact, while others crumpled at the roots' touch, turning to the consistency of ash with a faint hissing sound. Others broke into tiny pieces that scattered over the tabletop, but each time an invention died, the bud glowed a little brighter.

Rose could feel the magic that had once been bound to the inventions flowing into the bud like an invisible river. Her eyes travelled along the roots to the surface of the workbench, which had turned into something green and poisoned-looking. A brightly coloured object on the table exploded without warning and she let out a startled yelp.

"The invention's repairing itself!" screeched Mary, throwing her arms up over her head as glass and coloured pieces flew through the air.

The bud continued to destroy everything closest to it until its repairs were complete. The roots then retreated, wrapping themselves back around the base protectively, leaving Alison staring at the bud in surprise.

"It went for the strongest combined source of magical power in the room. Huh! Your grandpa didn't mention *that* in his reports …"

"Now we have to start all over again!" moaned Matt, his shoulders drooping.

Alison, however, looked as though she'd just been

given the answer she'd been searching for. Her expression lifted and she sprang into action. "But now we know how to weaken it, and this time we can stop it repairing itself. We'll move everything with magic downstairs. They'll be out of the bud's range there."

They bundled up all of the other inventions and took them into the living room, placing them in a heap on the coffee table. Alison plunged a hand into the pile and drew out an object containing the same glittering black liquid that powered the Shield.

"Inhibiting fluid," she muttered, turning it over in her hand. "It won't like that." She held the fluid up to the light, but it remained dark and impenetrable. She turned to Rose, Matt and Mary. "I think we can use this to help kill the prototype. Would you mind if we sacrificed this one invention?"

Rose shook her head.

"Do whatever you need to do. Mum and Dad would want the bud to be destroyed."

Alison grinned and took the little invention back upstairs, placing it on the edge of the table, close to the workbench.

"Now we have to make the Fragmenter send out roots again. We'll use the same combination of spells as before. They seemed to work well together. Ready?"

Matt nodded, his jaw set, and they tried again. The bud sprang back to life the moment their spells made contact, its tendrils curling back to expose the glass shards. Rose fixed her eyes on the centre of the invention and concentrated on her dissolution spell, imagining the bud's spells unravelling like a cloth.

The spell hit its mark with a sizzling sound and then rebounded back at her, forcing her to hop quickly out of the way so that it struck the wall behind her, leaving a long strip of blistered paint. Rose gasped and steadied herself on the doorframe.

"Is it me, or is the bud stronger than before?"

"The magic it absorbed from the other inventions will have made it more powerful," panted Alison, dodging another rebounding curse. "But we have to find a way to damage it again or it won't take up the inhibiting fluid."

The light from the glass shards glowed brightly now and Rose yawned, suddenly tired to her bones. She peered through heavy lids at Mary, who was blinking furiously. Matt's head was starting to nod and Rose could feel his spells becoming weaker.

"We haven't got much time left to do this," she said, shaking her head to clear it.

Alison nodded and conjured up a shield spell to protect herself as the Fragmenter continued to lash out.

"I'm going to try something different, but I'll need you all to do your best spells again," she called. "When you're ready."

Rose gathered her remaining strength and hurled one last spell at the Fragmenter, hoping that it would be enough. The others did the same, and finally, the bud began to shrivel. The base unfurled once more, but instead of reaching for the invention on the table, they wound their way towards Alison, spiralling down the leg of the workbench and creeping across the floor.

Rose, Matt and Mary shuffled backwards until they were almost in the hall. Alison, however, stood her ground and continued to work on the bud, even as the tendrils wrapped around her ankle. The pure white light radiating from the glass pieces was almost blinding now, and Rose fought the urge to drift off to sleep. She rubbed her eyes and surveyed the glowing invention.

Its surface was no longer smooth and pristine. Scorched and dented, some of the tendrils appeared to have died, leaving shrivelled brown stumps around the base of the bud. But the remaining roots had grown up to Alison's knee, preventing her escape, and the white light was growing stronger rather than fading.

Matt sank to his knees and Rose took hold of the door for support as her energy drained away. Mary slumped against the wall, watching with wide, fearful eyes. Alison seemed less steady on her feet now. She aimed another spell at the bud and it pushed it back at her, sending her reeling into the table beside her. Drops of blood stained the wood as broken invention pieces cut into her hands.

The tendrils wrapped around her waist, and Rose began to worry that their plan was not going to work. Aware that time was rapidly running out, she stumbled forward, determined to free Alison, but Matt reached out and held her back, giving her a warning look.

"You won't be helping her if you get stuck, too."

Rose stopped, caught between conflicting emotions. She wanted to help, but she knew Matt was right. Alison sent a string of spells at the bud, but they seemed to have little effect on the invention now, and it shrugged off a particularly strong curse with ease, sending it back at her with twice the force.

"We're not going to kill it in time! We have to leave!" cried Rose, her voice high with fear.

Alison stopped fighting the bud and leaned back, catching her breath. Sensing victory, the root-like tendrils around her legs contracted, holding her tighter, and she threw an arm out to regain her balance, gripping the edge of the table beside her. Her eyes met Rose's and she nodded.

"Go back to my place. Go now, before the invention completes the Fragmenting curse."

Rose, Matt and Mary glanced at each other.

"But what about you?"

"We can't just leave!"

"Can't you use a travel spell to get away?"

Alison yawned and sagged against the tendrils holding her. She shook her head.

"Travel spells won't work. And you promised to do as I say."

Rose knew that she'd promised, but she also knew that she would be ashamed of herself if she left her friend to such a fate. She glared at the invention containing the inhibiting fluid and forced herself to focus.

"Let's try one more time. If it doesn't work, then we'll go."

She turned to her brother and sister and they nodded, steeling themselves. Rose waited as they got to their feet, and the three of them positioned themselves in front of the bud. Rose threw everything she had left at it, her hatred of the bud and her fear for Alison making her spell stronger than she'd anticipated. The metal casing of the Fragmenter hummed as the spells made contact, but still, it showed no interest in the inhibiting fluid.

Rose gritted her teeth, sweat beading on her forehead. She met Alison's eyes and saw her jaw tighten. Alison took a deep breath and thrust her own spell at the bud, with enough force to make the light gathering at the tips of the bud's glass pieces dim.

For a moment the room was still as all four of them balled their fists, bearing down on the invention with their minds until a loud snap broke the silence and a crack appeared on the largest of the jagged glass pieces at the centre of the bud.

Rose let go of her spell gratefully, her head aching, and finally, slowly, the bud sprouted a single new root. Rose hurried even further backwards as it grew across the workbench, this time heading in her direction.

Matt and Mary followed Rose out into the hallway, ready to run. The root reached the edge of the table and a tiny shoot emerged from its side, touching the little invention containing the inhibiting fluid tentatively.

Mary whooped as the shoot seized it and began to absorb the dark fluid inside. Matt punched the air victoriously and leaned against the wall, looking like he'd just run a marathon.

"Yes!" Rose cried, as the shoot turned a bruised,

purple colour, which spread like rot to the tip of the root still threatening to follow her into the hall. It's growth began to slow as the inhibiting fluid did its job, and before long it had dried up, stretched out across the floor.

Rose sighed with relief as the bud collapsed in on itself, the glass pieces toppling and crumbling into sandy granules that scattered over the workbench. The roots wrapped around Alison withered and fell away, and the energy in the room faded, the white light dissipating and leaving everything looking comparatively dark.

"You did it!" said Mary, her eyes lined with tiredness. "It worked!"

Rose edged back into the room, careful not to touch the bud or its roots. Alison's hands shook as she brushed her hair out of her face and stepped out of the tangle of shrivelled roots.

"Well, that's out of the way," she said lightly, as though they'd just done something perfectly normal. "The three of you did so well. I'm glad I had help."

"I thought those roots were going to take your magic away!" moaned Rose in anguish.

"They would have if I'd stayed wrapped up in them for long enough." Alison healed the cuts on her hands with a glance and then smiled at them. "I was lucky I wasn't alone and that your grandpa included some safeguards when he made the bud. It can take someone's magic away and store it, and it can use the magic from other objects, but it can never use a person's magic to heal itself."

"What's the difference?" asked Mary, lifting a ruined invention up to her eyes. "This had Mum's magic on it until the bud killed it."

Mary held the cracked and blackened remains out in her hand so that the others could see it. Rose turned to the prototype thoughtfully as understanding dawned on her.

"Using the inhibiting fluid and the little bit of magic on those other inventions is one thing, but completely removing a person's abilities to heal itself would be a much bigger problem," she said.

Alison nodded.

"When you make an invention, the magic you put on it is always yours. It's extended out from yourself rather than separate from you. But it's a little different with the Fragmenter. Your grandpa had to find a balance between preserving the invention to protect any magic stored inside it and stopping it from taking too much power. So it can take energy away from minor sources to preserve itself, or it can remove and store energy from people it considers a threat to itself. It was all done to control the Fragmenter's behaviour and limit its abilities."

Matt gave a snort of laughter.

"Yeah, like it needs more power than it already has."

Alison chuckled and brushed herself off.

"Yes, exactly. Well, let's clean up in here and then we can rest for a bit. We can go and see my friend later. If we want to find the real Fragmenter we're going to need help from inside the Archives, and I can't be seen in there with Lawrence Hunter after me, so I think Ben might be able to help us. But we'll have to wait until he gets home, so we might as well go back to my place for a while. We'll be safer there."

They helped Alison take the other inventions back to the invention room and Alison vanished the remains of the bud, repairing the workbench and leaving no signs of the struggle that had taken place.

Rose placed the usual protective spells over the door before getting ready to leave. They reappeared in Alison's living room and Rose settled herself on the sofa gratefully between Matt and Mary. Alison collapsed into the armchair by the fireplace, looking exhausted. Rose frowned, suddenly concerned for the Archivist.

"Are you OK?"

Alison nodded.

"I'll be fine. I just need to rest. I haven't fought that hard with an invention in a long time."

They lapsed into thoughtful silence and Rose closed her eyes, enjoying the warm morning sunlight streaming in through the window. Her thoughts returned to the withered bud in the invention room, and she shuddered at the thought that a worse version existed somewhere in the world.

They spent the remainder of the morning resting and watching television, and Rose soon began to feel more like her usual self. It was close to midday when Alison got to her feet and stretched her arms above her head.

"I've got some errands I need to run in the city. Would you like to come? We can wander a bit and get lunch while we're there."

Rose looked up at her from the sofa. The colour had returned to her face and she seemed much happier as she rummaged in her bag for her keys. Rose attributed this to the prototype being destroyed and out of Hunter's reach, and she admitted to herself that it was a relief to know that it was gone.

"We've still got ages until Ben gets home and I need to pick up a few things for work," continued Alison. "But if you'd rather stay here that's OK, too."

"No, we'll come," said Matt with a grin. "It'll be fun."

"Yeah, I'd like to see the city again," said Rose as Mary got to her feet with a squeal of excitement.

They gathered around Alison and seconds later Rose opened her eyes to a wide street bustling with traffic. Putting a hand up to shield her face from the blazing sun, she peered up at a sign beside her and saw that they were in the heart of Sydney. The sun reflected off the pavement, dazzling her eyes and making everything seem over-bright. The shops beside them were crowded and dusty, and a strong smell of petrol fumes hung in the air.

"Wow," said Mary, staring up and down the street. "It's so busy!"

"I think Mum and Dad might have taken me here a few times when I was little," said Rose, trying to remember. "Matt was here, too, but he was only a baby then. Isn't this where the Archives are?"

"The building's a couple of streets down that way," said Alison, pointing to a road that swerved to the left before diving behind a tall, federation-style building that

Rose thought might be a pub. Mary leaned forward to look and Alison tugged her back onto the footpath as a bus roared past.

"Stay close," she yelled over the noise. "I don't want to lose you."

An idea flitted into Rose's mind and she turned to Alison.

"Hey, there wouldn't be a supplies shop somewhere around here for invention-making, would there? I could use some new pins for my Viewer!"

"Sure, there's a good one a few streets away." Alison pointed to the right this time. "It's actually where I'm headed. It's the biggest store in the country and it's got all of the rare pieces I need for work. Come on, I'll show you where it is."

They crossed the road and walked a little way down the crowded street. Enjoying the hustle and bustle, Rose peered into the shops as she passed them and watched the cars banked up on the road as far back as she could see. Alison let them admire the sights for a while before leading them over to a small shop beside a newsagent, right at the end of the street.

A sign overhead simply stated 'Robertson's Specialist Supplies'. It was plain and unremarkable from the outside, and if there hadn't been posters over most of the windows announcing a sale on magical compasses and technical equipment, Rose would have assumed that it was just another ordinary shop.

A doorbell tinkled as she followed Alison inside and Rose felt her jaw drop. It couldn't have been more different on the inside. Shelves ran in all directions and her eager eyes travelled over hundreds of boxes containing invention pieces in all shapes, colours and sizes. She hesitated, desperate to examine a collection of sparkling silver pieces under a sign reading 'For Illusion Effects'. Alison laughed.

"Why don't you go and explore while I get a few things and then I'll show you where the best pins are?"

"Thanks!" said Rose, running after Mary.

"I'm going to buy some more attachments for my Hook!" said Matt, disappearing down the aisle marked 'Miscellaneous'.

Rose pulled out a box containing pieces that changed colour depending on the angle you viewed them at, casting multi-coloured lights onto the walls and boxes around them.

"Wow! Rose, check these out!"

Rose turned to find Mary poring over a cluster of containers halfway down the aisle, where sets of beautiful, miniature pieces for tiny inventions were displayed in tubs. They were perfectly formed and identical to their full size counterparts in the row above, but as small as Mary's little fingernail. Rose picked out a piece with delicate interlocking strands that reminded her of the Fragmenter's casing, only to put it back with a shudder.

It wasn't long before Matt reappeared, looking thoroughly amused about something.

"Hey, Rose! Mary! You have to come and see this!"

They followed him through a shabby little door. Like

the main shop, this room was filled with rows of shelves and long lines of boxes, but looking closer, Rose saw that the shelves were stocked with completed inventions for sale, rather than separate parts and pieces.

Matt ushered them down one of the aisles and turned them around to face a row of inventions that looked very familiar.

"Mum and Dad's inventions!" cried Rose in surprise. "So this is who they sold these to!"

She picked up the nearest, gazing at it fondly. She'd always known that her parents sold finished pieces to most of the magical stores in the country, but she'd never seen them there before.

"The shop owner must know Mum and Dad, then, if they're selling these," said Matt. "It's so cool to see our family's inventions for sale. I can't wait to start selling my own."

"I know! I remember watching Mum and Dad make most of these."

Rose put the invention back on its shelf, suddenly feeling homesick. She looked down at Mary, who was regarding the inventions with an expression halfway between laughter and tears, and decided that it was time to move along.

Rose took her hand and pulled her away to explore the neighbouring aisles. They found Alison in a corner stacked to the ceiling with extra-bendable and malleable pieces designed to fit any gap or space and then beckoned to her to come and look at a section Mary wanted to see.

Rose glanced up at the sign reading 'For Medical Inventions and Spells' before examining the nearest boxes with fascination. She knew little about medical magic and was curious about how the invention pieces worked. Matt picked up a small, battered box of what appeared to be ordinary plastic strips, but which claimed on the back of the carton that they could heal any minor cuts or abrasions in less than twenty seconds. Alison eyed the box with amusement.

"Do you think these would work?" Matt asked her.

"I'm not sure," she said, looking doubtful. "I've never used anything like them before. I wouldn't count on them if I were you."

Matt snorted and took a box that wasn't so battered.

"I'm going to try them just to see what happens," he said with a grin.

Rose rolled her eyes and stalked off.

"If you want to waste your money, fine by me."

When they'd toured each part of the shop, including the section for old-fashioned creations, which held suitable pieces and materials for inventions crafted as early as the medieval period, and the section for multi-purpose inventions, where Rose found everything she could ever want for her Viewer, they left the shop with their wallets considerably lighter and crossed the street, wondering where they should go next.

"It's still only one o'clock," said Alison. "How about we get some lunch and find somewhere cool to sit?"

"Sounds good to me," said Rose, suddenly realising how hungry she was after the fight with the prototype.

They sat down twenty minutes later at a table in a shady park close to the water, bearing a package of hot chips. Matt waved to the small boats that came and went as they ate, and they watched birds duck beneath the surface of the water for fish. Mary threw a handful of her chips over to them and soon they were surrounded by the wildlife.

When they had nothing left to give to the birds, they left the park and wandered the streets. Mary was eager to see everything and insisted on stopping to peer through the windows of the shops they passed, keeping up a constant stream of chatter and pointing to things across the road that took her interest.

Heat rose in waves off the roads, and Alison bought them all sundaes from an ice cream parlour they discovered near the park. Matt devoured his in minutes while they explored, avoiding the sun whenever possible.

They were searching for a popular bookstore Rose thought was somewhere close by when Alison stopped in the middle of the pavement. She reached out and held Rose and Mary back as they continued along the pavement.

"Wait a moment."

Rose looked at her in confusion.

"What's the matter?"

"That man over by the bus stop," said Alison, her eyes narrowed. "He's one of Lawrence Hunter's friends."

Alarmed, Rose turned to see a man in a faded jacket and jeans staring at them. Recognition shot through her and she backed away.

"We need to go."

Alison whirled around and hurried back up the street. Rose, Matt and Mary kept close behind her, ducking through the crowd.

"It could be a coincidence that we saw him here," said Matt, moving closer to Rose as a throng of people in suits rushed to cross an intersection. A tall man pushed past them, accidentally striking Matt's elbow with his briefcase, and Matt muttered under his breath, rubbing his arm. "It's a big place, this."

"Maybe," said Alison, sounding unconvinced. "But I know for a fact that Hunter's been having me followed ever since your grandpa disappeared, and I don't want to take the chance."

"We'll be safe at your house, won't we?" asked Mary, jogging to keep up. "Even if they know we're there?"

"Oh, yes," said Alison. "They won't be able to do anything as long as we stay inside."

They stepped into the nearest alleyway, away from the crowd rushing past. They reappeared seconds later in Alison's living room, and Cocoa barked happily, getting up off the rug to meet them. Rose scratched behind his ears as Alison sat tensely in one of the armchairs. It was now past three o'clock, and she looked more nervous than ever as she picked up a magazine and flipped through it in an agitated sort of way.

Too preoccupied to try out her new pieces, Rose packed them away in her camping bag and went to join the others in the living room. She picked up a book instead and tried just as unsuccessfully as Alison to forget about what had happened. She was surprised that the man hadn't tried to follow them, but then she realised that he surely already knew where Alison lived. She shivered again and repressed the urge to glance out of the window towards the road.

Cocoa settled himself over her feet and she stroked him absent-mindedly while she waited for Alison's friend to get home from work. The sun was beginning to sink behind the trees when the clock over the mantelpiece finally struck half past five. Alison put down her magazine and stood up.

"Ben should be home by now," she announced, reaching for her bag.

Rose went down the hall, calling to Matt, who was experimenting with his Hook, and not knowing where they were going, they each took hold of Alison's sleeve, ready to use a travel spell. They arrived outside the little brick house she, Matt and Mary had gone to when they'd helped Alison repair her inventions.

"This is the same friend you stayed with before?" said Rose, looking up at the house.

"Yes," said Alison, opening the gate. "He's the only other Archivist besides me at the moment, so he already knows a bit about what your grandpa's been working on. He'd better be home."

They walked up the shadowy path to the front door and knocked, waiting impatiently until a light flickered on over the veranda and the door opened, revealing a tall young man around Alison's age, with freckles and loose, light brown curls.

"Alison!" he exclaimed, his eyes wide with surprise. "What are you doing here? Why haven't you been at work? It's been weeks and Miranda won't say what's going on."

He stood back to let them in and they hurried inside. As the man closed the door behind them, Rose noticed a long scar on the back of his right hand that looked like a bite mark, and was immediately reminded of the stories Alison had told her about the rogue, biting invention in the Archives.

The young man led them into the living room and motioned for them to sit down, smiling at them all in a cheerful, friendly way.

"I'll explain everything in a moment," promised Alison, "but first, I think you should meet Rose, Matt and Mary Stephensen." She indicated each of them as she named them, before adding, "This is Ben Atherton."

"Hi," said Ben, looking at them with curiosity. "So, you're Peter Williams' grandkids?"

The three of them nodded.

"I'm sorry about what happened to him. He's an amazing guy. I did my research at university on some of his earlier work. He's made some great inventions."

"Thanks," said Rose, pride swelling in her chest.

"Ben, their parents have disappeared now, too," said Alison. "That's why we're here. We need your help."

"What?" Ben's face darkened. "You don't think -"

"They found out where the real Fragmenter is?" said Alison in a rush. "They must have. But we need help figuring out where it is now, and if Lawrence Hunter has it. And to do that, I need to get into the Archives, but I can't go in there myself."

"Why not?" demanded Ben. "What's going on? And why have Hunter and his friends been looking for you?"

"He made it look like I was the one who made Peter disappear," Alison burst out angrily. "The only reason I haven't been arrested is because they don't have any real evidence against me. I found out Hunter was involved in having the Fragmenter made and he wanted me to make sure nobody linked him to it, but I refused to help and this is his payback."

Ben stared at her for a moment as though she'd gone mad, and Rose sat in silence, watching them both as they talked.

"So, you've been in hiding for the last couple of months?" said Ben, raising an eyebrow.

"You could say that," said Alison awkwardly. Ben ran a hand through his hair and scratched the stubble on his chin.

"When you said you needed somewhere safe to stay for a while to avoid someone, you didn't tell me it was Lawrence Hunter!"

"I didn't think you'd believe me and I didn't have time to go into detail," said Alison in a hurry, catching Rose's amused look. "I'm sorry, but the police were after me, I hadn't put protection around my place yet, and you were going away. But that's not why we've come. I wanted to ask if you'd help Rose, Matt and Mary go through the Archives to find the Fragmenter. I'd go myself, but like I said, I can't be seen in there, and they can't go in without supervision unless they're over eighteen."

"It might not even be in the Archives, you know," said Ben bracingly. "I'm sure Peter has plenty of good hiding places."

"I know, but it's a place to start, and we at least need to be sure it's not there before we go looking somewhere else."

"And if it *is* in Hunter's room, what will you do then?" asked Ben. "You'll never be able to break in. We don't know what he's got guarding the room."

"I know it won't be easy," pleaded Alison. "But we have to try. If he gets the invention before we do, their whole family will have their magic taken away from them."

She turned to her companions for support.

"We don't care what we have to do," said Rose, sounding far more confident than she felt. "We're going to get our family back again, whatever it takes."

Ben glanced uneasily at Alison.

"You know I'd be risking my job if I was caught anywhere near Hunter's room again ..."

"I'm not asking you to go into his room, or anything like that," said Alison quickly. "I just need you to take Rose, Matt and Mary into their own family's rooms, that's all."

She looked at him beseechingly. Ben hesitated for a moment and then sighed.

"All right, then. I'll help. But just to get into their family's rooms."

Alison nodded, and Rose relaxed. She, Matt and Mary thanked him profusely.

"We'll go early tomorrow morning," he said with a grim smile. "Hopefully Hunter won't be prowling around."

10

Into the Archives

Rose dressed at top speed the next morning. She had only been inside the Archives once or twice when she was very young, and she was eager to see them again. But she was also worried about what they would find when they got there and did not like the idea of possibly meeting Lawrence Hunter. Hoping today would be one of the days he didn't turn up, she went into the living room, where Alison was already pacing up and down, waiting for Ben to arrive.

Matt and Mary were at the kitchen table finishing their breakfast. They seemed as excited to explore the Archives as Rose was, and they swallowed the last of their cereal in a rush before hurrying back down the hall to get ready. At eight o'clock a knock on the door announced Ben's arrival and Alison disappeared down the hall to let him in.

"Hi," he said, following Alison into the living room and beaming around at them all. "Are you ready to go?"

Rose jumped up and nodded.

"Oh, if only I could come with you," fretted Alison. "What if Hunter's there?"

"If he's there, we'll just come back another time," said Ben simply. "Don't worry about us. Rose, Matt and

Mary are allowed to visit their own family's rooms."

"I know, but I still wish I could come. You'll let me know as soon as you can if you find the Fragmenter, won't you?"

Rose promised to tell her everything when they returned, and they all gathered around Ben. Alison waved as they vanished, looking a little forlorn.

"Good luck!"

The ground changed under her feet and Rose opened her eyes to find herself standing in a dusty street, not far from where she'd appeared with Alison the day before. Smoke haze filled the air already, stinging her eyes as she squinted through the bright sunlight at the imposing building before her.

Hemmed in by a towering block of apartments on one side and a post office on the other, it had been built with smoky grey bricks which glistened in the morning light, contrasting with the sandstone buildings on either side. The magical protection around the building was so intense that Rose could feel it even from the curb, and she shivered as the tiny hairs on the back of her neck and arms stood up, reacting to the spells.

Ben gave them an encouraging smile, leading them up the front steps and through a set of plain wooden doors. Beyond was a spacious, high-ceilinged room. Tall, narrow windows let in long shafts of sunlight that illuminated the faded portraits on the walls and a broad, spiral staircase that stood in the centre of the room.

Rose breathed in the faint scent of books and wood polish and was reminded of her school library as she followed Ben over to a reception desk, where a young woman with a round face and short, spiky red hair was waiting for them.

"Hi, Ben. You're not usually in on Wednesdays."

"I'm just taking some friends into their room," explained Ben. "They've never been in on their own before, so I thought I'd show them what to do."

"OK," said the woman. She turned to Rose, Matt and Mary. "I just need you to fill out a form and then you can go up."

She opened a drawer and placed a sheet of paper labelled 'Visitors' Log In' on the desktop. Rose picked up a pen and filled out their names and which rooms they would be going into. They all signed it at the bottom and Rose handed it back. The woman checked it and filed it away.

"That's all fine. Here's your key."

She held her hand out and an ordinary-looking key took shape in her palm. Rose took it with a word of thanks, her fingers tingling with magic as they made contact with the metal.

"We're all set, then," said Ben. "Follow me."

He turned and headed for the spiral staircase. Doors lined three of the walls here and Rose's gaze swept over them as she followed Ben, wondering how big the building really was.

"Where are all the keys kept?" asked Rose as they walked.

"They're locked in a magically-protected area on the ground floor," replied Ben. "The room vanishes once it's been sealed so that the keys can't be stolen from the building, and they're brought back into being when we need them. Most people choose to leave their key here for safekeeping when they're not using it, but others, like Hunter, prefer to keep it safe themselves."

Rose looked down as she began to climb the stairs, which continued to spiral down several levels underground.

"What's down there?"

"They're the experimenting stations," said Ben. "Miranda, the head of the Archives, wanted to put a few more floors on top of the private storage area, but the council wouldn't give permission so we had to go underground instead."

They reached the first floor landing and Rose found herself at the centre of an immense collection of documents. Books, boxes and folders stuffed full of papers filled the shelves in long rows, making her family's library at home seem woefully insignificant in comparison.

"This is where our records are kept," said Ben. "If any of you start selling inventions professionally down the track, you'll have to make a report on each of them and they'll come here to be checked and catalogued. It's a big job, as you can see."

Rose's eyes travelled along the shelves towards the opposite side of the room, expecting to find the far wall, but there were only files, stretching around the central staircase until a row of shelves running the other way blocked her view.

They continued up the stairs to the next floor, where hundreds of thousands of inventions were divided into categories. Rose gazed up at the nearest shelf, keen to take a closer look at a curious invention made from a shimmering, pale gold material. She turned her ear towards it, catching a sweet, tinkling sound like a wind chime in a gentle breeze. She looked at Ben beseechingly and he laughed.

"Just don't touch anything, and don't go too far!" he called, as Rose, Matt and Mary each raced down a different aisle. "You can get lost in here if you don't know where you're going!"

Rose couldn't believe the number of inventions she was seeing. It was as though every piece ever created sat right here, on a shelf with a little card in front of it, listing its function, maker and catalogue number. After wandering up and down the aisles for several minutes, Rose ran back to where Ben was waiting patiently and they all took the stairs to the top floor.

"What are the spells on the key for?" Rose asked, turning it over in her hand as they climbed.

"Each private room is protected by a physical lock and a unique magical one," answered Ben. "The spells on your key will open the magical locks on your family's room."

"So, say we do have to get into Lawrence Hunter's room," said Matt, lowering his voice and glancing behind him to check they were alone. "Wouldn't it be easy to just steal his key? If he takes it with him rather than leaving it here?"

Ben shook his head, his cheerful ease disappearing. He, too, checked that the upper and lower landings were deserted before answering, his expression tense.

"It's a bit more complicated than that, I'm afraid. Your key will only let you through the Archives' protection, and most people add magic of their own as an added barrier, just in case. I'm sure Hunter will have plenty of extra spells around his."

"What do you do if you need to get into a room but don't know what's guarding it?" said Mary, jumping up the steps two at a time.

"By law, the owner has to let us in. If they refuse, or if there's some other kind of problem, we can break in, but it doesn't often come to that. Most people are happy to cooperate."

Rose bit her lip, sincerely hoping that they wouldn't have to break into Hunter's room.

"What if you forget which spells you put on your own room?" asked Matt, pointedly ignoring Mary's snort of laughter.

"Then we have to force our way in," said Ben, his grin returning. "It's a complicated process and it can take a long time, depending on what's protecting the door. I've actually been working on an invention that'll make it easier to break into people's rooms if they refuse to let us in. It'll destroy just about any spell it comes near. I can't wait to try it out. Hunter was actually interested in it himself. Asked me if I'd consider selling it, but there's no way I'm letting *him* have it."

Mary looked up with interest at this. "You make

inventions, too?"

"Not often, and they're not as good as your family's," said Ben with a small smile. "I wanted to get into invention-making when I was a kid but I wasn't good enough at it, so I came to work here instead."

They reached the top floor and stepped out into a brick corridor. Instead of lines of shelves, plain, unremarkable doors stood at regular intervals along the hall until it turned a corner, out of sight. Ben rubbed his hands together.

"This is the floor we want. Your rooms aren't far from here."

He turned left and Rose hurried to keep up, looking curiously at each door she passed. Up close, her attention was caught by the smoky grey material running through the bricks. She touched the nearest with a tentative fingertip.

"What are the streaks for? I didn't notice them so much in the rest of the building."

"It's a kind of magical barrier, made by the Guild," Ben informed them as they continued down the corridor. "We needed to contain the influence and effects of some of the inventions kept here, and to increase the protection around certain areas, so the Spellmakers developed a substance that could be infused with the spells we wanted. The mixture was poured into the bricks before they were set, so the protective magic is literally built in. It covers the whole building, but the bricks in the high-security areas have more of the mixture in them, so they're darker and more noticeable."

Fascinated, Rose inspected the walls more closely as they walked further down the hall and saw that there was indeed a variation in colour in some places, where the pale grey deepened to a rich charcoal. She turned the corner and the walls became almost black. Motion sensor lights flickered on as Ben passed them, flooding the narrow corridor with light.

"Be careful along this stretch here," he called, waiting for Matt and Mary, who had stopped to examine the brickwork for themselves. "One of the inventions in the room coming up can play tricks on you if you're not paying attention."

Rose took a few steps forward and stumbled into the wall.

"Whoa!" she muttered, throwing out a hand to steady herself.

"I know the wall looks like it's curved, but it's actually straight," Ben warned them, as Matt promptly stubbed his toe.

Rose peered down the corridor and rubbed her eyes to check they were working properly. The wall appeared to bend, but as she put one hand up to the bricks and felt her way along, she discovered that Ben was right. Mary giggled and stretched out a hand for balance like Rose.

"It's kind of like being at the fair, standing in front of those mirrors that make you look tall and skinny!"

Rose took another cautious step forward and a door marked 'High Security Inventions – Senior Staff Only' loomed up out of the dark on her right. She joined Matt and Mary as they huddled around it, trying to peer through the small window set near the top.

Most of the room was obscured by darkness but, looking over Mary's head, she thought she could make out lines of shelves inside, resembling the floors below. Something in this room, however, seemed to emit a strange kind of attraction, and all three of them gazed over their shoulders as Ben chuckled and pulled them away.

"Why would someone make an invention that played tricks on you?" asked Mary in a hushed tone. Ben's pace slowed as he continued down the hall, checking the names on the doors as he went.

"It was more of an unintended side effect of the spells used to make it. Some of them do unusual things when they're combined, and it doesn't help that there are so many other strong inventions around here for it to interact with. You can imagine what its effects would be like if the Guild's barrier spells weren't on the building."

They passed another room with a sign reading 'Fragile Inventions' and Ben explained that these pieces were so old or delicate that they had to be kept in climate controlled areas to stop them from decaying. They passed through a door marked 'Storage Area – Private Rooms'. Halfway down this corridor, a door with a small sign bearing the name 'Williams, Peter Alfred', and beside it, 'Stephensen, Michael and Charlotte' came into view.

Rose's excitement climbed still higher as she took

the key out of her pocket. She didn't expect the Fragmenter to be in either room, or her parents would have found it long ago, but she was eager to explore them nonetheless. They stopped outside the room labelled 'Stephensen' first. Ben grinned at them.

"I hope you know which spells your parents have on the door. We've got three tries before everything locks down and the police arrive. And I'd rather not have to break in."

Mary bit her lip and Matt took a step back, looking alarmed.

"No one said anything about that!"

Rose hesitated, staring down at the key in her hand.

"I bet Mum and Dad would've used something we know, in case we ever had to go in here."

"Alison says you have an invention room at home," prompted Ben. "It might be similar to the spells on that."

"Good idea," said Rose with a rush of gratitude. "Let's try that."

She performed the usual protective spells and waited. The magic surrounding the room changed and she glanced up at Ben. Ben gave a satisfied nod and stood back.

"That must be it. Now it's safe to use your key."

She inserted the key into the lock on the door and turned it until a soft click sounded. The door swung open and Rose slipped the key back into her pocket, following Matt and Mary into the room. Ben hung back, politely waiting out in the hall, but Rose beckoned him inside. It couldn't hurt to have a trained pair of eyes to help them with their search.

Her first thought was that the space greatly resembled their invention room at home, except for the smoky grey bricks and the filing cabinets that had replaced the tool rack. A shabby desk held a small collection of unfamiliar inventions and a workbench stood along the far wall. There was no black cabinet.

"Have a good look around and then we'll go to your grandpa's room," said Ben, closing the door behind him and looking around with as much curiosity as the others.

"So these are all inventions that Mum and Dad didn't want to keep in the house?" asked Matt, opening the desk drawers. "I wonder why they didn't put the prototype in here?"

Rose snorted. "I bet it would've gone haywire in here with so much magic surrounding it. It would've started attacking everything in sight."

A quick glance around the room was enough to tell her that the Fragmenter wasn't there, so she opened the filing cabinets instead and pulled out the first folder, labelled 'January 2007', which held a complete record of all the inventions her parents had made and sold that month, followed by receipts and bookkeeping documents.

"Let's try next door," said Mary, once they'd checked everything.

Rose put the file back where she'd found it and closed the cabinet.

"I didn't think it would be here. It would've been too obvious."

Ben stepped back into the hall with Matt and Mary.

"I don't think it'll be in your grandpa's room, either, but I guess we need to be sure."

Rose glanced around the room one last time before joining the others, closing the door behind her with another soft click. The protective spells sealed the room shut and the group moved on.

"I have your grandpa's key here, seeing as he's not able to sign for it," said Ben, taking a key out of his pocket and turning to the neighbouring room. "I don't suppose you know how he's guarding the door?"

"No," said Matt and Mary together.

"I might be able to guess," said Rose, stepping forward. "It's been ages since I've had to take the spells off his invention room, but I think I can remember them."

She tried the combination she thought was most likely and Ben put the key into the door. It swung open without a sound. Matt and Mary cheered, and Rose breathed again.

"I'm glad Grandpa didn't change the spells. As much as I like the Archives, I don't fancy being locked in until the police found me."

"Or Lawrence Hunter," added Ben, with a pointed look back down the corridor. "He's always sneaking around. I'm surprised we haven't come across him already."

Mary wrapped her arms around herself tightly.

"I hope we don't! I want to keep my magic forever."

"Or at least until we save our family, anyway,"

murmured Rose. "As long as we get them back, I'd be happy either way."

Matt raised a disbelieving eyebrow at her and led the way into Grandpa's room. It, too, was laid out similar to his invention room at home, except for the filing cabinets that took up almost half of the available space in the tiny room. Rose's jaw dropped.

"Are all those files for inventions Grandpa's made?"

"He's been inventing for a long time," chuckled Ben. He scanned the labels on the cabinets. "These go back more than sixty years."

Matt and Mary pulled open a cabinet and began to read while Rose searched the workbench and the other half of the room. A small collection of inventions stood on an almost-bare shelf. Like her parents, Grandpa rarely used his room here and almost never made anything that could be considered dangerous. She swept her gaze across the shelf but none of the objects gathered there resembled the Fragmenter, so she turned her attention back to the workbench.

It was littered with ruined materials that she guessed had been part of the Fragmenter at some point, but had been discarded when they were unable to take the strain of the potent spells around them.

"Grandpa must have done some of his testing in here. In the beginning, at least. But that still doesn't explain why we didn't find anything in his invention room."

"It would've been safer to try out materials and spells in here," agreed Ben, holding one of the damaged pieces up to the light to reveal tiny fractures running through it.

Rose opened the first of the two narrow drawers along the front of the bench. Finding nothing, she proceeded to the second and discovered a jumble of tools, wires and screws. She was about to push the drawer back in when Ben put out a hand to stop her.

"Wait, what's this?" He lifted out a dull grey object that resembled a spinning top. "It's not a tool or an invention piece, and I can feel subtle deception spells on it."

The object was unlined and appeared to be solid. Ben pressed a thumb against the top and four triangular pieces opened up, revealing a hollow space inside. Rose blinked in surprise as he reached in and drew out a tiny speaker, roughly the size of Rose's thumbnail. He gazed at it admiringly before flipping it over and holding it out to Rose.

"Your grandpa must have left you a message."

"Ooh, let's hear it!" said Mary, running to Rose's side.

Rose stared at the speaker, unsure how to operate it, but at the sound of the word 'Grandpa', the speaker had fizzled to life, and a moment later a familiar, soft-spoken voice filled the room, sounding urgent and put-upon.

"For the record, the date is the twenty-fourth of November, and it's now seven in the morning. Charlotte, there are things I need to tell you about the Fragmenter that I can't tell you in person, so I'm recording this

message hoping you'll find it before Lawrence Hunter does. His gang has been waiting outside the house for hours now, making sure I can't leave or contact you directly, so I'll have to use magic to get this somewhere safe.

'The more I learn about the spells I've been using on the Fragmenter, the more uneasy I am. The magic I was ordered to put into it seems to have effects no one expected, making the invention react in ways I didn't plan for during the design process. I've decided that it's safer to continue making it elsewhere, as its defence system proved to be much stronger than I'd anticipated and the protective spells on my room here at home have not been able to withstand it."

Static drowned out Grandpa's voice as some kind of disturbance interrupted the recording, and they all leaned in closer to the speaker, desperate for more information.

"Well that explains why we didn't find anything at his house," murmured Rose in an undertone. "But if he wasn't working on the invention here, or at home, where was he making it?"

"Shh!"

Mary flapped her hands at Rose as Grandpa's voice became audible once more.

"When I ran my first tests on the invention it destroyed the casing I'd made, and I realised then how unstable and dangerous its defensive magic is. I haven't

told anyone how powerful it is, because it might prove to be a useful weapon against Hunter when he comes to claim the invention, but I want you to understand it in case things go wrong and it becomes your responsibility.

'I also think I should tell you to contact Alison Maxwell. I know Hunter has been trying to make everyone believe she's after the Fragmenter, but I think she could be helpful to you. The government is still under the impression that the Fragmenter is their own project, but I suspect that Hunter has been influencing it all for quite some time now, and of course, he won't allow them to just take it and use it on him. Alison told me that she's been threatened by him, too, and –"

Static overtook Grandpa's voice for a second time and Rose let out a growl of frustration. His voice returned a moment later, fainter than before, and Rose was forced to hold the speaker right up to her ear to make out the words.

"I've decided to hide the invention away in a fake, magically-made place, where it can't do any damage. Hunter will find it sooner or later no matter where I put it, but as you know me and my hiding places better than he does, I hope you'll get there first. But before I tell you where I've hidden it, there's something else I need to warn you about.

'As I said earlier, the invention has other unexpected abilities, and the research I did when I was preparing to make it has led me to believe that Hunter will not only

use it to strip magic away from other people, which is bad enough, but to turn the –"

A loud crackling sound interrupted for a third time. Rose waited, but Grandpa's voice remained inaudible, and after a moment, the speaker fell silent.

Rose tucked it into her pocket, battling a mixture of confusion and disappointment. Ben, who had been listening intently, was now staring unseeingly at the open spinning top with a look of incredulity.

"A magically-made place?" repeated Rose. "What does that even mean? What would it even look like? A fake room? Or a fake world? But magic can't create anything like that, can it?"

"I have no idea," said Ben, his eyes wide. "I've never heard of spells like that."

Matt and Mary stared at each other blankly.

"I wonder what happened to the rest of the recording?" murmured Rose, her mind reeling. "Mum and Dad once told me that strong spells can sound like bad reception on a phone. Maybe the magic in the Fragmenter was distorting or interrupting the message?"

"I bet it was," said Matt sourly.

"But how are we going to find the Fragmenter if it's not in a real place?" cried Mary, her eyes full of uncertainty.

"I don't know," said Rose. She looked at Matt and saw her own panic reflected in his face. What if they couldn't find this fake place and Hunter took her family's magic away?

"Isn't there anywhere else in the Archives Grandpa might have hidden something? Another clue?" she asked Ben desperately.

"I suppose he might have left something in one of the experimenting stations." Ben thought for a moment, running a hand through his curly hair. "It's unlikely, but we'll check anyway."

The door locked behind them and Ben led them back down the corridor, away from the private rooms. They followed him down the spiral staircase to the first underground level, and Rose felt her curiosity surge as they came to a new set of open-plan rooms that resembled magical workshops.

Her eyes wandered from the bays of invention pieces along one wall to the racks bearing every kind of tool an inventor could ever want, organised beside a long line of workbenches. An open area in the centre allowed space to experiment, but the tingling sensation on her skin told her that the room was heavily protected in case things got out of hand.

Turning her attention back to their search, Rose joined the others as they combed each corner of the enormous space, but as she had expected, there was nothing to be found except for a handful of scraps from random inventions.

"Are there many other places in here where Grandpa could hide something?" asked Mary, leaning against the nearest workbench while they considered what to do next.

"Loads," replied Ben, drumming his fingers on the

bench top. "But we don't have time to go looking through the whole of the Archives. It's huge, so we're going to have to think of a way to speed things up a bit, and I think I know how we can do it. An invention upstairs can be used to find things. The problem is that it's old and the only one of its kind, so I'll have to get permission to use it. If Miranda says no, we're going to have to think of some other way of finding this fake place. Let's go and ask her."

They followed him back upstairs and over to a staff room on the ground floor.

"Wait in here," Ben told them. "I'll only be a second."

Rose sank into one of the squashy chairs beside the window as Ben knocked on a door bearing a small plaque that read 'Head's Office' and disappeared inside. She waited impatiently, hoping they weren't about to hit yet another dead end. Matt sighed and folded himself into a chair opposite her.

"This is turning out to be even harder than I thought it would be."

"I know," murmured Rose. "At this rate, we'll be lucky to find our family at all."

"I still want to know what Grandpa meant by an unreal place," said Mary, looking amazed at the thought of such a thing. "How is something like that even possible?"

Rose stared down at her knees, trying to imagine what a place made entirely of magic might be like.

"It sounds strange, doesn't it? He must have used very advanced magic to do it. I bet it's part of what he was experimenting with before he disappeared."

She sat up straight as Ben reappeared, his grin back in place.

"We've got permission. Follow me."

Rose hurried after him, her hope returning.

"So, is this invention like a Scope, then?" she asked, panting a little as they ran back upstairs. "I've been making a Viewer at home to find Mum, Dad and Grandpa, but I think blocking spells are stopping it from working."

"It can be used in a similar way to a Scope, but it works very differently," said Ben, leading them through the shelves of inventions to a door at the far end of the hall. "It's called a Clarifier, and it was made to help people find answers to problems by encouraging them to think more clearly. It opens up the mind. But it can be used to find specific objects, too, if you use it the right way. The spells for both are related."

Doors lined this wall, too, and Rose felt more than ever like she was in a maze.

"You really could get lost in here, couldn't you?"

"Apprentices get lost in here all the time when they're starting out," replied Ben. "I got lost myself once or twice. It can be scary sometimes at night."

They laughed and followed him through the last door on the left. Rose's jaw dropped as she took in the immense object standing before her.

"That's an *invention*?"

"Yeah," said Ben, chuckling at the awe on their faces. "It was created in the eighteenth century."

The invention towered over them, almost filling the room.

"How'd they get it in here?" gasped Mary.

"With magic, of course," grinned Rose, staring up at the Clarifier.

An immense pentagonal structure made of glass and clear quartz sparkled in the light, dazzling Rose's eyes. Five crystal pillars stood around the edge of the platform, curving inwards but not touching, leaving an open space at the top. Each pillar contained swirling white mist, and a chair of glass and white quartz stood in the centre of the platform. It was by far the biggest and most ethereal-looking invention she had ever laid eyes on.

"If it can find things, couldn't we use it to see where our family is, too?" said Mary, her voice full of hope.

Ben gave her a sympathetic look.

"The invention is powerful, but if Rose is right and Hunter is using magical blocks to stop you from finding them, I doubt it will be able to break through them. Technology wasn't as good in the eighteenth century, and the Clarifier was intended to be more of a problem solver than anything else."

Mary's face fell, and Rose wrapped an arm around her sister.

"Well, let's hope it can find the Fragmenter, then," she breathed, turning her attention back to the enormous mass in front of her. Matt rushed forward, the light of the invention shining in his eyes.

"How do we use it? Can I do it?"

"Sure," said Ben. "All you have to do is sit in the

chair and relax your mind. The Clarifier will do the rest."

Matt tiptoed up the glass steps carved into the platform as though they might break at his touch. He sat down in the chair and placed his hands gingerly on the armrests.

"Wow, it looks even cooler from over here!"

He grinned at them and Rose rolled her eyes.

"OK, now calm your mind," called Ben as Matt fidgeted in his seat. "The Clarifier won't start working until you're relaxed. It's all about thinking clearly, remember."

Matt closed his eyes and became still. Rose stood beside the invention, waiting for something to happen, and soon the mist inside the pillars began to seep out onto the platform, surrounding Matt. His eyes snapped open as he realised something was happening.

"It's all right, just concentrate on staying calm and think about the problem you want help with," instructed Ben.

Matt settled himself more comfortably in the quartz chair, a look of concentration on his face. The mist continued to swirl aimlessly around him for a moment, and then, with a gentle rushing sound, it surged upwards and began to form shapes.

Rose gasped and edged closer, face to face with the milky white but immediately recognisable shape of Grandpa, working at a bench on a misty Fragmenter. She fought the urge to reach out and touch the vapour, certain that it would dissipate if she did.

Captivated, she watched as the image dissolved and

another appeared in its place: her parents holding a small object that Rose guessed must be another invention. It was roughly two inches long and made of delicate woven threads. It looked very familiar. Rose thought hard, trying to remember where she'd seen it when the mist surged and then changed again, this time showing a picture of the same tiny invention sitting in a tall glass case in an unfamiliar room.

Ben stepped forward, staring at the scene with dismay. He remained silent, however, until the vapour had settled and retreated back into the crystal pillars. Matt stood up and made his way over to them, his footsteps a little clumsy, as though he'd just woken from a deep sleep. Rose and Mary turned to him expectantly.

"What did it feel like?" prompted Mary.

"Peaceful," he said, with a sleepy smile. "It was kind of like an extra-realistic dream. I still feel half asleep."

Rose surveyed him with amusement.

"How long will the effects last?" she asked Ben.

"He might be a bit more perceptive than usual for a couple of hours, but he should be back to normal soon," replied Ben with a shrug.

"By the time it had stopped showing me things, I felt like I just *knew* where the Fragmenter was, without knowing how," said Matt serenely.

He looked up at Ben and his grin faltered. "What's wrong? Didn't it work?"

"No, it worked perfectly," said Ben in a low voice. "I know the room it showed us last. Alison told me all about it. That's Lawrence Hunter's room, here in the

Archives."

Rose's stomach lurched unpleasantly as she suddenly remembered where she'd seen the tiny invention.

"Oh, no!" She clapped a hand to her forehead. "The little invention it showed us … it was in Grandpa's house the day he disappeared. I took it home myself! I held it!"

She remembered picking the tiny object up and admiring its ornate workmanship. It was small and silver, and fit easily into the palm of her hand. It looked more like an ornament than an invention, covered with tiny metal embellishments that wove in and out of each other in a way that reminded her of the Fragmenter's green casing. She let out a groan of frustration.

"Mum and Dad must have seen it and realised what it was! And when they took it out to test it …"

"Hunter kidnapped your parents and stole the invention," finished Ben, his expression grave. Matt and Mary hung their heads.

"I don't suppose the Clarifier could be wrong?" said Rose, fighting to keep a tremble out of her voice.

"I doubt it," said Ben, "but I'll check the records. I suppose it's possible. It *is* hundreds of years old, after all."

Hope filled his face as he spoke these words.

"When exactly did your parents disappear?"

"The twenty-eighth of December," said Rose at once.

Ben marched back out of the room and over to the reception desk with Rose, Matt and Mary close at his heels.

"Abbie, did Lawrence Hunter put anything in his room on the twenty-eighth of December?"

The woman behind the counter checked something on her computer and nodded.

"Yes, an invention and two documents."

She blinked, her expression confused as Ben's face fell. He headed over to the spiral staircase and ran up to the library, counting aisles as he passed them.

"Where are you going?" called Rose, running to keep up with him.

"I want to check the records, just to be completely sure," he said, racing along a shelf marked with the letter 'H'. "If we're lucky, there might be more information there about the invention he deposited."

About halfway down, Ben yanked out a file and flipped through the pages until he came to a section that contained a long list of dates.

"December twenty-eighth … one invention made of silver, two inches long … function unknown … investigation required." He closed the file and put it back on the shelf, looking devastated. "It's in his room all right."

Matt and Mary groaned in unison and Rose leaned against the shelf dejectedly. How were they ever going to break into Lawrence Hunter's room without being caught?

11

Miranda's Warning

Unable to do anything more for now, they took both keys back to the reception desk and returned to the house, eager to tell Alison about their discovery. They found her in the kitchen making a cup of tea.

"How did it go? Did you find the Fragmenter?" she said in a rush as Matt perched himself dreamily on the edge of the sofa.

"We think so, but we haven't got it with us," said Ben, leaning against the counter. He glanced at Matt and his lips twitched with amusement. "We searched both rooms thoroughly and there was no sign of it, but we found a recording made by Peter the day before he disappeared. It gave us some useful information."

"A recording?"

Alison raised an eyebrow and Rose nodded.

"It's not what we were expecting, either. You can listen to it if you like."

She held the speaker out in her palm and spoke the activating word. Alison's expression became increasingly grave as the message played. She stared at the speaker, listening in silence until it shut off.

"In the end, I got permission to use the Clarifier and it showed Matt what I'm sure is Hunter's room," said

Ben. He described the scene to Alison and her shoulders slumped.

"Yes, that's it. I was hoping we wouldn't have to go in there! It was hard enough getting in the first time!"

"And he'll be expecting you to try again if he does have the Fragmenter," said Ben.

Alison eyed the speaker with a hint of uncertainty.

"Are you sure that this silver invention is what we're looking for? I've read all of Peter's reports and there's no mention of anything like it. It would be just like Hunter to try to trick us into going after the wrong invention. But I suppose Peter wouldn't mention it, would he? Not if he wanted to keep it secret."

There was a quiet desperation in her voice and Rose braced herself against a fresh wave of guilt as her thoughts wandered back to the little invention. If only she had realised then that it might be important …

"I concentrated really hard when I was using the Clarifier and it showed me the little silver thing straight away," insisted Matt. "It seemed really sure about it. And Ben checked the records. Hunter put the silver invention in his room the day our parents disappeared."

Alison sat down beside Matt, her head in her hands.

"So, it's an invention inside an invention. Huh! I've never heard of such a thing. Still, you have to admit it's clever. Peter knew everyone would be running around like idiots trying to find the Fragmenter once he'd finished it. Who would ever guess that he'd hidden it in a fake place?"

Her gaze was distant as she stared down at her hands.

"We're going to have to plan things very carefully before we try to break into that room. We have no idea what's guarding it. Hunter's not stupid. He'll have changed the spells after I got in last time."

She looked up at the other Archivist, her jaw set in a stubborn line that reminded Rose of Mary.

"I don't want you to risk your job, Ben. I got in once, I can do it again. You've already helped us a lot, and you didn't have to. We know a good deal more now than we did a couple of hours ago."

Ben hesitated, but Rose could see him coming to a decision, his face filling with determination.

"No, I'll help. I want to help. It's about time Hunter got what was coming to him."

Matt gave him a serene smile and Rose thanked him gratefully. She had full confidence in Alison's ability to get them inside Hunter's room, but she was sure that another ally could only be a good thing.

"How are we going to find out what's protecting the door?" asked Mary, her smile faltering.

"I've got some inventions that can help with that," said Alison at once, fetching a pen and paper. "The difficult part will be getting through the protection without Hunter knowing about it."

Matt shifted nervously.

"And what happens if we're caught?"

"We'll probably be arrested," admitted Alison. Mary blanched, and Alison said in a hurry, "But if the Fragmenter is inside that silver invention, we won't have much time before Hunter finds a way to retrieve it and use it on your family, so we'll have to figure something out fast."

She picked up the pen and began to write. Rose sank onto the sofa, thinking. She had little experience breaking through strong spells or enchantments. The only spells she'd learned that might be helpful were the dissolution spells she'd placed on her Viewer, but they were unlikely to be of much use against the door in the Archives.

"Hunter always keeps his key on him," said Ben. "Unless he wants one of his friends to take something out of the room for him. He'd never leave it at reception. It'd be too easy for us to access it."

"Stealing it is going to be a nightmare," Alison mused. "How are we even going to find out where it is? Any of his friends could have it and we can't use the Clarifier every time we want help. Miranda wouldn't allow it, and it wouldn't be practical."

Rose sat up straighter. She might be able to help after all. She pulled her Viewer out of her pocket and placed it on the table.

"Would this help?"

She had added her new pieces the night before and bound her strongest magic to them. She'd tested the completed invention thoroughly and found, to her disappointment, that it was still unable to break through the blocks preventing her from finding her family. But the Viewer had been able to find everything else, and it was possible that it might be able to locate Hunter's key. Rose doubted that Hunter would have put quite the same level of defences around it as he had put around her family.

Ben picked the Viewer up, spinning the moving pieces with a finger.

"Finding and dissolution spells, with added tracking and boosting abilities." He shot Rose a grin, looking impressed. "That's one hell of a combination. I think it'll do the job."

"That solves that problem, then," said Alison, beaming at Rose. "How are we going to get close enough to the key to take it, then? I think it would be easier to steal it from Hunter's friends than from Hunter himself." She thought for a moment, twisting the pen in her hands. "Maybe we should go for it when they're on the move? But they usually travel in groups and I don't think we'd come off best in a fight."

Ben made a sound of agreement and set the Viewer on the table.

"Fighting should be our last resort. I think we'll just have to distract them somehow. Wait for an opportunity and see how it goes."

"But we could wait for ages," said Matt, yawning deeply. The effects of the Clarifier were finally wearing off, leaving him looking tired but much more like his usual self. "We need to get inside the room as soon as possible."

Mary clapped her hands together eagerly.

"I know! What if we come up with a reason to take the key the next time they go to the Archives?"

"Yeah, we could complain that Hunter's stolen our

stuff, couldn't we?" agreed Matt, turning questioningly to Alison and Ben.

"We'd need proof that Hunter stole the silver invention," replied Ben, "and even if we got it, Hunter would realise we know he has the invention and move it somewhere else."

They lapsed into thoughtful silence for a moment, until Alison continued in a low voice.

"I think you're right, Ben. We'll just have to see how things play out. But I think we should go back to the Archives tomorrow and take a closer look at the spells on that door. That might be all we need to do to figure out what's protecting it."

"We could go early, then, before anyone else turns up," suggested Rose. "Or would it be better to go after hours? Then we wouldn't have to worry about being caught."

Alison and Ben glanced at each other, Ben's expression uncertain and Alison's impassive as she stared down at the notes she'd made.

"Hunter's been watching who comes and goes into the Archives at all hours, and I'm sure he knows Ben and I don't usually come in late. It would seem more suspicious. I think we should go in early and make it seem like we're going into your family's rooms again, just doing the usual thing."

The others agreed, and Alison added, "I'll use my Analyser on the door. It got me inside the first time, so maybe it can do it again."

They spent the rest of the day outlining a plan of

attack, writing down everything Alison had learned from her trip into Hunter's room. Ben questioned Alison minutely about how she'd broken into the room, pressing her for every detail. When it was almost too dark to read their notes, Rose glanced up at the light above their heads and it flared to life.

"It took me about fifteen minutes to break all of the spells on the door, even with the help of strong inventions," said Alison, while Ben scribbled on the paper. He stopped and scratched the stubble on his chin.

"Speaking of help, I wonder if we should talk to Miranda before we do anything too risky? She knows a lot of things about the rooms that we don't and she has a higher level of access than we do."

"I'm not sure," murmured Alison. "The way we've used the Clarifier to see into someone's room is technically against the rules. She might have stretched them a little to let us use it that way, but I don't think she'll let us try to force our way into a room, and if we tell her what we're up to she might try to stop us. Or she might sack us, and we need our jobs."

Anxiety clouded her face as she said this, but Ben pressed on.

"We might not have a choice. It would be quicker than breaking in."

Rose stared down at their notes, internally arguing with herself. She didn't like the idea of breaking into an Archives room, even if that room was Hunter's, but she was aware that their chances of reclaiming the silver invention without breaking in were very slim.

"What if we check the door out first, and if it seems like we're going to have serious trouble getting in, we'll ask Miranda for help?" she suggested.

Alison thought for a moment before relenting.

"That seems fair to me."

Ben agreed and the plan was decided. It was almost eleven o'clock when they gathered up their notes and Ben went to the door.

"I'll meet you early tomorrow, then," he said, waving goodbye.

He walked a short way down the garden path and then disappeared. Rose and Mary trudged wearily down the hall to their bedroom, and Rose crawled under her covers with a grateful sigh. She rolled onto her side, staring at the shafts of moonlight on the floor as her mind drifted back to the Archives.

The seemingly infinite shelves stacked with inventions and the winding passageways lined with mysterious and forbidden rooms made her wonder more than ever if she should become an Archivist herself one day. She loved the creativity and freedom of inventing, but the Archives could give her training and skills that she could get nowhere else, and watching Alison defeat the Fragmenter prototype had shown her a side to magic and inventions she'd never encountered before.

She sighed and closed her eyes, listening to the sound of crickets in the grass outside. A moment trickled by, and she had just started to doze off when Mary whispered Rose's name into the darkness.

Rose rubbed her eyes and saw that her sister was still

awake, staring up at the ceiling and winding a lock of hair around a finger. Rose propped herself up on one elbow.

"What's up?"

Mary's face was tense, and she rolled onto her side, her eyes glinting in the darkness.

"What if we can't get Grandpa's invention?" she fretted. "We'll all lose our magic and we'll never be able to make inventions again."

Rose felt a flutter of fear in her own chest as her sister spoke, but she shoved it down before it could show on her face.

"It won't come to that. We'll find a way in sooner or later. With Alison and Ben helping us, we'll be fine. They'll get us in."

"Yeah, I suppose."

Mary closed her eyes and settled down more comfortably. Rose pulled her own blankets up under her chin, slipping into dreams of doors that wouldn't open and dark rooms filled with silver objects.

It was overcast and drizzling when they arrived at the Archives the next morning. A chilly breeze whistled through the cracks in the building beside them and Rose wrapped her arms around herself, trying to keep warm as they crossed the street. They'd attempted to persuade Alison to stay at home, but she'd insisted on coming with them, claiming that she wasn't going to let Hunter bully her into hiding anymore.

Rose couldn't help but glance around for any sign

that they weren't alone as they hurried upstairs to the private rooms, sure that Hunter or his gang would show up. Ben led them down the other side of the corridor this time, away from Grandpa's room, finally stopping outside a door near the very end of the hall. It was plain and unremarkable, and identical to all of the others except for the name 'Hunter, Lawrence' printed across the front.

Alison and Ben began to examine the door, peering at it closely and prodding it here and there as though they could feel the magic guarding it. While they worked, Rose tiptoed to the end of the hall, where a tall window let in what little weak, grey light there was, and gazed down at the street below.

"Damn it!" Alison's voice was barely audible. "I knew he'd change the combination!"

"Oh well, it was bound to happen," Ben murmured.

"I can only pick up a couple of spells on it now," said Alison, her brow furrowed. "There must be more on it than that, surely?"

Ben nodded and beckoned to Rose.

"He must be disguising them. Let's see what the inventions can pick up."

Rose hurried back to the door, opening the woven bag slung over her shoulder. She'd filled it with anything they might find useful, including the Analyser, several of her parents' Spell Detectors and the Curse Breaker Alison had been working on before Mum and Dad had disappeared.

Alison had confessed earlier that morning that the

invention hadn't fallen apart due to old age after all, admitting that it had become damaged during her first journey into Hunter's room. She'd promised to let Rose use it if it was needed again, and Rose was eager to try it out.

They each took an invention and attempted to identify the spells on the door. After ten minutes of fruitless work, however, it became clear that the room was not about to give up its secrets so easily.

"These detectors aren't picking anything up," murmured Rose, putting her parents' inventions back in the bag. "I don't get it. They've always worked before."

"He's done something strange to this door!" said Ben in an agitated whisper. Alison stepped back and glanced down the hall.

"We're not getting anywhere and we can't afford to hang around. I think we should pack up and leave before anyone sees us. We can come back and try something else another time."

They put the rest of the inventions back into Rose's bag and crept over to the spiral staircase. By the time they'd reached the ground floor, Mary's eyes were wide and fearful again. She hurried to catch up with Rose and reached out to tug on her sister's sleeve.

"How are we going to break in if we can't tell what spells are on the door?" she fretted.

Alison gave her a mischievous smile.

"Don't worry. It might take a bit of wheedling, but we'll find out what's on it. We knew it would be harder breaking in a second time."

"I'm impressed you broke in the first time," chortled Ben.

The showers had let up and the group splashed their way out into the street. They reached the traffic lights and were about to cross the road when Rose glanced back at the Archives out of habit. She gasped, hanging back and pointing up at the window in the corridor they'd been working in moments earlier.

Someone was standing there, looking out at them. It was impossible to make out any distinguishing features from a distance, but Rose was sure she could guess at the figure's identity. Alison looked up, too, and gave a start.

"I bet you anything that's Lawrence Hunter!" Matt gulped.

"I think we got out just in time," breathed Alison, going pale.

Ben looked up at the figure with distaste. "I wonder where his little followers are? They usually creep around the Archives in packs."

The figure turned and disappeared.

"Come on," said Ben, pulling them all along. "Let's keep moving."

Ben said he wanted to pick up some pieces for his Dispeller while they were in town, and Rose, Matt and Mary were excited to visit the magical supplies store again, so they directed their steps towards the city centre. They walked fast, and Rose soon became aware that Alison and Ben were talking in hushed voices.

"I have no idea how he found out I was in there last

time, but his friends came in after me barely five minutes later," said Alison.

"Maybe we should have lookouts ourselves?" replied Ben.

"It might be a good idea. Rose, Matt and Mary could watch out for us while we search."

Rose glanced at her brother and sister, knowing full well what they would think of such an idea. Sure enough, a look of outrage appeared on Matt's face as they rounded the corner and came to a stop outside the supplies store.

"Wait a minute! You're not letting us come in with you?!"

Alison and Ben turned around in surprise.

"It wouldn't be right to take you with us," said Alison earnestly. "It's dangerous in that room. I've only seen a fraction of what's in there and I'm not looking forward to going back in myself! What would I tell your parents if you got cursed or something?"

"It's much better if we know you're safe," added Ben.

"But you need us!" Matt raged. "You need our help! This is our grandpa's invention! We can't let you do all the work as soon as it gets dangerous!"

"Keep your voice down," implored Ben.

Alison surveyed Matt and Mary's angry faces and sighed.

"Our parents went out looking for an invention and they never came back!" declared Rose. "I'm not going to be left behind this time!"

Mary folded her arms across her chest and glowered at the adults.

"We're coming with you, whether you like it or not."

Alison ran a hand through her dark, curly hair and Ben let out a sound of exasperation.

"But we don't know what's in there!" repeated Alison. "The whole reason we want you to stay behind is *because* your family was taken! Hunter has already had you followed once, remember, Rose? He'll be looking for any chance he can get to make sure none of you interfere with his plans!"

"He knows you're looking for the Fragmenter, too, and I don't think he appreciates the competition," said Ben. "We need to keep you safe!"

Rose unclenched her fists and took a deep breath to calm herself.

"We understand that. We know you're trying to protect us, but we want to help. If either of you got into trouble it would be because of us, and that's not fair!"

"Besides, you might need more than two people in there," argued Matt. "It's like you said, we don't know what we'll have to deal with until we're inside the room."

"If you let us come in, we swear we'll be good and do whatever you say!" Mary pleaded, almost jumping up and down in agitation.

Alison and Ben glanced at each other. Alison looked like she was about to refuse until Ben said in a resigned voice, "I suppose it would be better to have you with us …"

Alison hesitated before bowing her head in defeat.

"All right, then. I guess it is better if we're all together."

Matt and Mary's expressions cleared and Rose gave both Archivists a grateful smile as they all trooped into the supplies shop. Ben disappeared behind the sign for heavy duty pieces and Rose found herself heading down the aisles to where her parents' inventions sat on the shelves in a neat line, wishing more than ever that she had her family back and there was no need to break into Lawrence Hunter's room.

They took to the streets again once Ben had what he needed, spending the rest of the morning wandering the city and debating whether they should ask Miranda for help.

"I think we'll have to," said Ben, opening a brand-new box of the same tiny coloured pieces that filled the Curse Breaker. "Hunter seems to have learned his lesson. He's not going to fall for the same thing twice."

Alison propped her chin in her hand, her expression distant.

"I think you're right. It'll be quicker to go to some-one who can tell us what's on the door. I just hope Miranda can, or getting inside will take a lot longer."

"We should ask her soon, then," said Ben. "If that was Hunter watching us in the window this morning, he might have gone to her already, and I don't think she'll be pleased that we were trying to get into the room without permission."

Alison grimaced.

"Definitely not. OK, we'll go see her after her break."

They retraced their steps when they thought it was safe to go back, and stood outside the door marked 'Head's Office' on the ground floor. They didn't have long to wait before a tall, powerfully built woman with streaks of grey through her chocolate brown hair strode into sight.

Her mouth was pressed into a thin line and one hand was picking through a large set of keys in a harassed kind of way, but her eyes were warm and kind, and she smiled when she saw the group waiting outside her door.

"Ah, I've got company!"

Rose returned the smile shyly. Miranda looked particularly hard at Alison.

"I think you'd better come in before anyone sees you."

She unlocked the door and motioned for them to enter. They sat down in the small collection of squashy chairs facing the heavy desk that stood in the centre of the room, covered on one side with stacks of official-looking papers.

Rose glanced around her with curiosity. The room was spacious and comfortable, with paintings of landscapes on the walls, a set of filing cabinets in one corner and thick, dark carpet. A window on one side looked out onto the crowded street. It was open a crack, and the low rumbling of traffic filtered through into the room, along with snatches of conversation as people walked past.

Miranda settled herself behind the desk and folded

her hands in a business-like way.

"Lawrence Hunter was here this morning, wanting to know if I'd seen or heard anything from you, Alison."

Miranda's face was full of concern as Alison fidgeted in her chair, looking uncharacteristically abashed.

"What did you tell him?"

"I told him that if he didn't get out of the building, I'd call the police," said Miranda, as though it was obvious. "I'm sure they'd be happy to speak to him. I've had them here so many times lately, trying to catch him when he turns up, but he finds a way to avoid them every time. I wish I knew how he does it."

She sighed, frowning down at the desktop.

"It's not safe for you to be here. He's expecting you to turn up sooner or later, and he's always hanging around. He seems to have a real vendetta against you."

"I don't want to cause any trouble," said Alison in a rush. "I wouldn't be here at all if it wasn't important."

Miranda nodded and turned to the others.

"I'm guessing you three are Rose, Matthew and Mary Stephensen?" she asked, giving them another warm smile. Rose nodded and attempted to organise her thoughts to argue her case.

"I'm Miranda. It's good to meet you. I've only met your grandfather and parents a couple of times, but I liked them a lot. What did you want to see me about? Is it this invention your grandpa made?"

"Yes," said Rose, finally finding her voice. "We think it might be in Lawrence Hunter's room here and we wanted to ask if you'd be able to help us find a way inside, please."

"Yes, he suspected you were trying to get in there this morning." Miranda's voice filled with amusement. "What makes you think the invention's in there? I've been paying close attention to everything he's put in his room for a while now and I haven't seen anything that looks even remotely like the Fragmenter."

"When we checked their family's rooms, we found a message from Peter saying he'd hidden it in a magically-made environment," explained Ben. "That's why we wanted to use the Clarifier. Matt asked it where the Fragmenter was and it showed him the inside of Hunter's room."

Miranda lifted an eyebrow.

"A magically-made environment? Well, that explains a lot. I was wondering why it was taking Hunter so long to find it."

"So it *is* possible to keep something real in a fake space?" asked Alison.

"Yes, it is." Miranda leaned back in her chair and her eyes settled on Rose. "But it's going to be very difficult for you to get it back out of whatever place your grandfather's hidden it in."

"How come?" said Mary. "If the invention is real and it can go in there, we can too, can't we?"

Miranda paused for a moment. Rose could see that she was choosing her next words with care.

"Theoretically, yes, but there are lots of ways of putting a real object in a fake environment without going in yourself. Worlds made from magic are complex and all of the ones I've seen have been incomplete. You can probably stand inside your grandpa's world and move around in it, but it's just a mirror of the real world. No part of it was made by nature. I'm not sure spells have been invented yet for a lot of the things you'd need to make one habitable for real people, especially in the long term."

Alison groaned.

"I hadn't thought of that."

"Neither had I," said Ben, looking crestfallen.

Rose blinked in confusion.

"Uh, I don't think I understand."

"What I mean is, real people need real food, water and atmosphere to survive, not just illusions of them, and all of the magical environments I've seen have been missing at least one of these components," Miranda explained. "It wouldn't matter if your grandpa hid an invention in there because it's not alive. But it would make it difficult for a person to enter the fake world and survive long enough to find the Fragmenter and escape."

Disappointment dropped like a rock inside Rose's stomach as she understood what Miranda was saying. She stared down at her knees, feeling faintly sick.

"Oh. That changes things, then."

Miranda seemed to guess what Rose was thinking. Her voice was gentle as she said, "Yes, it's a clever plan, isn't it, putting the invention there? But the comfort is that Hunter and his friends are as real as any of us, so they're just as unable to go after the invention as we are."

Matt, however, sat up straighter in his chair, and his

face lit up with hope.

"But if no one can reach it we wouldn't have to bother with it, would we? We could leave it there and it would be safe from Hunter?"

Alison, Ben and Miranda exchanged dark looks at the mention of Hunter's name.

"There might be other ways of getting the Fragmenter out," said Ben. "Hunter can be smart when he wants something. I wouldn't count on him just never finding a way in if I were you."

Rose shuffled her feet, breathing slightly faster than normal as unwelcome images of Hunter tearing away her family's magic swirled through her mind.

"How are we going to get to it first, then?" she said.

"I have no idea," said Miranda softly. "I'm truly sorry I can't be of more help."

But Alison shook her head.

"We'll deal with that when we've got the silver invention. What we really came about was Hunter's room. Can you help us?"

Miranda put her elbows on the desk and gave both Alison and Ben a stern look.

"You know I'm not allowed to give out keys to people's rooms without their permission. It's against the law unless we can prove without a doubt that he's got something illegal in there. You know he wouldn't cooperate even if we accused him of stealing. He'd also realise you've worked out where the invention is and hide it somewhere else. And besides, he never leaves his key here, so even if I was allowed to help, I couldn't."

"But what about the protective spells over the door?" pleaded Alison. "This is Hunter we're talking about! We all know what he'll do if he gets his hands on that invention! Isn't there some excuse we could give to make him tell us what spells he's using?"

"I doubt it," said Miranda, her expression grim. She glanced at the open window and it snapped shut. "I can't help you with the key, I'm afraid, but I think you might find the spells a little easier to deal with."

Alison blinked at her in surprise.

"What do you mean?"

Miranda glanced at Rose, Matt and Mary, clearly doing some fast thinking.

"He has our family!" Rose said, fighting to keep the desperation out of her voice. "We'd be grateful if you could tell us anything at all!"

Miranda twisted her hands together and Ben's face stretched into a wide grin.

"You know what spells he has on his door, don't you?"

Miranda nodded.

"Like I said, I've been watching him and his room ever since he tried to blackmail Alison."

She opened the top drawer of her desk and took out a sheet of paper. Rose leaned forward to watch as Miranda drew a complicated kind of diagram on it. She caught a glimpse of a door covered in the strange symbols used to represent spells, with a series of lines connecting them in an elaborate pattern, before Miranda pushed the paper across the desk towards Alison.

"If he finds out I've told you, or if he catches you in his room, we'll all be in a lot of trouble. So please be careful when you go inside. I don't fancy a prison sentence."

Alison took the paper and relief flooded her face.

"Thank you! This is exactly what we need!"

Miranda smiled in a slightly guilty way and began searching through the piles of papers. "Just make sure you get that invention."

Rose thanked her again, and Matt and Mary exchanged gleeful looks as Alison led the way back to the reception area.

"I *knew* we should have asked her first!" laughed Ben.

12

Theft

"All we need now is the key!" said Rose.

She peered over Alison's shoulder at the sheet of paper Miranda had given them, trying to decipher the long strings of symbols. They had left the Archives immediately and shut themselves away in Ben's spare room, watching him fine-tune his Dispeller and trying to decide if it would be enough to break them into Hunter's room on its own.

"It's time to figure out how we're going to get it, then," declared Matt, sitting on the kitchen counter and swinging his legs.

Alison continued to study Miranda's diagram, a small crease between her eyes as she concentrated on the magical symbols covering the surface of the door. As Matt spoke, however, she blinked and finally glanced up, her eyes unfocused as though her mind was far away.

"Well, I still think it'll be too difficult to take it from Hunter himself, so I guess we'll have to take it off one of his friends the next time they get something out of his room for him."

"I could use my Viewer to see where it is right now?" offered Rose. Summoning her invention, she rotated the centre until the dark blue eye was horizontal.

"I've never used it on anything I haven't seen before, but I guess Hunter's key looks the same as Grandpa's?"

"They're identical except for the initials engraved on them," murmured Ben, rearranging tiny coloured pieces inside the Dispeller with his tongue between his teeth.

Rose turned back to her Viewer, allowing the image of a key to form in her mind and, not knowing what Lawrence Hunter looked like, she concentrated hard on his name at the same time, hoping that would be enough for the spells to work.

She waited as the centre of the invention began to move, twirling like a spinning top until it slowed and came to a halt. She peered into the pupil expectantly.

"It's not showing me anything," she said in a small voice, fighting back tears as disappointment and frustration bubbled up inside her once more. She folded the Viewer flat and shoved it unceremoniously into her pocket. "I thought I'd fixed it, but it's still completely useless!"

Ben paused in the process of placing a tiny green piece into the Dispeller's metal framework, his face full of sympathy.

"No, it's not! My spells fail every time I try to track Hunter, too. He uses magic to conceal himself. If you can't see anything, it just means that he has his key on him. I've never had any trouble tracking his friends, though."

"Your Viewer could be a useful way of letting us know when he gives the key to someone else," added Alison. "Keep trying it and tell us as soon as it shows you anything."

Rose nodded and put her chin in her hand with a sigh.

She used the Viewer over the next few days without success, gazing into the tiny lens at the centre of the eye, only to push it away, disappointed yet again. Her luck changed, however, just when she'd given up on her invention completely.

It was a humid, overcast afternoon, and she and Mary had come in from the backyard as thunder rolled overhead, threatening rain. Rose lay on her bed, listening to music and spinning the Viewer idly in her hand. She tapped the invention to activate it for the fifth time that day, feeling sure that if it hadn't shown her anything by now it was never going to, only to gasp in surprise as a tiny picture of a tall, burly man with blond hair appeared in the pupil. She lurched upright and stumbled out into the hall.

"I've found it!" She hurtled around the corner into the living room. "It worked! It actually worked!"

Alison dropped the book she'd been reading, looking startled.

"You saw where the key is?"

Rose nodded triumphantly and Mary, sprawled out on the floor watching television, pushed herself up into a sitting position.

"Awesome! Let's go, then!"

Rose made a sound of agreement and gave Alison the Viewer.

"It's with this guy."

There was a moment of silence as they both stared at the picture.

"I've seen him before," said Alison, "and he's a real idiot, so it might not be that hard to trick him. It looks like he's in one of those alleyways near the bank. It's only a block away from the Archives. And he's alone! This is perfect!"

Rose remained where she was, sure that Alison was going to demand that they stay behind, but Alison seemed to realise what would happen if she attempted this. Instead of warning them to stay put, she beckoned them to her.

"Let's follow him, quickly!"

Matt was still outside playing tug-of-war with Cocoa, and Rose pushed open the window to call to him. His eyes sparkled with mischief when she told him where they were going and he rushed through the back door to join them. A moment later they were off, and Rose found herself standing in the same dirty street the Viewer had shown her.

Alison pulled them back into the shadows and they began to search for the blond man. It wasn't long before Mary stopped and pointed down an alleyway beside them.

"Over there!"

Rose turned in time to see the back of the man's jacket disappearing around the corner, and Alison followed him, her footsteps silent as she signalled to the others to stay close. Rose did as she was told and hid behind a collection of tall rubbish bins lined up against the wall. The man reached the end of the alley and stopped with his back to them.

Rose tried to calm her nerves. She had no experience robbing people in the street. She was feeling more and more uncomfortable at the thought of what they were about to do, but she grit her teeth and forced herself to think of her family, locked away and bullied by Hunter and his gang.

There was a metallic glint, and she glimpsed something small clutched in the man's hand. Matt had clearly noticed it, too. He waited restlessly, staring at the key with narrowed eyes.

"I'm going to try to creep up on him," he whispered, starting to edge his way out from behind the bins. But Alison grabbed him and pulled him back.

"Wait a moment!"

Matt stopped struggling and stood still, listening. For several minutes Rose heard nothing but the low rumble of traffic in the next street, competing with the loud music and laughter issuing from one of the apartments nearby. But soon, the unmistakable sound of footsteps could be heard, approaching the corner behind them.

"I don't think he's alone after all," whispered Alison, her eyes wide.

Rose stared at the corner, rooted to the spot. She gulped as the footsteps grew louder.

"We can't go back the way we came, and we can't get out of this alleyway without *him* seeing us ..."

She nodded at the man waiting in the shadows.

"We're stuck!" gasped Mary.

Rose crouched further down behind the bins.

"Let's use a travel spell into another street!" she hissed. "Quick! Before they see us!"

But it was too late. Three others rounded the corner before she could begin the spell. Alison flung her arms out, pulling all three children flat against the wall beside her with a muffled curse. Rose held her breath, waiting for the newcomers to recognise them, but to her surprise, they walked past without a glance.

Letting her breath out in a rush, she turned to Alison, only to find that she had disappeared. Confused, she turned to her other side, where Matt and Mary had been standing mere seconds before, and saw nothing but brick wall. Blinking furiously, she looked down at her hand, closed tightly around Mary's wrist, and then down at her own body, which had taken on the exact colour and texture of the bricks behind her. But she could feel Mary's hand even if she couldn't see it, and she leaned back against the wall, concluding that Alison must be using a camouflage spell.

The group had now formed a small huddle, and were whispering together in urgent voices. Rose watched them as they talked, recognising two of them as the men who'd broken into her parents' house. The shorter of the pair was limping badly, while the man dressed all in black seemed angry and impatient. They appeared to be arguing in an undertone, and kept shooting furtive looks towards the main street. The fourth member of the party was an auburn-haired woman with pale skin and a scowl on her face.

"The old man's causing too much trouble," the injured man grumbled, turning his back to the street. Maybe we should separate him from the others. Might be easier to get information out of him that way."

With a thrill of excitement, Rose realised the man was talking about her family. Mary's hand twitched, and Rose bit her lip hard, forcing herself to remain silent.

"How can one old man be that hard to deal with?" retorted the man dressed all in black, his icy blue eyes narrowed. "Besides, I thought you said he'd already told you how to get the Fragmenter to cooperate?"

"I thought he had," replied the injured man. "But everything he's told me to do has just made things worse. Last time I did what he said, I got these!"

He pointed at the deep, jagged cuts on one side of his face. Rose stared at the gashes in shock. It looked more like an animal had attacked him than an invention. The blond man folded his arms across his chest and rolled his eyes.

"Well, you'd better get it out soon. It won't be long before his grandkids find out about the fake world he made. Lawrence saw them talking to Miranda. She would've told them everything. They'll be trying to break in any day now."

"I know, I know," said the injured man. "It's just a little hard to concentrate when that damned invention is chasing after you!"

"Well, figure something out," replied the blond man. He glanced at his watch. "I don't care what you have to do. I'll see you in a couple of days."

He gave the key to the man in black and then turned and walked away, disappearing into the crowded street beyond. The other three lingered in the alleyway, talking quietly among themselves. After a moment Rose felt a tug on her hand, and she allowed herself to be steered into a bright courtyard nearby. Alison removed her spell and Rose felt herself relax.

"Good thinking, Alison," she said in an undertone, patting her on the shoulder as several people laden with shopping bags passed by. Matt nodded, looking shaken.

"Yeah, I thought we were done for."

Alison leaned against the wall and took a deep breath. She brushed dust and dirt off her jeans and smiled innocently at the shoppers as they passed by.

"That was way too close," she murmured.

Rose laughed weakly, feeling more cheerful than she had in weeks.

"But now we know Mum, Dad and Grandpa are OK!"

She hadn't realised until now just how worried she'd been, especially about Grandpa, who'd always been frail. She wiped away the tears in her eyes, feeling like a weight had been lifted from her chest.

"I knew they would be," said Matt contentedly.

Mary beamed, her face pink with happiness.

"And I'm glad they're annoying Hunter. Ha! Too bad for him!"

Alison chuckled and led them out into the street.

"I'm glad, too. But I don't think they were ever

going to let Hunter have an easy time of it." They all laughed again and Alison ran a hand through her hair with a sigh. "Let's go back home. There's no point hanging around. We'll come back another time when we've planned this out a bit more."

Rose thought this was a good idea, and seconds later they all reappeared in Alison's living room.

"So," said Alison, her expression pensive as she paced up and down. "They've figured out how to get into the fake place your grandpa made. I was wondering how long that would take them."

"And it sounds like the only thing stopping them from getting at Grandpa's invention now is its defensive spells," said Matt, settling himself in an armchair. Rose watched Alison prowl around the room and thought about what Miranda had said about worlds made entirely from magic.

"But didn't Miranda say they wouldn't be able to find the Fragmenter before starving or something?"

Alison frowned, rubbing her temples.

"Your grandpa must have made it possible for people to return to the real world when they need to. There's definitely no way they could survive if they stayed in the fake world for any length of time."

She stopped pacing and pushed her curls out of her face.

"We've got to get that silver invention out of Hunter's room, and fast."

Rose shrugged and twirled the Viewer in her hand. She wasn't going to let Hunter have it all his own way if she could help it.

"Then we'll follow the key every day until we get it. We'll work it out, no matter what."

Filled with determination, they followed the various members of Hunter's gang into alleyways, stairwells and courtyards all over town for the next week, watching from a distance as the key was passed from person to person. But it always seemed to remain out of reach, and despite telling herself to be patient, Rose began to worry that if they didn't get their hands on it soon, Hunter would find a way to take the invention for himself and it would all be too late.

These trips were not always a waste of time, however, as they occasionally yielded useful snippets of conversation and hints about what Hunter was up to. From what Rose had overheard so far, she gathered that her family had attempted to escape on more than one occasion, and knowing that they hadn't given up filled her with fresh hope. She grinned as she and Alison hid behind a car in an underground car park, listening to the men's complaints.

They visited Ben late that afternoon to relay everything they'd learned and he ushered them all inside with an air of intense excitement.

"I'm glad you came," he said, leading them into the living room. "The Dispeller's finished! I've been testing it all day and I'm sure it'll work on Hunter's door."

"That's great, because we don't have much time left," said Alison tensely.

Mary launched into the story of their first disastrous attempt to steal the key, and Ben listened without interrupting, his excitement turning into alarm as she talked.

"You're lucky you got away! Next time you go out, let me know. I want to come. It might help to have an extra person."

"It's been worth going, though," Rose told him with satisfaction. "We've heard loads of things we wouldn't have known otherwise, and at least we know Mum, Dad and Grandpa are hanging in there."

"Yeah, I'm glad to hear it. I don't suppose anyone's mentioned where they're being kept?"

Rose frowned and shook her head.

"Ah well, we'll find out anyway." Ben grinned his usual grin and beckoned to them, his enthusiasm returning. "But for now, I'll show you the Dispeller if you like. You can try it out."

He led them into one of the bedrooms at the back of the house.

"I made a copy of Hunter's door using the information Miranda gave us. I wanted to be sure the Dispeller would work on these particular spells. We can't afford to have any problems or surprises at the last moment."

Rose edged into the room, stepping over piles of broken invention pieces to find a door with no handle standing unsupported in mid-air. It was in very bad shape. Deep scratches and what appeared to be scorch marks covered its surface, and it was hanging off invisible hinges.

"At first, I thought I could separate the door from the spells over it, but because of the type of magic Hunter's used, they're so intertwined that you can't destroy one without destroying the other," explained Ben. "So that's why this is in such bad condition."

He jerked his chin at the door suspended in front of him. Alison seemed unsurprised as she circled it, taking in every inch.

"We'll repair it before we leave. But seeing as we're breaking into the room to steal an invention, I don't suppose it'll matter all that much if we damage the door a bit."

"Yeah, if we get caught, we'll be done for anyway," agreed Matt.

Rose watched as Ben repaired the door and placed a swathe of defensive spells back over it.

"I'll show you how the Dispeller works," he said, picking a multi-coloured, circular object up off the floor. Looking more closely, Rose saw that it was comprised of nine concentric circles arranged inside a shiny silver band, each one smaller than the last and ending with a small opening in the centre.

Coloured pieces inscribed with symbols were fixed inside each ring, and wide silver spokes, similar to those on a bicycle, radiated out from the centre on all sides, protecting the interior.

"It looks complicated," remarked Rose. "How do you activate it?"

"You just have to twist the caps on either end at the

same time, but in opposite directions," said Ben, demonstrating. "Otherwise, it'll be locked and you won't be able to move the pieces. I had to make sure it couldn't be activated by mistake. The spells on it are strong. They can do a lot of damage if you're not careful."

He turned to face the copy of Hunter's door.

"Once it's activated, all you need to do is select the spells you want to remove. Each of these coloured pieces represents a different category of spell. You just move the outer ring until the coloured piece that matches the spell you want is in line with this black mark here," he indicated a black strip along the top of the silver band, "and then do the same with the other rings if there's more than one spell to remove. Then you look through the eyepiece in the centre to make sure you're aiming at the right object and push this button on the top to destroy the spells."

He aimed the invention at the door and pushed a small black button, like the shutter button on a camera. The Dispeller released a rush of energy and the air around the floating door began to churn. The magic over it began to weaken almost at once, and Rose watched in fascination as scorch marks and scratches reappeared on the door's surface.

Soon it began to blister and peel as though Ben had poured acid over it, and a moment later the spells supporting the door gave way. It hit the floor with a resounding crash, discoloured and riddled with holes.

"It doesn't work instantly," said Ben with an apologetic look. "It's faster on smaller, simpler objects, but Hunter has so many strong spells on his room that it takes a while to get through them all, particularly as most of them are disguised."

Alison bent to inspect the door more closely.

"No, this is great! It's perfect!"

Matt looked as though Christmas had come again. He bounded forward, nearly upsetting a pile of debris.

"Can I have a go?"

"Sure," said Ben with a grin. "Just don't aim it at anything living. It wouldn't be pretty."

While Matt, Mary and Ben had fun playing with the Dispeller, Rose and Alison returned to the living room and spent the rest of the afternoon tracking Hunter's key. Rose felt closer than ever to getting into his room, and she peered into the Viewer's eyepiece impatiently as the key changed hands once more, realising as she did so that the same four people carried it each time.

Today it was the man in shabby, faded clothing who took it from the auburn-haired woman and tucked it into his back pocket. His injuries seemed to have hardly healed at all. Fresh claw-like scratches ran down one side of his neck and back now, too, and his limp was worse than ever. Rose and Alison watched him through the Viewer, debating whether they should follow him when five others came into focus around him.

"I think we're just going to have to go for it," mused Alison, sitting cross-legged on the sofa beside Rose. "We've been trying to get one of them on their own for ages now and we've had no luck. We're running out of time."

"Well, there are six of them and five of us," said Rose, trying to ignore a stab of fear at the thought of confronting Hunter's gang. "We're almost equal."

Alison bit her lip, staring down at the Viewer with wary eyes.

"I don't want you fighting them. No, I'm still hoping we can trick them somehow."

She unfolded herself from the sofa and disappeared down the hall. Rose could hear smashing sounds and a great deal of raucous laughter coming from the last room. She slipped the Viewer into her pocket and got up to follow Alison, curious to see what Matt was destroying this time. Alison opened the door and Rose stared over her shoulder at the carnage inside.

The replica of Hunter's door was in worse condition than ever, and the piles of destroyed objects were considerably higher than they had been before. Rose watched as Mary picked up a small invention from a box on the floor and tossed it high into the air, while Matt held the Dispeller up and aimed it. There was a rush of energy and the little invention broke into tiny pieces like glass, its spells torn apart.

Matt threw his head back and laughed like a maniac. Rose hopped out of the way as a piece of invention shot across the room towards her and landed on the nearest pile of debris with a clatter. Mary tossed another invention over to Matt, and this time bright lights of all colours burst into being as the invention crumpled and died.

"Whoa!" Rose admired the lights as they sparkled

and faded. "What was that?"

"There must have been illusion or deception spells in that invention," said Alison, edging her way past the piles of broken pieces to where Ben stood hunched over with laughter. Rose smiled as Mary rummaged in the box again.

"That does look like fun."

"I love this thing!" said Matt, his cheeks flushed from laughing. "I wonder if Mum and Dad would let me have one?"

Rose gave a disbelieving laugh.

"Not a chance. The house would be demolished in a day."

Mary threw a third invention into the air and Alison pulled Ben out of the way as a large chunk of it hit the wall where his shoulder had been, leaving a long scratch.

"We know where the key is. I think we should have another go at taking it."

"All right." Ben wiped tears of laughter from his eyes and repaired the wall with a glance. "How many of them are there this time?"

"There are six, but it's not going to get any easier than this, is it?" said Alison quietly. "We have everything else we need to get into Hunter's room now. We need to get this over with."

"OK. Let's go now, in case more of them turn up."

Matt locked the Dispeller and set it down beside the floating door before joining the others. They huddled together to use a travel spell, arriving in a street near the centre of town, just as the light was beginning to fade from the sky. A cool breeze whispered through the trees lining the pavement, making the hairs on Rose's arms stand up. She shielded her eyes from the glare of the setting sun and searched the area for any sign of the group.

"I think they were headed this way," said Alison, zipping up her jacket and making for the intersection at the end of the road. Rose ran to catch up, shivering and trying to blend in with the townspeople doing their last-minute shopping. Hoping that Hunter's friends would be less likely to attack in a well-lit area with other people around, Rose glanced up at the street light beside her and it flickered to life, casting a wide pool of yellow light over the pavement.

Fingering her Viewer nervously, Rose pulled the invention out of her pocket and checked it once more. The gang was headed for the shopping complex beside the arcade that she, Matt and Mary had visited so often before Grandpa disappeared. Rose followed suit, leading the others.

It wasn't long before she caught sight of a huddle of people, one of them limping, by the arcade. The group stopped beside the steps and Rose crept to the back of the building, tucking a strand of hair behind her ear with a clammy hand. Ben turned to Alison.

"OK, I'll distract them and then you can sneak up on them."

Alison nodded and Ben rounded the corner, making his way past the arcade to the shops further along. The injured man glanced over his shoulder and caught sight of Ben walking down the footpath. Rose grinned and stifled a laugh as Ben pretended to notice the party and gave a convincing start of surprise.

"What are you doing here, Atherton?" growled the injured man. He limped up to Ben, flanked by his friends.

"I'm doing my shopping," said Ben matter-of-factly. "Not that it's any of your business."

The man stepped closer, but Ben didn't back away. Alison shuffled anxiously on the spot.

"Stay here," she told them. "I'll be back in a minute."

She disguised herself with another camouflage spell and disappeared. Rose listened to the sound of her footsteps moving out into the main street before edging closer to the corner with Matt and Mary so that she could watch Hunter's friends.

She waited in silence, listening to Ben talk. The Viewer had shown her the key in the limping man's back jeans pocket, and it suddenly occurred to her that Alison would not be able to get close enough to him without touching his companions.

"We need to think of a way to separate everyone," whispered Rose as the injured man glared at Ben. "Otherwise, that guy's friends will catch Alison and we'll be done for."

But Matt gave her a gleeful look and dug a hand into his pocket.

"No need. I've got just the thing."

"What are you going to do?" Rose's eyes narrowed as he copied Alison's camouflage spell and disappeared.

She grabbed his arm before he could move away.

"What are you going to do?!"

"Just trust me!" Matt hissed, shaking her off.

His footsteps hurried away out of earshot and Rose gave Mary a look of exasperation before peeking around the corner. She went back to watching the group by the arcade, trying to ignore the sinking feeling in her stomach.

"I have a terrible feeling this is all going to go wrong."

"I hope it doesn't," whispered Mary fervently.

Rose sighed, listening intently as the injured man's voice came floating back to her.

"I don't suppose you've heard anything from Alison Maxwell, have you?" he asked Ben, picking at the scratches on his face with a broken fingernail. "We haven't seen her at the Archives for quite some time now, and we were hoping to talk to her. You two are friends, aren't you? She must have told you where she is."

Ben looked down at the man coldly.

"No, I haven't heard from her. And if you haven't found her by now, I don't think you're going to."

An idea struck Rose as Ben prattled on, and she hastily camouflaged herself, too.

"Stay here, I'll only be a minute," she whispered to Mary, ignoring her sister's protests as she ran after Matt.

Creeping up behind the group, she got as close to the injured man as she dared, only to collide with something invisible. Quickly steadying herself, she groped around in the air and found Matt's arm and Alison's shoulder. She bent to whisper into Matt's ear but stopped when she noticed his Hook scuttling along the road on razor-sharp legs with prongs on each end, perfect for grabbing hold of small objects.

The invention was wrapped in black threads that appeared to radiate a strange kind of darkness. They immediately called to mind the invention for concealment that Alison had gifted Matt for Christmas, and Rose stifled a laugh as, like a centipede, the Hook crawled up the man's leg and into his back pocket. To Rose's relief, he and his friends didn't seem to notice. The Hook soon reappeared, retreating into Matt's hand with the key clutched in a pincer-like piece at the end of the stretchy wire.

Rose retrieved the key and used magic to copy it. Thrusting the copy into Matt's hand, she tried to tell him without words to place it in the man's pocket, and seconds later the fake key was safely tucked away.

She felt Alison and Matt retreat towards the corner where Mary waited, and Rose approached Ben, giving a small tug on his sleeve to signal they had what they needed. She edged around the group and had just reached the blond man when he took a step backwards, treading on her right foot.

Rose threw a hand out to regain her balance and the man glanced down, evidently wondering what he'd stepped on. Rose fell onto her hands and knees, still grasping the real key in her fist. She hastened to get out of the way as the man bent down and grabbed her ankle.

"There's someone else here," he said, his eyes narrowing.

Comprehension dawned on the injured man's face and, with a curse, he removed their camouflage spells, revealing Alison and Matt creeping away towards the other end of the street, and Rose on the pavement, struggling to get to her feet. Feeling the spells lift, Alison and Matt spun around. The injured man's gaze settled on Alison and his face twisted into a sneer.

"Finally! It's about time you showed up!"

He began to advance on her and Matt.

"They've got the key," snarled the auburn-haired woman at once, pointing at the glint of silver in Rose's clenched fist.

The blond man let go of her ankle and snatched hold of her wrist instead, attempting to wrestle it out of her hand, and Rose, desperately hanging onto the small piece of metal, looked up to see Mary launch herself onto the blond man's back.

With a cry of rage, Mary began beating at him with all of her strength, clawing him with her fingernails and sticking her fingers in his eyes until he let go, cursing and howling with pain. Rose scrambled up frantically.

"Run, Rose!" yelled Ben, rushing forward and getting in the way of the blond man as he shook Mary off and lurched forwards.

Without even thinking about where she was going, Rose grabbed Mary's hand and tore around the corner, racing off down the street. She could hear the others chasing after them and put on a burst of speed, stopping at the back entrance of the shopping complex, gasping for breath.

"Hide in the arcade until they stop chasing you and then meet up with Alison," she told Mary. "I've got the key, it's me they're after."

To Rose's immense relief, Mary nodded and sprinted towards the steps. Rose headed for the fruit market on the opposite side of the road, hoping to get far enough away to use a travel spell. She was almost there when she again collided with something solid. The auburn-haired woman had materialised right in front of her, almost knocking her to the ground. She gripped Rose's wrist tightly and began to prise the key from her hand. There was a scuffling sound behind her and Matt and Alison appeared out of nowhere.

"Alison! Here!" Rose yelled, throwing the key high into the air.

Alison caught it and they were off again. The auburn-haired woman promptly let go of Rose and sped after Alison instead, sending curses after her as she ran. Rose cancelled the curses and met up with Ben as he hurtled around the corner, pursued by the other five men. He had a split lip and a bruise was forming on his cheek. Rose caught sight of the men's livid faces and hurried to catch up to him.

"Who's got the key?" he panted as they ran.

"Alison has it," gasped Rose, indicating the fleeing figures ahead of them. She gritted her teeth, massaging the stitch in her side.

"We need to catch up with them," said Ben. "Hold on to me."

Rose took hold of his sleeve again. She felt herself

disappear and then reappear, looking over her shoulder to see Alison, Matt and Mary coming up behind them. Blocking the spells still being aimed at Alison, Rose and Ben waited for the others to reach them. Moments later they were all together again and Rose found herself back in Ben's living room, cringing in pain and thoroughly out of breath.

"I'm sorry!" she moaned. "That blond guy trod on my foot! I shouldn't have got so close."

"It's OK," panted Alison. "The main thing is we have the key."

She fixed her eyes on Ben and his injuries healed. He settled himself between Matt and Mary on the sofa, his grin already returning.

"Yeah, we got what we wanted. And even better, we got to annoy those guys."

Matt and Mary laughed and Rose couldn't help but join in.

"You're right, that is a bonus."

"It's a good thing you had your Hook with you, Matt," said Mary, her cheeks flushed from running. "No way could we have taken the key without it."

Matt beamed, patting the bulge in his shirt pocket fondly, where Rose assumed the Hook must now be lurking.

"And it was a good idea to copy the key," added Alison. "You're right, Rose, it would have been too obvious if they'd met us in the street and then suddenly it disappeared. I should have thought of that."

"I suppose it doesn't matter now." Rose pushed her

hair out of her face with a frown. "They saw me holding it, so they know we have it."

Alison took the key out of her pocket and held it out so that they could all see the initials 'LH' engraved on one side. Matt picked it up and twirled it between his fingers, his grin growing wider.

"So … when are we going in?"

13

Smoke and Spellwork

By now, Rose had been in and out of the Archives often enough that she had no difficulty in finding her way to Hunter's room, despite the dark and winding passageways. They'd wasted no time after stealing the key, stopping only to collect Ben's Dispeller before heading to the Archives.

The weather was changing rapidly. The sun had almost set and the atmosphere was tense. Dark clouds had gathered on the horizon and Rose could feel the electricity in the air as the storm approached. She hurried along the shadowy corridors with the others, reaching Hunter's door without meeting anyone.

They'd used Ben's after-hours card to enter the building, but Alison had warned them that, if they triggered the lockdown, it would take only minutes for security to arrive. There was also the problem that Hunter himself was sure to know by now that his key had been stolen and was likely already heading to this same spot to catch them. However, there was no way for them to prevent this, so Ben extracted his Dispeller from Alison's bag and rotated the caps to unlock it.

"Here goes," he muttered, facing the door and backing away several paces. He looked as nervous about what they were about to do as Rose was herself, his freckles clearly visible as he turned each of the inner circles to select the correct combination of spells.

Rose crossed all of her fingers and the rest of the group waited breathlessly as Ben held up the Dispeller and pressed the black button on top. There was a rush of energy and it began to work on the door.

It wasn't long before blisters and scorch marks appeared on its surface, just as they had on the replica hanging in Ben's spare room. The invention worked at full power, making the tiny hairs on Rose's arms stand up in response to the magic. After a tense moment of silence, the energy around the invention began to dissipate. It deactivated with a faint click, its job done, and Ben stepped forward to examine the smoking, blackened door. He grinned over his shoulder at Alison.

"It worked! Ha!"

Alison took a deep breath and Matt punched the air triumphantly. Rose stepped forward, fumbling with the key in her pocket, but stopped as something creaked beneath them. Her eyes darted over to the stairwell.

"I didn't see anyone on the way up here. Did you?"

She turned to the others and they shook their heads.

"I'll go and see if it's anything to worry about," said Alison. "It might just be the cleaners or something. Don't wait around for me, though, we don't have time to waste. If there's trouble I'll come and find you."

"All right, but be careful," Ben warned.

Alison nodded and tiptoed towards the stairs. Ben approached the ruined door, checking it for any traces of magic the Dispeller might have missed.

"Let's try the key."

Rose slipped the key out of her pocket and pushed it into the slot. Another soft click sounded and the battered door swung open.

"Yes!" crowed Mary. "We did it!"

Ben locked the Dispeller and tucked it into his jacket as Mary rushed forward into the room with Matt and Rose close at her heels. Their feet had barely crossed the threshold when an alarm sounded. Thick iron bars appeared across the doorway and around Ben so that Rose, Matt and Mary were trapped inside the room and Ben was caught outside it.

"Damn it! Hunter must have changed something before we got here to make sure we triggered the lockdown!"

Ben gripped the bars, looking devastated. Frantic footsteps echoed up the stairs and a second later Alison came tearing around the corner. She stared at them in horror.

"Hunter's coming himself, with his whole gang! They're all here! He must have been sure he was going to catch us! What are we going to do? Only Miranda can take the bars down and she's not here! By the time I go and get her, Hunter will be here and it'll be too late!"

"Go and get her anyway," urged Ben, his eyes fixed on the stairs. Alison disappeared again and Ben turned to Rose, Matt and Mary.

"You need to hide. Here, take this with you." He poked the Dispeller through the bars so that Rose could take it. It barely fit. "I don't want Hunter to have it."

"Can't we use it to break out of here?" cried Matt. "If it can kill Hunter's door, I bet it can get rid of these bars."

"No, it won't work on them." Ben sighed, his voice low as he pressed his forehead against the cold metal. "Alison's right, only Miranda can remove them. They're not made from the usual kind of magic, otherwise everyone would be able to escape. You can't use a travel spell out, either. Believe me, people have tried. We need Miranda. The spells will only obey her."

Rose thought she could hear a large group coming up the stairs now. She rattled the bars but they were solid and immovable.

"Hide!" Ben commanded. "Hunter can't know that you three are inside his room! It's illegal for a start, and you know he's after you!"

"But -"

"There's nothing you can do!" insisted Ben, prying their fingers off the bars. "Wait for Alison to come back with Miranda. They'll let you out. I notice security hasn't turned up yet. Hunter must have done something to stop the alerts."

He cursed and positioned himself so that he blocked the doorway from sight. When Rose, Matt and Mary refused to move he sent a spell at them, sending them reeling backwards, away from the door as the footsteps reached the hall. Laughter broke out, and Rose knew that Ben had been spotted. She gave him an apologetic look before pulling her brother and sister over to a shabby cupboard along the far wall, facing the hall. She threw it open.

One side was taken up by a line of shelves stuffed full of tools, but beside this was a narrow, open space containing long sheets of metal, bolts of canvas and other materials. Sweeping them aside, she ushered Matt and Mary into the cupboard and then squeezed herself in after them, leaving the door ajar so that she could watch the doorway. It was extremely uncomfortable.

Ben was soon surrounded by jeering faces. One of the men closest to the bars was the blond man they'd taken the key from earlier. She glared at them all as they laughed, their eyes travelling from the ruined door to Ben, caught in the cage. She wriggled with impatience, wishing Alison would hurry up.

"Hi, Ben," said a quiet voice further down the hall.

It was difficult to be sure with one ear squashed against the wall of the cupboard, but for a fraction of a second Rose thought that voice sounded familiar. Ben looked around and his expression soured.

"Hunter," he said, inclining his head.

"I was hoping we'd meet each other here," said the quiet voice, full of amusement.

"I'm sure you were," retorted Ben. Rose pinched Matt hard as he snorted with laughter behind her.

"What did you do to my door?" The quiet voice sounded curious rather than angry. "I have to admit, I didn't think you'd find a way through. But I guess I was wrong."

Ben simply shrugged, his expression full of disdain.

"Looks like it."

"It's a good thing I added a new spell to the room before you arrived, then," replied Hunter.

"Ah, I thought you must have," said Ben conversationally. "Where did you put it? Because I checked the door and we destroyed all the spells on it …"

"I placed it over the threshold, not the door."

Ben let out a groan and the men laughed again. Hunter waited for them to fall silent before saying, "Where are the others? I thought Alison would be here with you at least. Jacob here told me that you weren't alone when you took my key earlier, and you said 'we' instead of 'I' a moment ago."

The injured man's laughter faded as he glared at Ben.

"I told them to run when we triggered the lockdown," answered Ben, as though it was obvious. "You didn't think they'd wait around for you to arrive, did you?"

"Hmm."

Rose could tell that Hunter didn't believe him. Someone performed one of the most unusual spells Rose had ever encountered and all of the bars except for the ones across the doorway disappeared. Ben stared at them with a kind of resentful surprise.

"How did you do that? No one can remove those bars except Miranda!" His eyes widened with concern. "You haven't done anything to her, have you?"

"No, no, she's fine," said Hunter with a laugh. "But I'm sure you've heard by now, Ben, that I'm always looking for new ways to do things."

He didn't elaborate and silence filled the hall until

Ben spoke again.

"What about the bars over your door, then?"

"I see no reason to risk anyone else taking a night-time stroll in there," replied Hunter. "What if your friends decided to come back? This way nobody except myself can get in or out." He emphasised the last two words ever so slightly. "But if you're telling the truth and the others are gone, you've got nothing to worry about, have you?"

Ben glanced at the bars again, his face full of anxiety. Hunter said something inaudible and Jacob nodded.

"Take him to the house," Hunter's voice carried down the hall, loud enough for Rose to catch this time, "but keep him away from the other three. I don't want them talking."

She watched in pained silence as Jacob and the man in black grabbed Ben roughly by the arms and then disappeared. The others headed back down the hall, smirking and laughing among themselves.

Rose waited until she was sure the corridor was deserted before pushing the cupboard door open and disentangling herself from the metal sheets. Unlike her own family's rooms here in the Archives, carpet covered the floor of Hunter's room, and her steps were silent as she crept to the doorway and peered as far down the hall as the bars would allow. They were alone.

Rose signalled that it was safe to emerge and Matt and Mary tumbled out of the cupboard. Mary gripped Rose's arm with icy fingers and stared around the room.

"We're stuck in here until Alison comes back!"

"Or Hunter," added Matt with a dark look towards the stairs. Rose turned her back on the bars, her mind going over the plans they'd made. She smiled at Mary and tried to keep her voice steady.

"Alison must have told Miranda what's happened by now. I reckon they'll try to help Ben before they come here. We're safe for now, so we might as well do what we came here to do while we're waiting for them. Otherwise, all of this will have been for nothing. We know the silver invention is in here somewhere. Let's see if we can find it."

Keeping a firm grip on the Dispeller, Rose surveyed the room. It appeared suspiciously normal. Nothing on the set of shelves beside the door could be considered illegal or even dangerous and there were no documents at all. Apart from the shelves and the cupboard they'd hidden in, the room was bare.

"It's not here!" cried Mary, rummaging through the cupboard drawers for the third time. Matt pulled a face and tossed a silver-tipped tool aside with a clang.

"You know, now that I think about it, this isn't the room the Clarifier showed me when I asked it to find the Fragmenter."

Rose dropped the box of shiny silver clasps, screws and hooks she'd been picking through and whirled around to face him.

"Please tell me you're joking?"

Matt frowned and shook his head.

"Nope. I saw a darker room with a tall glass case."

Rose and Mary exchanged looks of horror.

"So we went to all this trouble just to break into the wrong room?" said Rose in a hollow voice.

Matt rattled the bars over the doorway in frustration. "I guess so."

Rose stared at the threadbare carpet, wondering how they could have made such a mistake. She turned to Matt again.

"But this can't be the wrong place. Remember when you described what you saw to Alison? She said it was Hunter's room, and she's been in here before, so she'd know."

Something stirred in her memory as she combed the room again with her eyes. Suddenly Alison's words came rushing back to her.

"Of course! He keeps it all hidden away so that the Archivists can't find it," she intoned. "That's what Alison said the first time we went to her house!"

"Well, that explains why we can't find anything unusual," said Matt, leaning against the bars, "but it doesn't help us get at the stuff he's hidden."

Rose shook her head, refusing to be put off.

"There must be some sign of concealed magic here."

She gazed around the room, taking in every detail. Reaching out with her mind, she searched for spells that might be disguised, or anything else that might help them, but found nothing. If there was concealed magic here, Hunter had done a good job of blending it seamlessly into the Archives' protective spells. Rose made a sound of impatience and roamed around the room, wondering what she was missing while Mary sat on the floor with her back to the wall, picking at a hole in the carpet.

"I guess we'll have to wait until Alison gets back."

Rose went to stand beside her brother, looking past him for any sign of movement down the hall.

"Hunter would've been expecting Alison, Miranda and Ben to do everything we've just done," said Matt. "He's not going to make it that easy, is he?"

"But spells always leave a signature," argued Rose. "That's just how it works. There has to be some sign of hidden magic in this room, but I just can't feel it."

Silence descended as each of them pondered this, waiting for Alison to return. Soon Mary began to wriggle uncomfortably against the wall, and her brow furrowed in confusion.

"Uh, I know this sounds weird, but it kind of feels like the wall behind me is vibrating."

She stood up and pressed her hands against it. Rose and Matt glanced at one another in surprise and crossed the room. Rose put a hand out tentatively, her fingers tingling with a static-like energy as they drew near the wall.

"This must be it! The glass case Matt saw must be here!"

Her eagerness returning in an instant, she placed both hands on the smooth stretch of wall, letting the energy wash over her. It was no wonder she'd missed it before. It was like trying to distinguish a single faraway voice while standing in the middle of a noisy crowd.

Clever, Rose thought dryly. Hunter must have used

the spells on the neighbouring rooms to drown out and disguise his own magic. Rose beamed at Mary.

"You did well to notice this. Hunter obviously didn't expect anyone to press themselves against the wall."

She and Mary chortled, poking at the seemingly empty space.

"How do we make whatever is hidden here show itself, then?" asked Matt, staring at the blank stretch with apprehension. Rose contemplated the wall, her mind going blank.

"I have no idea. I wonder what Alison did?"

"Probably something complicated," said Mary.

Matt sighed and rolled up his sleeves.

"Well, let's try some spells and see what happens."

He fixed his eyes on the middle of the wall and began to work on it. Rose and Mary joined in, focusing all of their energy on the same spot and allowing their combined magic to spread over it like ripples on the surface of a pond.

Minutes trickled by with no result, and Rose decided to try her dissolution spell again. She sent her best magic at the wall, her hands balling up into fists with the effort. For a brief moment, the area glowed with a faint light, illuminating their faces, but it soon faded, leaving the wall unaffected. Matt glared at it as though his frustration alone could burn a hole through it.

"Wait, I know what we should do!" cried Mary, her eyes bright. "Let's use the Dispeller again! It got us in here, didn't it?"

Rose blinked and held out the invention.

"Of course! Why didn't I think of that?"

They backed further away towards the corridor as Rose unlocked the invention and looked down at the coloured rings.

"I think I'll leave it on the settings Ben used," she said. "They might be strong enough to break through, even if the spells on the wall are different."

She aimed the invention and pressed the black button on top, watching the wall for signs of magical damage. The air around it began to churn, but instead of a cabinet, another unremarkable wooden door began to form in front of them, covered in blisters. It creaked open an inch or so, revealing darkness beyond. Rose couldn't believe their luck.

The Dispeller clicked and deactivated, wreathed in a haze of smoke. She tucked it into her pocket and Matt stretched out a hand to pull the door open.

A sense of foreboding swooped down on Rose the moment Matt's hand made contact, and she took an involuntary step back, her heart rate quickening as her eyes adjusted to the sudden darkness. Magic pressed in on her as she forced herself to step into the hallway, almost pushing her straight back out. They weren't supposed to be here …

"Whoa! How much stuff does he have in here?" she said in a hushed voice, her eyes making out the dim outlines of three more doorways further ahead in the gloom.

She took another step forward and stopped, almost overpowered by the urge to turn around. Shaking herself mentally, she did her best to overcome her instincts, reminding herself why they were there. It was just an empty hallway, after all. There was no reason to be afraid. Nevertheless, Hunter's spells continued to bear down on her, filling her with irrational fears.

"I really do hate mind magic," she muttered into the darkness.

Each step she took seemed to cost her more effort than usual, like she was wading through thick mud, and her feeling of dread only intensified as she approached the first room. Touching the doorknob with a fingertip, she wondered if there would be protective spells around it, too, but there was no layer of magic blocking her path this time. Instead, light from an unseen source flooded the hall, following her as she moved.

"This place is weird."

She stood on the threshold, fighting to regain her composure, her voice sounding small and out of place in the total silence.

"You're telling me," replied Matt, huddled close behind her.

Rose glanced back at her brother and sister. Both were unusually quiet, their faces ghostly in the unnatural light. Rose hesitated with her hand still outstretched.

"It's just magic," she told them, sounding more confident than she felt. "Another trick of Hunter's to stop anyone going near his stuff. There's nothing frightening in any of these rooms."

To prove herself right, she turned the knob and pulled the door open. The light fell on a cramped space filled with books and documents. Rose stared. Surely these weren't all reports for inventions Hunter had hidden?

She turned to the shelves beside her and wiped the dust off a black book with no title, battling a mix of emotions. She was itching to open the book and begin reading, but Hunter's spells pressed down on her relentlessly, making her want to run. Matt and Mary edged past her, staring around the room, and Rose stopped, arguing with herself. This was not the time to get distracted …

She half-turned towards the door, about to continue down the hall when a long shelf containing some of the largest books she'd ever seen caught her eye, and curiosity got the better of her. She bowed her head in resignation.

"We'll have a quick look around and then move on."

Matt and Mary made quiet sounds of agreement and fought their way over to the nearest bookshelf. Rose crossed the room to the shelf and took hold of a mossy green book that seemed perilously close to tumbling off onto the floor. Feeling a little guilty, she eased it from the shelf and opened it. Her suspicions were confirmed as she scanned the contents page.

"This is a collection of reports for inventions that weren't supposed to be made." She frowned, flicking through the pages with distaste. "I thought Hunter wasn't much of an inventor?"

"I bet they're not all his," guessed Matt. "They can't be. Not even Grandpa has made this many inventions. I bet Hunter's been collecting anything that took his fancy for ages."

"Hmm, I think you must be right."

Rose replaced the green book on the shelf with difficulty and turned to the others, standing on tiptoe for a closer look. Old and battered-looking books with peeling covers and yellowed pages filled the rest of the shelf. She pulled out a thick volume with a richly embellished red cover and opened it. It contained black magic rather than reports for illegal inventions, and Rose only read a few pages before putting it back. She picked up another, which proved to be just as awful.

"Anything good in that?" asked Matt from a set of filing cabinets, where he and Mary were studying the reports with great interest.

"No, it's horrible, like all the other books here," replied Rose, leafing through the pages. "The other book was filled with curses and this one tells you how to do spells that spread from person to person like a virus. As if you'd even want to know!"

She slammed it shut. Thumbing through the jumble of reports on a neighbouring shelf, she soon found one detailing a range of inventions Hunter had made himself. Curious, she opened it and began to read, a satisfied smile on her lips as she skimmed through the pages. Alison was right. Hunter wasn't an expert on invention-making.

His ideas were innovative and intelligent, but it seemed to Rose that he struggled to turn them into a working creation, resulting in overly complicated pieces that lacked the finesse of a professional invention. It seemed obvious now why he'd let Grandpa make the Fragmenter, rather than trying to make it himself. Feeling immensely proud of her grandfather, she put the collection of reports back and chose another.

"This one's interesting. It seems like Hunter's been following all of the new magical discoveries and trying to push the boundaries of what people are capable of for a long time. This paper talks about the fundamental principles of magic and how they limit what we can do with spells. Maybe that's one of the reasons why Grandpa's invention is so interesting to him. It pushes the boundaries more than anything I've ever seen! People will be able to do things they could never have done in the past. I can definitely see Hunter being interested in that."

A shabby book with a plain blue cover caught her eye at the end of the shelf. As she pulled it out, she saw that a dark, mysterious substance had spilled over it, and she grimaced as she opened the book and began to read, trying her best not to touch the splatters.

"Urgh!" She crinkled her nose in disgust. "This one lists loads of different magical poisons and potions. And it describes tests and experiments that have been done on people in the past. Some of them are pretty nasty, too." Her eyes travelled to the stains on the covers and she hastily set the book down on a pile of papers, propped open against the side of the shelf. "It says here that one person lost a finger when the poison started to destroy their skin."

She wiped her own hands on her jeans with a shudder. Mary pulled a face and eyed the book the way she would a slug.

"Urgh! Gross!"

A wave of nausea struck Rose as she reached the end of the page.

"It goes through all of the test subjects' symptoms and describes how the poisons work in detail. Eww, there are even sketches."

"Awesome! Let me see!" demanded Matt, coming over to look.

Mary tossed her papers aside and began to follow him. Rose hurriedly wrapped her hand in the cloth of her shirt and shoved the book back onto its shelf. Some of the effects described in it were so gruesome that she was reluctant to allow Mary to see them. Unperturbed, Matt yanked the book back out again, but Rose took hold of her sister's hand and steered her over to the door instead.

"We've let ourselves get distracted," she chided. "We're supposed to be looking for the silver invention and it's clearly not in here. Let's go to the next room. Come on, Matt!"

Matt tore himself away from the blue book with a sigh and they continued down the hall. Rose forced her feet to move, one in front of the other until she reached the second door, feeling increasingly unwelcome as she did so. She took a deep breath to calm the butterflies in her stomach and pushed the door open to find herself in a kind of storeroom.

Racks and even more shelves occupied every available space, full of materials. She crossed to a cupboard stocked with bunches of dried plants and sniffed at a sprig of leaves.

"Mint. I bet the ingredients for the experiments in that blue book are in here somewhere."

Matt stared around the room for a moment, looking puzzled. "I wonder what Hunter uses these things for? I've never seen Mum, Dad or Grandpa working with herbs."

"Hunter isn't an inventor like us, though," Mary reminded him. "Maybe he uses magic in a different way?"

Matt shrugged and turned to the apothecary cabinet beside him. Bunches of dried herbs littered the top, scattered among clusters of seashells and feathers. He opened the drawers at random, and Rose glimpsed mounds of chalks and other minerals, ground into fine powders, before a drawer full of sparkling gemstones slammed shut on Matt's hand with a sickening *crack*.

He let out a cry of surprise and pain. Bracing his other hand on the cabinet, he attempted to wrench himself free, but the drawer held tight. Rose hurried over and grabbed hold of the handle, pulling with all her might while Mary attempted to dig her fingers into the gap and pry it open.

"It's just getting tighter!" said Matt through clenched teeth.

A polished metal tray caught Rose's eye on a table nearby. Snatching it up, she wedged it into the gap beside Matt's fingers to stop the drawer from tightening any further. The wood groaned, straining against the tray, but Matt's breathing eased a little as some of the pressure shifted from his fingers.

Rose and Mary pulled hard on the drawer again, and Matt slowly wriggled each of his fingers free. Rose and Mary let go and the drawer snapped shut, swallowing the tray with a clatter. Matt rubbed his hand, eyeing the cabinet resentfully.

"Thanks," he said, flexing his fingers. "I don't think it did any damage."

He shot Rose and Mary a grateful look and they all took a wary step back from the cabinet. Rose took another deep breath.

"We need to be more careful. We can't afford to get hurt in here."

Matt and Mary nodded in agreement and they resumed their search of the room with more caution. Rose made her way over to a desk overflowing with beakers, measuring cups and other equipment, stepping over the baskets and boxes that littered the floor around it.

"I wonder what these are?" said Mary, pointing at something hidden behind a cluster of wicker baskets.

Rose leaned forward until she could see rows of glass bottles arranged on a small table, each containing a different coloured liquid. Matt held a black one up to the light, watching admiringly as it turned a deep blue.

"Nothing good, I'm sure," said Rose, looking at the liquids suspiciously.

She went back to examining the contents of the desk

with interest, poring over the more oddly-shaped pieces of equipment. After several minutes of quiet searching, Rose heard Mary gasp and glanced up to find her backing away from something behind the apothecary cabinet that had attacked Matt, her eyes wide with fear.

"Get it off!" she cried, shaking her left arm.

A rust-coloured liquid dripped from the trailing edge of her sleeve. It travelled up her arm with alarming speed, transforming the fabric into something soggy and reddish-brown as it spread. Rose almost tripped over a box as she rushed to her sister's side, feeling sure, without quite knowing how, that they couldn't allow the liquid to touch Mary's skin.

"How do I stop it?" Mary yelped.

She twisted her arm around, holding it out at an awkward angle to avoid touching the fabric. Without a word, Matt appeared from behind another cabinet and used a spell to tear the fabric off at Mary's elbow, tossing the sodden cloth onto the floor.

They all took a hasty step back as the liquid spread over the shred of sleeve and began to soak into the carpet and objects nearest to it, stopping only when it had consumed everything within a metre or so. Rose stared down at the mushy, rotten baskets and boxes with horror, her heart pounding in her chest.

"What the hell is that stuff?"

"And how did it spread so far?" demanded Mary. "I only got a tiny bit on my sleeve!"

Rose could only shake her head, unable to explain how this could be possible. She met Matt's eyes, but he seemed as bewildered as Rose. She peered at her sister closely, suspecting that Mary was beginning to regret her decision to enter Hunter's room, and Rose privately agreed that the sooner they left the better.

"OK, let's be extra careful not to spill anything," said Matt, carefully avoiding the nearest cabinet.

He worked his way back across the room to where he'd been studying a crate of vials. "I think these might be the poisons you were reading about before, Rose!"

He held up a crate of glass vials gingerly, keeping them at arm's length as though he thought they might bite if he got any closer. "They're all labelled with their names and the effects they have."

Rose turned away with a shiver.

"Put them back," she pleaded. "I don't want to see them."

She scanned the shelves beside the desk, looking for anything made of silver, but the only metal objects were a set of heavy, old-fashioned brass scales and a jumble of weights. Thinking that this was no surprise, as the room was clearly just a storeroom for supplies, she straightened up and headed for the door with relief.

"Let's try the last room. The invention must be in there somewhere."

She went to the very end of the hall this time and opened the last door, hoping there would be no more accidents. Her enthusiasm returned in a rush as the door swung open.

"This is more like it!"

Inventions twinkled down at them from every angle,

packed into glass cabinets. Two paths had been cleared through the clutter, disappearing quickly behind the towering cabinets standing back-to-back in the middle of the room. Rose turned to Matt.

"Is this the room the Clarifier showed you?"

Matt leaned forward, keen to take off down the nearest path.

"Yeah! But from a different angle."

"There's so much stuff in here," groaned Mary. "It'll take us ages to search through it all."

"Let's split up, then," said Matt. "Rose, you can take the left and we'll go right. Come on, Mary."

They disappeared and Rose set off down the other path, scanning each cabinet's contents before moving on. Time wore on and Rose's excitement soon became tempered by a sense of urgency.

It had now been over an hour since Hunter had left. How long would they have before he returned to the Archives to check on his hidden treasures? Trying not to dwell on this possibility, she turned her attention back to her task but quickened her pace all the same, eager to leave the Archives before they were discovered.

A flash of light caught her eye as she turned to search the next set of shelves, and she bent down to inspect the object more closely. It wasn't the silver invention, but it shone with the same tantalising, multi-coloured hues, and she couldn't resist stopping to investigate.

Etched with symbols and made of a material that resembled mother-of-pearl, the tiny object blossomed out at the base and narrowed at the top, mimicking the shape of a teardrop. Careful not to disturb the pieces clustered around it, she picked the invention up and weighed it in her hand. It was heavy for its size and fit easily in the palm of her hand. A jet of vapour smelling of sweet perfume billowed from an opening at the tip of the teardrop, dispersing into the air around it.

Rose gazed at it for a moment, admiring the little object, and then closed her eyes, breathing in the scent. It reminded her of the smell of spring in the bush at home. Feeling a little homesick, she opened her eyes and jumped in surprise. The little invention, now surrounded by a fine haze of vapour, had changed colour completely, as had the inventions around it.

Where they had appeared dim before, they now shone brightly with many-coloured lights. Remembering the deception spells sparkling in the air when the Dispeller destroyed them back at Ben's house, she wondered if the same kind of effect was happening here. She blinked furiously, but the glowing lights remained. Turning her head from side to side, she found that the lights became clearer as they neared the edge of her vision.

A small card sat on the shelf where the invention had stood. She lifted it out and read the tiny handwritten words 'Illuminator - makes all magic visible to the human eye' in black ink. Amazed, Rose glanced back up at the glowing inventions.

"So the colours are different spells," she murmured.

She moved the invention around so that the vapour

filtered around the room. It looked the same as ever. She closed her eyes as she had before, and then opened them, looking through the steam like a strange kind of filter. The room had transformed. Colours of all hues twinkled everywhere, illuminating the spells around her. She peered down the hall. The place where the hidden door stood open now shone bright and obvious.

The inventor in her took over, and she held the invention up to her eyes, eager to know how it had been made. Using the bright colours shining all over the Illuminator as a guide, she managed to identify all but one of the spells used on it. What amazed her most of all, however, was that none of these spells were compatible.

After working fruitlessly on her Viewer for so many months, she knew from experience what happened when someone attempted to bind incompatible magic, and she marvelled at the way the teardrops' spells had been encouraged to cooperate.

Assuming it must be the work of the mysterious purple spell gluing them all together, she tried to guess what it might be. With a thrill of excitement, she recognised it as a dissolution spell, but it felt nothing like the one she had used on her Viewer. Her spells had an irritating habit of butting heads with one another, but this spell mingled and blended with its companions seamlessly. The inventor had cleverly used the spell in such a way that its destroying abilities countered the other spells' incompatible features, allowing it to act as a custom-built bridge between them.

Intrigued and wondering if she'd been doing the

spell wrong all this time, she flipped the Illuminator's card over and stared down at the words 'Inventor: L. Hunter' printed across the bottom. Hardly able to believe her eyes, Rose hastily put the little invention back in its place with its card underneath it. She tore her gaze away from the glowing vapour, suddenly doubting Alison's claim that Hunter was a poor inventor, not to mention her own assumptions based on the reports she'd read in the first hidden room.

The room returned to normal when she moved out of the haze of steam, and she cast the invention one more admiring look before forcing herself to move on.

Wondering if Matt and Mary had found anything, she continued down the line of cases, peering into each of them. She'd barely gone ten steps when her attention was caught yet again, this time by a flash of silver, and she hurried over to it.

The dusty glass door of the cabinet made it difficult to see, so she opened it and craned her neck to see an unremarkable, vase-shaped silver bottle with hinges running around its base. It had been placed in the deep shadows at the back of the shelf, and she let her arm drop back to her side, feeling deflated.

The bottle had several grooves running around the outside, as though it could be unscrewed into pieces, and a slow, steady dripping sound issued from it, like a leaky tap. It looked nothing like an invention, but she reached up again, wondering if it concealed anything inside it.

Her fingers brushed a curious blood-red marble that contained a substance that pulsed like a beating heart, and she watched it with fascination before nudging it to one side, reaching for the silver bottle. She flinched as her fingers touched the metal. It was warm to the touch, almost too warm to hold, and she picked it up gingerly. She waited for some kind of reaction, but when the bottle remained just a bottle, she settled it more steadily in her palm and reached out with her other hand to unscrew the top. She twisted the cap and withdrew her fingers hastily with a sharp gasp of shock and pain.

The silvery surface of the bottle had sprouted hundreds of needle-sharp spines which grew deep into her palm, and she pried her hand free with difficulty, letting the bottle fall to the ground with a clang. The spines shrank back into smooth silver as they parted contact with her skin, and Rose stumbled backwards, away from it as it rolled across the floor.

"What happened?" Matt and Mary's voices came from somewhere behind the line of cases.

"It's nothing," Rose replied, cursing under her breath. "I hurt myself, that's all. Don't worry, it's fine."

"Be careful, won't you?" teased Matt.

Rose held her hand up to the light and saw a mass of tiny puncture marks. Blood oozed from several scattered wounds on her fingers, but most of the damage was contained to her palm. She prodded the marks gently. They felt deep.

"Damn it! Why did I have to pick it up?"

Furious with herself, she bent down to see where the silver bottle had got to. She found it underneath the cabinet beside her and crouched down for a better look, but the silvery surface was smooth and normal-looking once more. Judging by the steady dripping sound coming from the bottle, she doubted the invention they were looking for was inside it anyway, so she shrugged and left it on the floor, deciding that it was best to leave it alone. She then resumed her search, coming to a shelf stacked with more magical instruments.

She rubbed her hand as she raked the shelves with her eyes, trying to concentrate on her task, but the bleeding steadily became heavier, and she was forced to stop once more and search for something to use as a bandage. Finding only a small white cloth that had been wrapped around a delicate glass invention, she used magic to clean it and tie it around her palm awkwardly.

"That'll have to do, I suppose," she sighed, wincing as she tightened the clumsy knot.

Half-listening to Mary talking animatedly on the other side of the room, Rose approached a set of narrow plywood shelves only to stop as a rustling sound disturbed the stillness somewhere behind her.

Mary shrieked in alarm.

"What is it?" called Rose, dreading the answer and thinking of dangerous objects again. She looked for a quick way through into their part of the room, and was on the point of going all the way around when Mary's voice wafted back to her, halting and uncertain.

"I swear one of the inventions over here moved on its own!"

Matt cackled with laughter.

"Don't worry, Rose, we're fine!"

"It was *you* making it move, wasn't it?" Rose heard Mary say accusingly. "You're just trying to scare me!"

Matt muttered something under his breath that sounded rather like "peace and quiet", and Rose rolled her eyes, resuming her search of the shelves. Finding nothing silver, she moved on to the last cabinet, sweeping her eyes over the mess of inventions crammed inside it. For the second time, Rose caught a flash of bright silver.

She moved closer and stood on tiptoe to peer over a collection of green, poisonous-looking candles on the top shelf, clustered in front of the little invention and almost shielding it from view. It was hard to be sure through the grimy door, but it looked like the silver piece the Clarifier had shown them.

Her heart beating fast now, she tried to open the case, but the door was locked. Realising it was probably protected by magic, Rose took the Dispeller out of her pocket, aimed it at the cabinet and covered her face with her free arm. She pressed the black button and the door exploded, sending tiny shards of glass cascading onto the floor. Tucking the Dispeller away again, she reached into the cabinet, doing her best to avoid the broken glass, and with more caution this time, picked the silver object up.

She recognised it immediately as the invention she'd taken from Grandpa's house after he'd disappeared. The silver shone, reflecting rainbow colours over its surface as she moved it. Holding it in her good hand, she was struck again by how small the invention was. It would be easy to lose if she wasn't careful.

Flushed with victory, she repaired the cabinet's glass door with a glance and whirled around, calling to Matt and Mary.

"I've got it! It's here!"

There was a distant crash followed by the sound of running footsteps. They appeared a moment later, their faces eager as they hurtled around the corner. Rose stumbled a little, suddenly feeling unsteady on her feet, and she grasped the edge of a crowded table beside her.

"You found it! I can't believe it!" Mary cried, her voice shrill as she took the silver invention and inspected it for herself. Matt beamed at the sight of it. He looked up at Rose, and the triumph on his face vanished as he noticed her ragged breathing and the sweat beading on her forehead.

"Are you OK?"

Rose nodded and tried to smile naturally.

"Yeah, just a little dizzy, that's all," she said.

She cringed, trying to ignore the throbbing pain in her hand and the nausea that had been steadily building, threatening to overcome her. She glanced down at her injured palm. The cloth tied around the wound was now soaked in blood. Rose tried to hide it behind her back, but the movement only attracted her sister's attention, and she groaned as Mary caught sight of the bloody cloth and stopped cheering. She snatched up Rose's hand.

"What did that to you?!"

"Oh, it was some stupid bottle I picked up," said

Rose, waving a vague hand towards the cabinets behind her. "If it even *was* a bottle. Maybe it was an invention after all."

True panic spread across Mary's face now, and Rose continued in a rush, "But my hand's really not that bad. I don't know why there's so much blood. It's just a few puncture wounds."

She dragged a stool out from underneath the table and sat down, telling herself she wasn't going to throw up. Five minutes later, however, it was clear to her that she was in trouble. The pain in her hand was getting worse and her breathing was becoming more laboured. She unwound the cloth gingerly and saw that the torn skin had developed a greenish tinge.

"Eurgh!" Mary backed away in disgust. "Is that normal?"

"Huh, that *is* strange," Rose muttered, looking at the skin with a mix of curiosity and fear.

Matt stared at the holes in her hand in silence, a look of dread stealing over his face.

"There could have been something weird inside that bottle," he said in a hollow voice.

Rose had been trying hard not to dwell on this unpleasant idea, but now a stab of terror ran through her. Her thoughts went back to the list of poisons and potions in the other room, and the page describing the symptoms of the test subject who'd lost a finger. Another wave of nausea struck her.

"I hope it's not any of those poisons in the other room," she gasped, her throat and chest constricting.

"They all looked pretty awful to me."

Mary blanched at this, and Matt said, "But even if the invention was poisoned, how could it make you sick so quickly? Wouldn't it take a while?"

"I don't know," gulped Rose between deep breaths. Mary moaned in anguish and turned back to the open door.

"We need Alison to come back! I don't know what to do! Maybe you should lie down?"

"Yeah, that sounds like a good idea," mumbled Rose, her eyelids starting to droop. She lowered herself onto the floor with her back against the leg of the table. She sat still to catch her breath, her head still spinning, and then lay down on the carpet, her heart hammering against her ribs.

"What are we going to do?" Mary asked Matt, watching Rose gasp for breath.

Rose looked up at them from the floor. Their outlines were growing vague and hazy, and everything was going quiet.

"Something weird is happening to her!"

Mary's voice sounded distant as Matt crouched down beside Rose.

"I know. It's not like her to pass out from such a small injury …"

His expression was grim as he cleaned the cloth and wrapped her hand back up again. Mary disappeared down one of the pathways and returned with another strip of cloth, which she tied tightly around Rose's elbow.

"Maybe it'll help if she's been poisoned," she said,

looking up at Matt, who nodded his approval.

Rose lay still, listening to them arguing about what to do next. She thought she heard Matt ask her something, but she couldn't make out the words. She opened her mouth to tell him so, but speech seemed to have become much more difficult than usual.

"We need Alison to come back!" repeated Mary, sounding angry now. "Why is she taking so long?"

Matt bent his head down close to Rose's and spoke loudly. "Lie still and try to calm down, Rose. We'll get you out of here."

Rose nodded listlessly and concentrated on slowing her heart rate. Several minutes passed, while Matt and Mary whispered to each other and checked her bleeding hand, but Rose wasn't listening. She could feel Mary wrapping spells around the wounds, but nothing she did could stem the flow of blood.

Finally, after what felt like hours, a clanging sound from down the hall announced Alison's return, and Rose hoisted herself up onto one shaky elbow. Miranda was with her, and Mary dragged them over to where Rose lay.

There was a sharp intake of breath as Alison unwrapped her hand, and she stared up at the two women as they began to work on the injury. Alison's face was deathly white and stood out clearly against the dark wall behind her. The last thing Rose remembered was Miranda leaning over her anxiously before everything went black and she heard no more.

14

The Infuser

Rose gradually became aware that she was lying on something soft. Voices whispered close beside her in low, anxious tones. Sunlight streamed through her eyelids, warming them, but she kept them closed, letting herself wake up slowly.

The whispering stopped and somebody drew close, tucking something soft under her injured palm. The small movement sent a wave of pain up her arm, but it faded quickly and she relaxed again, focusing on the voices now speaking again beside her.

"She's looking really sick. Why can't we take her to the hospital?"

"Because there isn't a single doctor trained in magical injuries anywhere near here, and I'm not sure if it's safe to move her with a long distance travel spell. She's lost a surprising amount of blood for such a small injury."

The voices became clearer as Rose came to, and she realised that Matt and Mary were arguing with Alison.

"Mum and Dad always healed us when we were hurt," said Mary matter-of-factly.

"There's a big difference between an everyday kind of magical injury and what's happening to Rose," replied

Alison, prompting a sound of impatience from Matt.

"But *why* isn't there a magical doctor here?" he persisted. "What do people do when they're injured, then?"

"Matt, there are almost no magical people left these days and very few of them become doctors. If someone is badly hurt, they just have to hope they can get themselves to a town or city that does have one."

"But that's the stupidest thing I've ever heard!" raged Matt, his voice getting louder.

Alison's words were soft and soothing when she spoke again, but Rose could hear the strain in her voice.

"I agree with you. But unfortunately, it's just how things are."

"Are you sure it's magic doing this to her?" Mary whispered.

"What else could it be?" said Alison. "Look at her hand. Have you ever seen a normal wound like that?"

"No."

"Do you think it's a magical poison hurting her? Or a curse?" asked Matt, his voice tight with fear.

Alison hesitated.

"It could be either. She said it was a bottle-like object that stabbed her, so it might also have been an invention with a nasty defensive spell. Or it could be a combination of those things."

"What's the difference between a normal poison and a magical one, anyway?" said Mary.

"Magical poisons are infused with spells. The poison will act differently depending on the spells used."

Silence fell again, but still Rose kept her eyes closed.

"She isn't going to die, is she?" said Mary in a trembling voice.

"No, she won't die. It won't be easy, but we'll find a way to heal her."

Rose felt that this was a good time to let the others know she was awake. She opened her eyes slowly, her lids heavy. Sunlight filtered through the trees outside and a gentle breeze floated in through the window beside her. She was lying on the sofa in Alison's living room, wrapped in blankets. Half a dozen cushions had been stacked behind her head, and something sticky tugged at the skin on her injured hand.

Alison, Matt and Mary crowded around her. As she stirred, she became aware of a dull, throbbing pain in her palm. She glanced down at it, expecting to see the blood-soaked rag she'd tied around it in Hunter's room, but it was gone, along with Mary's tourniquet. With a weak cackle of laughter, she turned her hand over. Someone had applied the entire box of magical plastic strips from the supplies store to her hand. She gazed blearily up at Matt and he grinned at her.

"You were right. They're useless."

Rose laughed again and tried to ignore the pain spreading to her elbow. She gave her brother a triumphant grin.

"Told you so," she teased. "Mind you, I'm not sure if this really counts as a minor cut or abrasion," she added, indicating the punctures on her palm.

Alison immediately began to fuss over her, tucking

the blankets in around her and adding more cushions.

"How are you feeling?"

Rose shifted into a sitting position, only to lower herself back down onto her cushions, gasping and taking deep, slow breaths.

"I'm fine. Just a bit queasy, that's all."

Alison hovered by the sofa, her fingers clutching the fabric.

"You're as pale as a sheet. How's your hand? I've got some painkillers here if you need them." She held out pills and a glass of water.

"Thanks."

Rose swallowed the pills and downed the water in one long gulp. She peeked under the plasters. Her skin was swollen and red, and a distinct greenish-yellow ring had developed around the wounds.

"Can you move your fingers?" Alison asked.

"They're a little stiff, but I can move them easily enough," replied Rose, bending and stretching them gingerly.

Alison nodded, relief spreading over her face.

"I can't believe all this trouble was caused by a few holes in my hand," grimaced Rose.

Alison met her eyes for only a second before looking down at Rose's plaster-covered hand.

"We think there might have been some kind of magical poison in the invention that hurt you. That's not a normal injury. Matt and Mary told me about what happened. They said you started to get sick a few minutes after you were hurt, and I don't know any regular poisons that work that fast, or cause you to bleed that much."

She met Rose's gaze properly now, her eyes full of concern. Rose's chest constricted with fear, and Alison seemed to guess what she was about to say.

"But don't worry, I'm going to call all of the hospitals. We'll find a magical doctor that can help."

Rose nodded and tried to feel optimistic, but she knew magical doctors were hard to find and even more expensive to pay for. She glanced at Matt and Mary's drawn and exhausted faces and decided to turn the conversation to something else.

"So you managed to get us all out of Hunter's room without any problems?" she asked, as Alison whisked out her phone. "What held you up? Were you trying to save Ben?"

"Yeah," said Alison tonelessly. "I got to Miranda's house as fast as I could and told her what had happened, but Hunter and his gang had already surrounded you by the time we got back to the Archives. We were hiding just around the corner on the stairs, trying to decide what to do. There were too many of them for us to fight off on our own and we couldn't afford to give you three away, locked in Hunter's room, so Miranda thought it would be best to wait for them to take Ben away. We tried to follow them when they grabbed him and began the travel spell, but we didn't get very far. All we know for sure is that they took him somewhere near a river."

"Ben's gone for sure, then?" said Rose with a frown.

"I'm afraid so."

Alison bowed her head, staring down at her phone. She found the number she wanted and got to her feet, her face set.

"But we have to concentrate on you now. I think I'll call the hospitals in Sydney first. One of them must have a magical doctor."

Rose, Matt and Mary watched as she walked into the kitchen and started dialling. Rose turned to her brother and sister.

"What happened after Alison and Miranda found us?"

"Well, after they'd stopped your hand from bleeding, they wanted to know what stabbed you, and Miranda went looking for the invention," explained Matt, his eyes shadowed. "We had to take you down to the reception area so that we could use a travel spell back here. You kind of woke up a bit when we tried to move you, but you didn't take very well to travelling. You threw up and then blacked out again. Alison was really worried."

"Miranda came to check on you about half an hour later," added Mary. Her eyes were red and puffy as though she'd been crying, and she was still wearing the clothes she'd worn the day before. "She said she'd come back later. She went through everything in Hunter's rooms, looking for the thing that hurt you."

Matt got to his feet and took a silver bottle from the side table near the television, using a levitating spell to move it, rather than picking it up.

"Is this what did the damage?"

Rose sat up with a start and groaned as a sharp pain throbbed somewhere behind her eyes.

"Yeah, that's it!"

She lay back down on her cushions. The bottle was just as plain and unremarkable in the morning light as it had been in the half-dark of Hunter's room, and she eyed it warily as Matt settled it on the floor in front of the sofa.

"So it is an invention, then?"

"Alison reckons it's an Infuser," Mary informed her.

"I wish I hadn't picked the stupid thing up," Rose grumbled. "I should have known better, especially after what happened to both of you. I hope Alison destroys it."

"She's going to," Matt insisted. "She's only waiting because she wants to learn what she can about the poison in the Infuser first. Miranda might stop her, though. She wants to use it as evidence against Hunter."

Rose nodded with satisfaction. She worked her good hand into her pocket and a cold sweat broke out on her brow. It was empty.

"Oh no! Where's Grandpa's silver invention? I thought I had it on me. I didn't lose it, did I? That's all we need!"

"No, it's OK, I took it when you passed out," Mary told her.

She summoned it with a spell and it appeared in her palm. She offered it to Rose, who picked it up eagerly. Sunlight glinted off the silver threads, dazzling her eyes and somehow reflecting all of the colours of the rainbow.

"Illusion spells," she said, suddenly realising. "This is covered in them."

"It makes sense, I suppose," said Matt.

He looked at the invention suspiciously as Rose turned it over in her hand, taking in all of its delicate details.

"I wonder how you use it. Has anyone tried yet?" she asked.

Mary shook her head.

"We've all been more worried about you."

They glanced up as Alison made an irritated sound and sat on the floor in front of Rose. Her cheeks were flushed as though she'd been arguing and her dark curls were turning into a tangled mess from all the times she'd run her hands through them in frustration.

"I can't find a magical doctor anywhere!" she raged. "And no one can tell me where to look! Only one hospital gave me a name, but they said he's retired now."

Alison took a deep breath, and some of the tension seemed to seep from her features.

"The receptionist said she'd get in touch with him and then call me back. Even if he can't help us himself, he might be able to tell us where to find someone who can. Until then, we'll have to manage on our own. I might take a closer look at this invention. The more information we have about it the better."

She levitated the Infuser like Matt had done, and after contemplating it in silence for a moment, she summoned a pencil and jabbed the invention hard. Nothing happened. She touched the pencil to the lid of the Infuser and needle-like spines erupted all over the bottle, spearing the pencil before shrinking back into smooth silver. The pencil fell to the floor, covered in tiny green-tinged holes.

"Whoa!" Matt shuffled backwards as the pencil rolled towards him. "That's nasty!"

"Yes." Alison stared at the Infuser, lost in thought. "I guess that explains why Hunter didn't want anyone at the Archives to find it. An invention like this should be in the high-security area."

Matt wrapped his shirt around his hand and picked up the pencil, carefully avoiding the green substance clinging to the holes.

"So the invention uses the spines like syringes to inject whatever is inside it," mused Alison. She worked on the invention, removing the defensive spells. "There. It should be safe to handle now."

She pressed a small silver button on the lid and the four upper compartments of the invention separated from the bottle. Each was connected to a hinge at the base, so that the compartments sat in a ring around the Infuser.

Rose leaned forward, dreading what she was going to find. The first part held only steaming water, and she guessed that, without any obvious heat source, magic must be heating it. The second contained a basket filled with soggy herbs. Alison drained them and turned to the next compartment.

Rose eyed it suspiciously, expecting to see more herbs, but this time the water, now a rich golden colour, had pooled and combined with a deep blue gel that shimmered with a metallic sheen, swirling thickly around the basket before draining into the fourth compartment, which held more of the same blue gel. The holes in these last two baskets were so small that the sparkling liquid dripped out slowly, creating the steady dripping sound Rose had noticed when she'd first encountered the invention.

Summoning a bowl from the kitchen, Alison opened the base of the Infuser, releasing one of the strangest substances Rose had ever seen. It poured over the silver side of the bottle, bright blue-green and glutinous, sticking slightly to the sides of the bowl. As Alison moved it, however, it seemed to become thinner, flowing faster and smoother, much more like water.

She set the bowl down and the substance came back together into a thick, sticky mass that glistened in the light. A crease appeared between Alison's eyebrows as she stared down at the poison, and her voice, when she spoke, was dull and flat.

"I've never seen anything like this before."

She pressed the silver button a second time and the compartments snapped shut, one on top of the other, re-assembling the bottle. Rose stared at the Infuser with resentment, rubbing her injured palm and feeling contaminated.

"What will we do if we can't find a magical doctor soon?"

"We'll find someone, don't worry," repeated Alison, her expression suddenly fierce. "We'll manage, no matter what happens."

Rose didn't answer. She glanced at the strange poison one last time before before turning away, trying to ignore the uneasy thoughts swirling inside her head.

Miranda arrived as they were having lunch, looking harassed but rather pleased about something. Cocoa jumped up off the rug and bounded over to the door, and Rose sat up straight, keen to hear her opinion on the mysterious green substance.

Rose was starving, having missed breakfast, not to mention dinner the previous day, and she filled her bowl to the brim with vegetable soup. Alison ushered Miranda into the living room, where Rose sat propped up on the sofa between Matt and Mary. She smiled and waved to her with her good hand. Miranda settled herself in one of the armchairs and accepted a cup of tea from Alison.

"I thought I'd check in to see how you were doing. The last time I saw you, you were still unconscious, and I have to admit I was starting to worry."

"I'm OK," Rose insisted. "Alison's been great. She's been running around for me all day, even though she doesn't have to."

Miranda smiled.

"I knew she'd take good care of you. And I'm glad you're eating."

"We took the Infuser apart and found something unusual inside it," Alison informed her, passing her the bowl of blue-green ooze and sitting on the edge of the other armchair. "I've never seen anything like it before. Do you know what it is?"

Miranda set her tea down and inspected the poison, tilting it this way and that. She moved it into a shaft of sunlight and it gave off an acrid, burning scent. Her expression changed from suspicion to alarm.

"I'm not sure what the blue-green stuff is, but I do know what's making it glitter." She gave the bowl back to Alison. "It's a modifier. A type of spell that alters the ingredients or spells mixed with it," she added, seeing Rose's confusion. "It's often used by the Guild to create particular magical reactions."

Her eyes flickered down to her cup of tea, her expression troubled.

"The spell breaks down over time, but it - it creates damage as it decays. They're not supposed to be used on people."

Rose's breath caught in her lungs.

"What kind of damage? Can we stop it?"

"The effect it has will depend on the type of modifier used and what it's mixed with," said Miranda in a low voice. "If the green liquid is normally a fast-acting substance, the modifier might slow it down, sometimes creating delayed damage. We can't be sure what the effects of this particular mixture are until we've tested it."

Rose gulped, hoping dearly that the green mixture wasn't the kind that caused prolonged symptoms.

"But there might be a quicker way of figuring out exactly what's in it," Miranda added. She opened her bag and produced a ragged blue book that Rose recognised at once.

"The list of poisons!" Mary blurted out.

Miranda gave her a look of surprise and Mary blushed.

"Uh, we went through most of Hunter's stuff," she

admitted with a sheepish grin.

Miranda gave the book to Alison, who flicked through it with a shudder, handling the pages as though they themselves were poisonous. When she reached the end of the book, however, her expression had become hopeful.

"This might be just what we need! How did you make him give this up?"

"I almost didn't," Miranda admitted. "It took a lot of persuasion. He's been furious ever since he found out the four of you got away when he thought he had you cornered. I had to search his rooms myself because Rose was injured and I'm legally required to investigate what did the damage. He's been threatening me all day, trying to keep me out, but as I keep telling him, I've got to go by the rules. What a shame."

She smiled at Matt and he snorted with laughter.

"I didn't have time to investigate everything in all three rooms, but judging from what I did find, he's got an awful lot of dangerous things hidden away in there," Miranda continued. "It's going to be a big job cataloguing it all, but we'll finally have enough concrete evidence to have him charged."

A dreamy expression came over Alison's face at the idea.

Miranda took another sip of tea and then added, "I've been thinking about that river we followed Ben to, and it seemed to me like Hunter's gang intended to stop somewhere close by. What do you think?"

Alison considered this for a moment, staring down

at the tattered blue book before tossing it onto the coffee table.

"It did seem like they were getting ready to stop, but I didn't think there were any buildings in that area. It's all just empty fields and bushland out that way, isn't it?"

Miranda raised an eyebrow. "Perhaps not."

"I didn't know you could follow people using a travel spell," remarked Mary. "How can you tell where they wanted to go?"

"Well, when you start a travel spell, you're concentrating on the place you want to go," said Alison. "And when you hitch-hike off the back of someone else's spell, sometimes you can see in your mind where that person is intending to travel to. I didn't see exactly where they were going, but I did get the feeling that they were almost there."

Matt fidgeted in his seat as the others talked, his face shining with eagerness.

"If they were taking Ben there, our family must be there, too!"

He beamed at Rose and Mary, and Rose couldn't help but grin back.

"We might have our first clue about where they are," said Alison.

Miranda's phone rang and she checked the number.

"It's Abbie at the Archives. I'd better go, but I'll come back again tomorrow to check on you all. And I'll think some more about that river. We might be able to work out where they were going."

"Thanks," called Rose, Matt and Mary as a chorus.

Rose waved again and Miranda disappeared down the garden path.

Under Alison's watchful eye, Rose spent the afternoon lying on the sofa with Cocoa curled protectively over her feet, keeping herself occupied with the silver invention. Matt and Mary sat on the floor beside her, and the three of them took turns attempting to activate it.

They worked on the invention for hours, using every combination of activation spells and words they could think of, but it seemed determined to keep its secrets hidden. Rose soon found a way to make it hum quietly with energy, but they were all certain that this was not what they wanted.

More than once, they attempted to persuade Alison to help them. Rose was sure that she could be of great use to them, seeing as she did this kind of thing each day at the Archives, but she was too preoccupied with Rose's hand to spare much attention for the silver invention.

"As long as we have it, the Fragmenter's safe," she'd said when they'd asked her for the third time what she would do to activate it.

This irritated Matt and Mary, who were eager to retrieve the Fragmenter and turn their attention to finding their family. Guilt gnawed at Rose whenever she thought of the trouble she'd already caused Alison, and she was grateful for everything she'd done to make her comfortable. Therefore, she didn't badger her about the silver invention. Instead, she lay on the sofa and did as she was told while Alison cleaned the wounds and applied a fresh dressing.

Rose sighed and twirled the invention between her fingers, reminding herself of the first magic lessons she'd been given as a young child. Her parents had taught her that most inventions were activated either by touch, like her own Viewer, by speaking a particular word, or by performing a particular spell. She also knew that, like her parents, Grandpa mostly used touch, so that when they sold an invention to a non-magical person, they were able to use it.

The problem with this was that Grandpa would never have intended for a non-magical person to use the silver invention, and would therefore have been more likely to use a spell to activate it. This made their job much harder, and Rose sat for hours going over all of Grandpa's favourite spells in her mind, trying them on the invention one by one.

When each of these failed, she returned to non-magical methods out of desperation, tapping the invention here and there, commanding it to activate and rubbing it between her fingers, hoping for some kind of response. She even tried tickling it. Matt especially became more and more frustrated by their lack of progress, and when he finally suggested they try kicking it across the room, Rose decided they'd done enough for today and tucked the invention into her pocket.

She felt well enough to join the others at the dinner table that evening. Her stomach grumbling, she shovelled down her pasta as though she hadn't eaten in days. Alison's phone rang as they were clearing the dishes away. She answered it on the first ring and went into the hall.

Rose helped Matt pile up the plates, her nerves returning as she awaited the verdict. A moment later Alison reappeared in the room, her fingers drumming against her leg, betraying the look of forced calm on her face.

"That was the hospital I called this morning," she said. "Only two magical doctors in the country are still practising and they're both booked out. There's no way they can fit in another patient right now."

Rose's heart sank. She clutched her plate, trying just as unsuccessfully as Alison to hide her disappointment.

"My hand doesn't even hurt anymore. Maybe I'll get better on my own, without a doctor?

But Alison dismissed this idea with a shake of her head.

"I'd much rather have someone check that you're OK."

She lowered herself onto the sofa and put her head in her hands. Rose looked at Matt and Mary in surprise and hurried around the dining room table. She sat beside Alison, accidentally dislodging several cushions, and put her good arm around her shoulders.

"It's all right, Alison, we'll find someone else."

Matt stood behind the sofa awkwardly, apparently unsure what to say.

"This is all my fault!" Alison wailed, wiping her eyes with the back of her hand. "I should never have let any of you near that room!"

"But you tried to stop us going in, remember?" pressed Mary, sitting on Alison's other side. "You didn't want us to go in there! We nagged you until you gave up and let us come!"

"Yeah, we forced you to let us in," agreed Matt, finally finding his voice.

"That's no excuse!" insisted Alison. "This is why Archivists have to be trained before they can go into rooms like that. They're not places you should take children. I should have refused, no matter what you said."

"Do you really think we'd have listened?" challenged Matt, his voice heavy with scepticism. "I probably would have found a way in anyway."

He had the grace to look ashamed at this.

"Alison, it's my fault for picking the invention up in the first place!" urged Rose. "You told us so many times that it'd be dangerous in Hunter's room. I'm the one who was stupid enough to touch the Infuser!"

But Alison remained inconsolable.

"I should have been with you. All I can do now is make sure that you get better. I'll start calling hospitals again first thing in the morning. If I have to get a doctor from overseas, I will."

She gave them all ice cream for dessert and then ordered Rose to bed. Rose obediently changed into her pyjamas and climbed under the thick blankets Alison had piled on the bed, despite the summer heat.

Rose lay back and tucked the blankets in around herself, listening to the sounds of the others clearing away dinner. She really did feel almost normal again. The pain in her hand had ebbed away, but she was exhausted. The moon rose slowly outside her bedroom window and Rose tried to keep her mind off doctors and mysterious blue-green substances, sinking into a deep, dreamless sleep.

15

Breakthrough

Rose was still tired when she woke the next day. Cocoa had draped himself over her legs during the night, and she dragged herself out from underneath him with difficulty. She sat down at the table with Matt and Mary and buttered a slice of toast one-handed.

"You're not looking so good this morning," Matt informed her, surveying her over his cereal. "Maybe you should go back to bed."

Rose rubbed her eyes and picked up her toast.

"I can't sleep when everyone else is up. I feel like I should be doing something. I hate just lying around."

Alison bustled into the kitchen, checking her phone as she approached the table. She asked Rose to hold out her hand for inspection and Rose complied, peeling the bandage off to reveal the mess of holes in her palm. The greenish colour that had covered it yesterday had now spread along her fingers and down to her wrist. Glancing up, she saw Alison's lips press into a thin line, but they both remained silent and Alison continued to clean the skin thoroughly, applying a fresh dressing before wrapping up the wounds once more.

Rose picked up her toast but stopped before she could take another bite. Flinging her chair back, she ran for the kitchen, reaching it just in time to throw up in the sink. Alison hurried over and cleaned the mess up with a spell, wrapping a comforting arm around Rose's shoulders.

"The symptoms are getting worse, aren't they? Do you want something to drink instead? A glass of water might help."

Rose shook her head. Icy cold and trembling all over, she avoided Alison's eyes.

"That's OK. I think I will go back to bed after all."

Matt and Mary gave her looks of sympathy as she tottered past the table and back to her room. Her hand was beginning to hurt again, and she tried not to use it as she clambered awkwardly back into bed. Staring up at the ceiling, she tried not to think about what Miranda had said about modifiers. Alison was right. Her symptoms were getting worse, not better, and if they couldn't find a magical doctor soon …

Rose rolled onto her side and focused on the sound of the television down the hall, hoping to distract herself. She drifted in and out of consciousness for the rest of the day, occasionally catching Matt, Mary or Alison leaning around the door to check on her. The last thing she remembered before slipping back into a light, restless sleep was the music announcing the late-night news.

It was late afternoon when she opened her eyes the next day. She staggered out of bed, not noticing until she pulled fresh clothes out of her bag that her hand was no longer hurting. The pain had been replaced with an icy numbness that made it difficult to move her fingers. The skin felt rubbery and strange, and peeking under her bandages, she saw her palm had now turned a sickly yellow. Trying to keep calm, she dressed clumsily and joined the others in the living room.

Matt and Mary had already finished lunch and were playing with Cocoa while Alison sat tensely on the sofa, reading the tattered blue book from Hunter's room. There were shadows under her eyes and her shoulders were slumped. It was clear that she hadn't got much sleep last night, either.

"Ah! You're awake!"

She stood up, seeming to guess that something was wrong as Rose entered the room. She sighed in a defeated kind of way as Rose told her what had happened, and began her daily routine of cleaning the wounds before covering them with a fresh bandage.

"I had an idea last night that might help us," she said as she worked. "But I want your permission before I do anything. You're the one who's injured, after all." She pinned the end of the bandage in place and closed the first aid kit with a snap. "Do you remember me telling you about the invention that grew teeth and bit Ben when he and I were both still apprentices at the Archives?"

Rose nodded, thinking of the scars on the back of Ben's hand.

"Our supervisor dealt with the invention, but he also took care of Ben to make sure there was no magical damage to his hand before sending him to the hospital to get stitches."

Matt and Mary looked up at this, their faces full of hope.

"He's retired and an old man now, and he's not well himself," Alison continued in a rush, "and he's definitely not an expert on poisons -"

"But he must have dealt with loads of weird injuries, especially if he worked in the Archives for a long time!" interrupted Mary, scrambling up off the carpet. She'd been playing tug-of-war with Cocoa when Rose had emerged, but now that her attention was elsewhere, Cocoa gave a joyful bark and tugged the short length of rope out of her hand, bounding across the room with it.

"He was there for decades, but as I said, he's not a doctor," replied Alison. "He started studying magical medicine when he was young, but he quit to join the Guild, so he didn't finish his training and he doesn't have access to antidotes or any other supplies we might need."

Rose turned to her brother to see what he thought. He gave her an encouraging nod.

"It's not like we have any other options. I say it's worth a go."

"It wouldn't hurt to at least show him," agreed Mary.

Alison picked up the first aid kit.

"It's your decision, Rose. If you want me to ask him, I will."

Rose didn't hesitate.

"I think we should try, like Mary said. If he can't help, then we're back to where we are now, that's all."

The tension in Alison's shoulders seemed to ease.

"All right, then. I'll call him now."

Pulling her phone out of her pocket, she disappeared down the hall, returning a moment later with a weary smile.

"I described your symptoms to him, Rose, and he thinks he might be able to help."

Warmth flooded Rose's body.

"That's great!"

"He wants us all to stay with him," Alison said. "He's not well enough to travel often and there's not enough room for everyone here, so it'll be easier for him to treat you if we stay at his house."

"Oh. Maybe we shouldn't be bothering him if he's that unwell."

Rose tugged at her bandages, suddenly uncertain. But Alison shook her head, summoning a travelling bag and packing the blue book from Hunter's room into it.

"He seems excited at the idea of having company. I think he gets lonely living by himself. I go to visit him as often as I can, but sometimes I don't get the chance."

"Are you friends, then?" asked Matt. "What's his name? Would we know him?"

"His name's Nathaniel, but most people call him Nate, and I guess he's more like a parent to me than a friend," replied Alison. "He trained me when I started at the Archives. My dad died when I was five and Nate never had kids. His wife died years ago and he doesn't have any close family left, so when he got sick there was no one to take care of him. He spent a lot of his time alone, so I started checking on him to see how he was doing and helping him when he needed it."

"That was kind of you," said Rose, watching her transfer the poison from the bowl into a container. Alison smiled and packed the container in the bag, too.

"We got along well and I felt sorry for him. Besides, I was always a bit of a loner, so the company was good for me, too. Anyway, let's pack some clothes and then we can go. The sooner Nate starts work on your hand, the better."

Matt and Mary went back to their rooms while Alison helped Rose pack up her things. Matt called Cocoa to him with a whistle.

"Will Nate mind if Cocoa comes with us?"

"No, he likes dogs," replied Alison. "He's got a huge backyard, more like the one you've got at home. Cocoa will love it there."

Matt took hold of the dog's collar and they prepared to leave. Alison wrapped them all in a travel spell and a moment later they appeared beside a small iron gate. Rose leaned against it, her head swimming and her stomach heaving. Alison looked at her closely, as though afraid she might pass out again.

"Travel spells often make people feel worse when they're unwell," she said, holding Rose steady. "They're a bit disorienting."

Rose took a deep breath and smiled at Alison to show that she was fine. Unlatching the gate, she led the way down a paved driveway towards a modest, two-storey house with a lawn even larger than her parents'.

"This yard is huge!" she cried, her gaze wandering over the expanse of grass to the sweeping view of the city centre in the distance. The house, too, reminded her of home, from the weather-beaten façade to the dormer windows. This house, however, sported a small conservatory and a greenhouse, just visible on the other side of the building. Matt stared across the grounds with wide eyes.

"He lives here all by himself?"

"It is a bit much for one person," Alison admitted, "but it's been in his family for a long time and he's very fond of it. I don't think he'd ever sell it."

"I don't blame him!" said Mary. "I wouldn't either!"

Rose's heart sank at the thought of anyone living alone and unwell in such an isolated place. With a sigh, she followed the others down the driveway, glad that he at least had Alison for company.

Alison led them over to a wooden door with decorative glass panels and rang the doorbell. Soon Rose heard the sound of shuffling footsteps and an elderly man appeared in the doorway, leaning heavily on a walking stick and beaming at Alison.

"It's wonderful to see you," he said as she hugged him.

"Thanks for agreeing to help. We really appreciate it."

But the old man shook his head, turning his gaze on Rose, Matt and Mary.

"It's no problem. I'll do everything I can."

Alison stood back, pointing out each of them.

"This is Rose, Matt and Mary."

Rose gave Nate an awkward smile. She looked into his thin, pale face and once again wondered if she was right to intrude.

"Come in! Come in!" he said, beckoning them inside. "I'll show you around. You can settle in and then we can get down to business!"

Alison closed the door behind them and they followed Nate down a hallway decorated with pictures of people Rose assumed must be his family. She studied him as they walked down the hall. As Alison had warned them, he had the look of someone who had been unwell for a long time.

His skin was sallow and his hair was snowy white and wispy, but his eyes were sharp and calculating and he moved around the room with an air of determination and independence despite the walking stick clutched in his hand. He shuffled along at a surprisingly rapid pace, seeming happy enough as he chatted to them.

He led them through to a comfortable living room. The view of the city was clearer from here and Rose stared out at the distant cluster of rooftops glinting in the morning sun before turning to follow the others down another hall. They passed a small library and study that overlooked the garden and then headed upstairs, using a travel spell for Nate's sake.

Rose decided to take the stairs rather than risk being sick again, joining them a moment later on the landing, where Nate indicated a row of five bedrooms and allowed them to put their luggage away. The rooms were airy and well kept, but it was clear that most of them were rarely used.

Glass cases containing magical instruments and manuscripts lined the walls everywhere Rose looked, giving her the impression that she was in a strange kind of magical museum. Breathing in the faint scent of polished wood, she peered into each room as she followed Nate downstairs, past a cramped laundry and out into the backyard.

The greenhouse she'd spotted earlier took up most of one corner of the yard and appeared to be filled with ferns and other tropical plants. The other end of the yard contained a paved area, where a pool was fenced off and sheltered by a shade sail. Matt and Mary's faces lit up with excitement at this last discovery.

"Wow, you've got a pool? We've always wanted one at home, but Mum and Dad said no!"

Rose took another deep breath, enjoying the open, airy space. It was bare except for a single ash tree and a collection of tidy garden beds clustered around the greenhouse. With Nate's permission, Matt removed Cocoa's leash and they let him stretch his legs while they returned to the house.

"All right, then," wheezed Nate, lowering himself onto the sofa. "Let's have a look at your injury, if you don't mind, Rose."

Rose hesitated before unwrapping her hand. She'd never been to a magical doctor before, even a partially-trained one, and she wasn't sure what to expect.

"Why don't you tell me about how you got hurt?" suggested Nate, while Matt and Mary crowded around the sofa.

Alison stood behind them, out of the way, and Rose glanced up at her, unsure if she should tell Nate the whole truth about what had happened. But Alison nodded encouragingly, and so she gave a brief description of her encounter with the Infuser. Listing all of her symptoms, she tried not to let the fear in her voice show as she described how the invention had attacked her. Nate bent over her hand, examining the needle-like holes in her skin.

"My hand turned a yellowish colour this morning. Now everything is numb up to my wrist."

Rose's words tumbled out in a rush. She waited for him to speak, half expecting him to put her bandages back on and announce that there was nothing he could do, but Nate's face remained impassive as he asked her to flex her fingers, and Rose hoped that this was a positive sign.

Alison opened her bag, pulling out the container of poison and the herbs she'd extracted from the Infuser, along with the tattered blue book.

"I've destroyed the invention that did the damage, but I kept these so that you could study them."

Nate took the poison first, moving it around the container and watching the curious way it flowed like water before coming back together into a sticky mass.

"I'm afraid I have no idea what it is," he said. "I'll have to run some tests to find out more. But Miranda was right. The metallic sheen is a sure sign of a modifier." He set the container aside and sniffed at the herbs, separating them with the cloth Alison had wrapped them in. "Fortunately, I've got something that can identify most poisons and their components."

He summoned a small golden invention and folded out a delicate mesh grille. Fascinated, Rose leaned in and saw a range of attachments tucked into each side.

"Hey, that's cool," said Matt admiringly, as Nate held the grille up to Rose's hand and moved it over her palm like a metal detector.

"It was given to me when I started medical school," Nate chuckled. "Pieces like this are useful, but they're getting harder to find. There are very few magical inventors left these days, and there are even fewer with medical knowledge."

After a moment the golden grille began to glow. Rose opened her mouth to ask if this was a good thing, but stopped herself, allowing him to work in peace. He tried the next tiny golden attachment, holding it over Rose's hand for a second or two before moving on to the next until he'd used them all. He placed the invention carefully on the table, his face unreadable.

"Well, the first attachment resonated clearly with the poison, so that gives us a lead to follow, but overall it means that this must be a new creation. Not surprising, seeing as it was in Hunter's room. He's always been an experimenter. At the very least, that shortens our list of suspects."

He picked up the blue book and scanned the first page, his expression becoming increasingly stern as he did so. He turned to Alison.

"This was in Hunter's room, too?"

Alison gave a hesitant nod, fiddling with the cushions on the sofa.

"In the first hidden room, with the documents."

Nate looked down at the lists again with a disapproving frown. His eyes swept over the neat handwriting.

"All of these substances are prohibited, either because they do terrible things or because their effects aren't fully understood," he murmured. "I can't believe he'd even consider exposing a person to them."

Rose's stomach lurched as though she'd missed several steps going downstairs.

"Do - do you think the green stuff is one of them, then?" she gulped.

"No, I don't," said Nate confidently. "The invention I used a moment ago would have detected all of these."

He gave her a warm smile, his blue eyes full of reassurance.

"So how do we find out what's making Rose sick?" prompted Mary, peering over the back of the sofa with her hands tucked under her chin.

"First we'll run some tests on that green mixture," said Nate. "I'll get them running now. They'll take a few hours at least, so the sooner I get them going the better. Then we can concentrate on stopping the poison from doing any more damage. If your sister is feeling sick and lethargic it must have spread quite a bit already."

Leaning on his walking stick, he prised himself off the sofa and shuffled off towards the study, taking the container of sticky green ooze with him. Rose, Matt and Mary watched with curiosity as he hobbled past. He stopped and turned, and with another chuckle, gestured for them all to follow him.

Matt and Mary hurried over to his side and Rose got to her feet, keen to see what would happen next. Alison followed him to the study too, standing in the doorway while Nate moved the books on the desk to one side. His breathing became more laboured as he opened a narrow cupboard beside the window, revealing a collection of bottles, jars and other pieces of equipment.

"I don't do much experimenting or testing these days, but I still have some of the things I used as a student," he said between coughs, allowing Alison to take down a tripod, a set of beakers and some paper strips from the top shelf for him.

She placed the beakers in a row on the desk and Nate poured a small amount of the poison into each before turning back to the cupboard and picking out three glass jars containing what Rose could only assume were ingredients.

The energy around these ingredients told her that they contained powerful spells, and having never seen anyone experiment with magic like this, she crowded around the desk with Matt and Mary as Nate unscrewed the lid of a jar containing an orange powder.

"What are they for?" asked Mary, standing on tiptoe with her elbows on the desk.

"They'll help separate and identify the components that my invention didn't detect. Watch what happens when I add them to the beakers."

Taking a pinch of the powder, Nate sprinkled it into the first beaker. The poison began to react the second the powder made contact, glowing a fluorescent green which sparkled like glass for a moment before growing dark and dull, making the modifier's metallic sheen much easier to see.

He did the same with the next ingredient, adding a rich purple bead the size of a marble to the second beaker. The bead dissolved rapidly, transforming the poison into a dark, inky substance that rippled like water disturbed by a light breeze.

Finally, Nate placed a gauze mat over the tripod and set the last beaker on top before opening a jar containing dark brown curls of something that resembled shredded bark. He extracted a single curl from the jar with tweezers and added it to the beaker, stirring briskly with a spoon. The mixture hissed and bubbled, emitting a strong earthy scent.

Rose could feel the heat coming off it from where she stood, and she took a step back as the concoction began to spit violently. Nate packed the glass jars of ingredients away and inspected the bubbling, rippling and sparkling beakers with a satisfied expression. He checked his watch.

"They should be ready by about six o'clock. The spells in the ingredients work best when they're left to stew for a few hours. Until then, let's go back to the living room and I'll see if I can do anything to stop the modifier in your hand breaking down any further."

Rose nodded and followed him out of the room, attempting to squash the unwelcome thoughts that had pushed themselves to the forefront of her mind. What if there was no way to reverse the damage? She shuddered to think what kind of condition her hand would be in if things kept going the way they had been, but she banished these fears and placed her hand on the armrest of the sofa while Nate got to work.

It was nothing like visiting a normal doctor. Nate worked with his eyes closed, but it seemed to Rose that he could see past the skin on her hand, right down to the blood vessels and tissues. The sun had disappeared behind the trees and Mary had begun to fidget in her seat when Nate finally stopped and opened his eyes.

"That will have to do for today, I think." He leaned back in his chair, his face lined with exhaustion. "The modifier and the poison have already spread through your entire body. In this case, it appears that the modifier is causing the poison to spread much faster than normal, which is why it had such a strong effect on you right away. However, it's only started to break down up to your elbow, and that's what's creating the swelling and numbness. I did what I could to stop it going any further for now, but the spells won't stop it causing more damage from your elbow down. They'll keep the modifier in the rest of your body from breaking down for a few days, though, so that gives us some extra time to work out how to get rid of the poison properly."

Rose flexed her fingers again gingerly.

"Thanks. It actually feels a bit better."

The swelling had gone down a little, making it easier for her to move. Nate smiled and checked his watch again.

"Our ingredients will have finished stewing by now. They should be able to tell us something."

He got to his feet again and they followed him back to the study. The moon was rising outside the window, sending weak shafts of light into the room, but the three beakers glowed on the desktop. Instead of bubbling and rippling, they were now perfectly still, awaiting the next stage of the experiment.

Nate picked up the paper strips and inserted one into each beaker. The strips changed colour where they met the ingredients, becoming a muted yellow, a muddy purple and a dark rosy pink.

"These will tell us what the poison is made up of," he said, shuffling to the cupboard and searching the shelves before picking out a small invention with a series of open slots along one side. It looked rather like a harmonica, except for the screen that ran across its length.

Nate inserted another paper strip into the container of poison, coating the end with green goo before feeding the end of each strip into the side of the invention. He pressed a white button and Rose bit her lip as the invention began to analyse the samples, humming gently while a light flashed on one end.

"Not long to go now," he murmured, watching the screen. "Soon we'll know what we're dealing with."

Only a second later the light flashed green and Nate

read the text that had appeared on the screen. His eyebrows shot up.

"Well, we have a clear result. The poison is plant based, the active ingredient being Arnica. But the biggest cause of the trouble is the combination of spells that the Arnica has been infused with. There are eight, including the modifier."

Rose glanced at Alison, about to ask if this was unusual for magical poisons, when Alison said, "But will they be difficult to treat? That's a lot of spells, and they'll all be interacting with each other …"

Nate shook his head.

"The effects of these particular spells can be stubborn once they've taken hold, but if I use the right magic to deal with them, Rose will be fine. Arnica is definitely toxic when it's ingested, but I can counter that with magic, too."

Alison breathed a sigh of relief, and Rose relaxed for the first time since she'd been injured.

"The work I've done should be enough to stop the poison from spreading for now, but we'll continue first thing in the morning." Nate turned to Rose with another smile. "The best thing you can do right now is to get some rest."

Rose nodded, feeling drained despite having done very little. Thanking Nate for everything he'd done, she dragged herself up the stairs in search of the airy bedrooms she'd seen earlier.

She slept badly again, unable to get comfortable because

of the stinging, tingling sensation in her hand. She was relieved when morning finally arrived and sounds of movement could be heard downstairs. The numbness in her hand had now travelled up to her elbow, but thanks to Nate's work the night before, it had gone no further.

Her fingers were clumsy and stiff, and she dressed with difficulty, trying not to worry about what would happen if Nate was unable to reverse the damage permanently. She found Matt and Mary in the living room, watching the morning cartoons, and Alison in the kitchen, making breakfast.

"Good morning," she said as Rose pulled a tall stool out from beneath the counter. "Would you like some cereal? Or do you think toast would be better?"

Rose turned away from the milk, already feeling queasy.

"Toast is safer, I think."

She accepted a slice from the stack Alison offered her, and took a tentative bite. She'd managed to eat three pieces without any trouble and was beginning to feel a little better when Matt joined them in the kitchen to pour himself a glass of orange juice. Rose took one look at the glass in his hand and threw up all over his feet as he passed her.

"Urgh, Rose!"

Matt turned away, looking revolted.

"Yeah, Rose, he can't help what he looks like," teased Mary, pinching her nose.

"I'm sorry, Matt!" gasped Rose. "I didn't mean to!"

Alison vanished the mess, leaving Matt clean and dry.

"Give me some warning before you do that!" he told Rose, shaking his head as he walked away.

"Just sit quietly for a minute and you'll be OK," insisted Alison, pulling Rose's hair out of her face.

Nate shuffled in from in the garden a moment later with Cocoa at his heels. He was carrying a bunch of fresh herbs, which he set on the kitchen table. He peered at Rose, taking in her half-eaten piece of toast and the pinched look of her face, and seemed to understand.

"These herbs should help," he said, washing them in the sink. "I'll make a salve for you to put on the wounds, and something for you to drink, too."

Rose nodded, willing to try anything that might help. Nate used magic to cut up the herbs before adding them to a bowl of steaming water, leaving them to soak while he led a pale and trembling Rose into the conservatory at the front of the house.

"I thought we might work in here today."

He lowered himself into a padded chair and Rose did the same, looking around with interest. Plants filled the room in pots and hanging baskets, and sunlight streamed in through the windows, warming Rose's back. A cluster of showy orchids sat beside her armrest and she admired their bright colours before turning back to Nate. Cocoa joined them, his eyes closing as he lounged lazily in the sun beside Rose's chair.

Nate propped his walking stick against a nearby table and got to work, using spells that targeted the magical part of the poison directly this time. Rose stared out of the window, watching Matt and Mary race each other across the wide stretch of lawn.

After a minute or two Alison drifted into the room, looking preoccupied. She sat on the edge of the chair beside Rose, observing Nate's work for a moment before getting to her feet again and wandering restlessly between the plants. Nate looked up at her, a small smile on his face as she completed another circuit of the room, twirling a strand of her dark, curly hair around a finger.

"Perhaps it would be best if you took your mind off Rose's injury for a while," he suggested, his voice gentle. "Worrying isn't going to help either of you."

Alison blinked and stopped in her tracks.

"You're right," she said with a frown. "I was thinking last night that it was time I started tracking Hunter and his gang again. The Fragmenter is safe now that we have the silver invention, so we can concentrate on finding Ben and your family, Rose."

Rose looked up at her eagerly.

"Really? Do you want to borrow my Viewer?"

She summoned it from her bag and held it out to Alison. Alison smiled and slipped it into her pocket.

"Thanks. I think I'll explore the bushland along that river we tracked them to first. Miranda was certain they were going to stop somewhere there."

Nate gave Alison a look of concern.

"I don't like the idea of you tracking Hunter and his friends through the bush on your own. It's dangerous, and it would be difficult to find you if you got into trouble. Maybe you should ask Miranda to go with you? I'm sure she wouldn't mind."

"All right, then," said Alison peaceably. "If she doesn't have time, I'll come back."

She waved at them both and disappeared. Rose turned back to Nate, excitement bubbling up inside her.

"I hope she finds something."

A lump formed in her throat as she spoke.

"So do I," said Nate, his normally sharp eyes soft and sad.

"Well, that's about all I can do with conventional medical magic," he continued, distracting Rose from her thoughts. "But, if I have your permission, I think I might be able to create a new spell to remove the poison. It will take some experimenting to find the right one, but I think we'll have more success that way."

Rose stared at him in surprise.

"Sure, I don't mind. But I've never met anyone who could make their own spells before."

Nate shrugged as though inventing new magic was nothing special.

"It's a skill most people learn when they train with the Guild."

"I didn't know the Guild did that kind of thing, either," added Rose, thinking of the grey streaks in the bricks at the Archives. "I thought they made new magical materials and things like that."

"They do, but to make the new materials and do their experiments they often need to do magic that hasn't been done before, and that means creating new spells," explained Nate. "They're brilliant spellmakers. It was my favourite thing to do when I studied there. You can make a spell do almost anything, provided you can imagine it first and see the result you want clearly in your mind. I'll show you."

Rose watched, fascinated, as he created new spells on the spot. They came and went as he cancelled them and formed others, apparently with ease. He gave her a wide smile, chuckling at her obvious astonishment.

Nate continued to invent and test spells to draw out the poison until midday, when it became too hot to sit in the conservatory. As they got up to move into the shade, Rose heard a clatter of feet in the hall outside and turned to find her brother and sister standing in the doorway, their faces flushed from running. They grinned at Rose and approached Nate's chair. Matt nudged Mary forward.

"Would it be OK if we went swimming in your pool, please?" Mary asked, stepping up to Nate shyly.

Nate laughed.

"Of course! I'm glad someone's using it. No one's been in it since my great-nephews visited two years ago."

"Thanks!" said Matt and Mary together.

Rose rolled her eyes.

"I was wondering how long it would take them to ask."

Nate glanced at a clock on a shelf beside a hanging vine-like plant. "I think it's about time we took a break, anyway. Do you want to go swimming, too? I can put some spells on your bandages so that they stay dry if you like."

Rose shook her head, her mind lingering on the impressive collection of spell books in Nate's study.

"That's OK, it'll be nice just to sit in the shade with a book."

"No, come in with us!" Mary protested, taking hold of Rose's good hand and towing her down the hall to the back door.

"Maybe I'll put my feet in, then," Rose conceded with a laugh as Matt vaulted the fence, ran to the edge of the pool and threw himself in fully dressed.

"I don't even remember the last time we went for a swim!" he said, shaking water out of his eyes.

Nate came to sit in one of the chairs under the shade sail, beaming as Matt and Mary raced each other up and down the pool. Rose rolled up the legs of her jeans and sat on the edge, dangling her feet in the water and doing her best to avoid most of the splashing.

Alison returned not long after, accompanied by Miranda. They stood by the pool looking tired but pleased.

"Did you find anything?" Rose asked them.

"Well, we followed Jacob and that mean guy who always wears black for most of the morning, and listened to their conversations," replied Alison, giving Rose her Viewer back. "They didn't mention where your family is being kept, so we started tracking them like we did when they took Ben away. We couldn't find the place they kept returning to, but we're sure now that it's close to Stony River."

"We'll take a closer look at the area tomorrow, now that we know roughly where to search," said Miranda. "The river covers a lot of land, but it's a place to start."

Alison retreated inside with Miranda and Nate. Rose spun the Viewer in her palm, wishing she'd paid more attention in geography class and trying to remember how big the Stony River was. If it covered as much land as Alison and Miranda said, how were they ever going to find her family and Ben?

She glanced down at the Viewer, twirling in the sunlight. It would take a long time to investigate all of the bushland in the area, and her invention hadn't been able to locate her family like she'd hoped it would. She sighed as Matt and Mary tossed water in each other's faces, and a knot formed in her throat again. Her thoughts were cut short, however, when Mary decided to splash Rose, too. Sopping wet, Rose shook the water out of her hair with a laugh.

"I think that's my cue to go back inside."

She tucked the Viewer into her pocket and clambered to her feet, tiptoeing upstairs and along the hall to her bedroom, trying not to drip water on the floorboards. She sat on the edge of the bed and pulled her travelling bag towards her to search for dry clothes.

Her hand found the silver invention first. She set it aside and continued her search, pulling out a mixture of clothes and her grandmother's book of advanced magic. It already felt like an age had passed since Mum had given it to her. Tears prickled in her eyes as she found what she was looking for and changed.

Without thinking, she pulled the Viewer out of her soaked jeans pocket with her injured hand and reached out to place the invention on the bedside table. She fumbled with it for a second before it slipped through her numb fingers and fell onto the hardwood floor, smashing the glass pupil and dislodging the pins that held the pieces together. The spells on the invention broke as it came apart, the rings rolling across the floor and coming to a stop underneath the wardrobe.

Rose cursed and got to her knees, summoning the remains of the Viewer to her with a spell. They zoomed into her hands and she looked down at them ruefully, wondering if it was worth repairing the invention. It had taken months to get it the way she wanted and it still hadn't been able to find her family. Deciding she'd had enough this time, she scooped up the remains and put them in the wastepaper bin under the desk.

With a small sigh of disappointment, she closed her bedroom door and went back into the living room. Alison and Miranda were at the table talking over coffee while Nate worked on something in the kitchen. He beckoned to her as she entered the room, and she joined him beside the sink.

Two bottles of clear liquid stood before her. Nate took a collection of ingredients from the pantry and combined them in a bowl over the stovetop to make a white cream. Scooping the herbs out of the bowl of water, he shook them off and set them aside, adding the water to the cream in small amounts. Rose breathed in the fresh, clean scent of the herbs as he stirred the mixture. Then he began to add spells to the salve, blending them with the other ingredients.

"Let's have a look at the wounds now," he said,

spooning the salve into a jar. He tapped the jar and the salve rapidly cooled to room temperature. Rose took the dressing off her hand and held out her palm, allowing Nate to apply a small amount of salve to the broken skin.

"It doesn't sting, I hope?" he asked, wrapping her hand up once more. Rose shook her head.

"No, it feels cool and soothing."

"Excellent. Now I want you to drink some of this."

He poured a measure of the clear liquid into a glass. Rose sipped it, and her eyebrows shot up.

"It tastes good. Like mint tea."

Nate nodded in a satisfied kind of way.

"I'd like for you to drink some twice a day. It will counteract the magic in the poison and help to stop the modifier in the rest of your body from breaking down like it has in your hand. I also want to try out some more spells to draw out the poison, just to speed things along. We'll find something that works soon, I'm sure of it. I might try again first thing in the morning, to give the salve and the tonic time to start working."

"OK, thanks," she said gratefully as Nate stored both concoctions in the fridge.

Alison called Matt and Mary inside as the sun began to set. A strong wind had developed, rattling the windows and making the branches of the trees sway dangerously. Dark clouds had gathered on the horizon, blocking out what was left of the evening light.

"Well, I think it's time for me to go," said Miranda, nodding at the tempest brewing outside. "If you need me for anything, just call or text me."

Alison collected their mugs and followed her into the hall.

"Thanks for coming with me today. I think we're finally starting to get somewhere. I'll let you know if I go out looking again."

Miranda waved goodbye to Rose and Nate and vanished.

It stormed violently later that night. Rose sat cross-legged on the living room floor, listening to the evening news with the others and trying to piecc together her Viewer while the wind howled around the house and rain lashed against the windows.

She studied the invention pieces spread out in front of her, wondering where to start. She'd told Nate what had happened as they'd all sat down for dinner, and he'd urged her not to waste all of the pieces and time she'd put into it. So she picked through the parts now, searching for the right ones and doing her best to reassemble them.

"Hmm," she muttered, holding up a tiny hinge she'd just repaired.

She couldn't remember exactly where she'd put it last time, so she guessed as best she could and fitted it back on. While she worked, she found her mind going back to the Illuminator she'd discovered in Hunter's room. She remembered the shape and feel of the dissolution spell holding the incompatible magic in place, and she tried to recall in detail how the spell had been used as a kind of bridge between the various magical components.

She glanced at her brother and sister, knowing full well what they would think of her using anything she'd found in Hunter's room, even if it was just his unique version of a spell. The others were engrossed in their own activities, so she held the dissolution spell firmly in her mind and tried her best to mimic all of its intricacies, repeating to herself what Nate had said about the Spellmakers being able to create anything they wanted, provided they were able to picture the result.

Observing the way the dissolution spell worked physically had somehow made the pieces come together in Rose's mind in a way that they hadn't before, and soon all of the Viewer's pieces were back into place with fresh spells around them. Her numb hand made it much harder to assemble the invention this time, but finally the Viewer stood in one finished piece on the table.

Rose looked down at the completed invention as the clock struck nine o'clock, satisfaction coursing through her. She was sure she'd got it right this time. It was black outside now, and rain was coming down so heavily that the street lights down the road were barely visible. Nate sat in an armchair, studying the book of poisons and symptoms Miranda had extracted from the Archives and cursing Lawrence Hunter under his breath.

"You'd think he'd have better things to do with his time than to invent poisons and dangerous inventions, wouldn't you?" he said, turning the page with more force than was necessary. "It's ridiculous!"

Alison eyed the book with distaste.

"He's made that way," she said simply.

"You should see all of the other things he's got hidden," Mary told Nate, her eyes shining in the half-dark as she launched into a detailed description of their time in Hunter's rooms. "In the end, we searched all three rooms and there were horrible books, potions and inventions in all of them!" she finished, tucking a strand of hair behind an ear.

"No, that's not entirely true," said Rose, picking up the Viewer to test it. "There were some things in there that could be used to do good if Hunter wanted them to. I mean, some of his inventions weren't all that great, but there were more than a few where he got it right."

Nate and Alison looked at her with surprise and interest.

"Like what?"

Rose hesitated, wondering if she shouldn't have said anything.

"Like that Illuminator thing I found," she said eventually. "The card under it said it made magic visible. It put out loads of steam and when I looked through it, the spells Hunter had put on the room to hide it were lit up like a rainbow. It was pretty cool. An invention like that could be useful."

Nate scratched his chin and turned another page of the blue book.

"Hmm, that is a surprise."

"I wonder who he stole it from," murmured Alison darkly.

"It was definitely one of Hunter's creations," Rose informed her. "At least, that's what the identification card under it said."

But Alison stuck out her chin and said, "A single useful invention doesn't mean he's a real inventor."

Nate gave her a weary look.

"No, but it means he has potential. I know you don't like him because he framed you, and you're right to be angry. But I agree with what Rose said before. Imagine how much his work could have benefitted the world if he'd focused on helping people instead of pursuing his own agendas. It's a shame. He certainly had potential when I met him at the Guild."

Rose lowered her invention to stare up at Nate, her mouth open in surprise.

"You met Hunter at the Guild?"

Nate nodded.

"I was about to leave to start work at the Archives full time when he started his apprenticeship. He was only sixteen or so at the time, but he was already very talented."

"What was he like?" asked Matt, turning his back on the television and fixing his gaze on Nate instead.

"He was quiet and eager to please," said Nate simply. "And a hard worker. In his first year he helped another Guild member perfect a series of spells that are now used to fortify buildings against damage from earthquakes and other disasters."

Alison raised an eyebrow, her blue eyes full of astonishment.

"So what happened?"

Nate closed the book with a sigh.

"I can't be sure what caused him to change direction, but I think I can guess. The Guild held a presentation ceremony for the member that created the fortification spells and Hunter was offered an award, too, for his contribution. He'd brought his parents along to watch the ceremony, but it was clear to everyone there that they had no interest at all in their son or his achievements. I overheard the three of them arguing in a side room, just before the presentation. Hunter was yelling, saying that he could never makc his parents proud, no matter how hard he tried. They left before the ceremony began and Hunter was visibly upset. He didn't stay to receive his award. He left the Guild soon after and just disappeared. Neglect and indifference can do more harm than physical violence in some cases."

A stunned silence followed Nate's words. Rose blinked, struggling with a sudden wave of pity. Her own parents had always been openly affectionate, showering their children in love and acceptance, and Rose gulped, wondering what life might have been like for herself and her siblings if they had been deprived of that love and support.

"Huh, I never thought I'd feel bad for Hunter," said Matt, breaking the silence.

"Neither," agreed Mary in a small voice.

Alison stared unseeingly into the empty fireplace, her expression sombre.

"You're right, that is a shame," she murmured. "His parents seem horrible. It's not an excuse for the way he behaves now, but still."

Rose shifted uncomfortably, not sure what to say. Privately agreeing with Alison, she fixed her attention back onto her Viewer, placing a finger on the invention as the others went back to their activities. She waited for a moment and then nodded, confident that it was working as it should.

"I wonder if he knows we have Grandpa's silver invention?" said Mary with a cackle of laughter. "He might not have checked all of the stuff in his rooms yet."

"Oh no, he'd know by now for sure," replied Alison. "I bet the first thing he did when he found out you three had escaped was check on the invention. What I want to know is why he's been so quiet about it so far. That can't be a good sign."

"I heard Miranda saying that he was threatening to go to the police and tell them we'd broken into his rooms," said Matt, sitting on the floor with Cocoa's head on his knee. "He wouldn't do that, would he?"

Nate and Alison both laughed.

"No," Nate assured him. "If he did that, he'd have to tell them where he got the invention from in the first place, and he'd have to admit that he has three hidden and highly illegal rooms in the Archives. He's not stupid enough to do that. He's trying to scare you, that's all."

Matt looked deeply relieved at this.

"I don't fancy trying to explain what we were doing to the police."

They sat in silence for several minutes, listening to the news.

"When we were hiding in the cabinet, listening to

him talk, it sounded like he's keeping Mum, Dad and Grandpa all together," said Rose, twirling the Viewer in her hand as her thoughts wandered. "I wonder why he wanted Ben to be kept away from them?"

"I suppose they're more of a threat if they're all together," answered Nate, taking a sip of his tea. "Ben knows what's been going on all this time and your family doesn't. They probably have no idea what's happened to you three, or that you've managed to get the silver invention back. Hunter could use that against them. It makes sense for him to keep Ben isolated."

"Yeah, I guess," said Rose.

She went back to staring at the television. At half past nine, Mary stood up and announced that she was going to bed. A picture flashed into Rose's mind as Mary brushed past on her way to the stairs.

Three people stood huddled together in a shadowy room with a bare concrete floor and one tiny, dusty window. Rose gasped and nearly dropped her Viewer again. Everyone stared at her in surprise.

"What's the matter?" asked Alison, rising from her chair. "Is your hand hurting you again?"

"N-no, it's fine!" Rose stammered. "It's just - I just saw Mum, Dad and Grandpa! I saw where Hunter's keeping them!"

16

The Silver Archway

It took a few seconds for Rose's words to sink in. Mary spun around frantically and Matt scrambled up off the floor.

"Are you sure it was them?" pressed Alison.

Rose nodded and looked down at her Viewer with shock and excitement. She closed her eyes and concentrated on the scene in her mind. Grandpa was now sitting on an old sofa pushed up against the wall, his shoulders slumped as he said something inaudible. Mum and Dad stood nearby, staring out of a window set high up in the wall. The small amount of light it allowed in dimly illuminated the plastered walls and concrete floor. Rose tilted her head to one side.

"The room they're in looks new. Everything is rough, unfinished. Here, it'll be easier if I show you."

She opened her eyes and held the Viewer out. The others each placed a finger on it and Rose tried the invention again.

"Hmm." Nate set the blue book aside. "It looks to me like a basement that's been added in a hurry."

"I wish we could see out of the window," said Alison, studying the glass pupil. "The view might have given us some clues. Otherwise, the room looks like every other basement I've seen. That could be anywhere," she added with a frown.

Nate leaned forward, mulling over the tiny picture.

"What happens if you concentrate on the room or the house, rather than your family?"

Rose tried again, but the pupil remained clear and empty, reflecting the room around them.

"I don't think it works that way. I'd need to know the house's address, or at least what the place looks like from the outside so I can tell the Viewer what to search for. If I don't even know what I'm looking for myself, I don't suppose it can, either. I didn't think of that when I made it."

"Never mind, it can't be helped," said Nate gently as Rose folded the invention flat.

"I wonder why it worked this time, but not any of the other times we've used it?" said Matt with curiosity.

Rose's insides squirmed uncomfortably, and she wondered how the others would react if she told them the truth. Alison smiled at Matt.

"Rose must have done something differently this time. Or maybe it's all the practise you three have had, fighting your way through spells. You've been up against some strong magic thanks to your Grandpa's prototype and Hunter's room in the Archives, and your sister is better at the spells she used on her Viewer because of it."

Rose tried to smile naturally but only succeeded in producing a kind of grimace.

"Yeah, maybe. But it hasn't helped me much, has it? Like you said, that room we saw could be anywhere."

"Well, we know now that we're looking for somewhere close to Stony River and with a basement," said Alison encouragingly. "I'm guessing it's an old farmhouse or something like that. Hunter and his gang will want somewhere they can come and go without it looking suspicious."

Nate settled himself back in his chair, lost in thought.

"Yes, there are a lot of old, neglected houses out in the fields past the river. Some of them have been abandoned for a long time. It's the ideal place for Hunter to look for a hideout."

Rose hesitated, fighting back the flood of emotions coursing through her. She was itching to go and explore, even if it meant wandering through the bush in the rain-drenched darkness to find her family and Ben. But she knew that this would get her nowhere, so she held her tongue and forced herself to focus on the tiny picture at the centre of the Viewer instead. She glanced at Matt and Mary and saw her own emotions on their faces. Matt gripped the armrest of Nate's chair.

"How will we know which house we're after?" he asked. "We can't go searching all the old buildings along the river. Someone would call the police."

Alison got to her feet and wandered over to the window. The storm continued to rage outside and rain beat against the glass, almost drowning out the sound of her voice when she spoke.

"We'd just be watching the comings and goings from a distance, but I think, in the end, we'll have more luck if we keep tracking Hunter's friends."

"What do you think, Nate?" asked Rose, turning to him.

Nate looked as though the idea of doing either gave him no pleasure at all, but he sighed and bowed his head in resignation.

"I think it would be best to do both. You never know what you'll find until you look. But we'll have to be careful. I can help track Hunter's friends from here, but you'll have to follow them, I'm afraid, and I'd feel better about it if you took Miranda with you again."

Alison nodded and agreed to ask Miranda to accompany her early the next morning. In the meantime, Rose decided she would track Hunter's gang with the Viewer.

"With any luck, we'll know where your family is being kept soon," Alison told Rose, Matt and Mary, beaming at them.

Excitement rushed through Rose again at the thought of having her family back again, and she hugged her arms around herself, feeling more hopeful than she had in weeks.

The next morning dawned bright and clear. Rose stood in front of the wide living room windows as she ate breakfast, squinting in the summer sunlight glaring down on the wet rooftops in the distance, creating a fine haze that obscured the horizon.

Alison had already left for the Archives to meet up with Miranda as planned, and as soon as Rose had finished eating, Nate hobbled over to begin testing new spells on her arm. Before he began, however, he handed Rose a glass of the clear, minty concoction he'd mixed up the day before.

"Try this. I added some spells to it last night."

Rose took the glass with a word of thanks, downing it in one go. Nate looked pleased as he put the bottle back in the fridge.

"I'll give you some more to take later today. Now let's see how your hand is healing."

Rose peeled off the bandages and held her hand out for inspection.

"It's getting better!" she gasped, hardly able to believe her own eyes. The sickly yellow colour of the skin was fading and the swelling had disappeared. She prodded her palm with a finger. "I can feel it!"

Nate smiled as he applied more salve.

"The spells in the tonic work as fast as the modifier. The ones I'm going to use on your arm in a moment will help the tonic along. Let's try them out and see what happens."

He lowered himself onto the sofa and placed a small bowl on the coffee table.

"What's that for?" asked Rose, sitting beside him.

"That's to catch the poison in," Nate explained. "You'll see in a moment I hope."

Matt and Mary entered the room and, seeing that Nate was about to attempt more magic, gathered around to watch. Nate began his first spell and Rose waited for something to happen.

A quarter of an hour had passed before she began to

notice a strange crawling sensation throughout her entire body, as though the spells were creeping along her veins, drawing the poison back the way it had come. Soon the skin on her injured hand and arm was covered in angry, red marks that burned and itched. Her good hand twitched, but she forced herself not to scratch at the spots. Pain built up around the wounds again, but she said nothing, waiting for the spell to do its work.

Nate remained silent for almost an hour before finally lifting the spell and leaning back in his chair, sweat beading on his brow. He looked at Rose enquiringly and said, "That seems to have been successful. Can you feel anything?"

Rose struggled to find the right words.

"It's like all the poison has crawled back into my hand. Or like something is forcing it there."

"Good, that's what we want." Nate leaned forward again, all trace of exhaustion now gone. "We're ready for the next spell. This one should remove the poison altogether."

Matt and Mary leaned in, too, and Rose held her breath as Nate began to work. She waited, unsure what to expect, experiencing a slightly uncomfortable sensation in her hand, like tiny needles had been inserted into her skin. Nothing else happened for several minutes, until Nate's face suddenly broke into a wide smile.

"Ah! It's working!" he said. "Can you see it?"

Nonplussed, Rose bent down and looked more closely at her palm, wondering what she was missing. It took her a second to notice the minuscule beads of blue-green liquid building up as though tiny openings had formed all over her hand, allowing the poison to be extracted. The beads grew larger until Nate picked up the bowl and siphoned the ooze off into it. He repeated the process for hours, drawing out more and more of the poison and gathering it in the bowl until it seemed to have been removed.

Rose suppressed the urge to scratch at the wounds as the blue-green mixture irritated her skin, but the burning sensation gradually subsided, leaving her hand red and stiff, but much less painful. She flexed her fingers. They moved with ease.

"It's so much better already!"

"So does that mean the poison's all gone now? Rose is OK?" Mary asked, draped over the back of the sofa.

Nate summoned a facecloth and wiped the sticky green residue off Rose's skin.

"Yes, all of the poison is gone now. The tonic will take care of anything that's left."

Rose gave him a look full of gratitude and he smiled back at her, looking tired but elated.

"You're amazing, Nate!" said Matt earnestly, picking up the bowl of poison and swilling it around.

"Be careful!" Rose warned.

Matt rolled his eyes.

"You don't really think I'd touch it after seeing what it did to you, do you?"

"I think I'd better destroy this properly," chuckled Nate, taking the bowl back.

He conjured a fire in the empty grate and threw the

poison into it. It hissed and smoked, filling the room with its acrid, burning smell. Mary ran to the window and threw it open, coughing.

"Good idea," Matt choked, waving the smoke away and going to stand beside Mary. Rose remained on the sofa, bending her fingers again just to prove to herself that she could. She'd been sure that it would take weeks to heal, at least.

"I can't believe the poison is all gone!" she said. "It's so good to be able to feel and move my arm again. I can't wait to tell Alison!"

"The poison is gone, but we still have to repair the damage it did," Nate reminded her. "You'll still be tired and unwell for a while, so it's important for you to keep resting."

Rose nodded and obediently settled down with a book from Nate's library, waiting for Alison to return while Matt and Mary flicked through channels on the television. The evening wore on and Rose had just reached out to turn on the lights when Alison materialised beside her. Both of them jumped, startled.

"Sorry," said Alison with a laugh, as Rose relaxed and flicked on the light.

"Did you find anything?" asked Rose breathlessly. Mary turned around in her seat and gazed up at Alison expectantly.

"Not exactly, no," she said, her smile fading. "We didn't get a chance to go out looking because Hunter was at the Archives making trouble again."

Rose frowned.

"What kind of trouble?" she asked, as Nate shuffled into the room with a cup of tea for Alison.

Alison took the mug with a word of thanks and folded herself onto the sofa beside Matt.

"Hunter's noticed us following his gang around and searching the bushland near the river, and he doesn't appreciate Miranda getting involved. He was warning her to stay out of it. I think he's afraid that you three are getting close to finding your family and he's keen to make sure she doesn't give you any extra help."

"What did Miranda say?" asked Rose anxiously.

Alison's face broke into a grin.

"Oh, well, you know Miranda. She's not easy to intimidate. She told him that she'll give you as much help as she likes, and the fact that he came all the way to the Archives to tell her to stop looking for his hideout just proves that she's looking in the right spot." Alison laughed and took a sip of tea. "You should have seen the look on Hunter's face when he left the building!"

Rose snorted, picturing the scene in her mind and feeling a rush of gratitude towards Miranda.

"If Hunter wants her to let things be, he's going about it the wrong way," remarked Nate.

"Yeah, he'll just make her more determined." Alison put her feet up on the footstool and seemed to notice the look of intense excitement on Mary's face. "What did you all do today?"

The words had barely left Alison's lips before Mary piped up, "Nate got the poison out of Rose's hand!"

She picked up the empty bowl, which now contained

only the slightest trace of green liquid clinging to the edges, and held it up in front of Alison's face as proof. Alison stared at it for a moment as though sure she'd misheard. Regaining her senses, she looked at Nate silently for confirmation.

"You got it out!? All of it?"

"All of it," he repeated.

Rose held up her arm in demonstration, bending and stretching her fingers and elbow with relish.

"That's wonderful!"

Alison rushed to Rose's side. Taking her arm gently, she peeled back the bandages and surveyed the wounds. They were healing fast. The angry red spots had almost disappeared, leaving the skin looking surprisingly normal.

"I can't believe how much better it looks!" Alison's face was full of relief as she turned to beam at Nate. "You've done so well!"

"We're not finished yet," said Nate fairly. "We still have to repair the damage."

"It's a start, though! I knew you could do it!" Alison replaced the bandage. "This calls for a celebration! I think I'll -"

She got up and headed for the kitchen, but stopped when a sharp knock sounded on the door. She glanced at Nate.

"You weren't expecting anyone, were you?"

Nate shook his head and the knocking came again, more urgent this time. Alison disappeared down the hall. Rose had turned her attention back to her rapidly-healing hand when a loud shriek sent her, Matt and Mary scrambling to their feet.

They hurried into the hall, Nate shuffling at top speed behind them. Rose skidded to a halt, expecting Hunter's gang to be forcing their way into the house. But it wasn't Hunter's gang at all. Ben stood in the doorway, grinning back at them. Rose, Matt and Mary crowded around him eagerly.

"I thought Hunter locked you away!" cried Alison. "We saw his friends take you away!"

"They did, but I escaped before they locked me up," replied Ben, laughing at their astonishment. His hair was windswept and it looked like he'd been out in the bush for some time. Scratches covered his hands and face, and his clothes were torn and covered in dirt.

"Why don't we all go into the living room," said Nate, recovering first. "There's no need to stand here in the hallway."

Rose followed the others back down the hall, keen to hear Ben's story.

"They took me to their hideout right after we got caught in the Archives," he said, collapsing onto the sofa. "I saw your family. I'll show you where they are once it's dark. There was some kind of commotion inside as I got near the door. I think your family might have seen them bringing me in, and I got away while Hunter's friends were trying to deal with whatever was going on inside. I ran into the nearby bushland and hid there for a while. I had to go a fair way in before they gave up looking for me. I went to your place, Alison, but when you weren't there I figured you might be here."

"But you've been gone for days!" remarked Mary wonderingly.

"I didn't want to come back without any useful information," he said with a shrug. "I knew that this might be our only chance to find out where they're keeping your family. I couldn't get close enough to talk to them, but I've seen them."

Rose opened her mouth to speak, but her voice seemed to have deserted her.

"Are they OK?" said Matt and Mary together.

"They're fine" he assured them. "It was good to see how well they were all doing. By the looks of things, they haven't been making things so easy for Hunter."

Rose felt a fierce pride well up inside her at this news. Alison grinned, her cheeks flushed with happiness.

"You know, Rose saw them with her Viewer just yesterday!"

Ben looked deeply impressed at this.

"You must have made one hell of a Viewer, then! You should see the protection Hunter's put around the place. It makes his door in the Archives look like a joke." His grin faltered. "There's no way we'll get anywhere near it without being caught."

"It's no wonder I had so much trouble with my invention, then," said Rose. "But there must be a way to get in without being seen!"

Ben ran a hand through his tangled curls. Cocoa entered the room to investigate the newcomer and Ben scratched behind the dog's ears.

"There are loads of spells around the outside, but

they're nearly all to avoid detection, like repelling your Viewer, Rose. They aren't expecting us to find them to attack them. Only a few spells are for defence. The biggest problem isn't going to be breaking in. It'll be breaking in without them knowing about it."

"Where is it?" asked Alison urgently. "Miranda and I have been looking everywhere for it for days now, but we never found it."

Ben shook his head, looking unsurprised.

"It would be almost impossible to pinpoint the place with a travel spell, or even just to stumble across it unless you were invited in. It's this old abandoned house that Hunter's converted into a kind of lab. It's out in the middle of nowhere, in the fields beside the Stony River."

Alison's expression was gleeful.

"I knew it!" she crowed.

"As far as I can tell, the place has been empty for decades and Hunter just took it and started using it," continued Ben. "Since he put his spells on it, nobody seems to have remembered it even exists."

"I don't care how many spells are on it, I want to go to Mum, Dad and Grandpa!" Matt declared. He stood up, his face full of determination. "Can you show us where the house is? Why do we need to sit around and wait for it to get dark?"

"Yeah! Why can't we go now?" seconded Mary.

Ben gave them a sympathetic look, and when he spoke, his voice was gentle.

"We're outnumbered. If we don't find a way to draw Hunter's gang away, we'll never get in without being caught."

"It wouldn't be a good idea to go barging in with the whole lot of them there," agreed Alison. "It wouldn't help your family much, either. They need us to help them escape, and if we're caught, too, we won't be able to help at all."

Matt glowered at them.

"OK, then, we'll wait," Rose conceded, hoping to keep the peace. "But only until it's properly dark."

There was a tense silence. Rose drummed her fingers against her leg, trying to think of something to say.

"So, did you see inside the house?" she asked Ben.

He ducked his head apologetically.

"Not really, no. But I could see through some of the windows. It's a two-storey building with a basement. One side of the basement's ceiling is about two feet above the ground because the ground slopes down towards the river. On that side, a small window high up in the wall looks out onto the grass. I think there must be more spells around that area because every time I tried to get near it a couple of Hunter's friends came out to investigate. But your mum saw me running back into the trees, so she knows we've found them. Once you've seen the place, we can figure out how to get inside."

Ben leaned back in his chair, looking spent. Alison fetched him a glass of water and he gulped it down.

"Thanks. So why did you all come here instead of going back to your place, Alison?" Ben looked at her questioningly. "What happened in the Archives after they took me away?"

Alison explained how they'd found the silver invention and how Rose had been injured. Ben was keen to hear about the Infuser and looked angry, but not surprised, to discover how much Hunter had hidden in his rooms.

"You were always great with magical injuries, though, Nate," he said, looking down at the scar on his own hand. "Miranda always said she was lucky to have you working at the Archives."

Darkness descended around them as they filled Ben in on everything else that had happened while he'd been gone. Nate turned to Rose.

"I think it's time for you to take some more tonic," he told her, checking the clock on the mantelpiece. He took up his walking stick, but Alison shot up first.

"I'll get it. I need another drink anyway."

"Yeah, I might get another one, too," added Ben, following her. "I haven't drunk anything in days. I didn't want to risk going back to my place too often in case Hunter was looking for me there."

They'd barely disappeared from view when Cocoa cocked an ear in the direction of the kitchen. A stifled yelp from down the hall followed, and Rose, Matt and Mary leapt to their feet for a second time. Nate snatched up his walking stick and prised himself off the couch, wheezing.

"What's going on now?" said Matt, as they went down the hall towards the kitchen.

Rose rounded the corner and her breath caught in

her throat. She glimpsed Jacob, the short man with scars on his face, and counted eleven others that she didn't know, blocking off all of the exits so that Alison and Ben were trapped behind the kitchen counter.

Cocoa took one look at Jacob and launched himself towards the man, his teeth bared. With a look of alarm, Jacob backed away, slamming the door in their faces just as the dog reached it. Cocoa hurled himself against the wood, snarling and pawing at it.

"Alison!" cried Nate in horror.

"Run!" she yelled, her voice muffled behind the door.

Ignoring this, Rose put her hand on the doorknob, but immediately yanked it back. The door glowed red hot around the edges and she backed away as blistering heat radiated from it. It quickly subsided, leaving the door looking quite normal, but it refused to open, no matter how hard she, Matt and Mary pulled at it. It was as though it had become fused to the doorframe.

"Open up!" Rose screeched, beating at it with her fists.

"You won't open it now." Nate's voice was faint. He looked older than ever. "We'll have to find another way inside. They've stopped us from using travel spells, too. I can feel it."

Mary looked up at him, her eyes darting from him to the door and back again.

"But we have to help Alison and Ben!"

Nate suddenly looked fierce. He seized Matt and Mary's arms, towing them with a surprising amount of strength away from the kitchen and back down the hall.

"You'll let me deal with them," he declared. "You three have to stay safe. Come with me!"

Rose followed him into the study, where he locked the door and used the heavy chair under the desk to barricade it.

"Why aren't those guys following us?" Matt asked, in a tone that suggested he wasn't sure if he wanted to know the answer. A shadow passed over Nate's face as he placed spells over the door.

"They're trying to split us up. It will be easier for them to get what they want if they have us separated. More of them will come, don't you worry!"

Rose took a deep breath as Nate worked. How many more of them were there? Ben was right. They were seriously outnumbered. Wheezing, Nate hurried over to the desk and opened a drawer.

"Here, take these!"

He thrust three objects into Rose's arms. She looked down and saw the silver invention, Grandpa's pocket watch and a new, unfamiliar invention shaped a bit like a box.

"You're going to need these. Alison asked me to keep them safe while she was out looking for your family and Ben, in case she was caught. Take them quickly. That's what they're here for. They want the silver invention back!"

Mary pointed at the unfamiliar object.

"What's that?"

"It's something Miranda found in the Archives," Nate explained. "She repurposed it for you not long after you told her you were planning to go into your grandfather's fake world. It'll multiply the real food and water we bring into it so we can survive in there for longer. Its spells will wear out the more we use them, so we'll have to use the invention sparingly, but we'll think about that later. You just keep it safe for now."

Rose could hear the fear in Nate's voice, and her own heart hammered in her chest as the sound of footsteps drew closer. Cocoa let out another howl from somewhere in the direction of the living room, and Nate put himself between the door and the three children.

"You need to run! It's not safe for you here now. Go to Ben's house. He's got enough magical protection on the place to keep you safe even from Hunter. Go and wait there until we come for you."

Matt opened his mouth to protest, but Nate cut across him.

"You can't stay here. They know you're in the house somewhere."

"We can't just leave and let you deal with all of this on your own!" said Rose indignantly. She pushed the inventions back at Nate, but he refused to take them.

"We want to help! We're not leaving you!"

Nate sighed as Matt folded his arms across his chest, his feet planted firmly on the floor.

"Your safety is the most important thing. They mustn't find you here. I'll try to reach Alison and Ben and give you enough time to go out the window. Once you're far enough away you should be able to use a travel spell to Ben's house. Until then, I'll seal the door with spells and do what I can to keep Hunter's lot away from you."

Rose bit her lip as Nate began to invent a new spell. She wanted to say a proper goodbye, but he turned and walked through the wall, disappearing into the hallway before she could say a word. She could feel him surrounding the room with protective spells and disguising them so that their presence wouldn't give them away.

"How does he do that?" Matt asked, staring at the wall Nate had just passed through. Rose groaned and flipped the catch on the window.

"I have no idea."

A floorboard outside the study creaked, making all three of them jump. Rose felt a strange kind of wriggling in her left palm and looked down at it in confusion. The silver invention had begun to grow, spreading molten silver threads upwards, high over their heads and down to the floor until a slender archway stood before them. They stared, startled and amazed as it shone in the darkness. Mary turned to Rose with a gasp.

"What did you do?!"

Rose looked at her blankly.

"I don't know! I jumped when that floorboard creaked and I think I squeezed the invention. That's all!"

She took a tentative step towards the archway. Her eyes seemed to be drawn to the shadowy, unfamiliar passageway leading away from them. It continued for several paces before turning a corner and disappearing into darkness.

"We're going to have to go in there, aren't we?"

asked Matt in a hushed voice, peering down the passageway.

"Looks like it," said Rose, her breath quickening. Mary tugged on her good hand.

"When you got sick in the Archives, Alison said she was going to get the Fragmenter out of the fake world alone. She was so upset. I don't think Ben or Nate wanted us to go in there, either."

Rose blushed, regretting her stubborn insistence on going into Hunter's room, despite Alison's warnings. Guilt and uncertainty wracked her as she stood in the reflected light of the silver invention.

"I wish no one had to go in there. Maybe they're right, though, and we should stay away from the archway. It's not the test version of the Fragmenter in there. It's the real thing."

Rose hesitated, feeling more unprepared by the second.

"It's not going to be easy getting it out. I think it's going to take magic that's way beyond anything we can do. It'll probably be -"

There was another, louder creaking sound from behind the door this time, and she stopped talking. They watched the door nervously. Minutes trickled by and Rose began to breathe freely once more when Nate's protective spells suddenly broke. The door rattled as someone attempted to force it open.

"They've found us!" Rose gasped, backing away. "They know we're here!"

She started towards the window, but Mary pulled her

back, tears shining in her eyes.

"I don't want to run away and leave Nate. He needs us!"

"We have to go through the archway," urged Matt, walking around the gleaming invention.

When Rose and Mary hung back, he took hold of their hands and marched them over to it. Rose looked again at the dark stone passage and yanked herself free, hesitating on the threshold. She glanced down at the inventions clutched in her hands.

"We can't do this on our own, Matt!"

"We have to try! It's either that or we let Hunter's gang take us," said Matt as the chair in front of the door flung itself out of the way. "They won't let us just run off! If Hunter's as smart as everyone says he is, he'll have more people outside, waiting for us to try to escape. And you heard what Alison said after Mum and Dad disappeared. If Hunter gets the Fragmenter before we do, it's all over! We'll lose our magic forever."

He took one step into the stone passage. Mary followed a moment later and they both looked back at Rose. Rose groaned, trying to force her reluctant feet to move. She looked out of the window, searching for any signs of movement outside. Sure enough, several long shadows appeared, creeping along the side of the house.

Panic bubbled up inside her. She wasn't ready for this. Whenever her thoughts had strayed to Grandpa's fake world, she'd always pictured Alison at least being there to help them, and if Hunter himself had so far been unable to retrieve the Fragmenter from the illusion world, how could *she* possibly manage it?

There was a bang and a yell from somewhere down the hall and the door to the study burst open. Rose caught sight of a figure dressed all in black, standing in the doorway silently, watching them with cold blue eyes before fear propelled her forwards, through the gleaming silver archway after her brother and sister.

17

A City in Ruins

Rose spun around as the archway began to collapse. The man in black stood by the study door, still and silent, his face impassive as the silver of the invention flowed down towards the floor. It pooled like liquid metal, shutting him out with the rest of the real world and leaving Rose staring at the blank stone wall.

The puddle of silver wove itself back into its usual shape, shining on the rough floor. The corridor was dark and oppressive without the bright glow of the arch, and Rose's eyes travelled to the rectangular patch of light at the end of the narrow passage, where there was an open doorway.

Behind her, the corridor disappeared into darkness, a strange chill breathing off the stone. A shiver ran down Rose's spine as her eyes adjusted to the dense blackness around her. Matt frowned and bent down to retrieve the disguised archway.

"So all this time we've been trying to figure out how to activate this thing, and all we had to do was squeeze it!" He threw his hands up in the air. "That makes me feel loads better!"

Mary laughed. The sound died away quickly, creating no echo. Matt stretched out a finger and touched the nearest wall.

"Grandpa outdid himself this time. I could swear this place was real!"

Rose peered into the blackness beside her. It all *looked* real, but it felt entirely different to the world she'd just left. Taking a deep breath in, she immediately found that the air had changed. It seemed thin and insubstantial somehow, like it had lost some important quality. But at least she could breathe. She took several more breaths, getting used to the feeling.

"I guess it *is* real," she said in a hushed voice. "It's just been made with magic, that's all."

They spent another moment adjusting to their strange new surroundings, until Matt let his hand fall away from the stone wall and turned towards the patch of light.

"Well, we can't just stand here. Let's do what we came here to do."

He led the way down the corridor. The light grew stronger as they approached until they came to the doorway and stopped. Rose stuck her head around the corner. A dreary stone room met her gaze. It was cold and bare, with only one small, deeply-set window on the opposite side of the room.

The window was a simple square hole in the wall, without shutters, glass or anything else to keep the weather out. Rose rushed over to it with a groan of dismay. A wide road ran from left to right before her, revealing a crowded city street stretching as far as she could see. A thin light illuminated the silent and empty streets. It all would have been entirely ordinary if it weren't for the destruction that met her eyes wherever she looked.

"Uh, did we just miss a wrecking ball sweeping through the place or something?" she gasped.

Even as she watched, the awning of a tall building across the street gave way and hit the ground with a hollow crash. Rose's spirits fell with it. The city had a desolate, hopeless feel.

"How on earth are we going to find Grandpa's invention in a whole city?"

The others joined her by the window and Matt let out a low, impressed whistle.

"Looks like we've got our work cut out for us," he said weakly. He glanced at Rose and, seeing the despair on her face, quickly added, "But this city might not be as big as it seems. We can't really see all that much from here."

Rose gave him a look of mingled amusement and horror before turning back to stare at the carnage outside.

"What happened to all of the buildings?" Mary whispered.

"I have no idea," replied Rose. She tore her eyes away from the decimated buildings to look over the rest of the room. "You know, this place kind of reminds me of a bunker, except it's above ground, not below." She paced around the room, her unease growing with each step. "These walls must be almost two feet thick."

"Maybe it's a prison cell," suggested Matt, looking at

them with apprehension. "Only it feels more homely, somehow."

Two roughly-hewn shelves had been cut into the left-hand wall, littered with a handful of objects. Rose brushed the dust off a blank notebook with a torn cover and examined a stack of canvas sheets, scattered scraps of invention-making materials and a small leather bag containing an assortment of tools. The rest of the room was bare except for a low stone bench beside the doorway. Rosc returned the bag to the shelf, thinking that things were finally beginning to make sense.

"Grandpa made the Fragmenter in here. Mum and Dad said he wasn't making it in his invention room and we know he wasn't making it in the Archives. I bet he was working in here the whole time. He wouldn't have to worry about damaging anything and if this place is as deserted as it seems, there would have been no one else around to get hurt if things went wrong."

"I think you must be right," said Matt. "It would be a lot safer. But he didn't leave it in this room. I suppose if he had, Hunter would have found it by now." He took one more sweeping look around the space and headed for the hall. "We might as well keep moving, then."

Rose and Mary followed him, looking for a way out into the city. Darkness descended again until a thick stone door loomed up in front of them. Rose's spirits sank further still when she saw that it was locked all the way down to the floor with iron bolts. She eyed it suspiciously. Why were so many bolts necessary? Mary seemed to be having similar thoughts, glancing over her shoulder towards the room they'd just left.

"Are these locks here to keep something in or out?"

Rose lifted an eyebrow, considering them.

"Out I guess. Otherwise, they'd be on the other side of the door."

"Good point," said Mary with a grim laugh.

Sensing a change in the air beside her, Rose turned to her right and saw the dim outline of a stairway leading up into the darkness. Matt and Mary noticed it, too, and began to climb the steps. Rose kept close behind them, half expecting the Fragmenter's defensive spells to come swooping down on them at any second, but all she found when she reached the top of the stairs, however, was another bare stone room.

"This looks more like a storeroom."

She stepped into the tiny space. It was lined entirely with shelves except for the far wall, which held another deep-set window. A small collection of food scraps and water bottles was clustered on the shelves. Leftover, Rose guessed, from the many trips Hunter's gang must have made to this place to retrieve the Fragmenter.

Her eyes found a crushed packet of biscuits, a few slices of stale bread, tea bags and an assortment of dried fruit and nuts. Matt wrinkled his nose at the scraps.

"The food in here won't last long. We'd better find Grandpa's invention fast, or we'll have to open the archway again and go back into the real world to get more. Hunter's friends seemed to come and go out of here without any problems, didn't they?"

Rose nodded.

"It seems like it. That guy with scratches on his face, Jacob or whatever his name is, was always complaining about having to come back here."

"That's a relief," said Mary. "We don't know how long it'll take us to find the Fragmenter."

Rose said nothing. She went to the window and leaned out. They were now on the same level as the rooftops on the other side of the street. She could see a little further than before, enough to discern that the city must be quite large. Tall spires rose against the skyline, high above the city in the distance to the left, and on the right, much closer, was a tower.

"I think we should climb that tower over there." Rose pointed, shielding her eyes from the glare. "Then we can see for sure how big this place is."

"Should we take these with us?" Mary nodded at the food and water bottles as they left the room, and Rose stopped at the top of the stairs, thinking that it couldn't hurt to take some supplies.

"We'll take some of it. We can always come back if we need to."

She took a packet of fruit and nuts, along with one of only two unopened water bottles, and stumbled her way back down the dark stairs. Emptying the leather bag in the first room, she packed their supplies, the pocket watch, the silver archway and the invention Miranda had repurposed for them inside it.

They trooped down the passage to the door and drew back the metal bolts. The door was so heavy that it took all three of them pushing and heaving together to shift it. Finally it ground outward enough that they could squeeze around it, out into the street.

It was eerily still and silent. There was no wind, not even the faintest hint of a breeze, and the trees lining the road hung limp and lifeless. The only sounds were the occasional crash of a collapsing building. Rose stood in the road, staring over the rooftops before spotting the tower several blocks away. They made directly for it, peering into front gardens and deserted shops as they walked.

"Nobody forget the way back!" Matt said with a grin as they reached the end of the street. "We need to remember where the store of food and water is!"

Rose turned and studied the building they'd arrived in. Sitting in the middle of a long row of federation-style houses, it was small and oddly-shaped, looking more like a sloping, hollowed-out slab of stone than a house. Rough and strong, it was the only structure in sight that wasn't damaged in some way.

"Well, at least it'll be easy to recognise," she said. "We shouldn't have any problems."

Rose took in her surroundings more closely as they rounded the corner. Some of the houses possessed grand gardens, while others had high fences that obscured her view of the building beyond. She couldn't help but be reminded of the photos she'd seen of the city Grandpa had grown up in.

A creeper grew across the fence beside her and she stretched out a finger to touch it. The leaves were cool and smooth against her skin, and she withdrew her hand, feeling more and more impressed by the level of detail he'd put into the place.

"You know, I'm surprised Grandpa had time to do all of this while he was making the Fragmenter," she said. "Especially with Hunter and his gang after him."

"He probably started on it as soon as he found out Hunter wanted the Fragmenter," guessed Matt. "But I don't think this place is nearly as big and complicated as Grandpa made it seem."

"I hope you're right," replied Rose, as they entered the next street and set off across a park with lush green lawns and colourful flower beds. "I can feel illusion spells covering everything in this place. Once you get past how lifelike it all is, you can actually feel that it's made of magic. Everything here is pretending to be something else."

She saw that some of the trees here had been torn up by the roots, leaving branches and scraps of bark strewn over the grass, crushing a park bench and a swathe of flowers. Rose gazed up at the gnarled trunks, deciding she didn't want to know how such immense trees could have been ripped up like weeds.

The tower was close now, and they peered into a smashed-up fish and chip shop and a newsagent with no roof as they wended their way through the streets, goggling at the extent of the damage around them. Mary prodded a twisted traffic light with her toe. It had been bent almost to the ground before being tossed aside onto the road.

"It's so weird in here! There are so many houses and

shops, but it's all so quiet and still. There are no people, or birds or cars, or anything else you'd hear in a city. It doesn't feel right."

"That's because it *isn't* right," remarked Matt.

He gave the buildings a dark look. Rose remained silent and kept walking. *It is kind of stifling in here*, she thought, staring around at the empty streets. The whole place gave her the uneasy feeling of being caught in an enormous, invisible cage.

It had been night-time in the real world when they'd left it, but here it appeared to be late morning. The buildings around them glinted brightly in what appeared to be strong sunlight, but she could find no sun or any other light source. There was just clear blue sky everywhere she looked. Unsure what to make of this, she continued to the next intersection.

The tower loomed up on their right as they reached the corner. Rose came to a halt and let out a snort of laughter. It was a clock tower, but the clock had come loose and fallen on top of the shop beside it. Worse still, one side of the tower had partially crumbled away, exposing sections of the interior. It was the most dilapidated thing she had ever seen.

Rose thought it might even be on a slight slant, leaning dangerously towards the cluster of shops and houses hugging its right-hand side. It looked very precarious. Her eyes travelled to the ruined, open space near the top, where the clock should have been. It would be a good place to look out over the city …

Mary hung back, staring up at the tower while Rose

and Matt climbed the shallow stone steps at its base and approached the plain wooden door. Rose stopped, remembering that her sister was terrified of heights.

"Do you want to stay down here while I go into the tower with Matt?" Rose asked, watching the colour drain from Mary's face. "We won't be long. We'll meet you back here if you like."

Mary seemed to consider this for a moment, but then her face became set in a very Matt-like way, and she marched up the stone steps after Rose.

"No, I want to come," she declared, her voice wavering. "I just hope it's safe to go up there. It looks like the whole tower could come down on top of us."

"Well, we need a good view of the city, so we have to try it," said Matt simply. "It'll be OK, don't worry."

He stepped around Rose and opened the door, revealing a tight, spiral staircase. Mary groaned. The stairs were old and flimsy. She positioned herself in the middle of the group and they began to climb, testing each step before putting their weight on it.

After several minutes of anxiety where the exterior had fallen away, exposing a sheer drop inches from their feet, they all made it to the top, Mary trembling from head to foot and averting her eyes from the holes in the walls.

She stayed close to the steps while Rose and Matt crept out onto a ledge where the clock would normally be. The air was still, even at this height, and the sun, if there was one, remained hidden. Broken glass littered the floor along with other debris, and Rose stepped further out onto the ledge, gazing down at the wreckage of the clock far below her. The space where they stood would have been extremely uninteresting but for the wonderful view it offered of the city. Rose gulped and stared out over the rooftops as fear began to claw its way up her throat.

"This place is enormous!"

The city stretched around them in straight, neat rows. She could see an avenue of churches, a city hall and a library not far from the tower. Sections of the library's walls had caved in, scattering bricks throughout the street, and one of the churches had lost its spire. The jagged edges of the tiles still in place glinted in the light, making Rose's eyes water. She turned away, wishing she was back in Nate's study.

"It can't be this big!" said Matt in anguish, staring out at the sprawling city. "This is unbelievable! We're *never* going to find that damned invention now!"

Rose moved away from the edge, wondering if she, Matt and Mary had set themselves an impossible task. It was obvious now, why Hunter and his friends had failed to retrieve the Fragmenter.

"There must be an easier way," she exclaimed. "Grandpa hid his invention here to stop Hunter from finding it, but he had to have a way of finding it himself if he needed to, and I'm pretty sure he would have expected Mum and Dad, or at least Alison, to find it and destroy it if anything ever happened to him. No one could do that if they had to search blindly through a whole city. It'd take too long. There has to be an easier way to do it!"

"Well, if there is, nobody told me about it." Matt aimed a kick at the nearest bit of debris and it sailed out of the opening. Rose counted to six before she heard it hit the ground with a distant thud.

"I wonder what would happen if we used a finding spell," said Mary, shooting terrified glances at the open space.

"Probably nothing, like when we tried to find Grandpa after he disappeared," Matt growled.

Rose closed her eyes, doing her best to calm herself.

"I'm going to try anyway."

She quieted all of her anxious thoughts and began to search mentally, keeping the Fragmenter fixed in her mind. Matt and Mary waited in silence until her eyes opened.

"You're right, I'm not getting anything. Either the Fragmenter is blocking us, or we can't do those kinds of spells here. I wonder if we can use travel spells, then?"

She tried again, this time imagining herself standing beside Mary. She opened her eyes to find that she hadn't moved an inch.

"No finding spells and no travel spells! We're done for!"

Mary gave a gentle tug on her hand, pulling her away from the edge.

"I think we should start searching," she said. "We're wasting time."

Rose knew she was right. She sighed and marched over to the rickety stairs, leading the way back down to the street. Matt checked his watch as they followed the main road back the way they'd come. He looked up at the sky.

"It should be almost eleven o'clock at night by now."

"I noticed that, too," murmured Rose. "The daylight hours must be different here. Maybe it's still morning in this place."

"Let's have something to eat," pressed Matt, clutching his stomach. "Just a bit, while we decide where to start searching. It feels like it's been ages since lunch."

Mary seconded this, and they went back to the park they'd discovered earlier and sat on the swings, hanging still in the windless air. They did what they could to conserve their food and water, but none of them were used to going without either, and Rose felt a flurry of uneasiness as her eyes travelled over their half-eaten supplies.

"We'll save more next time," she vowed, packing the food back into her bag. Matt grumbled as he handed the water bottle over, too.

"I wish we'd been able to take more food in here with us. I'm still hungry!"

Rose rummaged in her bag and extracted the strange invention Miranda had found for them.

"I wonder how we use this?"

She turned it over in her hands.

"Nate said the spells on it would wear off the more we used it, didn't he?" said Matt, voicing yet another problem that had been worrying Rose. She pursed her lips before answering in an undertone.

"He did. But it's like you said. We'll just have to go back to the real world for more food soon. We're going to need it."

Matt twisted his swing around in circles and then tucked his legs up underneath him. When he put his feet down and lurched to a stop, Rose caught a hint of fear on his face for the first time since they'd walked through the silver archway.

"And if we can't? We've got a whole city to search, and almost no supplies …"

"We'll worry about that when we have to," replied Rose, hoping to distract the other two from thoughts of starvation. She took a shaky breath and forced herself to think about something else. "I hope Nate, Alison and Ben are OK."

"So do I," said Mary, staring up at the perfectly still tree above her.

"They'll be fine," said Matt in a falsely cheerful voice. "Ben got away from Hunter last time. They can all take care of themselves."

Rose packed Miranda's invention into the bag with their supplies and got to her feet.

"OK then, let's decide where to start searching."

The ruined city stretched around her, and she let her gaze wander over the devastated buildings, wondering where an invention would hide itself. It seemed unlikely to Rose that it would conceal itself inside an apartment or one of the fancy houses lining the streets, but nothing more fitting presented itself, so she simply chose a block of houses opposite the park.

"It's as good a place to start as any, I guess," said Mary as they opened the door of the nearest dwelling. Matt stepped into the neat living room, his gaze sweeping over the pristine white sofa to the empty fireplace.

"I reckon the more unlikely-looking the building is, the more likely we are to find the invention there," he remarked, proceeding to the kitchen, where he began opening all of the cupboards.

Rose tied her long hair back and got to work, trying hard to suppress the suspicion that she was wasting her time. They searched for hours, looking through every building in the area, including restaurants, a furniture warehouse and the remains of the smashed-up fish and chip shop. They combed through long rows of houses, turning over every room, attic, basement and yard without success.

Rose soon began to lag behind the other two, feeling tired to her bones. Her legs felt weak and shaky, and her hand occasionally twinged with pain when she used it, despite Nate having removed the poison.

"It's bound to take a while for you to recover completely," said Matt, noticing her drawn features as he tried unsuccessfully to open a small safe he'd discovered in an upstairs bedroom. "You didn't have much time to get better before we came here."

"What time is it?" Rose asked, flopping down on the edge of the bed. "It feels like it should be almost morning by now."

Matt checked his wristwatch.

"You're right! It's past six!"

He gave up trying to open the safe and peered out at the sky, clearly visible through the lacy curtains covering the nearest window.

"But it still looks like morning! If night has been and gone in the real world since we came here, it should at least be getting dark by now."

"Weird," said Mary. "Maybe there *is* no night-time here. I guess Grandpa couldn't do everything."

"I suppose so." Rose stifled a yawn with difficulty. "But I don't think I can walk much further today. Maybe we should go back to that stone safe house thing we arrived in and try to rest a bit? It will be less comfortable, but it'll be safer than out here."

She wasn't quite sure what they were in danger from, but she was convinced Grandpa wouldn't have made the fortress-like building for nothing. Knowing that the Fragmenter was lurking somewhere in the city was reason enough for her to seek safety, and she guessed that the tense, foreboding atmosphere that followed her wherever she went in this fake world was the invention's way of making its influence known.

"Yeah, let's stop for a while," said Mary, coming to sit beside Rose and resting her head against her sister's shoulder. She'd been dragging her feet down street after street for hours. "But I think we should go back through the archway first thing in the morning for more food. When we have more supplies we can start searching again."

Rose thought this was a good idea, and they headed back the way they'd come, looking for the long avenue of federation-style houses. They got as far as the park in which they'd had their meagre meal before noticing anything peculiar. Rose stopped in the road, wondering if she was losing her mind.

"Wait a moment! We should be back to that fish and chip shop by now!" She scanned the area, but was unable to find it. "We've come the wrong way!" She turned back around with a sigh of exasperation.

"We can't have," said Matt. "The park is right there." He pointed to his left, where a green stretch of grass was visible a block away.

"But where are the other buildings we saw when we were here before?" countered Rose. "That must be a different park, that's all."

She continued down the road for a clearer view. It was the same park, but the newsagent and all of the other shops were gone, replaced by a crowded car park. Rose scratched her head in confusion.

"Let's keep walking," said Matt. "We might see something else we recognise."

"We could look for the tower," suggested Mary.

"If it's still there," snorted Rose, fatigue getting the better of her.

They hurried on, down more streets and around two more corners, until they came to the right place. A memorial garden now resided there, with a stately brick building beside it. Rose read the words etched over the doors and realised it was the city hall she'd seen earlier. Her heart sank. What was going on?

"But we passed this place hours ago!" she said

indignantly.

She turned to Matt as though expecting him to understand, but he simply shrugged his shoulders and returned her puzzled expression.

"Just keep going," Mary urged, dragging them both down the road to the next street, where they stopped and checked their surroundings. "That way!" she called, pointing.

Rose and Matt followed her up the hill, and to their relief, the old, grand houses were there, bathed in fake sunlight two blocks away.

"We weren't careful enough when we tried to remember the way back, that's all," Mary chattered as they walked. "We forgot."

They rounded a corner and reached the long row of houses without further incident. Rose began to relax as the lush gardens came into view. Suddenly eager to be back inside the stone house, she ran the rest of the way, pulling up short outside the shopping complex that had materialised in front of her. She gasped for air with her hands on her knees, glaring up at it. The safe house had disappeared.

"I don't believe it!" she panted, sitting down on the low brick wall that enclosed the nearest front garden. A letterbox hung open beside her, with a jumble of letters poking out, one of which looked like an electricity bill. She slammed the letterbox shut with a huff. Matt sat down beside her, looking crestfallen.

"How can a building disappear?!" he demanded, staring up at the shopping centre.

They watched from the garden wall as Mary, determined to make sense of the situation, searched the area once more. She returned ten minutes later, looking put out.

"I can't find the stone place anywhere. It really is gone!"

Rose sat hunched over, staring at the spot the safe house had occupied, trying in vain to understand how this could be possible.

"Well, there's no point just sitting here," she said with a sigh. "We'd better find somewhere else to rest. I can't keep wandering anymore, even if it *does* still look like it's daytime."

"OK then, let's stay here," said Matt, looking up at the grand residence behind them.

"But it's so weird going into these houses," Mary protested. "It feels too much like we're walking into someone else's home."

Matt shrugged.

"None of these houses belong to anyone. They're just illusions. If anything, they're Grandpa's, seeing as he made this place."

"Matt's right, let's stay here," mumbled Rose, unlatching the gate and walking with aching feet up the garden path.

Mary grumbled as the others stepped onto the veranda and threw open the door, but she relented and followed them inside. Matt stopped and stared as they entered a spacious living room.

"Wow! I wish our house was like this!"

"What's wrong with our house?" said Rose defensively, letting herself fall backwards onto the luxurious sofa.

The house was much bigger than it had appeared from out in the street, and expensive furniture adorned what Rose could see of the rooms from her spot on the couch. It was the kind of house she had only ever seen in magazines, with a chandelier high above her, expensive curtains and a piano by the stairs.

Matt went upstairs to explore and Mary followed, calling out to Rose that she was going to bed. Exhausted, Rose kicked her shoes off and soon began to fall asleep on the sofa. Thinking she might as well go to bed, too, she staggered to her feet and trudged upstairs to see how Mary was getting on in her makeshift room.

"Come and look at this!" Mary trilled, pulling her over to the window. "You can see loads of the city from here. There's the tower we were in before! It really did move!"

"Cool," said Rose, regarding the dilapidated clock tower with contempt. "OK, time for bed. We have to keep searching tomorrow." She chivvied Mary into bed and then stood at the top of the stairs, calling to Matt, who was now inspecting the dining room. "Come on, Matt! I know it's still light outside, but we need to sleep."

"I'm not that tired, I'm going to stay down here for a while," he replied.

Rose shrugged and went back down the hall, choosing the bedroom along from Mary's. She tossed her shoes beside the bed and lay down fully dressed on the squashy mattress. The sheer curtains over the windows did little to block out the constant daylight, but she found herself nodding off almost as soon as her head touched the pillow, drifting into troubled dreams with all of the blankets pulled up over her head.

Rose threw back her blankets early the next morning, feeling refreshed for the first time in days, but also uneasy. She'd slept like a log, but nightmares had plagued her for most of the night, and unwelcome scenes came flooding back to her as she sat up.

She'd dreamt she was being kept prisoner in a room with no doors or windows. Unable to understand how she'd got in there, she'd rushed around the room like a panicked animal, beating at the walls and trying to find a way out. Her fear had reached an almost unbearable level when she'd awoken, gasping for breath and covered in sweat, deeply relieved that it had all been a dream.

Climbing out of bed, she tugged her shoes on, keen to start searching again. She could hear Matt snoring somewhere downstairs as she tied her shoelaces clumsily, fumbling with her injured hand. It was improving fast, but it was stiff from lack of use. Wondering what the time was, she opened the curtains onto the same sunless blue sky she'd closed them on before heading downstairs and roaming the house while she waited for the other two to get up.

On her third lap of the living room, she glanced out of the bay window and came to a stop. When she'd gone to bed, the house had been facing the immense shopping complex. This morning they were opposite a primary school. The playgrounds were empty and silent, as she had expected, with sports equipment sitting here and there in the grass as though it had been abandoned moments earlier.

She sat down in an armchair so as not to disturb Matt on the sofa, summoning her leather bag from upstairs. Extracting the silver archway, she twirled it between her fingers, watching the play of colours on the metal. There was a clattering of footsteps on the stairs and a second later Mary appeared, combing her hair with her fingers.

"Hi," she said, stifling a yawn. She sat down on the end of the sofa and Matt awoke with a start.

"We've moved again," Rose informed them as she hunted for food and water.

"Ooh! Where are we now?" Mary ran over to the window and parted the curtains. "A school? Eurgh!" She crinkled her nose and turned her back on the unpleasant scene.

"Time for some breakfast," said Matt, looking at Rose eagerly.

Rose handed him the water bottle, now only half full, and divided the last of the dried fruit into three. Matt took his portion, regarding it with distaste.

"I can't wait to have something else to eat."

Rose wolfed down her share. She still felt a little unwell, but her appetite was beginning to return. Mary downed her fruit in one go, took a mouthful of water and then handed the bottle to Rose. When they were packed and ready to go, Rose got to her feet and moved into the centre of the room, where the archway could expand. She held the silver invention out in her good hand as Matt and Mary gathered around her. Mary eyed Rose's palm.

"I wonder what the archway will open onto? If it opens onto Nate's study where we went through, Hunter's gang might be waiting for us …"

"I hope not," said Rose with a shudder. "We'll have to check it's safe before we go through. If we see any of Hunter's friends, we'll close the archway up and try again another time."

Matt and Mary agreed and Rose squeezed the tiny invention. She held her hand out flat, waiting for the silver to flow outward, and Matt and Mary crowded closer beside her, eager to get back to the real world.

Seconds stretched into minutes as they stood there, watching the invention expectantly, but it remained as it was, showing no signs of magical power at all. Rose blinked.

"Maybe I didn't squeeze it hard enough."

She repeated the process, waiting patiently for the archway to appear before her, but the invention lay still and lifeless in her hand. Bewildered, she glanced at her brother and sister. Mary's eyes widened in fear.

"Why isn't it working? Are we stuck here?"

Matt picked up the invention and turned it over.

"Are you sure you activated this by squeezing it, Rose?"

"Yeah, I'm sure!"

She thought for a moment while Matt and Mary took turns squeezing the concealed archway. Something stirred in her memory, and her thoughts strayed back to the conversation they'd had with Miranda about Grandpa's fake world. Suddenly Miranda's words came back to her in a rush.

"It would make it very difficult for a person to enter and survive long enough to find the Fragmenter and escape."

Rose's blood ran cold as ice.

"Oh no! Why didn't I realise this before?!"

Mary squeezed the archway forcefully, her cheeks turning pink with effort, while Matt's face filled with alarm. He fixed his eyes on Rose warily.

"Realise what before?"

"Grandpa must have made it so that the archway will only reopen if we have the Fragmenter with us," Rose whispered. "It would have made the bud much harder to steal. We're stuck here!"

18

Trapped

Matt and Mary stared blankly at the invention in Rose's hand.

"Remember what Miranda said when we asked her about this place?" she prompted.

"Of course I do! She said it would be hard for us to survive in here because -"

Matt stopped and thought for a moment before an expression of pure horror spread over his face. He gulped.

"But how could Miranda have known we'd need the Fragmenter to get out? It wasn't in Grandpa's report."

Rose hung her head, devastated.

"I think she guessed. And it looks like she was right." Rose opened the leather bag and pulled out the repurposed invention. "Why didn't we figure this out before?" she repeated. "Miranda even gave us something to extend our food and water supply! It should've been obvious!"

She groaned, regretting her decision to step through the archway more than ever. She'd thought the purpose of Miranda's invention was to *reduce* the number of trips they'd need to make to the real world, not to replace them altogether …

"But Hunter and his gang always seemed to come and go from here, and we know they don't have the Fragmenter because Jacob was always being told to find it," countered Mary. "How could they do that if the archway won't open without it?"

Rose pondered this for a moment.

"Everyone says Hunter is clever. I bet he found a way around Grandpa's rules. There must've been something Grandpa didn't think of when he made this place."

Mary sank back down onto the sofa, staring at the empty fruit packet.

"So we're trapped in here with almost no food and water until we find the Fragmenter," she said in a hollow voice.

Rose exchanged a fearful look with Matt, trying hard not to panic. Clutching Miranda's invention tightly in her hands, she swallowed the lump in her throat before speaking in a tone of forced calm.

"We've still got *this*, though. We'll figure out how to use it and get some more food this afternoon. If we haven't found the bud by then, I mean."

"Well, we'd better get going again," said Matt, gathering up the remains of breakfast and packing it all into Rose's bag. "Looks like we're in even more of a hurry than we realised."

Rose tucked the archway into her bag, too, and followed her siblings to the front door, trying hard not to think about what would happen to them all if they didn't find the Fragmenter soon. If the spells on Miranda's invention wore off the more they were used,

Rose wondered how long she, Matt and Mary had before the spells vanished completely.

She closed the garden gate behind her and crossed the road for a closer look at the deserted school as they walked down the street, unsure where to begin. They seemed to be in an unexplored part of the city this time. A railway station with smashed windows and a collapsed roof stood behind the school, and Rose stared up at it with interest, heading for a cluster of apartments covered with graffiti.

She tried to memorise the layout of the city, only to remember that it was pointless because it was constantly changing. They passed the graffiti-covered apartments and directed their steps towards the city centre, searching any likely-looking buildings they came across. The hours dragged on, and Mary had just suggested they stop for a break when they rounded a corner and Rose stopped dead in the middle of the footpath. Matt ran into her, muttering under his breath as he ducked out from behind her.

"What's the matter?"

Rose hesitated, mistrusting her own senses.

"Can't you feel it?" she asked in surprise.

Matt stared at her as though she'd gone mad.

"Feel what?"

Rose refrained from rolling her eyes with difficulty.

"That feeling you get when someone's watching you!" she replied impatiently.

The familiar sensation had been creeping up on her for the last several minutes. It had become so strong as she'd stepped into the next street that she'd almost expected to see the Fragmenter sitting on the footpath beside her feet. Mary glanced up at her.

"I can't feel anything. Maybe you're imagining it."

"I'm not! I felt it loads of times at home before Alison destroyed the Fragmenter prototype," retorted Rose.

She turned in a circle slowly, excited and terrified at the same time, scanning the silent street for any sign of the invention.

"You know what that means, don't you?" she added, as Matt and Mary continued to look mystified.

"The Fragmenter must be close by!" said Mary, finally catching on.

"Exactly! At home, it always sent out magic that made me feel like I was being spied on, and if the prototype does it, the real one must do it, too!"

Matt shivered.

"I thought Alison and Ben would be here to help us with this," he muttered, his usual self-confidence deserting him. "I don't want to go near that thing again. It was bad enough the first time."

Rose nodded bleakly. The idea of fighting something worse than the invention Alison had destroyed wasn't appealing to her, either.

"I know. But we've got no choice. We have to do it ourselves."

"How are we going to find it?" asked Mary. "Even if we know it's nearby, there are still loads of places for it to hide around here. It'll take us all day just to search this one block of buildings."

Rose continued along the footpath, wishing she had a better idea.

"There's no other way to do it. We'll just have to follow the bud's spells as best we can and then pick a place to start looking."

Moving on, they stopped here and there to check for the static-like sensation of the Fragmenter's defensive spells, following it right to the foot of the cathedral that had lost its spire. A narrow, grassy lane lined with pine trees ran along one side of the building, and Rose instinctively moved towards it.

"I think it's down here."

A two-storey house overgrown with ivy came into view as she pushed a hanging branch out of her way. The static-like feeling of magic became stronger as she led the way down the lane and stepped up to the front door. Old and worn, the house stood in the centre of a small clearing, only separated from the cathedral by the row of pine trees.

"The Fragmenter's somewhere inside the house," Rose said in a hushed voice, peeking through the panes of glass on either side of the door. "I think there's a faint light coming from upstairs."

"With any luck, we might be out of here sooner than we thought," said Mary. "I didn't think we'd find it so quickly."

"We haven't got it yet," Rose reminded her, still peering through the glass. "I'm sure it will try to stop us from taking it."

Matt hesitated on the doorstep before edging in front of Rose with the air of someone steeling himself for something unpleasant.

"I'll go in first, to see if it reacts," he said, with what was clearly a great effort. "Let's get this over with."

He squared his shoulders and pushed open the door. It swung inwards with a loud creak. The energy in the room intensified until Rose nearly backed straight out into the lane again. Matt flinched but pulled her into the room after him. Mary followed close behind, quivering from head to foot and glancing around the room from the threshold.

It was cold and austere, furnished with hard, wooden furniture and painted a stark white. But their eyes were immediately drawn to the wooden staircase, where a clear, bright light emanated from somewhere beyond the landing. Without saying a word, Rose crept over to the stairs and began to climb.

She knew where she needed to go, following the static up the stairs and along the hall, forcing her unwilling feet over to the very last door, where she stopped, her throat dry and her heart racing. Matt and Mary piled up behind her and Rose paused for a fraction of a second before stretching out a shaking hand and wrenching the door open.

They charged inside and spread out, ready to do battle. Rose spun around, seeking the source of the energy rippling through the air, but all she found was a small bed and a set of drawers in one corner. Confused, she got to her knees and checked under the bed, wondering how she could have been mistaken.

"But I felt it! I'm sure it was in here!"

She blinked and straightened up as Matt crossed to the set of drawers and yanked them open to reveal nothing but neatly folded clothes.

"We even saw the light coming from it!"

Mary went to the window and parted the curtains, her expression halfway between relief and disappointment. She turned to face them, her head inclined towards the stairs as though listening for something.

"I think it's downstairs," she said, tracing her steps back out into the hall.

Rose stood still, gauging the atmosphere. Realising that Mary was right, she and Matt returned to the living room, where the energy was strongest, but Rose knew at a glance that they wouldn't find the Fragmenter there, either.

"There's nowhere in here for an invention to hide," she remarked, contemplating the straight-backed chairs and the small wooden table in the centre of the room. The rest of the space was bare except for a shelf of books along the far wall, which she examined in a distracted sort of way.

"We're not getting anywhere," said Matt dejectedly, sitting in one of the chairs and staring around the room. "Maybe we were wrong and the Fragmenter's not here at all."

"I don't know … maybe we should try outside?" Mary suggested, half-turning towards the door.

Rose hummed uncertainly and flicked through the

nearest book again, only to remember that she had just done so. She placed it back on the shelf, slowly becoming aware of a vague numbness settling over her mind, making it hard for her to think clearly.

Before she could voice this concern to Matt and Mary, however, she stopped, her hand still outstretched, the static-like sensation settling over her for a third time. It was coming from the kitchen now, and Rose felt her eyes widen as she turned towards the doorway, realising what was happening.

"It *is* here, but it's playing tricks on us!"

Dodging the wooden table, she darted into the kitchen, hoping that if she was fast enough, she might catch the Fragmenter before it had a chance to fool them again. She skidded to a halt beside the sink, willing the Fragmenter to show itself.

Pots and pans hung from hooks along one wall and scraps of food were scattered over the benchtop as though someone had been interrupted in the process of preparing a meal, but she could see nothing unusual or out of place.

Undeterred, Rose knelt on the scuffed floorboards and opened all of the cupboards, peering into every shadow and corner. Matt mumbled something inaudible and came to help, checking the overhead cupboards while Mary scoured the pantry. Matt spoke in a low voice again from behind Rose as she closed one cupboard and crawled across the floor to inspect the one beside it.

"I'm sorry, what?" she asked him, shaking her head

in an attempt to clear it.

"Umm, nothing," he replied, after a pause. "I thought I saw something by the door, but there's nothing there. I must have been imagining it."

Still on her knees, Rose peered over the kitchen counter. The doorway was empty and she couldn't detect the Fragmenter's magic anywhere near it, so she shrugged and resumed her search of the cupboards. Mary pulled open the pantry door for a second time and glanced uncertainly down at Rose.

"What're we looking for again?"

She stared at the well-stocked shelves in front of her, her eyes unfocused and glassy.

"Uh … the Fragmenter, I think," murmured Rose, suddenly anything but sure herself.

The urge to go outside stole over her, and she was halfway to the door before she came to her senses and stopped. Matt and Mary were bottled up behind her with dreamy expressions on their faces. They'd followed her without thinking, but when Rose stopped moving they blinked and moved back into the kitchen like sleep-walkers.

Rose shook herself fiercely. The fogginess that had crept up on her seemed to clear somewhat as she became aware of it, enough for her to register the presence of strong magic upstairs once more.

"It's upstairs!" declared Rose, abandoning the kitchen and stumbling over to the staircase again.

"But we've already looked up there," insisted Matt, trudging after her. "Haven't we?"

Ignoring him, Rose approached the first room along the hall this time. She leaned in close to the door and paused. Certain that this was the right room, she opened the door and hurried inside.

"Not again!" groaned Mary, staring around the Fragmenter-free room. "I give up."

"No, not yet!"

Rose ran back out into the hall, sure that she was closing in on the invention.

"That's what it wants us to do!"

She went to the second room and turned the doorknob. The door remained shut, rattling around in the frame as she pulled at it.

"It's in here!"

She tried the doorknob again, the hairs on her arms and the back of her neck standing up.

"The door won't open!"

They beat at it, throwing their combined weight against the wood until it burst open and they all fell inside the room. Rose threw a hand out to steady herself on the wall and gave a cry of victory. The Fragmenter was there, gleaming bright green and deadly on the bedside table.

"Finally," breathed Matt, gently moving Mary aside and approaching the invention like someone attempting to corner a wild and vicious animal.

Rose tiptoed towards the bud, expecting to be attacked at any second, but no barrage of magic came, and she was able to put a hand on the invention without any resistance from it at all. She eyed the invention warily, suspicious of its strange lack of hostility.

Gripping it with both hands, she attempted to lift it from the table only to discover that it was stuck fast to the tabletop. She let out a growl of frustration.

"You've got to be kidding!"

Rose pulled hard on the casing, looking down at it with loathing.

"I'll take the whole table back through the archway if I have to," she warned it.

"It's all right, I can get it off."

Matt approached the table and began a severing spell. Rose backed away with a gasp, her foggy brain dimly remembering warnings against using aggressive magic near the unstable invention. But it was too late. Matt finished his spell before Rose could stop him and the tabletop cracked, releasing the Fragmenter and sending it tumbling onto the floor with a clang.

The bud flashed angrily, its casing unravelling faster than the prototype's had. There was a hum of energy from where it lay on the floor, and Rose tensed as the sound of breaking wood rent the silence. The floorboards beneath her feet began to splinter, forcing her to shuffle backwards as more cracks radiated out from the invention, travelling up the walls to the ceiling at a startling rate.

Energy built up around the bud like the pressure before a storm. Rose threw her arms up in front of her face with a yelp as the bare light bulb over her head exploded without warning and the glass in the window beside her shattered, the pieces raining down onto the grass outside.

The floor and ceiling began to sink, and Rose met Mary's terrified eyes briefly as everything around the Fragmenter was reduced to dust, crushed as though an invisible force was pressing down on it with unbelievable strength. Rose took a step toward the invention and stretched out her hand. If she could just reach it …

But the floor was too weak now to support her weight, and the broken floorboards shifted dangerously beneath her. Her eyes locked onto the bud and she inched forward, determined not to let their chance to return to the real world slip out of her reach.

The ceiling sank lower with a deep, low groan. Rose hesitated for a fraction of a second before turning towards the door instead, telling herself that it would be nothing short of stupidity to risk being crushed just to get her hands on the invention.

"It's time to go," she yelled over the grinding of wood and plaster.

She and Mary ran for the door. Everything around them began to shake, but Matt remained as though caught in a dream. Rose screamed his name and he gave a start, blinking furiously and staring around the room. Finally seeming to register the danger he was in, he glanced at the moving invention sinking into the floor beside him and then up at the ceiling before launching himself into the hall.

Rose led the way downstairs, leaping over the bottom steps and landing cat-like in the living room. The staircase collapsed with a crash before Matt reached the bottom, and Rose turned to find him half-buried in rubble, struggling to pull himself free with most of the upper landing threatening to come down on top of him.

She and Mary waded back through the mess of broken stairs and, with a great deal of effort, managed to pull him free of the wreckage and into the living room, gasping for breath and wiping dust out of their eyes.

"Thanks," Matt panted, limping over to one of the straight-backed chairs and lowering himself onto it with a wince. Rose shrugged to say it was nothing.

"H-how are we going to get the Fragmenter now?" coughed Mary, wiping more dust off her clothes with a trembling hand. "We almost had it!"

Rose opened her mouth to respond, but stopped when something rapped her hard on the top of her head. Looking up, she caught a glimpse of green falling through the ceiling. All three of them lunged for the bud as it bounced off the living room table and rolled across the floor, but it was soon lost among the ruined furniture and debris raining down from the floor above, covering them in white powder.

Rose shook her head to dislodge some of the plaster in her hair and eyebrows and scrambled over a toppled chair, plunging her hand into the pile of rubble. She could see the metal casing! It was so close, but her fingers couldn't quite reach.

"Watch out!" Mary screeched, pointing at the rapidly widening hole in the ceiling.

Rose shuffled backwards with a shriek as the remains of the bedside table came crashing down, breaking one of the straight-backed chairs. The bed and what remained of a wardrobe soon followed, landing in the middle of the room with a shuddering crash, narrowly avoiding Rose and burying the Fragmenter even deeper. Mary beckoned to her sister.

"We need to go now!"

Rose cast the now powdery-white invention a regretful look as the pulverised floorboards and furniture cascaded down on top of it. Running to the door, she threw it open, stumbling back out into the lane as most of the roof came down, tearing off a branch of the nearest pine tree with a resounding *snap*.

She took another step back as several roof tiles came sliding down, smashing on the doorstep at her feet. A shocked silence slowly settled.

"Of all the different kinds of magic, I like mind magic the least," she declared, fighting to clear the Fragmenter's influence from her head.

Matt draped himself over a statue that stood in the middle of a small flowerbed, one arm dangling as he stared ruefully at the demolished house.

"I shouldn't have used that severing spell. I'd forgotten how unstable the bud is. We might've had it under control by now otherwise."

Rose came to stand beside him, wiping the dust and plaster off the back of his shirt.

"Don't worry about it. It was playing tricks on all of us. None of us could think straight."

Matt jerked his chin towards the ruins and his voice became hopeful. "I wonder if the Fragmenter's been destroyed?"

"I don't know," said Rose, biting her lip. She glanced over her shoulder at the streets behind them. "It's been destroying the other buildings ever since Grandpa put it in here and it's obviously still working fine. I think it will have survived."

"Damn it." Matt picked at a tear in his sleeve. "I was hoping that if we couldn't control the stupid thing, we could at least destroy it."

"So was I!" Mary cried. "How are we going to get it back into the real world if it attacks us every time we go near it? I wish we could just leave it here forever!"

"Hunter would eventually find it," Rose reminded her. "It wouldn't be safe here forever."

Mary sat down in the lane and put her head in her hands, staring down at her trainers. "I know, but still."

"I wonder if we should try shifting some of this stuff?" said Rose, indicating the fallen walls, but Matt shook his head.

"It would be too hard to move most of it by hand and I bet the Fragmenter wouldn't let us use magic to help. It wouldn't be safe to try. Something could fall on top of us. The invention will move itself somewhere else soon. We'll wait for that."

It was now well past one in the afternoon, according to Matt's watch. They had very little food left to eat, so they skipped lunch and allowed themselves only a few mouthfuls of water each before setting off in search of Grandpa's stone house. It was their safe place, and they felt drawn to it whenever they needed to rest or think without fear of attack.

"I wonder if it'll be there this time?" said Mary as they hurried through the streets, wending their way back through the ever-changing maze of the city.

"We'll see soon enough, I guess," said Matt as they rounded a corner behind the bank.

Before long they'd found the long row of fancy houses, and to their great surprise and relief, the safe house stood waiting for them halfway down the road, as tough and unbreakable as ever.

"Yes!" crowed Mary, running the rest of the way.

Rose and Matt laughed, following her inside gratefully. Heaving the heavy door shut, Rose locked it and sat down beside the window in the downstairs room, her back against the cold stone, feeling exhausted and a little shaken.

"I'm so glad we found this place again!" She took a deep breath, gazing fondly around the bleak, bare room. "It's weird how such a cold, dreary place can seem so safe and home-like."

Matt managed a ghost of his usual grin as he sat opposite her.

"I know. I reckon it's Grandpa's spells. You can feel them all over this place. They're a lot like the ones around his house, so they make everything feel kind of familiar, if you know what I mean."

"I can't wait to see everyone again," murmured Mary. "It's weird being alone in here all the time."

Rose sighed and tucked her knees up under her chin.

"I hate it, too."

She winced as a building collapsed across the street.

"We'll be out of here soon," Matt reassured them as the rubble settled. "We've already come close to getting the Fragmenter once. We'll be back in the real world in no time."

He grinned at them properly this time, and Rose couldn't help but grin back.

19

The Watch and the Tower

They remained in the safe house for most of the afternoon, sitting cross-legged on the cold stone floor and discussing tactics. Rose was anxious to avoid a repeat of the events near the cathedral, and thought that they might have more success if they took some time to plan how they were going to keep the Fragmenter docile once they'd found it.

"It always uses magic to stop us getting close to it and there's no point in us running in circles trying not to get killed all the time," she said, winding the golden chain of the pocket watch around a finger. "So I think we should come up with a plan. Any ideas?"

"What if we distract it?" suggested Mary half-heartedly, getting to her feet and resting an elbow on the windowsill, looking out at the silent street.

Rose frowned, not sure if an invention *could* be distracted.

"Hmm. Maybe. It's not really like a person, though, is it? Even if all three of us attacked it from different directions, I bet it could take care of us all at once."

"I still wish we could destroy it," said Matt. "But now that I think about it, we wouldn't be able to open the archway if we did that."

"Besides, Alison had to use inhibiting fluid to kill the prototype, and we don't have anything like that here," Mary reminded him.

Rose tucked the pocket watch back into her bag, trying to think of a way to capture the invention without having to fight it.

"I think the best thing to do would be to not use magic around it, no matter what tricks it tries to play on us. It only reacts violently if we attack it or use spells that it doesn't like, so if we don't provoke it, maybe it will let us take it back through the archway. If it does anything dangerous, obviously we'll have to use magic to protect ourselves, but if we can avoid it, we should. What do you think?"

Matt almost choked on his water. He swallowed and turned disbelieving eyes on his sister.

"But that's going to be almost impossible! The Fragmenter's sneaky. It was playing with our minds before we even knew what was going on this morning. It knew exactly how to make me use that severing spell on it."

Rose put her chin in her hand and stared unseeingly at her trainers. She agreed that it would be difficult to avoid using magic, but there seemed to be no way around it.

"Hunter's friends have been using magic against the Fragmenter for ages now and it hasn't helped them at all," she pointed out. "We'll just have to be sneaky, too. If Alison's taught us anything, it's that defeating an invention, especially a powerful one, is more about outsmarting it than trying to force it under control."

"I think you're right," said Mary. "It's way too strong for us to fight. It would be stupid to even try."

Matt appeared to see the sense in this. He nodded in a conciliatory way, looking more cheerful now that they had a plan.

"OK, but we have pretty much nothing left to eat, so I think it's time we started searching again."

Rose stood up and headed for the stairs.

"I'll go and get what's left of the food and water in case this place moves again after we leave."

Packing her bag with one hand, she squeezed through the heavy stone door. The gold of the pocket watch glinted in the fake sunlight, catching her eye, and she wondered for the hundredth time what was so special about it.

Matt and Mary were already halfway down the street, and Rose tore her gaze away from the shining metal as Mary's voice carried back to her, warning her not to fall behind. Rose slung the bag over her shoulder and ran to catch up with the others. Now was not the time to get distracted.

They followed their usual routine, wandering the city and searching buildings until their feet were sore and their stomachs groaned with hunger. They trudged on, passing houses and shops that were now familiar, despite their habit of moving. Rose stayed alert for traces of the Fragmenter's magic, but all she felt was a deep longing for the real world and her family.

They headed further into the heart of the city and

discovered another stretch of parkland, where a river carved a wide path through the landscape. Light sparkled on the water's surface, dazzling Rose's eyes and making her wink back tears as she followed the meandering riverbank to a concrete bridge. Crossing quickly, they left the river behind and made for the city centre, admiring the blocks of apartments that soared high into the sky, blocking their view of the rest of the city. Mary ran ahead, eager to explore the unfamiliar area.

"Don't go too far! I don't want to lose you!" called Rose, watching her sister disappear down another street while she and Matt followed at a slower pace. Soon Mary's voice was calling back to them from around the corner.

"Come and see what I've found!"

Rose exchanged an apprehensive look with Matt and they both sprinted the rest of the way, tracing Mary's steps to what appeared to be a vast courtyard, surrounded by high-rise offices and apartments.

Rose arrived at Mary's side and stood with her hands propped on her knees, out of breath and suddenly realising what she was looking at. A block of buildings lay before her, so badly damaged that only the foundations were left, except for a tall brick chimney and one crumbling wall. The road had crumpled and lifted up in places as though an earthquake had shaken the place. Broken glass and bricks littered the ground.

"Whoa!" Matt's eyes were wide with shock. "Something big must have happened here."

A narrow alleyway lay before their feet, barely

distinguishable from the wreckage surrounding it. Rose thought it could be traversed if they were careful, and she led the way through the battle zone. Following what was left of the partially-standing wall, she clambered over the rubble and edged around shattered pieces of office furniture, only to come to a sudden stop as she reached the chimney and the wall ended. She took a hurried step backwards.

"What is *that*?!"

A huge black space yawned beside her on the other side of the bricks, stretching from the road at her feet to the top of the chimney.

"It - it kind of looks like the world's been broken open or something," stammered Matt, staring up at it with fascination and horror. He edged forward for a closer look.

"Maybe the Fragmenter caused so much damage in this spot that it even affected the spells that make up this place?" Mary suggested.

Rose glanced at her sister in surprise.

"I think you must be right. Hunter and his friends must have fought with it here for ages."

"Looks like things didn't go so well for them," observed Matt. "These buildings have been totally destroyed!"

Her curiosity getting the better of her, Rose took a few steps towards the void.

"I wonder what would happen if we threw something into this?"

In answer, Matt picked up a brick and hurled it in. It

disappeared without a sound.

"It's just a big stretch of nothing. Makes sense, I suppose."

"That's creepy!" gasped Mary with a shudder.

They sidestepped the black area carefully, heading further into the wreckage. It wasn't long before they discovered a second rift, cutting through the middle of a collapsed hotel, and a third, gaping like an abyss in the pavement beside a battered fruit shop.

This last one was smaller than the others and much harder to spot due to the debris scattered and piled up around it. Unaware of what she'd been about to step into, Mary had put out a foot to continue along the footpath when Rose, being taller and able to see further over the fallen bricks, had noticed the edge of an ominous shadow and snatched a hand out to pull her back. Horrified by what had almost happened, they'd stood huddled together beside the opening, staring down into the blackness, mesmerised, until Rose regained her senses and pulled them over to safer ground.

They spent some time exploring the area, paying close attention to where they put their feet. Rose still felt that it was pointless to search buildings at random in a city so large, but she could think of nothing else to do, so they continued down the road, becoming more frustrated and exhausted as the hours trickled by until finally they were forced to concede defeat for the day and find somewhere to sleep.

They'd decided not to return to the safe house this

time, so that they could explore further away, and they settled themselves in a sturdy-looking hotel, far away from the black fissures. They chose a room close to ground level (at Mary's insistence) but high enough to have a good view of their surroundings (at Matt's insistence).

Rose stretched out on the sofa and put her aching feet up while Matt relaxed on the narrow balcony running along the front of the apartment, enjoying the sights and pointing out buildings that might be worth investigating as though they were on holiday.

He and Mary decided to explore the cinema opposite the hotel just for fun before getting ready for bed, and as they left, chortling, Rose took up Matt's spot on the balcony, determined to teach herself how to use the invention Miranda had given them. She dug a hand into her bag and lifted out the invention as she sat in one of the flimsy chairs, looking down on the silent streets below.

She had voiced concerns about them splitting up, but Matt had assured her that if they kept in sight of the hotel, they wouldn't lose her. Nevertheless, Rose kept an eye on the road, hoping they would be back soon.

She set Miranda's invention on her knee and turned it over. It was box-shaped, with tapered ends. One of these ends bore a small handle, and the other a metal dial, which lined up with a white, blue or green marker. Lifting the lid, she discovered two compartments inside, one lined with red cloth and the other with black.

Each was large enough to accommodate their last

bottle of water, now barely half full, so she placed it in the black chamber. Closing the lid, she glanced at the dial and decided to try the white setting first. She turned the tiny handle, winding it up like a music box, and waited before opening the lid. The water bottle appeared unchanged and the red compartment remained empty.

Rose put the bottle in the red compartment instead, winding it up once more. She opened the lid, but still nothing had changed. Undeterred, she experimented with the other settings. By the time Matt and Mary had returned, giggling and claiming that the cinema was in fact working, but showing only one very old and boring film over and over again, Rose had got the hang of the invention and was keen to demonstrate for the other two.

"The white setting turns the invention off, the green one is for solids and the blue is for liquids," she explained as they stood beside her chair. "You just put something you want to multiply in the red compartment and wind the handle up, and a copy will appear in the black chamber." She indicated the two water bottles she'd managed to produce, each half full and identical to the original. "I'll show you!"

She poured the contents of one bottle into the other so that they had one full bottle of water and placed it into the red compartment. Setting the dial to blue, she turned the handle until it stopped. It slowly unwound, finally issuing a loud *ping*, like the timer on a microwave. She opened the lid and lifted out two identical bottles. She gave the copy to Matt and he took a sip. His eyebrows shot up.

"It tastes like real water!" He drank more deeply and then handed the bottle to Mary.

"This is great," exclaimed Mary, drinking her fill.

"We'll have to be careful not to rely on it too much, though," said Rose. "I know it tastes real, but I don't think magic can copy food and water exactly, with all of the vitamins and stuff. I think it just gives the impression of the real thing. That must be what Nate meant when he said the spells would wear off. They become diluted. The more we copy something the less nutrients it will have."

"Well, either way, we'll have to remember to thank Miranda the next time we see her," said Mary, sipping the water with relish. "I bet it took some serious magic to make the invention do this. I wonder what its real use is?"

"Probably multiplying stuff in general," replied Matt with a shrug. "Not food or water, though. But you're right, Miranda must have gone to a lot of trouble for us."

"And she must be very good at magic," said Rose, admiring the invention on her lap. "Not many people can do spells like these."

"Maybe that's why Hunter hates her so much," said Matt with a twisted grin.

Mary choked on her water and Rose patted her on the back, laughing as she pulled what was left of their food out of her bag to create a proper meal. By the time they'd eaten the last scraps, saving enough for breakfast the next day, their moods had improved considerably.

Pleased with themselves, and confident that they weren't going to starve for at least a while to come, they relaxed in the hotel, talking and wondering what was going on in the real world. Rose summoned her bag from the balcony and emptied it onto the cushion beside her.

Hopeful that she might discover its secret now that her stomach was full, she held the pocket watch up by its chain, watching it twirl and shine in the artificial light. Nate had told them it would be useful in here, but why? And how?

Her mind went back to the days leading up to the Magicked Masterclass, when everyone had been so desperate to get their hands on it. She remembered how she had tried and failed to repair it, before it had been stolen and then retrieved by Alison. Alison had told them that she didn't think the watch was what it seemed …

Opening the golden case, Rose leaned back with her head on the headrest, expecting to find the hands drifting aimlessly. She sat up. Now that it was inside the fake city, both hands were still, pointing at ten minutes past two.

"The hands on Grandpa's pocket watch have stopped moving!" she told Matt and Mary, who were now playing hangman in the dust on the floor by the window. "Why would they suddenly do that?"

Matt shrugged his shoulders and drew another line in the dust.

"Maybe it's died. Nothing lasts forever and it must

be pretty old by now. Grandpa's had it for ages."

Rose frowned.

"I hope not. Nate said we'd need it in here and Hunter was interested enough in it to steal it."

"It might be another invention," conceded Matt. "But Alison had it for a fair while and even she couldn't figure out what's supposed to be so special about it, so it could be just a broken watch after all."

"It hasn't been much help to us so far," admitted Mary, drawing the final line on the floor and hanging the dust man. "We've got other things to think about right now."

"I suppose."

Rose tossed the watch onto the sofa cushion with a sigh. Matt and Mary went back to playing games and Rose sat by the window, battling a mixture of weariness and restlessness. She stared down at the street below, wondering what the others were doing back in the real world. Soon Mary's eyelids began to droop and Rose decided it was time to go to bed.

Matt and Mary disappeared down the hall in search of bedrooms, but this time it was Rose's turn to lie awake on the sofa for what felt like hours, the deep silence shattered occasionally by the distant sound of yet another building collapsing.

She was feeling more and more on edge. The buildings might change around them, but the environment itself never did, and this, together with the almost total lack of other people, was making her depressed. She knew that her surroundings were just an illusion, and she was beginning to ache for the real world.

Guessing that it must be close to midnight by now, she gave up on sleep and dragged herself upright, looking for something to do. She wandered around the room, listening to Matt's snoring. Glancing out of the window, she saw that their surroundings had changed since Matt and Mary had gone to bed. She looked down at the city library, once again trying to shake off the feeling of being trapped in an enormous cage.

Crossing the room, she came to a stop beside the table, where the pocket watch lay untouched. She picked it up and opened it again. The hands were pointing at five minutes past one.

Frustration bubbled up inside her and she folded herself onto the sofa. As she did so, the hands shifted to twenty-five minutes to seven. A vague idea that the watch reminded her of something nagged at her, but she couldn't think what. Setting it aside, too tired to make sense of it all, she lay back down, telling herself she really did need to sleep. If they found the Fragmenter the next time they went out searching, she would need all of her strength to outsmart it. Her eyelids grew heavy and she fell into a light doze.

It seemed as though she'd barely drifted off to sleep when Mary was shaking her awake again.

"Time to get up!" she said, moving aside to reveal Matt, sitting on the floor with Miranda's invention on his lap, surrounded by bottles of water, packets of crushed biscuits and trail mix.

Rose sat up and pushed her hair out of her face, not

feeling remotely hungry. Taking a handful of dried fruit anyway, she glanced at the pocket watch that had fallen to the floor beside her as she slept, the lid still open. There was something familiar about it. She snatched it up as a thought flashed into her mind.

"I've got it!" she cried. "How could we have been so stupid?! It seems so obvious now!"

"What's obvious? What are you going on about?" asked Matt, still concentrating on his breakfast.

"The watch!" said Rose ecstatically, turning it this way and that and noting its reaction. "That's why we need it in here! It's not a watch at all! It's a compass!"

Matt and Mary stared.

"And I think I can guess what it points to!" continued Rose, standing up eagerly.

The hands sat on twenty-five minutes to seven. She turned in a circle, watching as the hands stayed put, pointing in the same direction out into the street. Rose looked up at Matt and Mary, excitement buzzing inside her.

"I knew there must be an easier way to find the Fragmenter than just wandering around!"

She gave the watch to Mary, who tried it for herself, moving about the room to test it.

"Ha! You're right! It *is* a compass! That's why it didn't work in the real world! The bud's not *in* the real world!"

Matt scrambled up, scattering water bottles in his haste.

"What are we waiting for, then? Let's go! With any

luck, we might be back with Alison, Nate and Ben today!"

They packed up their supplies and rushed out into the street. Rose held the watch out in front of her, letting it guide them. It directed them to the left, past the library and through the park with the fallen trees. Soon a familiar sensation began to creep over her, and she quickened her pace, sure they were going in the right direction.

Her spirits fell, however, as she realised where they were being led. She checked the watch again, hoping she'd read it wrong. Both hands pointed squarely at the shallow steps leading up to the clock tower. Mary groaned and threw her head back in despair.

The tower had sustained even more damage since they'd last climbed it. Large sections of the exterior had fallen away entirely on the sloping side and it was leaning at an even more alarming angle, overshadowing the cluster of houses beside it.

"Here we go again!" grumbled Mary, as Rose opened the door onto the rickety stairs. "It was bad enough going up here once! And now we have the Fragmenter waiting for us at the top! The stupid tower really *will* come down!"

"C'mon, let's get this over with," said Matt, edging past her and starting up the stairs.

They made their way towards the top of the tower and Rose stowed the watch in her bag as they approached the ledge where the clock had once been. They came to a halt several steps down from the narrow space beyond.

"Can you see anything?" Rose whispered to Matt, a step above her. He leaned forward and stuck his head around the corner.

"I can't see the Fragmenter, but I can see the white light coming from it," he whispered back. "It must be close!"

Rose edged forward to look over his shoulder and saw that he was right. The open space glowed with a clear white light, illuminating the dust and sparkling on the broken glass scattered over the floor. She put a foot on the top step, preparing to charge into the room, but stopped abruptly when a shadow flickered past, disappearing seconds later as though something had come between them and the invention.

Rose tensed, the hair on the back of her neck standing up.

"What was that?!" yelped Mary. "Only something solid could block out light, but this place is deserted! If there were other people here, we would've seen them!"

Matt raised an eyebrow a fraction and Rose guessed what he was thinking.

"The Fragmenter's playing tricks on us again," she agreed, taking a deep, steadying breath. "Well, we've come this far, we might as well stick to the plan. Remember, only do magic if you absolutely have to," she reminded the other two.

They nodded, Matt pale and Mary trembling. The shadow flicked past a second time, making Rose and Mary jump, but Matt charged out onto the ledge. Rose hurried after him with Mary at her heels.

The Fragmenter was there, sitting peacefully on the open ledge. Rose pounced on the invention without hesitation, gripping it with both hands. Matt cheered and Mary called back to Rose, "Let's take it back to ground level before it starts playing tricks again!"

Rose thought this was a very good idea. She turned to follow them, holding the invention as though it were a bomb. Her foot touched the top step and the wood broke with a loud *crack,* sending her stumbling. With a gasp, she threw an arm out to regain her balance as her foot slipped through the broken wood and came to a stop several steps below it.

The Fragmenter shot out of her hand, suddenly slippery like a bar of soap, and rolled along the ledge, prompting another horrified squeak from Mary. Rose swore as the invention came dangerously close to the opening, but a twisted lump of metal blocked its path, and the bud bounced off with a clang, stopping on the ledge.

Rose squared her shoulders and began to clamber back up towards the landing, becoming aware of a strange sinking feeling in the pit of her stomach as she climbed. Pausing beneath the broken step, she looked down at her feet, wondering what was going on.

The wood appeared to be getting softer, and the step sagged lower, threatening to break at any second. She moved back, away from the Fragmenter. The further she retreated, the firmer the wood became.

Rose glared at the invention. Deciding to take the top steps as fast as possible, she used the handrail to propel herself up, but they splintered at the merest touch and she hit the lower landing with a bone-jarring crunch at her brother and sister's feet. She winced as she pushed herself onto her knees.

"That didn't go the way I wanted it to."

Mary gave her a look of concern, but the corners of Matt's lips twitched with amusement.

"It was worth a try," he said, helping her up. "Are you OK?"

Rose opened her mouth to answer but stopped as a tremor ran through the building. Mary's eyes widened in terror and she clutched at Matt desperately.

"We're going to fall!" she shrieked. "We need to go back down! Please, let's just go back!"

She grabbed Matt's hand and attempted to tug him back down the steps, but he resisted, staring up at the Fragmenter, seemingly caught between fear and the desire to go after the invention. A hole gaped in the exterior beside the landing and Rose gazed down at the ground, far below them. A memory from the Archives flashed into her mind and she suddenly understood what was happening.

"We're not going to fall," she told Mary urgently, standing on her sister's other side and taking her hand in what she hoped was a comforting grip. "The bud's trying to scare us away, that's all. Remember that invention in the high-security section of the Archives? The one that made the walls look like they were curved when they were really straight? The Fragmenter's doing the same thing! It's like a dream. It feels like real life at the time, but then you wake up and you realise it's not!"

Matt remained rooted to the spot, his face full of doubt.

"How can you be so sure?" Mary gasped, tears streaking her face.

"Just trust me!"

Rose held onto Mary tightly and tried to ignore the grinding sounds coming from the building. "We can still do this!"

The tower shook more violently. Several loose bricks in the walls around them rattled and slid to the ground, impacting the road with a distant thud. Soon the landing beneath them had begun to soften, too, and Rose struggled to fight her own instincts.

A disorienting wave of energy emanated from the bud and Rose gulped, convinced that she was slipping on the sagging floorboards. They had tilted back somehow, tipping her towards the long drop beside her. Squeezing her eyes shut, she wrapped her arms tighter around Mary, telling herself that it was all imaginary.

Roaring filled her ears as the tower began to crumble, and Rose's eyes shot open. There was only one way to end this.

"It's OK, Mary, I promise! We're not sliding, it just feels like we are!" she repeated, trying to calm her sister, who was now talking incessantly to distract herself. "I'm going to go and get the Fragmenter. Then this will all be over."

"Be careful," said Matt simply. His face was pale and his voice was strained, but he stood his ground, looking very much like he wished he was anywhere else but here.

Rose turned back to the steps above her. Her hands shook as she took hold of the splintered wood, fighting her way to the upper landing. A horrible moment of stillness settled over the tower. Rose paused with one foot on the last step, her hand outstretched, reaching for the invention. She waited, not daring even to breathe. Her stomach lurched and the tower began to sink, gathering speed as it hurtled towards the ground.

Rose gave a panicked cry and Matt clung to whatever he could reach, but it was too much for Mary. With a shuddering breath, she flung out a spell, fighting to free her mind from the invention's grip. The illusion shattered the moment Mary used her magic. Rose staggered as the world righted itself, the steps suddenly becoming stable and steady beneath her.

Mary sobbed with relief. A flash of green caught Rose's eye and she looked up to see the bud's casing unravelling, recognising attack. The air seethed and crackled with energy. In seconds the invention's defensive magic had surrounded her, pressing in on her until she felt she could hardly breathe.

She doubled over, wondering if her bones were about to break. Through watering eyes, she saw the bricks in the walls reduced to dust around her, crushed by some unseen force. It was as though the Fragmenter had put out a giant, invisible hand and pressed down on them. The pressure continued to build and a groan escaped Rose's clenched teeth as the building began to tremble for a second time.

"Now it really *is* coming down!"

Mary stared at the nearest hole in the wall with fresh horror before turning and racing back down the steps. Matt and Rose followed without a word, fighting against the crushing pressure and frantically sending out spells to stabilise and repair the tower as they fled. They stumbled back out into the street as the top of the tower broke off, slamming into the houses hugging its base and taking the Fragmenter with it.

Rose felt the earth beneath her shake as the top of the tower sent debris flying through the streets. The invention continued to bear down on them, and Rose could do nothing but wait for the pressure to pass, not daring to use any more magic. Matt and Mary were doubled over beside her, gritting their teeth in the middle of the road.

Rose's knees were almost ready to give way when it stopped, leaving her gasping for breath and aching all over. The three of them stood huddled together, watching in shock as the tower settled and silence fell.

"Well, that was a disaster," panted Mary, her face filled with guilt now that she was back on solid ground.

"And we still don't have the Fragmenter!" said Matt. He ran a hand through his hair and shot a look of purest loathing in the direction of the buried invention. "I'm going back before it disappears again."

He marched down the street towards the crushed houses, his shoulders slumped. Rose groaned and ran to catch up with him. The tower had completely destroyed the nearest house and blocked the entrance with rubble, and they had to push at the door for several minutes until the opening was big enough for them to squeeze through. Rose ducked her head under an enormous wooden beam that had forced its way through the ceiling and stared around at the mess.

"It's going to be impossible to find the bud in all of this!" she cried, stepping into the room and sinking up to her knees in the wreckage. It reached the ceiling in some places, and she struggled to keep her balance as she forced her way further inside, looking for a glint of green. "I'm not sure we'll be able to reach the other parts of the house."

She placed a foot on top of a jumble of bricks and splintered wood that blocked the doorway to the adjoining room, but it collapsed as she shifted her weight. She stepped back, extracting her leg while Mary stood by the front door, peering into the rubble's depths. She pointed to the far end of the room, where a corner of the mantelpiece was visible.

"Is it me, or is there a faint glow coming from over there?"

Rose bent down and saw a gap in the broken floorboards, out of which a clear white light shone.

"How're we going to get over there?" Matt asked.

Mary took a tentative step forward, her eyes narrowed as she sized up the pile of rubbish.

"I'm the smallest. I might fit through?"

She ducked under the wooden beam and clambered over a tumble of bricks and tiles, working her way over to the opposite wall. Rose watched nervously, wishing she could use another spell to keep the rubbish from falling on her, but Mary managed to wriggle into the opening without difficulty. Stretching out a hand, she reached down into the dark gap beneath the floor.

"I've got it!" Mary's voice rang out from under the debris.

Rose punched the air.

"Yes! Brilliant! You've done great, Mary!"

Matt climbed over the mess, getting as close as possible without disturbing the mounds.

"Wait, what happened to the door?"

He stopped and stared back the way they'd come. Rose looked over her shoulder to find the roof, windows and doors shrinking and turning into blank grey walls, just as they had in her dreams, days before. Terror turned her insides to ice. Her nightmares had come to life!

"It's trapping us in here!" she gasped.

Desperate to run, she began to scramble for the exit, but stopped, forcing herself to stay put. They were too close to give up now. Matt's expression turned to alarm as the walls closed up. He bent down and called to Mary, still grappling with the Fragmenter.

"Is everything OK under there?" he asked in a falsely-calm voice.

Claustrophobia settled over Rose like a suffocating blanket as the doors and windows vanished entirely, leaving them with no way out. Her heart thudded frantically in her chest. The bud was playing tricks again, that was all.

"The windows and doors are still there," she murmured. "It just wants you to *think* you're trapped. Nothing has changed."

She turned back to her sister.

"I can't get it out," Mary called, pulling hard enough to make the rubble above her wobble. "It's caught on something."

Rose swallowed loudly, her throat dry as paper. The light from the Fragmenter was brighter now, and there was a sleepy, serene note to Mary's voice that worried her. Matt glanced at Rose, clearly thinking something similar. They both crowded around the gap Mary had all but disappeared into.

"We need to go now," urged Rose, attempting to drag her back out by her feet, the only part of her she could now reach.

"Not without the invention!" Mary protested, gripping the broken floorboards with stubborn fingers.

"Leave it!" insisted Matt, taking hold of Mary's legs and pulling. "It's not worth losing your magic for."

Mary backed out of the rubble with a yelp.

"The Fragmenter's working," she said stiffly, confirming Rose's fears. "I tried to grab it, but it put out a tendril and tried to take hold of me!" She staggered to her feet and stopped.

"The door's gone," she said in confusion.

"It's not really," replied Matt. "We just need to find it again."

Rose stumbled over to where the door had been moments earlier and began running her hands over the blank wall, trying in vain to find the doorknob, but the spell was strong, and her hands swept over the wall without success.

"Let's look for a window instead," she suggested, clambering over to roughly the right spot.

The light from the Fragmenter was blinding now, and Rose felt herself beginning to tire. She ran her hands over the wall again, with the same result. Refusing to be put off, she scrambled over the rubble into the next room and tried again. Finding nothing, she backed into the corner, as far away from the invention as she could get.

"How far away do we need to be from the Fragmenter to be safe from it?" asked Matt, as he and Mary worked their way towards her. Rose gave an involuntary shudder.

"I don't know, but I'm sure we need to be further away than this. I can still feel its magic from here."

"We're not going to get out in time," said Mary faintly, hiding behind the rubble as though she thought it would protect her from the bud's curse.

Matt let his hands fall to his sides and leaned against the wall. Weariness washed over Rose's limbs, but she couldn't bear the thought of standing here huddled in the corner, doing nothing while the invention slowly drained her. She reached into the wreckage.

"We will. We have to."

Her fingers closed around a sturdy piece of wood and she wrenched it free, smashing it against the walls.

"It's no use, it's too late," muttered Matt, lowering

himself onto a fallen roof tile.

Mary watched with dim eyes as Rose worked her way around the room. Her arms screamed with tiredness, and she was having difficulty moving further through the debris, but the sight of her brother and sister sprawled out listlessly over the broken boards was enough to sustain her.

She struck another section of the wall and the sound of breaking glass rang out, sharp and clear. She stopped with the piece of wood protruding from what appeared to be solid wall. Matt blinked and surged to his feet. He and Mary threw themselves over to where Rose stood, helping her clear the rest of the glass out of the window before scrambling out through the hole. Mary went through first, disappearing from sight the moment she cleared the windowsill, but her voice called back to the others.

"I can see you both! The window's right in front of you!"

Matt propelled himself through like a diver coming up for air. When he was safely outside, Rose tossed her plank aside and followed him, landing painfully on her knees on the narrow stretch of lawn beneath the window. Free at last, her eyes drank in the cool green of the garden beds around her.

"We're not out of trouble yet," warned Matt, pointing at the sky. "I think we're about to find out how Jacob got all those weird injuries …"

Rose looked up and her breath caught in her throat. For the first time since they'd arrived in this world, the atmosphere was changing. The clear blue sky above the house was rapidly disappearing, replaced instead by low, dark storm clouds. Rose clambered up off the grass, feeling like her legs were made of putty.

She remembered Alison telling her that the invention's defensive spells were able to travel a long way away from the bud itself. The energy around the house intensified, and she knew that the Fragmenter wasn't going to let them go this time. Magic surged out of the ruined building towards them and Rose found strength she didn't know she possessed.

"Run! We need to get back to the safe house!"

"It might not even be there anymore!" panted Mary, her feet scraping the concrete as Rose tugged her down the garden path and out into the road.

Ignoring this, Rose glanced over her shoulder as she ran, suddenly truly afraid. There was nothing to see behind them, but she could feel the magic following them. It was all around her, like heat from a fire, invisible but deadly. They reached the end of the street and stopped, unsure which way to go, and Rose gave a shout of surprise and delight. By some miracle, the safe house was there, its door open and waiting for them beside the city bank.

Unable to believe their luck, Rose ran towards it, her feet pounding the road. She could hear the usual destruction following the Fragmenter as it chased them and she wondered if they were going to reach safety in time. They were only a block away from the open door when Rose realised that it was becoming more and more difficult to run. The road was turning into thick, sticky tar, catching her feet and holding her back.

She lurched to a stop as her feet stuck fast, sinking into the road. Matt and Mary were now further ahead and had almost reached the stone house. Ripping their shoes out of the road, they crossed the threshold and hurled themselves into the hall, safe at last. Rose tugged at her feet, but she was unable to pull herself free from the road.

"Come on, you're almost there!" Matt called, while Mary jumped up and down in agitation.

A pattering sound reached Rose's ears. Rain began to fall, and she flinched as a droplet struck her with enough force to scratch her skin.

"Ow!" she cried, rubbing her neck and hands as heat bit into her skin. "What the -?"

The scorching rain became thicker and she threw her arms up over her head. Droplets tore into her like daggers of molten metal, drawing blood and leaving blisters on any exposed flesh it could find. The smell of burning hair and skin filled Rose's nostrils, and the bank beside her, already barely standing, groaned and collapsed, the bricks sizzling like hot oven stones.

Desperate now, Rose slipped out of her trainers, hopping and stumbling the rest of the way through the tar in her socks, leaving her shoes embedded in the road. Matt and Mary moved out of the way and Rose crashed into the door, using the bolts to pull herself up as the Fragmenter descended on her.

"Close the door, quick!" Mary shrieked, backing

away down the hall. But it was too late.

Rose hauled herself over the threshold as the storm of magic reached the safe house and surged up to the open doorway. Rose threw her arms up over her head, waiting for an attack that never came. A shadow flitted past the doorway and Rose jumped with fright.

"Why isn't it coming inside? The door's open!"

The Fragmenter's magic roamed around the building, searching for a way in. The shadow flitted past once more, disappearing so quickly that Rose couldn't be certain she'd seen it, and the energy outside seemed to churn and focus itself into a single spot.

A figure of a person appeared in the doorway. Rose shrieked and backed away, staring at the copy of herself that had materialised. Matt and Mary gasped in shock. The figure resembled Rose perfectly, but its hazel eyes were hollow and empty, devoid of any human quality.

It returned Rose's stare, its face blank and expressionless. It looked at the open door with its many bolts and then stared at Matt and Mary, huddled at the end of the passageway. Putting out a foot, it attempted to step into the building, but the spells over the building were enough to prevent it from moving past the threshold. Rose's clone stretched out a hand instead and felt the air over the doorway, a flicker of frustration chasing across it's face. Intrigued and disturbed in equal measure, Rose edged towards the doorway.

"Leave it alone, Rose!" Matt called in a warning voice.

Rose went right up to the door, face to face with

herself. It looked her in the eye unblinkingly, and a shiver ran down Rose's spine. Unnerved, she reached out and slammed the door in the figure's face, bolting it shut. She retreated to the room at the end of the hall.

"That was so creepy!" whispered Mary, lowering herself shakily onto the stone bench beside Matt. "I didn't know it could do that!"

"Neither did I," said Rose, taking a steadying breath. "But it's pure magic, so I guess it can do whatever it likes."

She eyed the window uneasily.

"Maybe we should cover both windows up. I know it can't get in, but I think we'd feel better if they were boarded up or something."

Matt and Mary agreed without hesitation. They fixed a sheet of canvas over the window in the workshop, then hurried upstairs to do the same in the pantry. Reassured, they went back downstairs and settled themselves on the tiny stone bench. Rose sat on the floor with her back pressed against the wall, enjoying the cool feel of the stone against her burns. She looked ruefully at her raw and blistered hands, and her tar-covered socks, wanting nothing more than to curl into a ball and forget about the Fragmenter.

"That was close," breathed Mary. "I thought we were done for!"

"I'm glad it can't come in here," said Matt in a low voice. "I'd like to know what spells Grandpa put on this place to keep that thing out!"

Rose nodded, cringing in pain but trying not to let

the other two see.

"What time is it?" she asked.

Matt checked his watch.

"It's only ten o'clock, but I'm going to need a moment to rest before I can fight with that monster out there again!"

"I don't want to go out there ever again!" cried Mary. "Those defence spells are scary!"

Rose sighed and drew her knees up under her chin.

"We'll try again tomorrow," she said. "I don't want to go out there, either. Matt's right. We need to rest."

They sat quietly, listening to the occasional rustling and creaking sounds from outside. Now and then a shadow would move past the window, dark against the cream coloured cloth as the magic of the Fragmenter continued to prowl the perimeter, searching for a way in. Rose shivered and turned to face the wall instead.

20

The Fragmenter at Last

They removed the canvas over the windows to find that the safe house had changed location. The Fragmenter had abandoned the building in what should have been the early morning hours, disappearing to defend the bud as the city rearranged itself and the invention moved further away, finally allowing Rose, Matt and Mary to sleep.

Rose rubbed her eyes with a red and blistered hand and picked out a packet of biscuits for breakfast, looking out of the window at the dilapidated post office across the road. The windows were broken and the front door was barely hanging on, reminding her of Hunter's door in the Archives. The sky had returned to its usual clear blue state, the fake sunlight shining with eye-watering brightness on the tiled roofs across the street.

"I wish we had some of Mum and Dad's inventions in here with us," said Matt wistfully as he ate. "It'd make everything so much easier."

"Why don't we make something, then?" suggested Mary. "That's what we do best, isn't it?"

Matt glanced around the bare room and arched an eyebrow.

"There's nothing here to make an invention out of!"

"And even if there was, what could we possibly make that could control the Fragmenter?" wondered Rose. "It's made of pure magic. At best, any invention would only be equal to it in strength, and we need something stronger."

Matt finished eating and brushed the crumbs off his shirt, his eyes bright with excitement.

"But it's like you said before, Rose! Beating an invention isn't always about fighting it. I bet Grandpa knew that, too. Everyone says Hunter isn't much of an inventor, right? I bet Grandpa used that to his advantage, somehow."

Rose broke a biscuit into pieces and let it dissolve in her mouth while she thought, unsure if adding another invention to the mix was wise. What if it only made things worse?

"Are you sure you want to add more magic to this place?" she said eventually. "What if the Fragmenter uses it to make itself stronger, like the prototype did? And besides, we still don't know how the bud works. How can we counter it if we don't understand it?"

But she could tell that Matt was committed to the idea now. He sat on the stone bench with his hands clasped over his knees, his face full of determination.

"We might not have to know everything about it! We just need to block it out! What if we make an extra strong shield or something?"

Rose glanced at her sister, remembering what had happened to their parents' Shield when confronted with the Fragmenter. Mary seemed pensive as she scrunched up her empty packet of dried fruit and poked it into Rose's bag.

"We might as well give it a try. We don't have any other plans."

Matt jumped up from the bench so enthusiastically that he knocked it over.

"Wait! I have the perfect idea! And we wouldn't even have to do any of the hard work ourselves! Even better!"

He let out a cackle of laughter, his expression gleeful. Rose washed her biscuit down with a gulp of water and waited for Matt to speak.

"What is it? What are you talking about?" she said finally, when Matt didn't elaborate.

Matt set the bench upright and sat cross-legged on it again, his eyes sparkling with mischief.

"We're safe in this house because of the spells Grandpa put on it, right? We saw last night that the Fragmenter can't come in here, even when it really wants to, and we need a way of getting close to the invention without it attacking us. So why don't we just shift the protective spells from this building onto something we can carry around with us? We'd be protected no matter where we went, even if the Fragmenter was nearby and we attacked it!"

Rose's mouth fell open. She stared at Matt for a moment, thinking his plan through. Mary, as usual, found her voice first.

"Yeah! Why didn't we think of that before?!"

Rose leapt to her feet, all of her weariness forgotten

in an instant. Matt was right. It was so simple!

"Matt, that's brilliant! I really think you've got it!"

Her eyes raked over the room, her heart pounding in her chest as the possibilities presented themselves to her. "What are we going to shift the spells onto?"

Matt headed for the hall, looking smug.

"Well, let's collect everything we can find in here and upstairs, to see what we've got to work with."

He disappeared down the passageway, leaving Rose and Mary to search the room they were in. He returned several minutes later and they gathered together all of the discarded scraps, materials and tools from both rooms, placing them in a pile on the bench.

"So," said Matt, inspecting their collection. "Let's have a look at what we've got."

"It should be something that won't get in the way when we're carrying it, and won't get lost if we drop it when we're running or something," insisted Mary, eyeing the long, awkward rolls of canvas. Rose closed her eyes as though listening for some distant sound.

"The spells on the building were designed to protect whatever is inside them," she murmured, assessing the magic on the room the way Alison and Ben had analysed Hunter's room at the Archives. "If we're outside the building, they can't protect us. If we transfer them onto an object, it'll be the same. They'll only protect whatever is inside the object and we'll be outside it."

"Not if we increase its range," said Matt. "If we push the spells out from the object, so that it protects not just itself, but whatever's near it, we should be fine," said

Matt, sorting through the pile almost feverishly.

His energy was infectious, and soon Rose and Mary found themselves copying him, picking out anything they thought might stand a chance of holding the safe house's spells.

"We're going to do it this time, I know it!" sang Mary as they worked.

Rose smiled. Between the pocket watch compass and Grandpa's protective spells, it would be difficult to fail, and hope flared up inside her for the first time since they'd discovered the watch's secret. If they were successful, they could be back in the real world in a matter of hours, but there was one problem, as Matt soon discovered.

"Didn't Grandpa say in his reports that the first casings he used to make the invention weren't able to withstand the spells he'd put on them? They all fell to pieces until he found something strong enough."

Rose considered the chisel in her hand, her mouth pulled down into a frown.

"Yes, you're right. Most of the stuff we have here won't be able to contain the protective spells on this building, either. If they can hold the Fragmenter back, they must be strong."

"And if we take the spells off the house, only to put them on something that breaks, what will that do to the spells?" asked Mary in a tone that suggested she could guess the answer.

"They'd dissipate," replied Rose, "and we'd be without any protection at all."

Mary blanched.

"Uh, maybe we should test everything first, then. To make sure they'll hold up."

"Yeah, I think that's a good idea," laughed Rose. She nodded at the bench, feeling increasingly uncomfortable about what they were about to do. "These are hardly invention-making materials, that's for sure."

Matt said nothing but proceeded to put his strongest magic on each item, standing back to let Rose and Mary do the same. It was amazing, thought Rose, how differently each material reacted to the same magic. She wasn't surprised when the canvas was reduced to trailing threads, but the iron tools, which she had expected to hold up best, were now twisted and riddled with tiny holes. She pushed forward the scraps of invention pieces next, curious to see how they would fare. The three of them cast their spells and then stood back, waiting for the verdict.

"Come on, you can do it!" Mary encouraged them as they began to glow with a wavering blue light, but Rose felt them failing long before she noticed any visible signs of decay, and sure enough, the pieces broke apart with a sharp *snap*. Matt let out an exasperated sigh and Mary pouted.

"Wait, we haven't tried everything yet," said Rose, running down the hall and shoving the door open. As a last resort, she fetched some broken glass and bricks from the street, placing them on the bench before subjecting them to the same treatment.

Her spirits sank as the glass was reduced to sandy

grains. The bricks survived longest of all, but even they crumbled after a minute or two of pressure. The only untested objects in the room were the blank notebooks and Rose's bag. She shook her head, certain that neither would have a chance of surviving. She stared around the room, refusing to be put off.

"Hmm. How about this, then?"

She took the ruined chisel from the heap of tools and, using magic to help it along, chipped off a jagged, knife-sized piece of the stone wall.

"It's had Grandpa's spells on it since this place was made and it's survived," she said, placing the stone on the bench beside the destroyed items.

Rose crossed all of her fingers as they tested it and waited for the spells to settle. Seconds turned into minutes, but the stone piece remained unharmed.

"It's holding it!" cried Mary, doing a victory dance around the room.

She high-fived Matt and they cleared away the other materials, gathering around the stone for the next stage of their experiment. Rose took a deep breath. They only had one chance to get this right.

"This had better work. If it goes wrong and we end up with no protection in here, we're going to be in real trouble."

"It'll work," said Matt, sounding more desperate than confident. "I hope! On the count of three, we'll move the spells. Ready? One, two, three!"

Rose screwed up her eyes and balled up her fists, bracing herself as the pressure of the spells shifted from the building onto herself. She was soon panting with the effort of holding them in place. They were so strong! So strong that she almost couldn't contain them.

Quickly, before she ran out of willpower, she directed the magic onto the piece of stone, willing it to stay put. She wrapped the spells around the stone, binding them to it, and then pushed them out like she was blowing up a balloon, expanding them until they filled the room.

She opened her eyes. The stone remained in one piece, and while it looked the same as ever, it now felt very different, emitting waves of energy that tingled on Rose's skin. They'd done it! Rose let out a giddy sigh of relief as Matt and Mary whooped and cheered.

"How far can we go from the stone before it stops protecting us?" she wondered.

She retreated slowly, feeling for the edge of the spells and stopping when their influence was lost.

"We've got about four metres in each direction," said Matt, looking impressed. "We did pretty well."

Like the stone, the safe house appeared unchanged, but Rose no longer felt safe inside its walls the way she always had in the past. She hoped they'd made the right decision. A mixture of nerves and excitement fluttered in her stomach as Matt turned the stone over in his hand, looking down at it with pride.

"Soon we'll have night again!" said Mary. "And real food and water!"

"Let's go, then," urged Matt. "What's the point in hanging around?"

In answer, Rose and Mary charged over to the door, heaving it open. Rose held her bag out to Matt.

"Put the stone in here. It'll be safe with everything else."

Matt complied and Rose checked that the archway and Miranda's invention were inside, ready to return to the real world. She slung the bag over her shoulder and, after a moment's thought, bent down and tugged off her tar-covered socks, flinging them into the corner.

She marched out into the street with the stone at her side, barefoot and wondering where they were going to find the Fragmenter this time. Holding the watch out in front of her, she allowed it to guide her into the heart of the city, past the park with the fallen trees, to an area where the road forked.

The left-hand route skirted around the city centre for some way before diving between the high-rise offices, past a sprawling city hospital, a swimming centre with signs out the front advertising heated pools, and the well-kept grass of a football field, while the right led to a row of very ordinary-looking townhouses.

Rose stopped at the corner between the two, wondering which path they should take. She glanced down at the watch doubtfully. The hands pointed in opposite directions, the hour hand indicating the street on the left, the minute hand the street on the right.

"I guess that means there are two ways of getting to the invention from here. Which one do you want to try?"

Matt shaded his eyes with his hands and peered in each direction before turning left.

"Let's go this way. It looks more interesting."

He stepped out onto the road towards the sports field. Rose quickened her pace to keep up with him, eyeing the hazy outline of the high-rise buildings with trepidation.

Unlike most of the buildings she'd seen so far, the stands around the sports field were entirely undamaged. Rose slowed her steps, peering up at the structure and shielding her eyes from the glare as she walked past, but there was nothing of interest to see and she moved on.

They continued along the road until the watch shifted, pointing them down a dirty alleyway that opened up onto another heavily damaged section of the city. Rose stopped and looked around her, wary of any black fissures that might be lurking nearby. Matt and Mary seemed to think this was wise, and they proceeded with more caution, working their way back towards the heart of the city.

Rose checked the watch once more, hoping that it would direct them away from the ruins, but it led them right up to the door of an unstable-looking office block at a wide intersection. Rose looked up at the bare, bleak building and counted four levels. It was a strange, irregular shape and gave off a rather dismal air. Rose heaved a deep sigh.

"Don't worry, it'll be the last time we have to do this," Matt assured her. But Rose paused on the doorstep, clutching her bag closer.

"What are we going to do if this sets the Fragmenter off?" She indicated the bulge where the stone lay. "If it doesn't like us doing magic around it, it won't like Grandpa's safe spells."

Matt approached the door with a look of unconcern. "It won't matter. As long as we're in the stone's range we'll be protected. We'll be fine, you'll see."

He threw the door open and stepped inside. Rose and Mary followed him more cautiously and immediately came to a halt.

"Whoa!" Rose let out a disbelieving laugh. "Something must have gone really wrong with the magic in this place!"

A jumble of confused stairways was visible beyond a cramped reception area, one leading up into the dark, a second that began halfway up the wall, and a third that led into solid brick. Like the rest of this world, the building was eerie and silent.

"This has to be the weirdest place I've ever been in," Rose exclaimed in a hushed voice, following the watch's directions to the only staircase that looked functional, hoping it would take them to the first floor. "It's like the building's been scrambled or something!"

The stairs did indeed lead to the first floor, but they fell short of the landing by roughly four feet, leaving Rose, Matt and Mary stuck at the top of the stairs, faced with another blank stretch of wall. With a kind of awkward running jump, Rose and Matt managed to clamber up onto the landing, but Mary, being smaller, needed to be pulled up.

Rose allowed her eyes to adjust to the darkness before stepping into the corridor. It soon veered out of sight, and she walked cautiously, her feet silent on the threadbare carpet. Windows were scarce and as misplaced as the stairs. Rose let out a snort of laughter as she contemplated the nearest, which provided a strip of light an inch high before the glass disappeared beneath the carpet.

She continued down the corridor, peering into offices as she passed them and doing her best to follow the watch's directions. The whole building seemed to be made up of separate pieces that didn't fit together. Rose wasn't quite sure what to make of it. Had the Fragmenter done this? Or had the spells on the building been damaged in some other way?

Her thoughts went back months ago to when Mum had tasked them with placing defensive spells around the house. Remembering the resulting mess of magic when the Fragmenter had altered everything to its liking, she nodded, certain now that the invention was to blame.

They searched the first floor quickly, weaving their way through office compartments and meeting rooms, searching through lockers and drawers. Frustratingly, the watch kept steering them towards the interior of the building, straight into solid brick wall. After ten minutes or so of fruitless searching, Rose turned her back on the offices and headed for the door at the far end of the room.

"Let's keep going. There might be a hallway or something on the right further on," she said.

To her relief, another staircase did indeed branch off the hall, and Rose led the way upstairs. The upper levels looked much the same as the ones below, but the windows were situated above the floor, allowing the light to stream in through the grimy glass and showing up the old, shabby furniture and peeling paint on the walls.

Rose noticed the atmosphere growing tense as she approached the top floor, and felt the tiny hairs on the back of her neck standing up, telling her that they must be getting close now. Emerging from the stairs, they stepped out into a tea room, with snacks and a freshly brewed cup of coffee sitting on the table.

Rose's gaze travelled from the fridge humming in the corner to the tap dripping in the kitchen. She stopped underneath a flickering light panel, facing yet another blank stretch of brick wall.

"I don't get it. We've searched every floor and the Fragmenter's not in any of the offices on the other side of that wall!"

She let her breath out in a rush and turned to see what Matt and Mary made of this bizarre situation, finally noticing Mary poking at a dark hole in the wall.

"What is that?"

She and Matt came to look, too, and the three of them bent over the hole. Like the misplaced windows, it was an inch above the floor, but it extended far enough into the brickwork for Mary to insert her arm inside it. Matt brushed a hand over the wall, slowly moving back the way they'd come. He let out a yell near the stairs.

"There's another one over here!"

Rose and Mary hurried over to find a hole nestled

close to the top step, big enough to fit Matt's foot inside. He and Mary exchanged a confused look, and Rose bent down to examine the space, an idea developing in her mind.

"I might be crazy, but I think these gaps might be corridors or rooms that tried to form and failed. The spells on this building are so scrambled that parts of it didn't take shape properly."

She left the other two inspecting the hole while she raced downstairs to the floor below, checking the rooms more closely this time. Within minutes she'd found another six gaps, each of them terminating in a dead end between the walls of the building.

"Rose! Over here!"

Matt's voice called down the stairs, full of urgency. Rose straightened up, reluctantly leaving the promising-looking space she'd found in the locker room floor. Running up the steps, she came to a halt outside the tea room, panting. Matt and Mary were gathered around the door, looking both excited and annoyed.

"No wonder we didn't notice it the first time!" grumbled Mary, beckoning to her sister. "It's behind the door!"

Matt swung the door closed. A brick had been dislodged higher up in the wall, creating a hole large enough for them to reach into. A very familiar light emanated from it as Rose stood on tiptoe to look through the opening.

"I knew it!" she groaned.

The room was just another ordinary office, with

scratched desks, rows of computers and a photocopier. But it seemed to Rose that it had sunk several feet, so that it sat somewhere between this floor and the one below.

Rose didn't bother to try to understand how this was possible. Instead, she focused her attention on the bright green invention perched serenely upon the desk across the room, out of reach.

The only door was bizarrely located in the floor and the windows looked out onto solid brick. Rose took a step back, wondering whether to laugh out loud or yell in frustration. She took a seat at the tea room table, her mind racing.

"How on earth are we going to get in there?"

She placed the watch on the table. Both hands were now moving around the clock face, backwards and forwards. It knew they'd found the Fragmenter …

Matt pounded the bricks around the opening with a fist, but they held firm. He stopped, glaring at the invention.

"If only I had my Hook with me! It could bring the bud to us! One of the last attachments I installed is enchanted to make things fit through spaces that are too small!"

He leaned against the wall, looking devastated. Rose felt truly bewildered. Wandering up and down the stairs, she looked for a way inside the room, but without success. Whenever they were on the top level, they were too high to access the room, but when they descended to the floor below they weren't high enough. All she could think to do was to continue checking for misplaced or half-formed openings, sure that there must be a way in somewhere.

"How did it even get *in* there?" demanded Matt, his temper flaring. The idea of the Fragmenter being so close, but just out of reach, seemed to be too much for him to bear. He, Rose and Mary roamed up and down a few more times before conceding defeat, sitting on the steps between floors.

"If this place is as messed up as it seems, there might not even *be* a way in," said Mary, her arms wrapped around her knees. Rose picked at a blister on her hand, thinking.

"Maybe we should wait for it to shift location," she suggested. "It always moves sooner or later."

"But what if it keeps putting itself in places like this?" countered Matt. "We can't afford to keep waiting around. The Fragmenter's always going to make it difficult for us. It's managed to stop us every time we get near it! It'll just find a different way of stopping us next time. We have to do it now."

They considered getting the invention's defensive spells to destroy the wall for them by attacking it through the gap in the brickwork, but they soon decided against this. As Mary pointed out, it would most likely result in the bud being buried. It would damage everything around it, not just the one wall they wanted.

Rose stood up abruptly, remembering the hole in the locker room she'd been investigating before Matt had distracted her. She found the second-floor landing and ran back down the hall.

"Where are you going?" called Mary, following her.

Rose found the opening and stared uneasily at the space leading down into the darkness. She got down onto her knees and stuck her head into the hole.

"Anything in there?"

Matt's voice became louder as his footsteps drew nearer. Rose straightened up and dusted her jeans off.

"I can't see very much. It's too dark. I'll need to go further in."

She folded her arms across her chest, contemplating the neat rectangular shape in the floor. It was very narrow. After a moment of deliberation, she lay flat on the floor and slid her shoulders through the opening. Blinking dust and dirt out of her eyes, she stared around, allowing her eyes to adjust to the darkness.

"Yeah, I think we should have a closer look inside here," she said, hoisting herself back up and sitting on the edge so that she could lower her legs into the dark space instead. "It looks like the passageway heads away from the sunken room, but there's nothing blocking it for a fair way. For all we know it turns around further down. I'll see if it goes anywhere useful."

"OK, but be careful," said Matt, peering down at the hard floor below.

Rose lowered herself into the gap until her legs dangled awkwardly, the rough edges of the concrete biting into her hands. The space was deeper than she'd thought. She let go and hit the floor with a huff, rolling a short way before coming to a stop.

"Are you OK?"

Matt and Mary's voices came floating down to her, their faces peering at her from high above.

"I'm fine," said Rose through gritted teeth.

She clambered up and took in her surroundings, becoming aware that she was standing on a smooth stretch of concrete that sloped downwards before turning a corner and plunging down into total darkness.

"What can you see?" called Matt eagerly from above.

Rose looked up at the roof and stopped.

"Uh, this isn't a corridor after all," she chortled, still gazing up at the ceiling. "It's another staircase, only the stairs are on the ceiling instead of on the floor."

Matt and Mary exchanged a look before calling down to her again.

"How far does it go?"

Rose edged forward, breathing in the scent of dust as she approached the corner. The floor sloped at a sharp angle to follow the stairs and she had to be careful not to slide. Reaching the corner, she stared down into the blackness. It was impossible to say how far the passage extended. She traced her steps back to the opening and called to her brother and sister.

"I don't know. I'll have to go down there and see where it leads."

"We're coming with you," said Matt, sliding feet first through the gap and landing beside Rose with a thud. Rose helped steady him as he stumbled forward. He beckoned to Mary.

"Jump and I'll catch you."

Mary looked at the concrete below her with apprehension before swinging her legs into the hole and sliding in. Matt caught her and set her down on the sloping floor, while Rose repositioned her bag over her shoulder, ready to set off.

The other two stared up at the misplaced stairs and followed Rose over to the corner, descending into the darkness. Rose pressed her hands up against the walls on either side of her, feeling her way along until she walked into solid wall. She backed up a step, rubbing the end of her nose and muttering under her breath.

"There's another corner here," she warned the others.

She put her hands out again and felt around in the air. Her right hand met concrete, but her left found only emptiness, so she turned and stumbled on, treading carefully until she noticed a faint white light emanating from somewhere up ahead.

The stairway came to an abrupt end and another wall loomed up before them, blocking their path. Rose craned her head back, struggling to distinguish the outline of the stairs in the gloom. She considered using magic to light the space but decided against it. They couldn't afford to risk triggering the Fragmenter, especially now that they were bringing Grandpa's safe spells so close to the bud.

The ceiling had smoothed out into another corridor, devoid of any features at all except for a single doorway. It, too, was misplaced, sitting squarely over their heads. White light issued from the cracks around the door, illuminating their faces and casting an eerie glow over the corridor. Rose could already feel the pressure building in the narrow hall, and she braced herself, knowing that the invention would be ready to attack the moment they were within reach.

"I think it's time to take the stone out," she said, slinging her bag off her shoulder and hunting inside it. Clutching the stone in one hand and feeling more nervous than ever, she looked up at the door in the ceiling.

"Er, how are we going to get up there?"

There was nothing to climb on, and with magic ruled out, it would be difficult to access the sunken room.

"I could stand on your shoulders and you could push me up?" suggested Mary in a small voice.

"Hmm."

Rose didn't like the sound of this plan, but she could think of no alternative. Matt was thin and wiry, but Mary was smaller, and Rose thought she could lift her more easily than her brother. Matt, too, seemed uneasy at the thought of Mary facing the Fragmenter alone, but he nodded once, his expression grim.

Rose passed the stone to Mary, who took it with a word of thanks. Climbing onto Rose's shoulders, she reached up and opened the door. It swung upwards as Rose pushed Mary higher, and Mary took hold of the doorframe, hoisting herself into the room.

Rose tensed as she watched Mary's feet disappear into the space, coming back into view a second later as she straightened up and took a step across the room.

"Can you reach the Frag-"

A loud ringing sound filled the corridor, drowning Matt's words, and he let out a yelp, covering his ears with both hands. The sound bounced around Rose's skull and she clapped her hands over her own ears as the sound only intensified. Something raked across her face and she shrieked, flinching as invisible fingernails clawed at her neck and face. A yell from Matt suggested that he was suffering the same fate.

Rose cursed. They must be out of range of the stone piece. She looked up to find Mary running towards the open door, unscratched but cringing with discomfort. The invisible hands ceased their attack as soon as Mary drew near, and Rose rubbed her raw skin.

Mary held the Fragmenter tightly, her expression a mix of confusion and fear as bursts of light popped into existence and disappeared around her like lightning. Spots of colour remained suspended in the air, fading slowly.

"Yes! I knew Grandpa's spells would keep us safe!" Matt crowed, keeping close to the stone.

As he'd promised, the Fragmenter was active but unable to harm them. The air churned and raged around them as the invention attempted to fend them off. Grandpa's safe spells had done their job.

"What's going on?" Mary screeched, as the lights became larger and more numerous, glowing in the dark corridor.

Rose winced as another stab of light flashed close to her face. Breathing in the smell of smoke, she moved closer to her sister, away from the long streak of blue light hovering in the air beside her, immediately reminded of the colourful lights Ben and Matt had created when they'd destroyed the little invention containing illusion spells. Horror constricted her chest as comprehension dawned on her.

"The bud's not supposed to go inside the safe house and we've taken it right inside the range of Grandpa's safe spells! They're trying to fight each other off! This world is made almost entirely of illusion spells. These flashing lights are the spells being destroyed by the Fragmenter!"

The flashes grew more frequent, dazzling her eyes. She could feel the already scrambled spells of the building changing around her, reacting to the storm of magic. Matt swore as a tremor ran through the corridor, making the walls shiver. Energy tingled on Rose's skin as she desperately tried to deactivate the bud. It seemed ridiculous to her that she'd never thought to ask Alison how to do it.

Heat built up against her hip and she looked down, groping around in her bag. Her fingers closed on a searing hot piece of metal and she gasped in pain, wrapping her hand in her sleeve to lift out the silver archway, shining in her hand.

The bud glowed more brightly with each second that passed, while the archway and the stone piece in Mary's hand appeared to diminish, and Rose knew that the Fragmenter would suck the magic out of both to repair itself if left to its devices for too much longer.

Feeling faintly sick, she suspected that, like the building itself, the archway's spells had already been damaged by the two fighting inventions. Bolts of light struck the archway as she held it, and she jumped, almost dropping it in her surprise. She shoved it back into her bag.

"How do we deactivate the Fragmenter?" she cried, her heart pounding much too fast as she tried anything she could think of. But Matt could only shake his head, his eyes wide with fear.

Mary struck the invention with one hand forcibly and commanded it to stop the way Alison had done when Rose had been bitten by the Booster. Heat and smoke haze now filled the corridor and tremors continued to rumble through the building.

Rose's claustrophobia gripped her as a particularly violent shudder shook the corridor, and she gasped in fear, staring up at the room above her, suddenly terrified that the building would collapse and bury her alive. With a groan of desperation, she forced her attention back to the Fragmenter, her hands shaking as they clutched the leather strap of her bag.

She and Matt huddled close to the doorway, seeking the safety of Grandpa's spells, while Mary bent over the bud in the room above. Using every deactivation spell they'd been taught, they bombarded the bud with magic until finally, their spells hit it in unison.

The ringing stopped, leaving a deafening silence in its place. Coloured scars hung in the air everywhere Rose looked, bright but fading slowly. There was no time to ask what spells the others had used to deactivate the bud. She reached up to Mary, ready to catch her so that they could leave, but Mary's eyes were fixed on something further up the stone passage. Rose turned and let out a strangled gasp.

A large section of the floor and walls had disappeared. The dying lights in the air were enough to illuminate the immense black void stretching across the corridor, barely six feet from where they stood. Too wide to jump across, it cut deeply into both walls, trapping them where they stood.

"How are we going to get out?" Mary cried.

Matt tore his eyes away from the black abyss to look up at her.

"We'll all just have to go up into the room with you and hope there's another way out."

He turned to Rose.

"Do you think you can lift me up there?"

Rose nodded. "I think so."

She knelt so that he could climb onto her shoulders, using the wall for stability. Wobbling a little, Rose stood up, pushing him higher until he could get a grip on the doorframe. Mary grabbed his arms and pulled, and soon he was through, leaving Rose alone below. She looked uncertainly at the ceiling. Rose was slim, but definitely not athletic, and she was certain she wouldn't be able to pull herself up without help.

"Hang on," Matt called.

He disappeared, returning a second later with a high-backed wooden chair and a small desk, which he eased through the doorway. Rose felt a rush of gratitude.

"Thanks."

She stepped up onto the desk and set the chair on top. With some help from the other two, she managed to pull herself up into the room. The space was as cold, bare and uninteresting as it had appeared from the hall, and Rose wasted no time in searching for another way out.

She ran to the hole in the wall that looked out onto the tea room, now covered in a sheet of dust. To her intense relief, the repeated tremors had loosened many of the bricks in the wall, enough that she was able to beat the hole wider with another chair, allowing them to squeeze through.

"Yes!" cried Mary triumphantly, stepping up out of the sunken room and hugging the Fragmenter close to her chest.

Rose soon discovered a smaller void gaping beside the stairwell and began to feel uneasy, fearing that substantial damage must have been done to Grandpa's fake world. She averted her eyes from the misplaced windows, afraid of what she would find outside.

They hurried downstairs, pulling up short at the base of the staircase. Rose muttered an oath under her breath. It was the staircase that ended halfway up the wall. She and Matt jumped the rest of the way down, landing hard on the stone floor, catching Mary as she leapt from the bottom step. They ran for the door and threw it open. Rose stared at the scene before her, speechless.

"No!" cried Mary faintly. "What have we done?"

Voids sliced into the air, scarring the landscape wherever Rose looked. Much of the colour had drained from the world, giving it the look of a faded photograph. The spells that had withstood the Fragmenter's assault now felt fragile and unstable, causing many of the buildings to crumble as the world deteriorated.

Rose reached into her bag and lifted out the archway, knowing full well what would happen if their doorway back into the real world was destroyed or damaged beyond repair. The silver was scratched, pitted and bent out of its decorative shape. Its surface had become dull and it had lost the many-coloured sheen that she had always admired.

Matt stood rooted to the spot with his back against the building, his face a mask of despair. He lowered himself onto the shattered doorstep, his hands splayed out in the dust.

"It was my idea to take the Fragmenter into the range of the safe spells," he murmured. He looked up at the enormous black fissures above him and shuddered. "I've destroyed the world!"

Mary gave him a reassuring pat on the shoulder.

"No, you haven't. We only need the archway to open once and we'll be out of here."

Rose waited breathlessly as her sister took the silver invention and squeezed it. The metal flowed up to half its normal height, forming one side of a feeble, twisted arch before collapsing back to the earth.

"We're done for!" Matt cried, his expression slightly wild.

Fighting back tears and trying hard not to panic, Rose rummaged in her bag. Miranda's invention had, by some miracle, escaped the bud's attack.

"We'll keep trying it," declared Rose in a falsely-hopeful voice. She and Mary sat on either side of Matt, squeezing the invention again and again.

"Come on, you can do it!" Mary urged it, on the rare occasion when it began to take shape. It struggled to rise more than a few inches, sending out feeble threads of silver that quivered before giving up and sinking back to the ground. Matt moaned in anguish, his head in his hands.

"If we'd just kept the archway at a safe distance from Grandpa's safe spells it wouldn't have been damaged in the fight and we'd be back in the real world already!"

Rose and Mary glanced at each other, at a loss for what to say.

"Let's find somewhere to rest for a while," said Mary, as the silence stretched on. "We can't sit here in the road forever."

When Matt showed no sign of moving, Rose pulled him to his feet and looped an arm around his shoulders.

"We'll be OK, you'll see."

They took to the streets, looking for a place to stay, but most of the buildings had been too badly damaged. Rose shook her head at more than one house with a teetering veranda or crumbling walls. They continued wandering until they reached the site of their second battle with the Fragmenter, now situated beside the green swathe of parkland. Rose gave a cry and pointed further down the street.

"Hey! My shoes!"

She ran to retrieve them. They were right where she'd left them, embedded in the buckled and scorched road with the heels protruding from the asphalt. She took hold of the tongues of her sneakers and pulled, but they were stuck fast, and after several minutes of fruitless tugging she sighed and straightened up.

"Fine, then! Keep them!" she growled, earning a small smile from Matt.

They wandered on in search of a safe place to stay, eventually choosing a sturdy stone house out past the aquatic centre. Making their way inside, Rose used Miranda's invention to create a frugal lunch, after which they set about trying to repair some of the damage to the archway.

The two girls settled themselves in the armchairs beside the empty fireplace while Matt stretched out on the sofa despondently, and with his and Mary's help, Rose did what she could.

They worked on it for hours, passing it round and round between them. Calling on all of her knowledge and experience in repairing magical objects, Rose soon managed to restore parts of the invention's original shape and smooth out some of the minor scratches, but it remained unable to fully form the archway.

Many of the illusion spells had been damaged or removed entirely, and Rose knew as she twirled the invention between her fingers that she would never be able to replace them. With a sigh, she set it on the table beside her and leaned back in her chair, attempting to hide her emotions from the other two.

"Well, I don't know what else to try. I've never worked on anything this advanced before."

Matt fidgeted on the sofa. Some of his natural confidence had returned as they'd worked, but Rose caught another flicker of anxiety on his face before he looked away.

Five days trickled by in a dull blur. The archway remained damaged and Rose had begun to feel desperate. Worse still, the magic on Miranda's invention had worn off, just as Nate had warned them it would. Things were beginning to look grim and Rose was plagued with near-constant worry that they would never get back to the real world.

Food and water lost its substance, leaving Rose feeling unsatisfied no matter how much she consumed. Until now, Miranda's invention had given them just enough sustenance to keep them energised, but now Rose was reminded once again that copies of food were exactly that, just copies. They could never replace real nutrients.

"We'd better save the spells as much as we can, in case we're stuck here for a long time," she said dismally. "Even if it means we have to go hungry sometimes."

Matt and Mary nodded and said nothing. Meanwhile, Rose lay on the sofa, berating herself and feeling exhausted despite having done very little. Why had they got involved in all of this? She fumed in silence. Mum and Dad had tried so hard to keep herself, Matt and Mary away from the Fragmenter. Why hadn't she listened to her parents?

It was early afternoon, and her mind had wandered to wherever her family was, like it always did these days when she had given up her attempts to repair the archway and had nothing else to do. She had just asked Matt what day it would be out in the real world, when Mary sat up with a start.

"The twenty-ninth?! It's been my birthday for eight hours and I didn't even know it!"

Rose blinked in surprise.

"Why didn't I remember?!" She clapped a hand to her forehead. "You're ten today! Double digits!" she exclaimed, imitating her mother. Matt snorted with laughter.

"I can't believe I'm having my birthday in *here*!" wailed Mary.

"Yeah, when we pictured your tenth birthday party, none of us imagined it would be in a -," began Matt with a laugh.

Rose aimed a kick at his legs and he abruptly changed tack.

"Yeah, that is pretty unfortunate," he finished lamely.

"Don't listen to him!" Rose gave her sister a sunny smile. "We can still have a bit of a party, even if we're stuck in this place."

Matt swung his feet off the table and ran a hand through his unkempt hair.

"Rose, everything's half demolished and nothing's real!"

Rose gazed around the room for inspiration, refusing to take no for an answer.

"I know what we should do! Let's go down to that aquatic centre and have a pool party!"

"If we can find it," muttered Matt.

"We can get some junk food from the store on the way there," continued Rose. "We probably shouldn't use Miranda's invention on it. The spells on it are almost gone, anyway, but we can still get some food."

Mary's eyes brightened at this proposal. Rose gathered the archway and her bag containing the Fragmenter, unwilling to part with it for even a second after all they'd endured to get their hands on it, and they walked to the supermarket that had occupied the block two streets down the day before.

They went carefully, in case any buildings collapsed around them. Only yesterday, Rose had narrowly avoided being crushed by a half-destroyed house that had suddenly given way as she'd walked past. Since there was no need to worry about traffic, she, Matt and Mary had taken to walking in the centre of the road as they traversed the streets.

Rose cleared the corner and was surprised to see that the supermarket hadn't moved. Wandering from aisle to aisle, they had fun selecting the sweets they wanted from the shelves, while Rose picked out balloons and streamers so that she could decorate the house when they returned. Setting out with their shopping, they located the aquatic centre and opened the gate.

"Why didn't we think to bring our swimming gear with us?" joked Matt. "How stupid of us!"

"Who cares!" cried Mary, tossing herself into the nearest pool fully dressed.

They spent the rest of the afternoon swimming, only heading back to the house when all three of them were thoroughly water-logged and had temporarily forgotten their problems. Rose hung up her decorations and they began their meagre feast.

The hours went by, and Rose couldn't help but notice how empty she felt despite all of the food she'd eaten. She wondered how much longer they could survive like this, but said nothing, not wanting to ruin Mary's fun by worrying about supplies.

"Well, we've had a good time, haven't we?" asked Rose eventually, trying to sound positive. "The party wasn't so bad after all."

"Yeah, it was great," said Matt, his voice heavy with sarcasm. "No, it was unreal! Get it?"

He doubled up with laughter. Rose turned to Mary and rolled her eyes, unamused.

"I think the lack of real food has sent him around the bend," she said in a resigned voice.

She grinned at Mary, expecting her to laugh, but instead caught her brushing away a tear. Rose opened her mouth to ask what was the matter, but stopped herself. She was fairly certain she could guess what was upsetting her sister.

"I wish we were with Mum and Dad," mumbled

Mary miserably.

Matt sobered up enough to offer her the last chocolate bar and Rose drew her sister into a hug, trying hard not to cry herself.

"I miss them, too. But we'll be back with them again soon. We'll keep working on the archway first thing in the morning."

Mary placed her uneaten potato chips back onto the pile of food.

"I think I'll just go to bed."

Rose watched her disappear down the hall before snatching up the silver invention and squeezing it again.

"I don't think that's going to work," said Matt from the sofa, his expression sombre as he bit a piece off a roll of liquorice.

"We have to keep trying," replied Rose, watching the silver rise a few feet, only to cascade back to the ground. "Otherwise we really *will* die in here."

Matt helped her experiment for a while and then waved good night when he started to yawn, heading down the hall after Mary. Rose placed the archway back in her bag and took the remaining bedroom for herself, no longer feeling hungry. She lay on the squashy bed and stared up at the ceiling, trying not to think.

Rose stood in front of the bathroom mirror two days later, combing her long hair with weary fingers before braiding it. She surveyed her reflection as she braided, noticing the unhealthy pallor of her skin and the way her clothes hung more loosely on her frame. She sighed and made her way into the living room where Matt and Mary were working feverishly on the archway.

Her eyes immediately darted to their faces, pale and sickly, and the anxiety that had taken up residence somewhere in the back of her mind pushed its way to the surface once more. The spells on Miranda's invention had long since disappeared. Food and water no longer sustained them, and Rose found herself trying to ignore constant hunger and thirst.

The reality that she might never see her family again became more and more real with each passing day, and in an effort to distract herself, she took to roaming the streets alone whenever she wasn't working on the archway. Between the three of them, they worked on the invention ceaselessly, willing it to open just once so that they could be free.

Rose crossed the room, mumbling to Matt and Mary that she was going to take a walk. They nodded listlessly, barely taking their eyes off the shining silver. Rose turned towards the park and the supermarket beside it, thinking that she could use the time to replenish their supplies, despite their limited effect.

She walked far enough down the street to see the aquatic centre rising above the surrounding houses, but not far enough away to risk being separated from the others if the buildings rearranged themselves, and was on her way back when she saw Mary racing down the street towards her, screaming her name. Wondering what had happened this time, Rose sped up to meet her.

"What is it? What's wrong?!" said Rose, checking her

sister for signs of injury.

"The archway!" Mary gasped. "I got it open and it's waiting for us! We can go home!"

Rose gaped at her for a second, hardly able to believe her ears. She raced Mary back to the house, running as fast as her weak legs would carry her. They crashed through the door to see Matt jumping up and down in agitation.

The archway was pitted and twisted, but it was there, fully formed in the middle of the living room and looking out onto a shadowy room. Tears of happiness welled up in Rose's eyes at the sight.

"Quick! Before it collapses again!" Matt cried.

They rushed around the house, gathering all of their things and packing them into Rose's bag with the Fragmenter.

"You go through first, Mary!" insisted Rose, hurrying her forward.

Mary stepped through and gazed around, laughing delightedly. Matt went through next and Rose followed him. The archway began to sink towards the ground the moment her feet crossed the threshold, pooling and then hardening into its ruined form.

Rose picked it up and stared around to see where they were, her eyes struggling to adjust to the darkness after spending so long in the light. They were back in Nate's study.

She gazed around at the familiar, wonderfully real room, her throat too thick to speak. She wiped away tears and stretched out an arm to open the door and shout for Nate when movement from behind caught her eye. A dozen figures loomed out of the shadows from all sides of the room, surrounding them. They seized Rose, Matt and Mary roughly by the arms.

"Oh, damn!" said Matt weakly, twisting around to look up at the man dressed all in black behind him.

They'd finally been captured.

21

Lawrence Hunter

"About time!" exclaimed Mary's captor. "We'd started to think you weren't coming back out."

It was the auburn-haired woman. Her long hair hung around her face in thick curtains and her skin was so pale that she appeared to glow in the dark. She smirked as Mary lashed out, scratching at the woman's hands and kicking at her shins, but she was unable to pull free and soon gave up, out of breath and glaring at everyone in the room. Jacob sauntered out from the shadows beside the door with a look of impatience.

"Just look in the bag," he growled. "Have they got it or not?"

Someone snatched Rose's bag from her hand and tossed it to Jacob, who opened it and began pulling out the contents. With a snarl of anger, Rose lunged forward to snatch the bag back, but the man nearest her took hold of her wrists, twisting them painfully behind her.

Rose stamped on his foot and tried to pull her hands free, but she was exhausted from lack of food and water, and like Mary, she soon tired. She watched, fuming, as Jacob lifted out the silver archway, the pocket watch, Miranda's invention and finally the Fragmenter.

The men cheered at the sight of it. Jacob held the

invention up to the dim light, his gaze resentful as he checked the bud for damage.

"You did well to get this out. None of us thought you'd do it."

Rose said nothing as one of the group drew up three chairs from the edges of the room. The man holding her wrists let go and pushed her onto a chair beside Matt, who scowled and attempted to fight his way back onto his feet, struggling up only to be pulled back down by the spells binding him to the wood.

"Tell Lawrence we've got the kids and the Fragmenter," Jacob said gloatingly to the man in black, who seemed to disappear in the darkness. Rose turned her head in time to see him give a curt nod and leave the room. A floorboard creaked overhead and she realised there must be others upstairs.

"Let us go!" demanded Matt. "You've already got what you wanted, so why -"

"Be quiet!" Jacob barked. He glared at them for a moment, as though daring them to make a sound, before marching away down the hall.

Rose struggled against the spell holding her, her insides squirming with anger and fear. Craning her neck to look awkwardly over her shoulder, she found the last of the sun's glow fading on the horizon. The sting of tears pricked the corners of her eyes as she stared around the room. They had risked so much to recover the Fragmenter, only to have Hunter's gang take it from them the moment they stepped back into the real world!

She fought the tears back with annoyance and

listened to the sound of low voices outside in the hall, hoping to distract herself, while Mary wriggled impatiently and Matt yawned, his eyes red with tiredness. Rose strained her ears to catch the whispered conversation. The door stood open a crack and the voices carried clearly in the still evening air.

"-almost ready to take them over now," said a rough voice that sounded very much like Jacob's. "We've got a space ready near the hall, so we can keep them away from the others until we're done with them."

Rose gulped and glanced at Matt and Mary. Both of them fell still, their eyes fixed on the door.

"I thought Lawrence wanted to question them first?" said a second, unfamiliar voice.

"He does. He'll be here in a moment. Any sign of Alison or Ben yet? Or Miranda?"

"No, but we'll be ready for them, too. They're bound to show up sooner or later to help the kids. We sent Alison a message letting her know we've caught them."

"Good," replied Jacob in a satisfied tone, before both speakers moved away, out of earshot.

A moment later Jacob was back, standing outside the door like a sentinel. Rose could see a sliver of his faded jacket and curly hair from where she sat. Wishing he would go away, she lowered her voice to a murmur and turned to her brother and sister.

"Did you hear that?! Nate and the others must have escaped! They're OK!"

Relief flooded Matt and Mary's faces, and Rose

wondered where the others were now.

"I bet they went to Ben's house," whispered Matt. "It's the most heavily protected."

Rose agreed, thinking of the magical barriers she'd had to force herself through just to cross the threshold. They were still whispering together when Rose heard footsteps coming down the hall. She caught a glimpse of Jacob, stretching out a hand towards a small ornament sitting on a side table in the hall. Her mouth fell open in indignation. She was about to protest when another voice sounded down the hall.

"Put it back, Jacob. We're here for the Fragmenter, not useless trinkets."

Jacob scowled and placed the ornament back on the table. Seconds later the door was pushed open to reveal a man standing silently in the doorway. It was Dave. He dragged over another chair and sat down facing them, while Rose, Matt and Mary stared at him in shock.

"You … you …!" Rose gasped, speechless with rage.

"*You're* Lawrence Hunter?!" said Mary in disbelief.

Dave nodded.

"But - you can't be!" spluttered Matt. "You work for the police! How could they not know who you are?"

"I've always been careful to hide my identity," said Dave lightly. "I took care to set up in a place where no one else knew me. And I've never been in the police force."

He paused for a moment, looking at them with an elbow propped up on one knee. The shadow of a grin appeared on his face.

"I have to admit, I thought you three would have worked all of this out on your own by now. You seem to be fairly good at figuring out the truth usually. Just like your parents."

"Is that why you kidnapped them, too?" retorted Rose, seething.

"Not entirely, no," said Dave.

"Why, then? You'd already taken Grandpa, why did you have to take our parents as well?" yelled Matt, his voice loud enough to carry down the hall.

Dave sighed and leaned back in his chair.

"Maybe things would make more sense if I started at the beginning …"

He reached inside his jacket and drew out the Fragmenter, the metal casing gleaming even in the darkness. He held it up, his gaze fixed on the interlocking threads.

"I've always had an interest in magical inventions," he said. "But my main interest is in experimentation. I never had the patience to piece together a complicated invention. I'm good with magic and spells, but I'm not as good at turning ideas into functional inventions, and it was always so much easier to have a professional inventor make one for me. When I was fifteen, I joined the Guild and started to do proper experiments of my own. After I left, I set up my own place to experiment, and I've managed to come up with quite a few new creations since then."

"Alison says you use magic to make illegal things," declared Matt in a dismissive tone. "She says you make a habit of stealing inventions …"

Dave scowled at the mention of Alison's name.

"Actually, most of it has been completely legal, even if the government doesn't like it," he replied, a trace of irritation in his voice. "And if I need materials or information for an experiment that I can't come by in the normal way, then yes, I will find another way of acquiring it, but generally, I like to avoid stealing. I'd rather create something with my own hands if I'm able to."

He placed the Fragmenter on the desk beside him.

"I don't have to be an expert inventor myself to appreciate a clever or beautiful invention. Now and then, one of my tests will call for a substance that's restricted, and sometimes it takes a lot of negotiation to procure it."

His eyes settled on Rose as a grin twisted on his face.

"How's your hand, by the way? The Infuser that stabbed you contains a very rare and hard-to-source liquid. I intended to use it in one of my inventions, and I was curious about the effect it might be having on you."

"I'm fine," said Rose haughtily. "Nate got the poison out ages ago."

Dave's grin widened at the hostility in her voice and Rose's temper flared.

"Stick to the story," she growled. "I want to know why you tricked us all into thinking you were helping us and then kidnapped Mum, Dad and Grandpa!"

"And why is it so important for you to have the Fragmenter in the first place?" said Mary.

Dave folded his arms across his chest.

"If someone is making an invention to take away your magic, it makes sense not to let them keep it," he explained, with the air of explaining that two and two equals four. "That's why I went to so much trouble pretending to be a policeman and to become friends with your family when I heard that the government wanted to have the Fragmenter made. I couldn't stop them from making it, but I could steal it once it was built, and besides, it could be useful to me."

Rose scoffed.

"Useful for what?"

"For revenge," said Dave, as though it was obvious. He leaned forward in his chair to look them in the eyes, making no attempt to hide the resentment on his face.

"Do you realise that some of the people who passed that law to take away a person's magic are magical themselves? They know exactly what it would mean to someone to have their abilities taken away by force and still they see no problem with it! I can't believe they even suggested making it legal! We might as well be in the Dark Ages, cutting people's hands off for stealing. It's barbaric!"

Dave took a deep breath and seemed to calm himself a little.

"But I thought you *wanted* the invention to be made!" cried Rose in exasperation.

Dave raised an eyebrow.

"Definitely not! By the time I heard the invention had been approved, work had already begun! I thought that, seeing as it was going ahead, I might as well influence and shape it as much as possible, so that I could use it for my own purposes instead."

"But if you use the bud on them, you'll be as bad as they are!" Rose protested.

"They did this to themselves," said Dave, his tone icy. "They want to take away my magic, so I'll take away theirs. They deserve a taste of their own medicine. Once I've done what I want with it, the invention will be destroyed."

Matt pulled against his chair, looking increasingly irate.

"So why are you after *us*, then? We had nothing to do with making the Fragmenter legal! None of us wanted it to be made, either. Grandpa had to be forced into it! *You* forced him with those notes you sent him!"

Dave looked perplexed at this.

"No, I never sent him any notes. I don't know anything about that."

Rose let out a snort of derisive laughter.

"But it had to be you! Who else would've been threatening Mum and Dad?"

She glanced at Matt and Mary, who both nodded fiercely, but Dave continued to look confused.

"No, really. It must have been someone from the government. Someone who stood to gain from the bud being made and used on me. Sending cryptic notes isn't my style."

"But kidnapping is?" replied Matt dryly.

Dave ignored him.

"I can imagine, though, that all they had to say to

change your grandpa's mind was that I would be free to do as I please if he refused, and it would be all his fault."

It was Dave's turn to laugh.

"The usual drivel."

Rose wasn't sure she believed him, but one thing was undeniable: Dave and his friends had brought this on themselves. It was, after all, their bad behaviour that had given magical people a bad reputation and prompted the government's decision to make the Fragmenter.

"By the time the authorities approached your grandpa, I'd already decided to make everyone involved pay for passing that law," declared Dave. "I needed the invention to do that, and at first I thought about making it myself, but as you already know, I'm not much of a magical inventor."

Rose's insides squirmed again as she thought of the little tear-shaped invention in the Archives, the reason for her success with her Viewer. She beat back unpleasant thoughts that her invention was tainted in some way, forcing her attention back to the conversation as Dave continued in a low voice.

"I decided to let your grandpa make it, and I would steal it once he was done. But even without the invention, your family would have tried to stop me from carrying out my plans and experiments, and I can't have that."

He ran a hand through his black hair distractedly, staring down at the invention in his lap.

"As I said, when I heard the government had asked your family to make it, I took pains to get to know you all. It's so much quicker and easier to get what you want from people if they think you're a friend, and I assumed your family must be used to people trying to steal inventions. But if I was in charge of your protection, I'd know what kinds of magical defence you were using and I'd be able to quietly influence the construction of the bud at the same time."

"But Grandpa must have figured out the truth or he wouldn't have hidden the bud," said Matt with relish.

Dave's face darkened again.

"Yes, you can thank your friend Alison for that. She became suspicious when she met my friends and I in the Archives. I wanted to look through your grandpa's reports, but she got there first, no doubt trying to find out if I was involved in the making of the invention."

He shrugged dismissively and turned to Rose. She had opened her mouth to speak, but Dave seemed to guess what she was thinking.

"Why did I need the reports when I already had your grandpa?"

He paused for a moment, considering his response.

"I wanted to be sure he wasn't leaving out any important information. He was very reticent about the finer details of the Fragmenter when I questioned him about it. But of course, Alison found me reading the reports and went to Peter. She told him everything she'd seen and urged him to be careful in case I tried to take the invention. Between the two of them they figured out the truth, but I think they were both too afraid to tell your parents in case you three got dragged into it."

Mary gave a miserable sigh. She'd been unusually quiet since returning to the real world. Rose frowned, noticing the lines under her sister's eyes. The sudden change to night after spending so long in the perpetual daylight of the ruined city must have taken its toll.

"The Fragmenter was gone by the time I took your grandpa away," said Dave. "He knew I'd stationed my gang all around his house, of course, and that he'd never get the chance to give it to the government, so he hid it away instead."

"And that's really why you kidnapped him, then? To make him tell you where he'd hidden it?"

Matt looked at Dave with contempt, and Dave smiled.

"Partly. I also wanted to know how to control the thing once I'd found it. Certain tricks can be used to manipulate it, but your grandpa conveniently left them out of his reports. He might be useful to me. But of course, Alison had other ideas. She did everything she could to stop me, breaking into my rooms in the Archives and ruining my plans."

"So you decided to frame her, to keep her from interfering?" glared Rose.

"Well, yes," replied Dave. "I set your family against her by telling you she'd been seen sneaking around your grandpa's room in the Archives and creating trouble so that you wouldn't believe anything she told you. It was also useful to have the real police looking for her instead of me, and getting your parents to hunt her created the perfect diversion while I kidnapped your grandfather.

My identity was safe for a while longer."

Rose sat in stunned silence as her mind drifted back to the conversation she'd overheard with Matt and Mary outside the library the night Grandpa had disappeared. The last pieces of the puzzle were finally falling into place.

"I convinced your parents that it must have been Alison that had taken Peter, and they believed me," continued Dave. "They were so upset that they probably would have believed anything I told them. Using the information in your grandpa's reports, they took the prototype he'd made and fixed it up as close to the real thing as possible, just like the government told them to. It made no difference to me which version of the bud I got, as long as it was capable of carrying out my plans.

"More than once my friends searched through the reports in your library and found a passing reference to a compass, but I had no idea what it had to do with the Fragmenter, and your parents swore that Peter had never mentioned it, so I kept watching and waiting while your parents worked on the prototype and tried to keep you three away from it."

All of Rose's old feelings of guilt surged back into being, and she dropped her gaze to her knees.

"I used inventions in the Archives to discover that the compass was disguised as a pocket watch, and I saw that *you* had it in your jacket pocket."

Dave's grey eyes locked onto Rose's.

"I needed to take it from you, but I couldn't break into the house with your Shield working and I couldn't search the place while you were all at home, so I sent three of my friends to patrol the area around your house, but none of you seemed to want to leave."

He paused for a moment and Rose grimaced, remembering all too clearly what had happened next. She wriggled in her chair, wishing she could stretch her legs.

"Soon Adrian had an idea. Maybe you'd come out if you saw your beloved pet being attacked? Jacob tried it and the three of you came out to investigate."

Dave laughed, his eyes gleaming in the dark.

"You were even wearing the jacket with the watch in the pocket, Rose! I couldn't believe my luck. I was in the library with your parents at the time, as I'm sure you remember, and I watched you all head off down the road into the forest. I kept your parents occupied while my gang followed you. You can imagine how annoyed I was when I walked down your driveway to see them still chasing after you.

"I still needed my cover, so I couldn't attack you myself, and you'd already seen me coming out of the house. I had to help you and pretend I didn't know my friends, who went back to watching the house. But I realised too late that your Shield's influence stretched as far as the road. It must have been a last-minute change made by your parents. When I reached out to pull you up, I couldn't get a grip on your wrist. The spells on the Shield must have been protecting you. I was afraid you'd notice and realise I wasn't your friend, but you didn't, much to my relief."

"I thought it must have been the rain, that's all," Rose lied. Truthfully, she hadn't noticed anything at all at the time and was now feeling rather stupid.

"We both told your parents what had happened and then you took the watch out for us all to see," said Dave in a vexed tone. "Your dad even gave it to me! I thought about making up some excuse to keep it for a while, but by then you'd taken it back. I was sure from examining it that it must be the compass I was looking for, I just had to find a way of taking it without being discovered.

"I left my friends watching the house in case you decided to come out again, but I knew you wouldn't. I decided to wait until the masterclass instead, when it would be easier for someone to slip into the house undetected. I guessed that your parents would have to partially disable your Shield to let everyone inside."

"But you were outside the whole time! I saw you!" cried Matt. "We'd have noticed if you'd disappeared!"

"I meant for you to see me so I'd have an alibi when you discovered the watch was missing," said Dave with a shrug. "I sent Jacob and Adrian into the house to retrieve it. Jacob is a talented thief. It's about all he's good at."

Rose's mind went back to the Magicked Masterclass. She'd been so sure that she'd seen Jacob disappearing down the side of the house. How long had he been sneaking around the property before Rose had glimpsed him?

"I watched your parents come and go over the next few weeks, looking for the real Fragmenter and putting extra protection over your house and yard," said Dave. "I couldn't believe that none of you had worked out the truth about me by then."

"They might not have known for sure, but I think Mum and Dad were starting to suspect you," said Rose slowly. "They must've figured out that the pocket watch was a compass, too, and they didn't tell you. They even asked Alison to look at it for them." She turned to Matt and Mary. "And remember what they said when they dropped us off to help Alison repair those inventions?"

Mary nodded and grinned at Dave gloatingly.

"They told us to go to Alison if anything happened to them, not to you, even though you'd been protecting us!"

"It was like they knew something was going to happen," said Matt, his brow furrowed.

"Yes, I think the repeated breaches of your protection did make them suspicious," agreed Dave. "Particularly just before they discovered the archway."

"And it was why they wanted to put protection of their own around the house," mused Rose.

"It did make things harder for me," Dave admitted. "And it all got worse when Alison turned up on your doorstep. I thought I'd done enough to turn you all against her, but she still managed to convince your parents that she was innocent. The last thing I wanted was someone who knew the truth about me talking to you all. It almost ruined everything."

Matt snorted with laughter.

"Alison said she broke into your room in the

Archives and stole Grandpa's watch back to prove she was telling us the truth."

Dave shifted in his chair in an irritated kind of way.

"She did. And it set me back weeks. I had to change the protective spells on the door to stop her from getting in a second time. It caused me a lot of trouble. I needed the watch to find the Fragmenter and it was going to be much harder to steal it a second time."

Rose couldn't help but smile to herself, picturing the scene in her mind's eye.

"I had to do something about her," said Dave quietly, as though talking to himself. "I tried to keep you apart as much as possible, but your parents must have changed your Shield so that she could use a travel spell right into its field of protection. By the time my gang had spotted her, she was already safe and there was nothing I could do to keep her away."

"How did you know the Fragmenter was inside the silver invention?" asked Matt, his voice shaking with anger.

"I bet you found the recording Grandpa left in the Archives," answered Rose. "His room was probably the first place you looked when you couldn't find the invention at his house."

Dave nodded.

"It told me all I needed to know. I began searching for the archway at once. The magical disturbance from the Fragmenter ruined some key parts of the recording, but your parents discovered the archway anyway when they checked the inventions they'd moved from your grandpa's house. Its spells are subtle but distinctive, and your mother knows Peter's magical style better than anyone else. He obviously counted on that when he made it. It didn't take her long to notice the similarities."

"The day Mum and Dad disappeared, they told us they were going out to look for the Fragmenter again," said Rose, thinking out loud. "But if they already knew it was inside the silver invention, why did they go out? They could've opened the archway inside the house, with the Shield, where it was safe."

"That was exactly why they had to leave," explained Dave. "They knew the magic in the Fragmenter would be free to come and go through the archway the moment they opened it, and the Shield would be no protection. You saw what happened at your grandpa's house before I took him away. The fight between the two inventions tore the place apart. The Shield wouldn't let your parents try the archway out in peace, and the prototype had already caused enough trouble with the Shield. They didn't want to risk destroying the only safe place you three had, so they decided to test the archway somewhere else, somewhere without magical disruption or interference."

Rose blinked, fighting back tears. Their parents had done everything to protect herself, Matt and Mary. They'd sorted everything out on their own, not telling Rose and her siblings anything so they wouldn't have to worry, risking their own safety just so that their children would have a safe place to return to. Rose wiped her cheek dry on her shoulder awkwardly, wishing more than ever that she hadn't been so stubborn.

"My gang warned me when your parents left the house, and I followed them, watching from a distance as they opened the archway," Dave continued, getting to his feet and pacing around Nate's study, his gaze travelling over the jars of magical ingredients clustered on the desktop.

"And then you locked them away with Grandpa and took the silver invention," Mary added in a monotone.

"I hid it in the Archives, hoping Alison and Miranda would think it was too obvious for me to hide it there," shrugged Dave. "But they decided to check anyway. While you three helped Alison repair the inventions she broke trying to get into my room, I waited for the prototype to block your Shield and then sent some of my friends into the house to look for the watch. I thought she must have returned it to you by then, but they couldn't find it. Your parents didn't have it on them when I captured them, so I assumed Alison must have kept it. While I was figuring out how I was going to take it from her, I turned my attention to you."

"What did you need *us* for?" retorted Matt. "You already had our family. You can't seriously have thought that *we'd* be able to stop you?"

Dave gave him a shrewd look.

"I figured you might create problems for me, even with the rest of your family gone. And you have. You're young, but you're smart. The first thing you did was to start going through all of your grandpa's reports, learning everything you could about the Fragmenter, and

I was afraid you'd go straight to Alison once you'd discovered your parents were gone. I'd hoped you'd come to me first, seeing as you still thought I was your friend at the time and I'd been responsible for your protection throughout the whole business. But you didn't, and that confused me.

"I started to wonder if you'd learned the truth about me. I decided to wait, hoping to see what your plan was, but when days went by and you started looking for Alison, not realising you already knew her, I thought it was time for me to intervene. I decided it would be better if you were out of the way. I knew I wouldn't be able to attack you inside the house with all of the protective spells you'd put over it, so I thought if I lured you outside where you weren't so heavily protected, I could get to you then. Once again, I waited until your Shield had stopped working and then I visited you, pretending to be surprised that your parents had gone missing."

Rose remembered how Dave had tried to persuade them that they weren't safe in the house alone, that they'd be better off going to a safe place with him, and how annoyed he'd been when they'd refused to leave. He'd seemed like just another concerned adult at the time …

"When you wouldn't come out, I decided to wait, hoping you'd come out willingly once you'd run out of food and money," said Dave. "You proved to be more stubborn and independent than I'd anticipated. I told my friends to back off and watch from a distance, hoping that would entice you outside. It was only a matter of time. Meanwhile, I sent Jacob and some of the others into your grandfather's fake world, looking for the Fragmenter while I kept your family under control. Needless to say, they had no luck.

"And then you ran off to Alison's house, using a travel spell from inside the house so that my gang didn't realise you'd gone until later in the day," said Dave resentfully. "And by then the damage had been done. You were safe and had your Shield for protection as well as Alison and Ben's defences.

"With Alison helping you, I was sure you'd work out where the Fragmenter was, so I took considerable care to keep my key hidden. I watched you come and go from the Archives, and threatened Miranda with legal proceedings if she helped you get into my room, but I couldn't afford to push the matter too far. Miranda can be difficult to deal with, and as the head of the Archives, she's quite powerful in her own way. She also claimed to have evidence she could use against me. Things Alison claimed to have glimpsed in my room during her little excursion in there, so I had to just make sure the spells on my door were enough to keep you out."

"But they didn't keep us out," Matt crowed. "Ben's invention got through your defensive spells without any trouble at all!"

"All but one," Dave reminded him. "I was glad to have him out of the way. He'd been almost as bad as Alison, snooping around outside my room every opportunity he got. And depriving you of an ally seemed like a good idea. When you stole my key, I knew I'd have to act fast."

"Did you know we were trapped inside your room then?" asked Mary. "It sounded like you did."

"I suspected you were, though I didn't know for sure." Dave's voice was light, but his expression was tense as he met Mary's gaze. "I didn't think you three would let Alison and Ben go into my room alone. I'd seen how determined you were to do things for yourselves."

"You thought you had us cornered, but you didn't," said Rose with satisfaction. "We found your hidden rooms, got the silver invention and escaped, all before you could lock Ben up."

"Yes, I was surprised that you managed to even find the hidden areas, let alone escape during the lock-down," said Dave reluctantly. "I was angry about that at first, but after some thought I figured I could use it to my advantage."

"You thought you'd let us get the Fragmenter out of the fake world for you?" guessed Rose, heartily wishing she'd never stepped foot through the silver archway.

"Well, why not?" said Dave with a wry smile. "Jacob and the others had failed to retrieve it. Why not let you do it for me? You know your grandfather better than I do, you know how he works and thinks, the kinds of spells he uses most, so I thought you might know something I don't. You'd already been surprisingly successful getting into my Archives rooms, maybe you'd be just as successful in this fake world? And I was right, wasn't I?

You got the Fragmenter out. As you saw, I had people waiting for you to come back out. It took so long that I'd started to think you might have died in there. It was a relief to finally see the archway open."

Dave gave them a questioning look as he continued to roam around the room.

"I couldn't understand how you'd managed to stay alive for so long in there until I found this in your bag."

He summoned Miranda's invention and held it up for them to see.

"I've never seen anything like it before. How does it work?"

Rose sighed and explained how the invention worked, while Dave opened the lid and peered inside.

"Very clever," he said admiringly, placing it on the desk beside the bud. "Did you make it yourselves?"

"No, Miranda took it out of the Archives for us." Rose shook her head as she spoke. Something didn't tally up, but she couldn't quite see what.

"Wait a moment, how could you have sent people through the archway to search for the bud when it only opens if you have it with you?" she demanded. "We tried opening it without the bud ourselves and it didn't work!"

Dave turned around to face them, outlined against the window, and his grin returned.

"You're right, it doesn't. Your grandpa intended for it to be that way. But I soon found that a person could come and go if they deliberately kept the door open when they went through."

He laughed at the looks of astonishment and horror on their faces.

"It's one of the many tricks your grandpa kept to himself. If something is placed under the archway before it collapses, it will stay open, otherwise you're stuck. But if the archway is open, you have to leave it where it is, you can't carry the open door around with you.

"In the end, all we had to do was place a chair under the archway and we were able to come and go as we pleased, not that it helped much, seeing as everything kept changing up. There were quite a few times when I thought Jacob wasn't going to make it back out. Just because the doorway is open, doesn't mean you'll be able to find it again."

Rose's blood turned to ice and Dave chuckled again.

"Your grandpa needed to have a way of entering and leaving the place without the Fragmenter to work on it, didn't he?"

Rose hadn't considered this, but now that Dave said it out loud it seemed ludicrously obvious. There was a moment of silence before he spoke again.

"I have to ask. How did you manage to get the Fragmenter out when all of my friends failed?"

Rose could tell that he'd been dying to ask them this from the moment they'd begun talking. Matt smirked.

"It was easy, really. It had nothing to do with fighting the invention. All we had to do was shift the protective spells from the safe house onto an object we could carry around with us."

It was Dave's turn to look surprised.

"I'm impressed," he said after a pause.

"So if you wanted us to bring the bud back for you, why did your gang attack us right before we went through the archway?" demanded Mary, prompting Dave to raise an eyebrow.

"I thought that would be fairly obvious. Ben had seen too much and I didn't want him blabbing to you all about where my hideout was. He was bound to find you and tell you everything, so I waited for him to show up. I never had any intention of stopping you going through the archway. My goal was to recapture Ben, or at least keep him from talking to you."

"That reminds me," said Rose, suddenly urgent. "What happened to Ben and the others after we went into the ruined city?"

A flicker of irritation crossed Dave's face, and Rose guessed that they'd been causing him a fair amount of trouble while she, Matt and Mary had been absent.

"They went to Ben's house, where they've been hiding ever since," replied Dave. "I'm guessing they've been trying to figure out how to free your family while they wait for you to reappear. They all seem very anxious about you."

The tight knot in Rose's chest eased a little.

"I hope they've been giving you a hard time?" she said. "And Mum, Dad and Grandpa?"

"They have," said Dave solemnly. "They've been very uncooperative ever since I brought them in."

"Good!" exclaimed Matt, looking pleased. "Once we're all back together again, it'll be *your* turn to try being locked up."

"I doubt it," said Dave with a short laugh. "You don't know the best thing about the Fragmenter yet. It can do so much more than just remove a person's magic and store it away. I've found a way of moving the stored magic onto someone else."

Rose stared at him in stunned disbelief.

"By the time you're reunited with your family, I'll have your magic myself and the Fragmenter will be destroyed," said Dave with a smile.

He called to his gang down the hall and they took hold of Rose, Matt and Mary, releasing them from their chairs. The auburn-haired woman grabbed Rose roughly by one arm, her fingernails biting into Rose's skin, while Jacob took hold of Mary. The man in black melted out of the darkness as though he'd always been there, and pulled Matt to his feet.

"You can take them to the house now," Dave told them.

The woman gripping Rose's arm began a travel spell and Rose felt herself being pulled away.

22

Stony River

The sound of running water met her ears as the ground changed under her feet, her bare toes landing on soil and rock. She breathed in the scent of earth and gum trees as the gang pushed her along an over-grown dirt path through the bush.

It had rained recently, and she stepped through the undergrowth carefully, relishing the sensation of the cool water against her skin. Someone stumbled on the rocky ground behind her, and she looked over her shoulder to see the man in black hauling Matt to his feet with a muffled curse.

Matt shoved him away and almost broke free, but the man caught him by one arm and dragged him back. He raised a fist, ready to strike, and Rose whirled around, ignoring the auburn-haired woman's attempts to get her to move.

"Hit him and I'll do worse than just burn a hole in your boot," she burst out, meeting the man's cold eyes unflinchingly.

He glared at her for a long moment but said nothing, grabbing Matt's shoulders and forcing him further along the path. Matt, and Mary behind him, stared at her as though she'd gone mad, and Rose took a deep, steadying breath as she continued down the trail, wondering if they were right.

She paid careful attention to her surroundings. As Ben had warned them, they appeared to be well out of town. There was no sound of traffic nearby, or any other signs of life except for the distant hoot of an owl.

Rose struggled to make out any defining features amid the sea of trees. A shallow river followed the path on her right for a short distance, cutting through the bush and bubbling away among the rocks before swerving around a large boulder and disappearing from view.

A gentle breeze rustled the leaves over her head and Rose felt another rush of gratitude to be back in the real world, even if it meant she would be trapped once again. After several minutes of silent walking, the path widened and the trees began to thin. Soon Rose found herself facing a stretch of grassy fields.

A derelict farmhouse stood alone among them, projecting an air of dismal decay. She stared up at it as she drew nearer. It appeared to have been painted a crisp white at some point in the past, but it was now so worn and dirty that it was closer to brown in places. The roof sagged over the entrance and most of the windows on the ground level were broken.

Rose understood why Dave, or Hunter, she reminded herself with a scowl, had chosen the place. Nobody was ever likely to want to go near it. It was possible that most people weren't even aware that the old house existed. If Ben could keep his house protected from unwanted visitors using magic, Hunter no doubt could, too.

The building looked even more uninviting up close, but despite its dilapidated appearance, she sensed that it, like Grandpa's fake world, was not as it seemed. The house positively buzzed with magic. Rose found spells everywhere she looked, layered and blended so that they formed a thick shell around the building. Ben was right. Hunter's rooms in the Archives were nothing compared to what stood before her.

The gang brought Rose, Matt and Mary to a stop a few feet away from the front steps, and Rose waited sullenly as one of the group approached the door and knocked, murmuring something inaudible. The door swung open with a loud creak, revealing a dark, empty hallway.

"Get going," hissed the auburn-haired woman, pushing Rose up the cracked concrete steps.

The appearance of neglect vanished the moment Rose's feet crossed the threshold. The paint on the walls became clean and fresh, reflecting coloured lights from something in one of the rooms off the hall, and the dirty floor transformed into smooth, polished wood.

Rose looked eagerly into each room as she passed it, catching glimpses of tables and workbenches covered in magical equipment, clusters of vials, jars and bottles, and scattered books, giving her the impression that she had just entered a kind of magical laboratory.

Thinking that this was no surprise, as Hunter himself had told her that he had been a member of the Guild at one time and had mentioned his experiments, she peered through the steam and dim lights issuing from several of the jars and bottles, noticing a narrow wooden staircase at the other end of the hall. Her eyes followed the stairs up one level and stopped as they turned a corner.

She continued towards the stairs, passing a cramped living area, but was dragged back and shoved into the small room just beside the stairs. Matt and Mary were forced in behind her.

"Where's our family?" she demanded, peering back down the hall.

Jacob ignored her, placing spells across the doorway before heading upstairs with the others, leaving Rose, Matt and Mary alone in the dark room. Rose rested her head against the doorframe.

"Well, at least we're stuck in a real place this time."

Matt snorted with laughter.

"Yeah, it's definitely an improvement."

"I wonder what's in there?" said Mary, pointing to the room opposite them.

The door was shut, but a curious amber-coloured steam seeped into the hall through the gap underneath, bringing an even more curious scent with it. Now and then a bright orange light would flicker under the door, as though the room was on fire, but none of the people passing by seemed the slightest bit concerned.

"It smells a bit like maple syrup, only with a metallic edge to it," said Matt, sniffing at the air and pressing himself as close against the doorway as the spells over it would allow. "Is it me, or is there a whistling sound coming from in there?"

Rose turned an ear towards the door and found that he was right. Underneath the steady dripping from something in the equipment-filled room, there was a faint whistle like an old-fashioned kettle.

"That's weird. I wonder what it is?"

"If someone goes in there we might be able to see something while the door's open," said Matt hopefully, as Jacob and the man in black emerged from the stairs. They paid no attention to the three children, walking past without so much as a glance in their direction.

"Oh well," said Rose in an undertone. "Something tells me we'll find out soon enough."

The night wore on and Rose had nothing to do but watch the comings and goings in the hall. The night deepened around them and the house fell still and silent, except for the occasional creaking from somewhere above them.

"I wonder what's upstairs?" said Mary, glancing up at the ceiling as another creak issued from the upper floor. "It sounds like someone's moving around up there."

Rose shrugged and wrapped her arms around her knees for warmth.

"Hunter's probably got more experiments and stuff up there."

Several minutes later footsteps sounded on the stairs and she narrowed her eyes suspiciously as Hunter himself made a surprise appearance in their doorway, carrying an armful of thick blankets. She watched in silence as he stepped into the room and the magical barrier simply parted around him. He placed the pile on the floor and straightened up, his face unreadable.

"You'll be needing these," he said, already turning to leave.

He disappeared without another word and Rose spun around to inspect the blankets. They would indeed be better than sleeping on the hard wooden floor.

Unfolding the first four, she tossed them to her brother and sister, who looked at them grudgingly for a second before accepting them with thanks. Rose saved the last two for herself, wrapping one around her like a sleeping bag and using the other as a pillow.

She settled down beside Mary, and one by one, the last of Hunter's gang left, leaving the house still and quiet. Rose shivered and yawned, exhaustion creeping up on her at last. She'd stopped counting the days inside the ruined city, and now she wondered how long it had been since she'd had a proper night's sleep.

She glanced over at the other two. Their eyelids were beginning to droop and Mary's head had lolled onto Matt's shoulder, but both of them sat with their backs to the wall, facing the doorway and doing their best to stay awake. Rose sighed and lay down.

"Come on, let's get some rest," she yawned. "We're stuck here for now. There's no way we can reach Mum, Dad and Grandpa, even with Hunter's friends gone. We might as well sleep while we can."

Matt and Mary mumbled in agreement and the three of them lay in a huddle together on the floor. Cool drafts found their way into the house through cracks in the walls and windows, but the blankets and the heat from the steam room kept them comfortably warm.

Shadows lengthened in the hallway and the light under the steam room door glowed brighter as the darkness deepened. Matt and Mary fell asleep almost at once, but Rose forced herself to stay awake for just a little while longer, enjoying the dark and listening to the small sounds of crickets outside in the fields.

The clouds shifted, uncovering a sky studded with stars, and she stared out of the window, glimpsing a bright glow low on the horizon, just visible through the dusty glass. The moon crept higher and the stars became brighter, lulling her into sleep so gradually that she hardly even noticed herself nodding off.

Rose awoke early the next morning to find Mary prodding her with a finger.

"Are you hungry?" she asked with a teasing grin, moving aside to reveal the plate of sandwiches in the doorway.

Hungry was an understatement, thought Rose as she sat up. Stiff from sleeping on the floor, she rubbed her neck with one hand and chose a cheese and tomato sandwich with the other, devouring it in seconds. She took another and forced herself to eat more slowly, resuming her watch in the doorway as she chewed.

She soon discovered that she could get a decent view of the entrance to the house if she pressed herself right up against the spells sealing them in. The three of them settled themselves on the floor, watching as Hunter's friends rushed back and forth, sometimes carrying equipment, books or papers. All of them, however, had the same air of anticipation, and Rose began to feel uneasy as the day wore on without any break or pause in the frantic activity.

"Why haven't they used the Fragmenter on us already?" she said after a while. "What are they all doing?"

Matt's eyes followed Jacob as he hurried past, looking bad-tempered and carrying a spell book and a hammer.

"I don't know, but they must have a reason."

He propped his chin in his hand and stared moodily down the hall. Rose did her best to not think about the Fragmenter, focusing instead on the vision her Viewer had shown her of her family somewhere in the house below her. She knew that they were being held in a basement of some sort, but she'd seen no sign of the basement window Ben had mentioned when Hunter's gang had brought her in.

She roamed around the room restlessly while Mary turned her back to the wall and hummed to herself, winding a lock of hair around a finger in a bored kind of way. Matt, however, expressed his feelings by lounging in the doorway and doing his best to be as obnoxious as possible, complaining loudly and hurling taunts at Hunter's gang as they walked past.

"How much longer are we going to have to sit here?" he demanded as the auburn-haired woman cast spells over the steam room door and did something to adjust the magic over the entrance to the house. She turned to face Matt with a sneer.

"You'll be out of there soon enough, don't you worry."

She sauntered off without another word, leaving Matt to resume his criticisms. Most of Hunter's gang ignored him, looking down at him with contempt, but after nearly an hour of this, Jacob finally lost his temper, coming to a stop outside their door. His face white with fury, he advanced on Matt, brandishing the hammer clutched in his fist.

"Shut up!" he roared. "Shut up or I'll curse you!"

Matt opened his mouth to protest, but Rose cut across him quickly.

"I think you'd better stop now, Matt. You've had your fun."

Jacob glared at Matt for a moment before stumping away, cursing under his breath. Mary stifled a giggle as he marched out the front door, and Rose shook her head, trying hard not to let her amusement show.

"What?" said Matt innocently, grinning up at her.

Rose rolled her eyes, and before she knew it all three of them were laughing. The sound carried clearly down the hall and Rose was sure she heard Jacob let out another snarl of rage from somewhere near the entrance. Rose let herself laugh until her stomach hurt, relishing the feeling. It had been far too long since she'd had anything to laugh about.

There was a flurry of activity outside and Rose wiped tears from her eyes so that she could peer down the hall.

The sun was beginning to sink behind the trees, casting long shadows across the fields around the house and turning the tips of the long grass gold.

"I wish we could see what they're doing out there!" she said for the fifth time, standing on tiptoe.

"They're probably trying to find a way to bring the Fragmenter in here without destroying all the magic on this place," sniggered Matt. "It's going to go crazy as soon as they bring it to the door."

Almost as if to prove him right, the blond man Rose had stolen Hunter's key from appeared at the entrance, carrying something that flashed a vivid green in the evening light. Rose felt the laughter die in her throat. She gulped and nudged Matt with her foot.

"They're about to bring it in!"

Jacob reappeared a moment later, his scowl replaced with a malicious grin.

"I think it's about time we let your family know you're here," he said as he passed Matt.

Matt and Mary shot to their feet and stood on either side of Rose, pressed against the barrier over the doorway to see where Jacob went. He stepped into the room full of equipment and disappeared. Rose listened to the sound of his boots on the wooden floor until they faded away, out of earshot.

She stood rooted to the spot, her breathing coming much faster than normal, desperate to hear a voice or anything at all. She didn't have long to wait before two very familiar voices could be heard, raised in anger.

"Mum and Dad!" cried Mary in anguish. "I think

they're right underneath us!" She got to her hands and knees and turned an ear to the floor. "I wish we could get to them!"

Jacob reappeared a moment later, his expression smug. He marched back outside, calling instructions to the men working in the other rooms as he went.

"This is ridiculous!" cried Rose, staring around the room. "There must be a way out of here!" She pressed her hands against the window. "I wonder if we can break this?" She reached out with her mind and discovered yet more spells reinforcing this weak spot. She shrugged and continued, "I bet we can't, but let's try anyway."

Mary slipped a shoe off her foot and handed it to Rose.

"Here, use this!"

Rose gripped it firmly and smashed at the window pane. The shoe bounced off the glass, leaving it entirely undamaged. Refusing to be put off, Rose raised the shoe for a second assault, but Matt held a finger to his lips, pointing down the hall.

Rose stopped, one arm still raised to attack. Two more angry voices caught her attention near the entrance. Peering out of the window, she saw that Jacob and the blond man were now arguing just outside the house, the sound drowning out her family below.

"Just do it!" snarled Jacob, tossing his hammer aside with a crash. "It's taking too long. The sooner we get it inside, the sooner we're done with them all!"

The blond man looked like he was about to refuse,

but he glanced up and his eyes settled on Rose, Matt and Mary, all watching avidly. His expression soured and he gave a curt nod before approaching the doorstep, the Fragmenter glinting in his hands. Rose swallowed the lump that had lodged in her throat.

"Looks like time's up," she whispered to Matt.

Matt opened his mouth to reply, but no sound came out. He was paler than Rose had ever seen him, and this, somehow, made Rose's panic more real to her. She remembered saying once that she'd rather be normal and fit in with everyone else than be magical and an outcast. Now that she was faced with the prospect of exactly this, the words suddenly seemed hollow and insincere. She shook her head, wondering what she'd been thinking.

Matt, however, had always seen his difference as something to be proud of, and she knew that he would take the loss of his magic the hardest. Mary squeezed herself underneath Rose's arm and stared up at her with wide eyes, her fingers clutching at Rose in terror.

"Didn't Alison say that taking someone's magic away by force can kill them?" she choked out.

Rose looked down at her, not knowing what to say.

"We're not going to die, and neither is anyone else," she finally managed, sounding much calmer than she felt. "Mum, Dad and Grandpa are tough, and so are we. We've made it this far, haven't we?"

Her stomach lurched uncomfortably at the mention of Grandpa. He would be most likely to suffer from the effects of the Fragmenter, being eighty-one years old and, if the scene her Viewer had shown her was accurate, having been kept in poor conditions for many weeks, and it was for him that she was most worried.

There was another flurry of movement outside as most of Hunter's gang gathered around the house. Rose watched with a mixture of apprehension and amusement as the blond man approached the front steps with the Fragmenter, holding it at arm's length as though he thought it might explode in his face. She rushed back to the doorway for a clear view of his progress. Her eyes locked onto the bud, and she silently willed it to do its worst.

Just as she'd hoped it would, the invention's peaceful demeanour shattered the moment the man's foot crossed the threshold. The spells around the building strained and buckled as the invention sprang to life, flashing menacingly. Ignoring this, the blond man took a step further inside, and Rose cringed as the house began to groan.

The floorboards creaked loudly and cracks ran down the glass panes of the window. A sharp snap and a crash sounded from somewhere overhead, and Matt cackled with laughter as several roof tiles rained down onto the doorstep in pieces. Shards of glass from one of the upstairs windows followed, along with a string of muffled swear words from Hunter's gang outside.

The blond man took another step, and this time the bud's casing began to unravel. He hesitated, looking like he wanted nothing more than to toss the invention as far away as possible, but he continued resolutely down the hall to the first room, where smoke haze issued from

Hunter's many experiments.

The Fragmenter sent out a wave of energy in protest and Rose gasped as it struck her chest like a physical blow. The air seethed, and the hall appeared to twist and distort, like ripples disturbing the surface of a pond. She blinked several times to make sure her eyes were working properly, reminded once again of the way the Archives corridor had appeared to bend outside the high-security area.

"What's going on?" said Mary, shaking her head to clear it.

"There's too much magic in the house!" Rose cried, as smashing sounds issued from the experimenting area.

A boom and the squeal of twisting metal came from inside the steam room, and a burning, roaring sound filled the air. The orange glare under the door flared red hot and a golden liquid seeped out, along with a cloud of searing hot steam. Rose took a hurried step back as it flowed across the hall, scorching the wooden floor.

The spells around the house gave way and the building glowed with multicoloured lights as the illusion and disguise spells were destroyed. At the same time, the coloured lights from the experiment down the hall flickered on and off, slowly dying away. The thin plumes of steam billowing from another experiment turned into thick, acrid smoke, staining the ceiling a dirty grey. The paint on the walls peeled and blistered, and Rose jumped, startled, as their window suddenly shattered.

The blond man stopped in his tracks, holding the Fragmenter out in both hands. Rose chuckled, admiring the distorted lights outside the broken window until something dark caught her eye out in the fields. She nudged Matt and Mary.

"Hey, what's that? I didn't notice anything there when they brought us in …"

Matt and Mary turned to the window to look, but before either of them could say a word, the man in black came thundering down the stairs, his face twisted in fury.

"Get that damned thing out of here!" he roared, nodding at the glowing Fragmenter. "We're not ready for it yet! What do you think we've been doing for the last week?"

He looked down at the gushing golden liquid filling the hall and used a travel spell, appearing in the entrance to the house. The blond man seemed to give up, running for his life, back out the door. Rose's vision returned to normal as soon as the invention left the building, and she grinned, listening to the man in black yelling outside, his voice echoing across the grounds.

"Deactivate it! If you don't know how, go and ask the old man!"

Mary laughed as Jacob and the blond man struggled with the Fragmenter, attempting to wrestle it under control as the tendrils of the casing began to wind themselves around both men's wrists.

"They don't even know how to turn it off!" she said.

"Well, to be fair, neither do we," Rose reminded her, suppressing a grin with difficulty. Matt snorted.

"Yeah, we were just lucky that we did it by accident in Grandpa's city."

A shadow appeared by the entrance, and a second later Hunter had materialised at Jacob's side. He blinked, his gaze travelling from the attacking Fragmenter to the roof tiles and broken glass on the doorstep, and on to the scorched and blackened floorboards down the hall. He sighed and tapped the bud. It reluctantly released both men, retreating into its usual shape.

The blond man hastily thrust the dormant invention into Hunter's outstretched hand and Hunter took it without a word, walking down the hall to where the golden liquid was pooling. He ran a hand through his hair, looking exhausted. His eyes were red-rimmed as he glanced ruefully down the hall towards the ruined experiments in the other room. The man in black stood behind him silently, awaiting orders.

"We need more layers next time," Hunter told him in an undertone, using a spell to force the liquid back into the steam room. "At least twice as many. We just need the last one to hold. Let the gel thicken overnight. It should be almost ready by morning. And make sure this is locked in the area we prepared."

He gave the now-docile Fragmenter to the other man, who nodded and left. Matt watched him go with a grin and said to Hunter, "You need to keep a closer eye on those guys."

Rose shot her brother another warning look, but the ghost of a smile flitted across Hunter's face before he opened the steam room door and disappeared behind it, sending a wave of blistering heat down the hall.

"If they can't activate the bud in here to use it on us,

I wonder why they don't take us outside to the bud?" Mary said, going back to the window and staring out at the fields.

"They don't want to risk us getting away," replied Rose. She folded her arms across her chest as Hunter's gang began the repairs to the house. "It took them this long to catch us. If they let us go outside it would be easier for us to escape like Ben did."

"I thought they'd have trouble bringing the bud in here," grinned Matt. "I wonder how Hunter plans to get it inside?"

"Maybe they won't!" said Mary, her face lighting up with hope. "Then they won't be able to use it on us!"

"They'll find a way, sooner or later," sighed Rose.

Jacob appeared as she spoke, bearing a large plate of food and a handful of water bottles, which he shoved through the magical barrier without a word. Rose hadn't realised how hungry she was until she saw it all. She ate at top speed, savouring the taste of the chicken and pasta salad.

"It's so good to have real food to eat again!"

She settled back against the wall, licking grease off her fingers. Matt nodded enthusiastically, his mouth too full for him to answer.

"I forgot what it was like to feel full," agreed Mary, gulping down most of a bottle of water in one go. Rose rested her chin in her hand and stared outside at the setting sun.

"I wish Alison and Ben would turn up and get us out of here," she remarked as the last of Hunter's friends left, slamming the door behind them. "I wonder if those guys are going off to terrorise them now?"

"It wouldn't surprise me," replied Matt, watching them trek across the grounds. "But I don't think Alison and Ben will be able to help us this time. Ben might have escaped before he was locked up here, but I can't see them taking on Hunter and his entire gang and winning."

He glanced down at his trainers, his expression uncharacteristically forlorn, and Rose bit her lip, telling herself that he was wrong. He had to be.

She awoke with a jolt as someone opened the steam room door and a blast of searing heat hit her.

"Morning," said Matt, standing in the doorway again with Mary beside him, watching the goings on with interest. There was a sense of urgency in the air, and Rose felt a flutter of anxiety as she sat up, sure she knew what was coming.

"Whatever Hunter hoped would be ready today seems to be almost done," Matt informed her in an undertone.

Mary's face puckered.

"We're toast."

Rose grimaced. She stretched her legs and joined their watch. The steam room door opened again and Hunter stepped out, looking pleased. Jacob and the blond man hurried over, awaiting the verdict.

"It's nearly thick enough," said Hunter. "Give it another thirty minutes and we'll try again."

All three disappeared up the narrow wooden steps at

the end of the hall. Mary watched them go with a scowl.

"I hate how we just have to sit here, waiting for them to take our magic away!"

It felt like no time at all before Hunter returned. Rose held her breath as he emerged from the steam room once more, carrying a large, blackened basin in both hands, his face flushed from the intense heat.

"It's ready. Bring the Fragmenter in."

Jacob shot a malevolent grin at Matt and stalked outside. He reappeared a moment later, carrying the shining green invention. Rose couldn't see inside the basin, but its contents smoked with the same amber steam that filled the searing-hot room opposite them, and a strong smell of maple syrup filled her nostrils as Hunter brought it out into the hall.

He carried it right up to the front door, and Rose ran to the window to watch as Jacob lowered the bud into the basin, wincing at the heat. Energy rushed down the hall as the invention detected the spells around the house and surged back to life, but no barrage of magic came.

Hunter took a tentative step backwards, past the threshold. A tense silence filled the hall as everyone waited. Seconds stretched into minutes, and still the Fragmenter remained docile. Hunter turned and brought the basin further inside, his expression triumphant as his friends cheered around him.

"I think we'll take it downstairs first."

Jacob took the basin from Hunter and directed his steps towards the experiment room, followed by the rest of the gang.

"No!" screamed Rose, Matt and Mary together, beating their fists against the magical barrier over the doorway. Hunter ignored them and followed his friends.

"What are we going to do?" cried Mary, her voice high-pitched with terror. She attacked the doorway with both hands, seeming on the verge of hysteria.

"There's nothing we can do!" gasped Matt, sending spells at the doorway which merely vanished on contact.

Rose continued to beat and tear at the barrier as tears welled up in her eyes, blinding her. Energy built up underneath them, and Rose knew that in a matter of minutes it would be too late for her family. The energy continued to intensify, building until the spells barring their door strained and gave way. Rose stood stunned for a second, staring at her fist, extended out into the hall, before lurching out of the room with Matt and Mary close at her heels.

She charged into the first room off the hall, ignoring several magical instruments that she would otherwise have been keenly interested in, knocking over bottles and flasks in her haste as she fought her way through the clutter. The sound of voices grew louder and Hunter's gang entered the room, jeering and grinning, their job almost done. Their grins grew wider still as Rose, Matt and Mary barrelled into them, scratching and pushing, attempting to force their way through.

"Get out of the way!" snarled Rose, shoving one of the men into an experiment behind him and destroying the fragile glass dome that shielded it.

She could hear Matt and Mary behind her, calling loudly for their parents. Her eyes found the hall at the other side of the room and she hurled herself towards it. Before she could take a step further, one of the men grabbed her arm and pulled her back the way she'd come.

"It's your turn now," said the man with a laugh, carting her back down the hall and into the tiny room beside the stairs.

The man in black replaced the barrier over the doorway before disappearing with the others. Matt and Mary lay in a heap on the floor, their breathing ragged and their faces flushed with anger. Rose collapsed against the wall feeling slightly sick. All was quiet below. The Fragmenter must have done its job.

"They did it!" said Mary, tears streaking her face. "I can't believe they actually did it!"

Matt got to his feet and leaned against the wall, his face a mask of shock and despair. Soon footsteps could be heard approaching the room, and Rose backed away.

Jacob and the man in black had returned, carrying the smoking basin between them. Both men stood back, waiting, and a moment later bars just like the ones in the Archives appeared in the doorway, replacing the magical barrier and separating them from the small table Jacob had produced.

He set the Fragmenter on top of it, just out of reach. Three of the glass shards now glowed with a piercing white light, and Rose shuddered, sure that it must be because there were now three people without magic somewhere beneath them.

The man in black waved his hand a second time and a golden substance flew out of the basin. Rose recoiled as it crawled through the air towards her, forming a thick bubble around herself, Matt, Mary and the bud.

"Don't worry, the gel won't hurt you."

Rose peered through the amber wall with difficulty. Hunter had joined them, standing well back from the bars. Unlike his friends, his expression was determined rather than gloating. For a fleeting moment, Rose wondered if there was any point in pleading, but her voice seemed to have deserted her.

"What is this stuff?" asked Matt, standing as far away from the strange substance as possible.

"It's a kind of magical shock absorber," replied Hunter. "It will stop the Fragmenter from affecting the magic outside this room."

"Better make it thicker this time," remarked the man in black. "These three escaped last time."

Jacob complied and the men backed off. Rose's heart thudded painfully fast as Hunter activated the Fragmenter from a distance. The casing began to move, shrinking back into the braided base. The remaining glass shards began to glow much too soon, the white light gathering at the jagged tips, and Rose panicked as weariness crept over her.

"No, no, no!" cried Mary, searching in vain for a way out.

Soon Rose found herself sinking to her knees. Matt was already half unconscious beside her, his shoulders slumped and his head lolling. Rose felt herself hit the floor. She lay looking up at the Fragmenter, glowing like a beacon in front of her.

She willed herself to get up, but she was so very tired, too tired even to lift her head. Mary fell on top of her, limp and silent, before everything became a whirl of light and she knew no more.

23

Reunited

Rose came to slowly. Her body felt heavy and lethargic. She rolled onto her side, the cold, hard floor pressed against her cheek. A hand pushed her hair back out of her face gently and Rose's eyes snapped open. Mum was kneeling beside her on the concrete floor. Rose opened her mouth, but her throat was too thick to speak, so she wrapped her arms around her mother instead.

Mum's face was thin and pale, but her eyes shone with happiness as she beamed at her daughter. Rose swallowed and tried again.

"Mum! Are you OK?"

Mum nodded, still holding Rose tightly.

"We're fine. It's you three we've been worried about."

Rose released her mother and brushed away a tear. There was movement behind her and she turned to see Matt sitting cross-legged on the floor. He was white and shivering, wrapped in a thick woollen blanket.

"Hey," he said, managing a weak grin. "You look as bad as I feel."

Rose stuck her tongue out at him.

"Gee, thanks."

She sat up properly, feeling like she was getting over a bad cold. Her head throbbed and her limbs shook, and there was a disturbing emptiness somewhere deep inside her, gaping like a chasm. It was a kind of numb disconnectedness that she'd never experienced before, and she blinked back fresh tears, grappling with the loss of her abilities.

Mum immediately began fussing over her, checking her temperature and pressing a bottle of water into her hands.

"How are you feeling? They haven't been starving you, have they?" She lifted Rose's chin, muttering disapprovingly at how prominent her cheekbones had become. "Here, have something to drink."

"I'm OK, Mum," Rose assured her.

Mum put down the water bottle and began wrapping Rose up in blankets instead.

"I know, but Matt had a bad reaction when he woke up, and -"

"I'm fine!" said Matt adamantly. He gave Rose a look of exasperation but allowed Mum to hold a hand to his forehead.

"We need to keep you warm and hydrated," Mum finished. Rose looked at Matt with curiosity.

"What happened to him?"

"He threw up and started shaking badly," said Mum, her eyes full of concern. "We'll have to keep a close eye on Mary when she wakes up."

Rose followed her gaze to where Dad and Grandpa were kneeling beside the sofa. Mary lay curled up on it, unconscious and deathly white. Rose gathered her blanket around her like a shawl and attempted to stand.

Staggering a little, she took hold of Mum's shoulder for balance, her head swimming. Mum held on tight to her until she was steady.

"Be careful. The dizziness should go soon. Just watch your step."

Rose nodded and made her way over to where Mary lay. Dad wrapped his arms around her.

"It's so good to see you three again!" he exclaimed. "We've missed you all so much."

"We've missed you, too," said Rose, burying her face in his shoulder. She took a step back and looked up at him with a grin. He was clean shaven, but his hair stuck out oddly at different angles. She chuckled.

"Mum's been cutting your hair again, hasn't she?"

"I did the best I could," said Mum with mock indignance as Dad ran his hands ruefully through his uneven hair.

Rose turned to Grandpa, still kneeling beside Mary. He, too, was thin and pale, and his wispy white hair had been cut short as awkwardly as Dad's had been. His normally clear blue eyes seemed watery behind his glasses, but he smiled up at Rose as she approached.

"Grandpa!" she cried, hugging him gently. "It's been so long since we've seen you!"

"Yes, can you believe it's been more than two months," he said wonderingly, hugging her back. "Damn Lawrence Hunter!"

"And damn the Fragmenter," added Rose. "Hunter said it was the fight between it and the Shield that let him take you away!"

Grandpa nodded, his lined face filled with regret.

"It had to happen, I suppose. There was no way to avoid it."

He glanced up with a rueful smile and, seeing Rose's confusion, explained in a low voice.

"The best way to keep the invention from him was to leave it in the ruined city. The Shield would allow me to open the archway and enter the city with it only when the bud was deactivated, otherwise the two inventions would fight. But I needed to leave the city with the bud active."

"So that Hunter couldn't just open the archway, walk up to the bud and take it?" guessed Rose.

"That's right," said Grandpa. "So, when my work was done, I held the Fragmenter in one hand and activated it, opening the archway with the other, but of course, the Shield began to fight with the bud, sensing the threat. I hurried back into the real world and placed the bud on the road of the ruined city, closing the archway behind me while Hunter's gang broke into the house. At least the distraction allowed me to drop the archway into the rubble created by the fight, where it wouldn't be noticed. I'd hoped that Alison would realise what the compass was and destroy it so that the Fragmenter would stay lost in the ruined city for good."

He sighed and resumed his watch at Mary's side. Rose stared at him, taken aback. She'd always assumed that the fight between the two inventions had taken Grandpa by surprise.

"But there must have been some way of leaving the

bud activated in the city without setting the Shield off!" she cried.

"A bit of this amber substance Hunter's created would've been useful back then, wouldn't it?" chuckled Grandpa. "It might have been enough to stop the inventions attacking each other."

He wrapped an arm around Rose as she settled herself on the floor beside him, and they both watched Mary's slow breathing. Grandpa looked down at Rose's bare feet with amusement.

"What happened to your shoes and socks?"

Rose wiggled her toes and gave him a sheepish grin.

"Well, they kind of got stuck in the road in your ruined city," she admitted, ducking her head.

Grandpa pursed his lips, but his eyes were bright with mirth.

"Oh dear. Maybe you should tell me the whole story. It sounds thrilling."

"It is," said Matt seriously, joining them by the window. "And it's all thanks to me that we got the Fragmenter out, you know." He shot Rose a teasing grin and Rose rolled her eyes.

"Go on, then, genius," she said with a laugh. "Why don't you tell everyone the story?"

Rearranging the blanket around his shoulders, Matt sat with his back to the wall and recounted their adventures. Rose tuned out, focusing instead on her surroundings. Looking around with curiosity, she saw all of the things her Viewer had shown her. Nate had been right when he'd said that the room looked like a basement that had been added in a hurry.

The room was almost bare and smelled of fresh plaster and sawdust. There was another tiny room attached to the basement, out of which a steady dripping could be heard, informing Rose that this must be a bathroom. The sofa was pushed up against the wall underneath the dusty window, which looked out onto the expanse of fields. The only other objects in the room were three mattresses laid out on the bare floor, a small table and chairs, and a basket of the same thick blankets she, Matt and Mary were now wrapped up in.

Finally, when there was nothing left in the room to distract herself with, she gulped and turned her attention to the energy over the doorway, keeping them all inside. Reaching out with her mind, she attempted to pick the spells apart the way Mum had shown her, but they no longer responded to her. She could feel them without difficulty and could distinguish one spell from another, but it was impossible for her to influence them.

Turning away from the doorway, she bit her lip hard to keep it from quivering as Matt finished describing Rose's encounter with the Infuser.

"Miranda had better destroy everything in those rooms before I get out of here," said Dad threateningly.

"But how did Hunter manage to sneak a poison into his room in the first place?" Mum demanded, looking outraged.

"Miranda reckons he brought the ingredients in one by one and made everything inside his room," explained Matt. "As they are, the ingredients are OK. It's what he combined them to make that's the problem."

"What did you do?" pressed Grandpa. "I didn't think there were any doctors left in the country who could deal with that kind of injury."

Rose stared down at her left hand, lost in memories.

"There isn't, really."

She told them about Alison's attempts to find a doctor who could help them, and how Nate had been forced to invent new spells to remove the poison. Grandpa looked both intrigued and impressed.

"He's a Spellmaker? Why isn't he working in a hospital? He could make a fortune with skills like those! Spellmaking is incredibly complicated, and not everyone is up to it."

"Alison says he's not very well himself and he isn't fully accredited," replied Rose.

She resumed her story, explaining how she'd seen Hunter's hiding place in her Viewer, and how they'd discovered the archway leading to Grandpa's fake world. By the time she'd finished describing Mary's pitiful birthday party, Mum's eyes were sparkling with tears.

Rose continued, telling them about Matt's plan to shift the magic from the safe house onto something portable. Matt, who was now looking much more like his usual self, glowed with pride.

"We knew you'd figure it out," said Dad, patting him on the back. Rose tucked her hair behind her ears and looked at Mary.

"Why isn't she waking up?" she asked, trying to hide the fear in her voice.

"She's much younger and smaller than the rest of us," said Grandpa. "It will have been more of a shock to her."

"If only we'd been able to keep the Fragmenter away from Hunter," Rose replied gloomily, but Dad shook his head and lifted Mary's unconscious form onto his lap, holding her close.

"You should be proud of yourselves for keeping it away from him for as long as you did."

"Before you three went through the archway, Jacob and some of the others had been through more than a dozen times," laughed Grandpa. "They all insisted on using force, which is useless. It never seemed to occur to them that there could be a quicker and much simpler way of dealing with it."

Mum perched on the armrest of the sofa with a satisfied smile.

"Hunter was always coming down here to try to get your grandpa to tell him how to do it, but we thought it would take all the fun away if we told him."

Rose and Matt chortled.

"So Hunter was waiting for you when you came back through the archway?" guessed Dad, tucking the blanket in under Mary's chin.

Rose nodded.

"He took everything we had and then brought us here."

She stopped as Mary began to stir. They all huddled around her.

"Finally!" exclaimed Grandpa, leaning forward. "I

have to admit, I was starting to worry."

Mary's eyelids fluttered and then opened. She turned her head, staring at Matt's sneakers, obviously wondering where she was.

"It's OK, you're safe with us," Dad told her, giving her a quick kiss on the forehead. Mary looked up at her father and began to cry.

"Dad!" she sobbed, clinging onto his arm with both hands. Dad chuckled and held her tighter.

"It's good to see you awake," he said, his voice wavering.

"How are you feeling, darling?" asked Mum, kneeling close beside them. Mary went to sit up, reaching out for her mother. Almost at once, the colour drained out of her face and she began to tremble violently.

"She's having a reaction, just like Matt," said Mum anxiously.

"If we keep her warm and hydrated and she should be OK," instructed Grandpa, holding a bottle of water up to Mary's lips so that she could take a sip. Rose shifted closer, using her own body heat to warm her sister. Mary slowly stopped shivering, settling down more comfortably on Dad's lap, and Rose turned to her parents.

"If we don't do something, Hunter will have Alison and Ben in here, too. They're bound to come here to help us."

Mum lowered herself onto the sofa and ran a hand through her hair.

"There's not much we can do at the moment. There are spells all around this room keeping us in, and we can't do magic now. We don't have anything in here that could break us out. All we can do is wait for the Fragmenter to help us."

Rose looked at her mother in surprise.

"It'll help us?"

Grandpa grinned a slightly impish grin.

"That amber shock-absorber Hunter's made will reduce the damage the bud does, but it won't block it out entirely. It won't be long before it starts to affect the spells on this place, and then we might be able to escape. We can't rely on Alison and Ben now. The last thing we want is for them to be caught trying to help us, so we have to assume we're on our own for now."

"But even if we do get out, Hunter's going to have the bud locked away somewhere surrounded by magic so that we can't touch it," Rose reminded them.

"He's got a lot of inventions and magical objects in this house," said Mum. "There's a chance we might find something helpful."

"And then we can destroy the Fragmenter!" said Matt, his eyes becoming misty at the thought. But Mum, Dad and Grandpa shook their heads. Matt raised an eyebrow in confusion.

"You don't want to destroy it?! But why not? I thought you'd *want* it gone! If we destroyed it we could stop Hunter using it on anyone else!"

"We'll destroy it, yes, but not just yet!" explained Grandpa. "The timing is important. We'll have to wait until we've taken our magic back first."

Rose's heart leapt at these words. She looked at Grandpa as though waiting for him to announce that he was joking.

"Can we really get our magic back? How?"

"Once someone's magic has been stripped, the Fragmenter stores it away inside the glass pieces," he explained. "But if you repeat the process it should also give the person their magic back again. It was obvious when I was making the bud that some people would try to misuse it, so I had to incorporate a way of reversing its effects. But if the invention is destroyed while magic is stored inside the glass shards, it will dissipate and be lost."

Matt shot to his feet and began roaming around the basement restlessly. It seemed to be costing him all of his self-control to stop himself from attacking the spells over the doorway with his bare hands.

"I had no idea," said Rose, stunned.

"Yes, Hunter came for the invention before I had the chance to finish my reports," remarked Grandpa, watching Matt's progress around the room with a small smile. "But that's helped us a bit because Hunter doesn't understand how the Fragmenter works in detail. It's also why he hasn't thrown us out of the house now that we can't do magic. He doesn't want us free until he's done what he wants and destroyed the invention."

"I can't believe we just have to stay down here and wait!" cried Matt.

Mum chuckled and reached out to take hold of him

as he began another circuit around the room, pulling him down onto the sofa beside her, where he sighed and began picking at the cushions moodily.

"It might not take as long as you think for the Fragmenter to free us. You're forgetting just how powerful it is."

"So, our plan is to wait until the bud interferes with the spells over the doorway, so we can find where Hunter's keeping it and then use it on him and his friends?" replied Matt, a hint of scepticism creeping into his voice. "That's going to be almost impossible! Couldn't we get our magic back first and then go after Hunter? It'd be easier that way."

"If we can, we will," said Mum. "But I doubt we'll get the chance. We were all unconscious for about twenty minutes after the Fragmenter was used on us, and it'll do the same when we reverse its effects. Hunter will know as soon as we start using it because of the effect it has on everything around it. That gives him a lot of time to find us and lock us back up. It would be better to have him and his friends out of the way while we're using it."

Rose looked uneasily out of the window, where several of Hunter's gang could be seen making repairs to the roof over the entrance. Matt folded his legs up underneath him, his eyes fixed on the doorway.

"I guess we wait, then."

Several days went by without incident. Rose occupied herself by staring out at the grounds, watching the people outside rushing about, attempting another round of repairs. As Grandpa had predicted, the Fragmenter had begun to take a toll on the building both magically and structurally, forcing Hunter and his friends to patch things up more and more frequently.

Rose did a quick headcount while most of the gang was outdoors and came to a total of fifteen including Hunter, who was by the treeline, replacing the magic that concealed the area from unwanted visitors. She frowned. How on earth were six people without magic supposed to overcome a group of fifteen? Even with the Fragmenter's influence, Rose couldn't help but fear that Matt was right. The odds of winning were not good …

Mum joined her by the window, carrying salad rolls for each of them. Rose peered across the grass to a woman she'd never seen before. Her short, dark hair obscured her face as she bent over her work, but Rose could see that her skin was an olive colour. She and the auburn-haired woman were perched on the roof at the entrance to the house, assisting Jacob as he attempted to etch fresh disguise spells into the building and repair sections of the tiling.

"Mum, how're we going to take out all of Hunter's friends?" Rose asked her. "We don't have magic anymore *and* we're seriously outnumbered!"

Mum took a bite of her roll and followed Rose's gaze to the hive of activity outside.

"It might not be so bad," she replied. "Only four of them are magical."

Rose turned to her mother in surprise.

"Really? Are you sure?"

She had always assumed that most of the gang could do magic, and she soon found herself wondering what use the other members could be to Hunter if they were unable to cast even the simplest of spells.

"Apart from Hunter, only those two on the roof," Mum indicated Jacob and the auburn-haired woman, "that guy over there," she nodded at the blond man, "and the one who always wears black can do magic. I think his name is Adrian … he's a nasty piece of work, anyway."

She jerked her chin in the direction of the auburn-haired woman again.

"That one's name is Maria. She joined the group later than the others, about a week or so after your dad and I were put here. I'm not sure what made her want to help Hunter, but she clearly has no love for the Fragmenter."

Matt snorted.

"Well, to be fair, neither do we," he joked. "No offence, Grandpa."

Grandpa chuckled and took another roll from the bag of food.

"None taken. It's certainly not the invention I wanted to make."

"So that's why Hunter only ever gave his Archives key to those four," remarked Rose, understanding at last. "The others wouldn't be able to do the magic to open his door even if they had the key!"

"That's right," said Mum with a smile. "And it's also

why they do most of the work around here. The others are just as unable to use magic as we are now, and that's bound to help us. We'll be out of here soon, don't worry. The Fragmenter will let us out."

And much to Rose's surprise, it did. Rose had devoured her lunch and was sitting on the sofa, bored and wishing there was something to do when the sound of yelling voices and running feet broke out upstairs. She heard a crash as the front door was thrown open and rushed to the window in time to see Hunter's gang charging out into the fields.

"What's going on?" said Matt eagerly, coming to stand beside Rose.

Grandpa joined them and together they watched as the group ran towards the river, where something seemed to be causing a disturbance. The sound of voices raised in anger floated back to them, and soon the gang was fighting with someone hidden among the trees.

"I bet it's Alison and Ben out there!" Rose cried.

Most of Hunter's friends were unable to defend themselves against the spells being aimed at them from the treeline, and several of them crumpled in the long grass while the others ducked for cover. Rose could just make out the heads of Jacob and the auburn-haired woman, crouched in the grass so that they were barely visible, sending spells back at their attackers. The fight became more intense, and before long Rose became aware of energy building somewhere close by.

"They're upsetting the Fragmenter!" she laughed, standing on tiptoe for a clearer view.

Jacob yelled something indistinct and hurled a curse at the trees, causing several of them to topple.

"No, don't do that, you fool!" cried Grandpa, as the Fragmenter reacted more forcefully, sending a rippling wave of energy through the house.

"Yes, do it!" urged Matt with a mischievous grin, his hands gripping the window ledge.

The house began to groan as the magic outside continued. Rose cringed as cracks appeared in the basement walls and the familiar sound of breaking glass rang out across the grounds. Soon a bizarre crunching sound met her ears and she pressed her face up against the window to see the farmhouse's cladding peeling away where Jacob and the auburn-haired woman had etched their spells, like skin peeling off after a bad sunburn.

"Interesting," said Grandpa, taking a bite out of his roll and chewing thoughtfully. "I've never seen those particular spells scrambled like that. I'll have to remember that combination the next time I'm inventing."

Rose and Matt both chortled and, without warning, the spells over the basement doorway strained and broke. Mary surged to her feet with a gasp. Rose and Matt exchanged looks of surprise before racing each other to the steps, but Dad rushed forward, blocking their path.

"Wait! I'll go and check the way is clear first."

Rose swallowed her impatience and nodded, recognising that this was probably a good idea. She stayed put while Dad approached the stairwell and peered up into the hall beyond. Mum made a warning sound and Dad hastily retreated as footsteps sounded on the wooden floor above them. A moment later the man in black descended into view, giving them all a look of contempt before replacing the spells with a wave of his hand.

Rose went back to the window, cursing the man in black under her breath. All was silent and still outside now. Hunter's gang was returning to the house, many of them limping or rubbing a shoulder where they'd hit the ground.

"Does the Fragmenter always destroy the buildings around it?" asked Rose, turning to Grandpa. He brushed the crumbs off his shirt.

"Only if the building is covered in magic, like this one. It won't cause any problems if it's stored properly, away from anything that could set it off, but Hunter has so many spells etched into this house that destroying one will only destroy the other. If he doesn't move the invention away or destroy it soon, it will slowly tear this place apart. It would have been much better to choose a house with no magical disruption to hide out in, but I suppose then he wouldn't have been able to keep us under control, would he?"

He turned away from the window with a smile. The afternoon trickled by uneventfully and Rose watched the sun begin to sink. Most of Hunter's gang had left for the night, and Mum and Dad were heaping blankets onto the mattresses on the floor as the temperature dropped. Darkness fell, and soon the only light source was the eerie glow of the experiments upstairs, illuminating the stairs with dim blue light.

Rose was settling down onto a mattress beside Mary when she felt the magic sealing the basement give out once more. She sat bolt upright. There was the sound of a blanket being flung back and the dark outline of her grandfather appeared, approaching the stairs.

"That'll be Hunter, trying to get our magic out of the Fragmenter, wherever he's hiding it!" he said in an agitated tone.

He placed a foot on the bottom step, but Dad stopped him, placing a hand on his shoulder gently.

"I'll go and have a look around."

"I'm coming with you."

Mum marched over to his side, her expression determined.

"But if I find Hunter -" Dad began.

"If you find Hunter, you'll need backup," said Mum. "You can't do magic anymore and I doubt he'll fight fair."

"Why don't we all go, then?" suggested Rose, tossing her own blankets aside. "He can't fight all of us at once, even with magic!"

Matt and Mary both voiced their agreement, but Mum and Dad shushed them.

"No, you need to stay here in case someone comes to check on us. Your grandpa can protect you."

Grandpa hesitated for a moment before looking at his grandchildren and nodding once. He went back to where Matt was kneeling on the mattress, ready to follow his parents.

"Back into bed," said Grandpa, covering Matt with

blankets and sitting beside him. "We'll need to keep a lookout while they're away."

Rose thought of the guilt she'd felt for not listening to her parents months ago, and sat back down beside Mary, giving Matt a meaningful look. For the first time since they'd become embroiled in the search for the Fragmenter, he sighed and, with a long look at Rose, lay down without arguing. Mum and Dad made sounds of relief and disappeared up the steps.

"Be careful!" Grandpa called after them.

Rose tucked her blankets up under her chin, trying to ignore her anxious thoughts.

"I hope no one realises Mum and Dad are out," she whispered into the dark.

"They'll be OK," replied Grandpa. "There are never many people about here at night. Most of Hunter's lot are usually off causing mayhem somewhere else, and the ones that do stay here aren't very observant. After you three went through the archway, Alison and Ben tried to get us out of here quite a few times. Nobody noticed them, but they couldn't find a way through the magic protecting the house without giving themselves away."

This news didn't surprise Rose. She'd seen for herself just how useless most of Hunter's friends were when she'd helped to steal his key. But it didn't stop her worrying that one of them might catch her parents. The hours crept by without any sound from above, and she eventually fell asleep waiting for them to return.

Moonlight was streaming in through the window when she was awoken by a loud *boom*, followed by the sound of rushing water. She sprang to her feet, staring around for the source of the disturbance.

"That didn't sound good," remarked Matt, sitting up.

"Are Mum and Dad back yet?" yawned Mary, stumbling her way over to the bottom of the stairs. Rose caught sight of Matt's wristwatch, glowing in the dark. It was one o'clock.

"No, they're not back yet."

Grandpa's voice rang out, strained but alert. As Rose's eyes adjusted to the half-light, she saw him hobbling over to the tiny bathroom, where the rushing sound was loudest. She, Matt and Mary gathered behind him and peered into the room.

A water pipe had burst and was now spraying torrents of cold water onto the floor, which was rapidly resembling a swimming pool.

"Well, that's just brilliant," said Rose, throwing up her hands in exasperation.

"How did it break? Was it the Fragmenter again?" asked Matt, scratching his head, his blond hair tousled from sleep.

There was a pause before Grandpa said in a quiet voice, "It gave out when someone used magic upstairs."

Rose glanced nervously at the stairwell. Had her parents been caught? She met Grandpa's eyes briefly and knew from the concern on his face that he was wondering the same thing. All was still and silent upstairs. Rose began to feel more and more afraid that something had happened to Mum and Dad. She perched on the edge of the sofa, too agitated to sleep.

Hours trickled by in silence, and soon light began to glow on the horizon. Water continued to rise around them until the mattresses were soaked through. Matt's watch beeped, announcing that it was now six o'clock, and a minute later footsteps clattered softly on the steps. Mum appeared, looking stressed but very pleased about something.

"Mum!" cried Rose, Matt and Mary in a chorus, gathering around her at the foot of the stairs. "Where's Dad?"

"Did you find the Fragmenter?"

"Who was doing magic?"

Mum put a finger to her lips and whispered, "Dad's coming now. We didn't find Hunter or the Fragmenter, but there are two locked rooms on the top floor. Now that Hunter's made that amber gel, he's most likely keeping the invention somewhere in the house. We tried to pick the locks but couldn't get in without triggering the spells sealing the doors." She stopped and looked down at her feet. "Why is there water on the floor?"

Rose began to answer but was interrupted by a beam of light approaching the stairwell. Mum gave Grandpa an alarmed look and rushed back into the room, pulling her children along with her as one of Hunter's friends appeared in the doorway, carrying a flashlight.

To Rose's relief, he was one of the non-magical members of the group and seemed entirely oblivious to the absence of spells across the doorway. He shone the light into each of their faces and stared down at the rippling water covering the floor. His mouth fell open in surprise, his eyes narrowing.

"Where's your dad?" he demanded of Matt, who was closest.

Matt shrugged and replied with a perfectly straight face.

"He's in the shower."

Rose fought to keep herself from laughing as the man glanced towards the bathroom, where the sound of gushing water was clearly audible. The man raised an eyebrow, not noticing the pair of feet that had appeared on the steps behind him. Rose tried not to react as Dad crept closer, staring at the man's back pocket. He stretched out a hand, reaching for something that caught the early morning light.

He froze, hand outstretched as the sound of movement from the floor above carried down the steps. The man whirled around. He and Dad stared at each other for a moment, startled, and Rose saw what had attracted her father's attention. A bunch of silver keys protruded from the man's pocket.

Dad pushed him before he could respond, sending him flying backwards into the basement. He hit the floor with a splash and began to climb to his feet, but Mum, Grandpa, Rose, Matt and Mary heaped themselves on top of him, holding him down. Mary clamped a hand over his mouth, stifling his cry for help, while Grandpa wrestled the keys out of his pocket.

Dad ran upstairs and returned a moment later with a length of extension cord, which he used to tie the man's hands behind his back. Climbing over a sodden mattress,

Rose pulled the cover off a pillow and used it as a gag so that Mary could let go, and they all straightened up.

"What're we going to do with him?" Rose asked, panting. "Someone's going to realise he's missing …"

"We'll put him in the bathroom for now," decided Grandpa. "At least no one will be able to see him tied up. But they're going to come looking for him at some point." He held up the bundle of keys. "We should get going now, while we have the advantage," he insisted. "If we -"

There was a low, impressed whistle from the doorway and Grandpa stopped. Everyone whirled around, and the man on the floor lifted his head to stare. Alison and Ben were standing at the foot of the stairs, beaming at them.

"One down, thirteen to go," remarked Ben, his grin growing wider. "Well, fourteen, including Hunter." He looked down at the water lapping at his feet. "Huh. So that's what made the crashing sound. Oops."

"That was *you*?" said Matt.

"Well, it was both of us, actually," admitted Alison, biting her lip. She splashed her way into the bathroom and the sound of rushing water stopped. "That's better."

She emerged a moment later and stood beside Rose, drying herself off with another spell. Rose gave her an approving nod.

"I knew you'd break in here sooner or later! You were out in the bush fighting Hunter's friends yesterday, weren't you?"

Alison's face broke into the kind of grin Rose was

more accustomed to seeing on her brother.

"It was very satisfying to torment them while we got the Fragmenter to weaken the defensive spells around the house for us. It was Ben's idea. Why shouldn't the bud help us for once?"

"We've been out there all day, waiting for nightfall, knowing that most of the gang would leave," continued Ben. "We put the two guys on guard duty to sleep and tied them up. Your mum and dad found us searching the house and we helped them break through some of the barrier spells upstairs, but we weren't expecting this guy to come back so early."

His gaze fell on the gagged man, who was now sitting upright, following the conversation with wary eyes.

"Most of Hunter's friends have gone to Ben's house to try and capture us both," added Alison. "Miranda and Nate are there now, keeping them all busy, so as long as the gang stays there, distracted, we should have time to take the Fragmenter back."

Grandpa nodded and turned to look inquisitively at Ben.

"We haven't met before, have we?" he said, holding out his hand. "I'm afraid I don't use the Archives as much as I should. I only know Alison and Miranda."

Ben stepped forward and shook hands, looking uncharacteristically awkward.

"Ben Atherton," he said. "It's great meeting you. I studied some of your work at university."

"Did you really?" replied Grandpa wonderingly. He

gave Ben another appraising look and said, "Maybe we should work together after all this is over."

Rose chuckled at the shock on Ben's face. He seemed to struggle to find the right words for a moment before finally finding his voice.

"That would be great!"

"And thanks again for looking after the kids," added Mum. "I don't know what we'd have done without you."

Alison smiled and shrugged as though it was nothing. "We were happy to help."

Matt gave his parents an impatient look and moved towards the stairs, apparently unable to contain himself any longer.

"So what's the plan?" he pressed. "Hunter's lot could be back at any minute. Are we going to check out these rooms upstairs or not?"

Without waiting for an answer, he took off up the stairs.

"Can we go upstairs, too?" asked Mary.

Mum glanced at Dad before nodding in a resigned kind of way.

"We won't be coming back down here again. Come on. Let's go find the Fragmenter."

24

A Trail of Inventions

Mary ran after her brother without another word.

"Be careful up there!" Mum called, as she and the rest of the party made their way upstairs. "There are experiments everywhere, so don't touch anything!"

Ben nudged the gagged man with his toe.

"We should move this guy into the living room with his friends. We can put him to sleep, too, so he doesn't bother us."

He and Alison dragged the protesting man to his feet and forced him up the stairs. Dripping water all over the floor, Rose stepped out onto the landing, relishing her freedom and trying to ignore the sense of urgency gnawing at her. Would Hunter have already taken her family's magic for his own? Would she know it if he had?

Pushing these thoughts to the back of her mind, she crossed the hall and took her first proper look at the room beyond. Herbs and magical equipment hung from the ceiling, still dark in the early morning light. A mortar and pestle were grinding something black and sparkling into a fine powder on a bench beside her. Several inventions nearby hovered inches above the benchtop, constructing themselves out of a jumble of pieces on the table beneath them.

The Fragmenter had taken a larger toll on the building than she'd realised while locked in the basement. The cracks in the ceiling and walls had deepened considerably since she'd last been upstairs, despite everything Hunter and his friends had done to prevent it, and the magic on the house had a fragile, brittle feel to it that hadn't been there when she'd arrived.

She edged around a desk overflowing with spell books and smoking beakers that left the scent of tar in the air. Some of the books were propped open, and she bent down to read the nearest, immediately recognising Hunter's handwriting.

Both pages were filled with long strings of the magical symbols that represented spells, and Rose scratched her head, at a loss to understand most of it. She reached out to turn the page, only to stop, remembering all too clearly what had happened the last time she'd touched Hunter's belongings. Glancing around, she snatched up a pen and prodded the book firmly. Nothing happened. Rose let her breath out in a rush and turned the page.

She glimpsed more of the same neat handwriting before the page flipped back over to its original position with a rustle. Rose stared. She turned the page over again, with the same result.

"One more time," she murmured.

She picked up the front cover of the book and closed it. This time she was forced to move her hand quickly out of the way as the book threw itself open with a thud, settling on the same page of writing.

"OK, fine!"

Rose grumbled and straightened up, her hands in the air in surrender.

"Come on, Rose!"

Mary's voice carried down the hall, where Alison and Ben could be seen wrestling the gagged man towards the cramped living room Rose had glimpsed beside the entrance. She hurried to catch up, joining the others in time to see Alison place a sleeping spell on the man before unceremoniously pushing him into the room.

"Sweet dreams," she said with a grin.

Rose stuck her head around the doorframe and saw three people collapsed on a sofa just like the one downstairs. Two of the men were tied up with thick cords, but all three were fast asleep, their heads lolling onto their shoulders. She let out a snort of laughter and continued along the hall.

Mum, Dad and Grandpa headed for the narrow flight of wooden steps, but Matt hung back, stopping outside the steam room door.

"Hold on! I have to see what's in here!"

He put his hand on the doorknob, but Rose pressed on towards the stairs.

"We already know. Hunter made his shock absorber stuff in there."

She motioned for him to follow the rest of the group, but he remained where he was.

"I still want to see!"

"Me too!" cried Mary, turning back.

Rose sighed. "Of course you do. OK, let's be quick,

then. You were the one saying we needed to get a move on, remember?"

Matt opened the door and a rush of hot air swept into the hall. An amber glow lit up the walls, making them appear to be on fire, and Rose stepped into the room, shielding her face from the glare.

"Wow," said Mary, standing behind her.

Rose moved aside so that her sister could see inside the room, leaving the door open so that she could more easily tolerate the heat. A large boiler took up half of the available space, creating the burning sound she'd noticed while locked in the room across the hall.

Taking a step closer, she peered at the liquid inside. Just as she knew it would be, it was the same amber substance Hunter had used to control the Fragmenter, but under such heat, it was closer to the consistency of water than the thick gel Hunter had used. Rose backed away, sure that her skin must be blistering.

"It's like being inside a pressure cooker," she gasped, retreating to the doorway.

Even as she watched, the amber liquid seemed to thicken, sticking to the sides of the boiler. A table covered in heat resistant spells stood along the opposite wall, bearing a collection of tubs filled with water, which Rose guessed must have been used to top up the boiler as the amber substance cooked. Deciding she'd seen enough, she went out into the hall, shivering in the comparative cool.

"OK, you've seen what's in there, now we have to keep moving."

She beckoned to Matt and Mary, who seemed transfixed by the bright, bubbling liquid, and pulled them out of the room, leaving the door ajar. She looked down at the legs of her jeans as she climbed the stairs.

"At least the heat from the boiler dried our clothes," she remarked with a laugh.

The stairs turned a corner, revealing another hallway. There were no windows here, making it much darker than downstairs. A door stood open on the left at the far end of the hall, however, bathing the walls and floorboards in golden light. Rose, Matt and Mary hurried towards this room, passing a closed door on their right, and found the rest of the group searching a room full of experiments like the one downstairs.

Rose stared around at the clutter, her excitement ebbing. The absence of the Fragmenter's powerful energy told her that they would not find the invention in this room, and she wondered why her parents were bothering to search in here at all. A wide window looked out over the fields and the bushland by the river, and Rose winked back tears as rays of sunlight broke through the treetops.

"Well, the Fragmenter's not in here, so it must be in the room across the hall," said Grandpa, glancing up from a rust-coloured invention made of a coarse material like sandpaper. It spiralled inward in a funnel shape, collecting beads of water that travelled down into its depths.

"What's that?" asked Mary, running to his side and leaning over the table for a closer look. Grandpa wrapped an arm around her waist, holding her back with a warning look.

"Be careful. It's covered in desiccation spells. Watch this."

He took a fresh flower from a glass jar and dropped it into the centre of the invention, where it hung suspended, trapped by the Desiccator's spells. The flower began to shrivel, curling in on itself. Grandpa waited a second before opening a compartment at the base of the invention, where a tiny reservoir contained droplets of moisture.

"It's got some clever magic on it, this one," he said with a regretful sigh. "If things had been different, Hunter could have been a great magical scientist and done the world some good."

"Come on, let's look next door," said Dad, leading the way back down the hall.

Ben stepped forward and began to break down the spells guarding the door, leaving it scarred, pitted and smoking slightly in the morning light. He produced the keys and, after several unsuccessful attempts to find the correct one, slipped a small brass key into the lock and turned.

There was a click and the door swung open. Matt let out a loud groan. The room greatly resembled the last of Hunter's secret rooms in the Archives. Cabinets and shelves filled every space, filled with inventions.

"This is going to take a while," said Alison, bending to inspect a stack of boxes on the floor beside her.

Rose picked her way towards the back wall, stepping

over crates and more boxes containing inventions that had either been partly finished or partly deconstructed. The pieces sparkled and glinted in the early morning light, many of them broken or damaged.

She edged past two rickety-looking shelves holding such a large number of objects that they were on the verge of collapsing. A spindly table wobbled under the weight of a pile of heavy spell books, which had spilled over onto the floor. Rose stared around the room, wondering where to begin searching.

"I don't know about you, but I can't see Hunter leaving the Fragmenter on a shelf like this," said Alison, picking through the contents of a cabinet.

Grandpa nodded, surveying the room from the doorway.

"You're right. The Fragmenter puts out so much magical energy that we'd be able to feel it if it was in here." He bent down to retrieve a tiny invention that had rolled onto the floor and placed it back on the nearest shelf. "Most of these pieces hold magic that would react with it anyway. He wouldn't be able to keep it here."

Mum turned around slowly, taking in the room from every angle, her expression desperate.

"But it must be here somewhere! We've searched the whole house!"

Rose racked her brain for answers, thinking of Hunter's rooms in the Archives and the mind games the bud had played on them in the ruined city.

"Are you sure it's inside the house?"

"It wouldn't be affecting the house so badly if it wasn't close by," insisted Grandpa. "Besides, the whole reason Hunter made the shock absorber was so that he could bring the Fragmenter inside. I can't see him going to that much effort just to keep it outside somewhere. There *is* nowhere outside to keep it, just fields and bushland. The nearest buildings are miles away."

Mum ran her hands through her hair.

"This is ridiculous!" she cried. "There's no use looking through the house again. We're just wasting time. And we've searched the downstairs rooms even more thoroughly than the ones up here."

They all moved out into the hall, scratching their heads and looking at each other in silence, perplexed and defeated. Matt kicked the toe of his shoe against the skirting board, his expression troubled.

"Let's hope Hunter's gang doesn't come back any time soon," he murmured.

"But the bud has to be here somewhere," repeated Rose. "It's like Grandpa said. It wouldn't be reacting with the spells on this place if it wasn't close by!"

Unable to think of anything else to do, she returned to the cluttered room. Mary sighed and came to help, sorting through the inventions trailing over an ornate desk.

"You're wasting your time in there," Matt called. Rose ignored him and continued her search.

"We must have missed something, that's all," she insisted, trying to convince herself as well as her brother.

"What about hidden places, like in the Archives?"

suggested Mary, looking up at her parents. But Grandpa shook his head.

"Alison and Ben would have felt it. Working in the Archives, they're very good at detecting concealment." He turned to the two Archivists. "You didn't feel anything, did you?"

"No, there's nothing hidden anywhere in here," said Alison, her lips pursed. "I'm guessing Hunter chose an isolated place like this so that he wouldn't *have* to conceal everything."

Rose moved from cabinet to cabinet, her hope shrinking fast.

"What time is it?" she asked Matt.

He held up his hand so that she could see the glowing numbers on his wristwatch. It was now almost seven o'clock. They were running out of time. She was about to voice this concern to her parents when Mary made a sound of outrage.

"Hey, some of this stuff is ours!"

She plunged her hand into the pile of inventions and pulled out Grandpa's pocket watch, dangling from its long, golden chain. She opened the watch to show the hands, drifting aimlessly around the clock face.

"Wait, that points towards the Fragmenter, doesn't it?" Rose cried, rushing to Mary's side. "It could show us where it is!" The words had barely left her mouth when she stopped. "Oh, yeah. Hunter's spells will be blocking it, just like they blocked my Viewer."

She turned away, her spirits sinking further. Mary dug her hand deeper into the pile and tipped it over, scattering the contents all over the desktop.

"The invention Miranda let us use!" cried Rose.

"My Hook!" said Matt, his face echoing Mary's outrage. "Why would Hunter want that?"

"He must have thought it could be useful," replied Mum, standing behind Mary and gazing down at the inventions. They continued their search, but found only unfamiliar pieces that bore Hunter's magical signature.

Even without his abilities, Matt seemed to have a certain amount of control over the Hook. He beckoned to it and it scuttled out of Mary's hand and across the floor. With a look of surprise, he scooped it up and tucked it into his shirt pocket. He looked up at Dad questioningly and Dad smiled.

"You're its maker. Your magic is inside it, and it'll respond to you, even if you can't do magic right now."

Mum stretched out a hand and plucked something that flashed blue and silver from the mess, holding it out to Rose with a wide smile.

"My Viewer!" Rose took the invention and checked it for damage. "Thanks!"

"Ah, I'm not surprised he wanted that," said Alison seriously. "That's a powerful invention. More than once after Hunter dragged you three off to this house, I suspected he was using it to find me, Ben and Nate. There was no other way he could have known where we were. It even saw through all of the spells on Ben's house, and that's saying something."

She and Ben both laughed, and Rose looked down at the Viewer, feeling proud of her little invention for the first time. Placing a finger on the outer ring, she concentrated on the Fragmenter but saw only blackness, with a faint light glowing at the centre of the scene, dimly illuminating an intricate green casing. Unsure what to make of this, she lifted her finger and folded the invention flat, her mind racing.

"Is it working?" Mary asked eagerly.

Rose hummed, tucking the Viewer into her pocket.

"It's definitely working. I can see the bud, but it's somewhere dark. Too dark for me to see anything that might help us find it. I *think* the room it's in might be circular, but I can't be sure."

Grandpa, Alison and Ben glanced at one another.

"A circular room? That would mean it's not in the house," mused Matt. "But there aren't any other buildings nearby."

"Unless there *is* a hidden area in here and we're just missing it," said Alison, her face clouding with worry.

"We need to keep searching," insisted Grandpa. "You're right, Alison. We must be missing something."

"But, just say we don't find the Fragmenter in time," said Matt, glancing over his shoulder towards the stairs. "What are we going to do when Hunter's friends come back? I mean, we could all run now, and at least we'd be free, but we'd be giving up on getting our magic back, wouldn't we?" He turned to the rest of the group beseechingly. "I don't think any of us want to do that. So we need to come up with a plan to fight them, or at least keep them out of the way while we search, and then get our magic back before Hunter takes it for himself."

"I don't know why he hasn't done it already," said Mum uneasily. Alison gasped.

"What?! But the Fragmenter can't do that, can it? I thought it only removed and returned magic."

Ben looked at Grandpa for confirmation, his freckles standing out clearly as the colour drained from his face.

"As usual, Hunter has found a way to misuse it," said Grandpa contemptuously.

"But how are we going to stop the whole gang without magic?" urged Matt. "Even with Alison and Ben here, we're outnumbered."

Grandpa nodded, his gaze distant and thoughtful.

"What we need is a way to get the gang out of the way indefinitely, so we can look for the bud without interruption."

Catching a glimpse of bright metal on the floor, Rose snatched up one final invention and turned back to face the others, holding out her hand so that they could all see the tiny object.

"And I've got the perfect idea!"

Matt, Mary, Ben and Alison looked down at the invention and then up at Rose, staring at her as though she'd lost her mind. Dad grinned, and Mum looked uncertain, but Grandpa burst out laughing. He shuffled forward and picked up the twisted remains of the silver archway.

"I thought you must be exaggerating when you said you'd destroyed this," he said, holding it up to the light and inspecting the many scratches and dents in the metal. "But look at the state of it!"

He chuckled again and squeezed the invention to test how much damage had been done. The silver spread upwards, feebly imitating half an arch before giving up and melting back into its deformed shape.

"But that's - no way!" spluttered Matt. "We nearly died inside that thing! I never want to go near it again!"

Rose gave him an impatient look.

"You won't have to! But Hunter was happy to let us go in there for him and he got his friends to go in there, too. I think it's about time he saw for himself what it's really like!"

"But it doesn't work anymore," protested Mary. "And Grandpa can't fix it now."

"Alison and Ben can still do magic," Rose pressed. "Grandpa could tell them how to repair it. If we could fix it, we wouldn't have to worry about anyone stopping us!"

She looked imploringly at her grandfather. It seemed to her to be the perfect plan, as they had no idea how long it would take them to find the Fragmenter, or where to look next.

"How would we get them all back out afterwards?" asked Mum. "The buildings move around all the time, don't they? We'd never find Hunter's friends again once we put them inside."

Grandpa weighed the remains of the archway in his hand musingly.

"Normally, yes," he said. "But we could change it a little this time. What do you think?"

He turned to Alison and Ben, who exchanged looks

of uncertainty.

"It's worth a try I guess."

"What do we need to do?"

Grandpa issued a string of instructions, which Rose only partly understood. The two Archivists, however, nodded and stepped forward as Grandpa held out the archway.

"You'll need to repair the metal part first, so that the archway can form properly," he told them. "Have you done shaping spells before? The shape of the invention when deactivated is important because it determines how the spells form the arch."

Alison took the invention tentatively. Fixing her eyes on the twisted metal, she sent it soaring into the air, hovering in front of her.

"I've done them a few times, but I'm not great at them," she admitted.

"It's not a complicated shape," insisted Grandpa. "It's the illusion spells that are most important, but we'll get to them in a moment."

Rose watched the repairs, wondering if they would be finished in time. Alison and Ben worked quickly, and soon the silver glowed hot, reshaping itself and erasing all of the damage. There was a brief pause, and Alison's eyebrows came together in confusion.

"I can see the final shape clearly in my mind, so why isn't the metal doing what I want?"

Grandpa observed in silence before holding a hand up to stop them.

"Just one of you should do the shaping. You both

see the invention slightly differently in your mind's eye and the silver is trying to obey both of you at once."

Alison took a step back.

"Ben's better at it than I am, he can do it," she said.

Moments later, the metal threads were smooth and perfectly sculpted, and after some more spellwork, the archway opened, fully formed in front of them. Grandpa smiled.

"Wonderful! Now we need to take care of the illusion spells!"

Alison joined in again here, replacing the magic that kept the ruined city changing up.

"I think we'd better make the city smaller, too," suggested Rose. "The way it is, it's so huge that it'd take us forever to find anyone, even if the layout didn't keep changing."

Ben adjusted the spells with a nod.

"Wait a minute, didn't Hunter say his friends could come and go out of the city as long as they kept the arch open?" cried Mary, turning to her brother and sister urgently. "We'll have to change it so that no one can get out once they go through, even if the arch stays open!"

"Good thinking, Mary," said Rose with a grin, giving her a pat on the back.

Soon the invention was completed, and Grandpa inspected it, surveying the improvements. The interior had been restricted to the city centre, and featured many of the landmarks Rose remembered from her time there, including the collapsed clock tower. They had seen no reason to waste time repairing the buildings.

"Should we disguise it, do you think?" asked Mum. "So we can leave it open? Or should we not bother -"

The sound of a creaking floorboard carried down the hall and Mum stopped. They all turned towards the stairwell. Ben approached the top step, peering down towards the ground floor. There was another sound of movement and Ben darted forward, dragging a figure out of hiding.

It was one of the men that had been knocked out with sleeping spells, and he regarded the silver archway with suspicious eyes as he grappled with Ben. Alison pursed her lips as Ben hauled the man closer.

"Huh. I guess our sleeping spells wore off …"

"We should have tied them all up better," panted Ben, struggling to hold his captive down. "Oh well, it can't be helped."

Alison shrugged and gave the man a sunny smile.

"Looks like you're going in first, then."

She and Ben each took hold of an arm and forced him up to the archway, pushing him over the threshold. Catching himself on the brick wall of the nearest building, he clutched at his throat and took several long, deep breaths, getting used to the strange air inside the city. Whirling around, he stared at his surroundings with bemusement before hurling himself at the opening, only to bounce off an invisible barrier.

"Awesome! He can't leave without the bud," said Rose, grinning.

Grandpa tapped the archway three times, causing it to collapse into its usual shape. Horror spread over the man's face as the metal flowed down around him, separating him from the real world. Alison picked up the invention and pocketed it.

"Not unless we choose to let him out," Grandpa said, his eyes twinkling behind his glasses. "Let's go put those other two idiots in there, too, before they wake up."

Mary giggled and the group moved towards the stairs. She looked up at Grandpa and spoke in a voice too low for Rose to catch, and Grandpa replied with a reassuring smile.

"It's just like a normal magical invention, made for non-magic people," he said. "We can use it and move it around, even if we can't do magic. When we -"

They reached the landing and came to an abrupt halt. Mary gasped and backed away. Ben swore and ran to the front of the group, quickly followed by Alison. Edging forward to see what was going on, Rose found a mass of people waiting silently downstairs, glaring up at them.

The sleeping spells Alison and Ben had placed on the men in the living room hadn't worn off. They'd been removed. Hunter's gang had returned, and now Rose and the others had nowhere to run but back upstairs.

25

The Battle

Rose retreated as the gang surged forward. Spells hit the walls on either side of her and the blond man jostled his way to the front of the group, reaching out to take hold of Grandpa.

"Go hide upstairs!" Ben yelled, throwing up a barrier that filled the space between the two parties, forcing the blond man back.

Rose glanced back over her shoulder as she followed her mother. The air shimmered where the spell blocked the hall, but she could make out the form of the man in black striding towards them, pushing the others out of his way.

"How're we going to hold them off?" gasped Mary, almost tripping over her own feet in her haste.

"I don't know, but I'm glad Alison and Ben are here to help us," murmured Rose, hurrying after her.

Reaching the upstairs landing, she followed Grandpa and Matt into the nearest room while her parents and Mary disappeared into the second room with Alison, who stood her ground in the doorway, ready to attack. Ben appeared last and stationed himself in front of Grandpa, shielding himself with the open door.

"We need weapons!" cried Rose, her eyes sweeping

the room frantically. Matt opened a drawer in the ornate desk and extracted a letter opener, holding it out like a knife.

"How about this?"

"Good one," Rose replied, turning back to the room.

Her gaze settled on the wooden shelves, still barely supporting the weight of the objects heaped upon them. She wrenched the lower shelf off the wall, sending inventions tumbling to the floor, and considered it for a moment, brushing a finger over the nails protruding from each end.

"It's not great, but it'll have to do."

Ben looked over his shoulder at the shelf and his face lit up with amusement.

"It's creative, I'll give you that," he said with a wicked grin. "I just hope you don't give anyone tetanus."

Matt snorted with laughter, twirling the letter opener in his hand.

"I think that's the least of our problems right now."

Grandpa sighed and shook his head, searching the mess on the table. Most of the inventions in the room had not been designed for combat, but finally, he plunged his hand into the pile and drew out an object with a ring of short metal spikes along the base, connecting it to the casing.

The sound of Ben's barrier shattering carried up the stairs, followed by the footfalls of many feet, and Rose braced herself, feeling completely unprepared for the coming fight. Grandpa dismantled the invention quickly, tossing parts aside until he was left with the spiked metal ring, which he slipped over his knuckles just as the first spell hit Ben's door, leaving the scent of charred wood in the air.

Rose stared at her grandfather in surprise. She had never seen him do anything remotely warlike. Straightening up, he turned to face the door and met Rose's eyes. He gave her a resigned look.

"Sometimes you've got no choice but to do things you'd rather not do," he said.

The footsteps became louder and Rose tensed, expecting the gang to appear at any second and force their way into the room. Ben peeked around the door and aimed a spell towards the stairs. A shout echoed down the hall, and a moment later the doorway was buzzing with energy as spells flew back and forth.

There was a commotion outside and a hand gripped the edge of the door. Rose ran to help Ben, who had braced himself against the wood as someone attempted to shut them inside the room.

"We can't let them trap us in here," he cried, thrusting a hand outwards. The spell hurled the man out of the way, and Rose heard a sickening crack, followed by the thud of a body hitting the floor. Glancing into the hall, she saw a man slumped on the floorboards, a large hole in the wall above him.

"Who's got the archway again?" cried Ben, using magic to drag the man into the room. The body skidded across the floor and struck the legs of the desk before falling still.

"Alison has it," said Grandpa, bending down to lift

one of the man's eyelids. A strip of white was all that could be seen, and Grandpa straightened up with a satisfied nod. "We shouldn't have separated. Matt, don't move!"

Grandpa's voice rang out urgently as Matt shifted away from the door, his foot disturbing a small glass vial containing a familiar rust-coloured liquid that had fallen from Rose's shelf. Matt glanced down and, with a yelp, took a hasty step away from the bottle, eyeing it like it was a poisonous snake.

"Argh! Not that stuff again!"

"I've always wanted some," said Grandpa longingly, backing away. Rose raised an eyebrow and Grandpa gave her a sheepish look.

"It's got amazing magical qualities when it's used the right way, mostly for cleansing spells from invention pieces so that they can be reused," he explained. "But it's restricted by law and you've got to store it properly, otherwise it -"

A spell shot past him, narrowly missing the glass bottle rolling across the floor. Ben cursed and sent a retaliatory spell into the hall.

"It spreads?" offered Rose, watching the bottle's progress across the floorboards with apprehension.

"Well, yes," admitted Grandpa.

"Exactly how far would a whole bottle of it spread?" asked Matt, bending down to retrieve the vial with careful fingers.

"And what happens if we touch it?" Rose asked, only to add, "On second thought, don't tell me. I'm not sure I want to kn-"

She stopped as the groan of wood filled the air and the house began to shake around them. Fresh cracks appeared in the window pane and pressure began to build around the house. A familiar feeling of foreboding swooped down on Rose, just like it had so many times in Grandpa's fake city when she'd been chasing the bud.

"Put the bottle in here." Grandpa opened the desk drawer so that Matt could deposit the grainy liquid inside. "It'll be safer there than on the floor."

His voice was drowned out by a deafening grinding. Rose cringed, hardly daring to move until the sounds stopped.

"This place is going to come down around our ears if we can't get Hunter's friends under control soon," said Grandpa, glancing up at the sagging ceiling.

"We only need it to hold up a bit longer," said Matt as the sound of breaking glass rang out from the next room. "Come on Ben, you can take those guys out!"

Rose and Matt cheered and encouraged Ben as he sent more and more spells down the hall, and soon a second unconscious man was dragged into the room to join the first. Rose clutched her shelf tightly, hoping that Alison and the others were safe.

Spells shot through the open door under Ben's elbow, leaving long scratches in the wood and knocking a leg off of a cabinet, which teetered for a moment before crashing to the floor, sending inventions cascading across the room. A faintly pink liquid began to leak from a cracked glass bottle onto a charcoal grey object underneath it, catching fire the instant it made contact.

Rose coughed and waved a hand in front of her face as thick smoke filled the room. Grandpa stamped out the rapidly growing flames with his shoe, but Ben darted forward and scooped the smouldering, smoking object up before Grandpa could kick it aside.

"Wait, I can put it to good use!"

He lobbed the charred thing into the hall, where it struck Jacob as he attempted to push his way into the room, shattering his shield spell and breaking his nose. Jacob pinched it hard to stem the flow, glaring at Ben before his friends hauled him out of the way. Smoke filled the corridor, and the sound of coughing intermingled with swear words as Hunter's gang struggled to see. Leaving the door open a crack, Ben used the time to reinforce the room with more magic.

"Hey, what's going on with these inventions?" cried Matt, indicating the objects littering the floor around the fallen cabinet.

A small flute made of black glass and etched with golden symbols was emitting a high-pitched scream, causing many of the inventions around it to hum like angry bees.

"Some of them have defensive spells," said Grandpa, coming up for a closer look. "The fighting combined with the pressure from the Fragmenter is setting them all off."

Rose put her hands to her ears as the screaming grew louder, feeling like her head was about to burst.

"How do we stop it?"

Many of the inventions surrounding the strange black flute did indeed explode, sending pieces clattering throughout the room. Several of the men in the hall were groaning in pain, as they, too, suffered the effects of the flute. A shimmering blue crystal ball exploded on the top of the bookshelf, expelling a mauve-coloured dust onto the books and equipment beneath it. Rose's vision grew hazy until the air cleared, and she bit down hard on her tongue, her head throbbing painfully.

"Hold on," grunted Ben, slamming the door closed and standing with his back against it, holding it closed while Hunter's gang hammered on it.

He fixed his gaze on the screaming invention. The ceiling sank lower, almost level with their heads, and the door rattled in its frame. Rose, Matt and Grandpa fled to Ben's side, desperately trying to keep it closed.

Rose looked on helplessly, wishing she could do more to help as Ben, cringing with pain, turned his attention from the flute to the ceiling. A surge of energy rippled over them and the flute fell silent, crushed into black sand in an instant. Rose and Matt exchanged looks of surprise and relief.

"I guess the Fragmenter didn't like the sound any more than we did," said Rose with a sigh, the pounding in her head finally easing.

Ben quickly covered the ceiling with reinforcement spells. There was a moment of stillness, followed by a resounding crack as the door was knocked almost off its hinges.

All four of them were thrown forward into the room

as Hunter's gang burst inside. The smoke had disappeared, leaving behind blackened walls and a strong smell of ash. Grandpa staggered but remained on his feet, while Rose and Matt fell to their knees, forced to scramble out of the way to avoid being trampled.

Ben caught himself on the ornate desk as Jacob and the auburn-haired woman advanced on him, their faces livid. Rose got to her feet, catching sight of the man in black, shielding his friends from Alison's attack at the end of the hall. Jacob's clothes were splattered with blood, and he straightened his nose with a sickening crunch.

"You're going to regret that, Atherton," he growled, taking a knife out of his jacket and brandishing it at Ben. He regarded Rose, Matt and Grandpa with contempt before taking another step towards Ben, ignoring the others.

Rose felt a flicker of annoyance mingle with her concern for Ben. Did Jacob think that she and her family were harmless just because they were unable to use magic?

She raised her eyebrows at Matt and Grandpa and then jerked her head ever so slightly at Jacob, hoping they would understand. To her relief, each of them responded with an almost-imperceptible nod.

The woman hurled a curse at Ben, and at the same moment, Rose, Matt and Grandpa threw themselves on top of Jacob, dragging him the the ground before he could put up another shield.

"What the -? Get out of it!" he snarled, rolling onto

his side. He swung his knife at Grandpa and Rose flung herself in front of him, holding her shelf up defensively.

"Rose, no!" cried Grandpa.

The blade slipped between the two planks of wood and Rose gave a shriek of horror as it stopped inches from her shoulder.

"That was awesome!" said Matt with a delighted laugh.

Rose gave him a tremulous smile before jumping, startled, as a spell wrapped around the knife, bending the blade so that Jacob was unable to remove it. With a roar of rage, Jacob tossed the shelf aside and attempted to stand. Grandpa drove his metal spikes into the man's leg, and he dropped back to the ground with a cry with Matt twisting his arm behind his back.

The cabinet door behind them creaked open and Jacob vanished the shelves. With a rush of air, Matt was sucked into the space, the door slamming shut on him. Jacob locked it with a wave of his hand.

"Let him out!" Rose cried, listening to her brother's muffled yells as he beat at it, unable to get out.

From the other side of the room, Ben fixed his eyes on the door, his face full of concern, and the auburn-haired woman leapt over Grandpa and Jacob, landing like a cat in front of the cabinet before sending another curse in Ben's direction, forcing his attention away from the others.

Pain shot through Rose's hands and she let go of Jacob with a gasp, wincing at the blisters erupting on her skin. He got to his feet and grinned down at Grandpa.

Ropes wrapped around the older man and Jacob bent down to tear the ring of spikes from his hand. Rose felt her pulse pounding in her veins as she retrieved the shelf from the floor.

"No you don't!" she yelled, swinging it high above her head.

It struck Jacob's ribs with a *thwack* and he staggered forward. She raised the shelf a second time, this time catching his head with enough force to send him crashing to the ground like a rock. She turned and struck two more non-magical members of the gang as they forced their way into the room.

Pushing her hair out of her face, Rose stood with the shelf balanced on her shoulder as she watched them, wanting to be sure they were unconscious before giving Grandpa another shaky grin and turning her attention to the auburn-haired woman.

Ben was out of breath now. His lip was bleeding and he was still supporting most of the ceiling, but he stared at the frozen form of his opponent, who appeared to be caught in mid-air. A mass of spells surrounded the woman, holding her in place like a fly caught in a web. She struggled against the tangle of spells, but to no avail.

"She won't be able to use magic while she's trapped, but it won't hold her for long," panted Ben, leaning against the desk. "We need the archway."

He repaired the ceiling and vanished the ropes binding Grandpa before glancing at the cabinet. It burst open, expelling Matt with a jumble of inventions.

"Thanks," he said, brushing dust off his clothes and

giving Ben a grateful look.

"The other room's completely blocked," said Rose, going to the door and peeking out at what was left of the gang. Two men lay sprawled out on the floor among chunks of the ceiling, one fast asleep, and the other sporting a nasty gash on his forehead. Only three people remained, fighting their way through the wreckage towards the last doorway. Rose raised an eyebrow, impressed. Alison and Ben had fought well.

Sounds of breaking glass and falling furniture told her that Alison was battling yet another member of the gang further inside the room. Rose made a sound of irritation, tired of feeling useless and wishing for what felt like the hundredth time that she had her magic back. The others gathered behind her, keeping out of view of the men in the hall.

"Here, I can get the archway."

Matt dug his hand into his shirt pocket and lifted out his Hook. The invention had curled itself into a ball, but it stirred as Matt turned his gaze on it, ready to do its master's bidding. Matt placed it gently on the floor and it scuttled out of the room, wending its way between the men's feet.

"I hope no one steps on it," he murmured, clutching the edge of the door and biting his lip.

The fight inside the other room sounded fierce, and Rose flinched as spells and pieces of broken furniture flew out into the hall. A pause in the fight allowed the three men to charge inside, leaving the hall unguarded, and Rose shuffled on the spot uneasily.

"Come on, come on," she whispered, willing the Hook to hurry up. She glanced over her shoulder to ask Matt if the Hook would be able to defend itself if attacked when movement caught her eye and she gave a shout.

"Hey!"

Ben and Grandpa spun around. The auburn-haired woman had almost fought her way free of the spells holding her. She glared at Ben, her eyes promising murder as she struggled against the invisible bonds. Ben hurriedly added more spells before resuming his watch by the door, ignoring the woman's growl of rage.

Minutes stretched by, and Rose began to wonder if the Hook had been discovered, or perhaps destroyed. Another tremor ran through the house as the storm of magic down the hall continued and several books fell from the rickety shelf. The auburn-haired woman staggered, regaining control of her right side, and Rose clutched at her face until it hurt.

She was about to give up hope when the Hook reappeared with the archway clamped in its pincers. Matt groaned in relief and stretched a hand out towards it.

"That's it, you can do it!" urged Rose, watching the invention crawl around the chunks of plaster.

There was a triumphant yell from inside the other room and the blond man was sent reeling backwards into the hall, hitting the wall with a crash. Blood streamed from a cut over his left eye. He stumbled, but managed to remain upright, one booted foot landing on a metal leg.

The Hook let out a tinny whine, unable to pull itself free. Noticing the flash of metal at his feet, the man bent to pick the Hook up, only to recoil as the invention reared a sting-like attachment at the end of the wire, jabbing at the man's outstretched hand and leaving a large red welt. The man raised his other foot instead, ready to crush the invention and the archway.

"No! No! Leave it alone!" Rose moaned, while Matt clutched the doorframe, his fingernails biting into the wood.

"If we attack him, it'll just draw attention to us!" he cried.

Ben straightened up behind them, peering over Rose's shoulder.

"It's worth it," he said, watching the fight outside. "We can't let them get their hands on the archway, and it'll make Alison's job easier if those guys are being attacked on both sides."

Pulling itself free just in time, the Hook crawled along the wall to where Matt crouched, waiting. Moving awkwardly with one leg bent the wrong way, it deposited the archway into his waiting hand before scuttling up his shirt and retreating into his pocket.

"Come on, let's do this quickly!" urged Ben, glancing back down the hall towards Alison's room.

Matt gave the Hook an appreciative pat and then squeezed the archway, moving back to allow the metal to spread. The auburn-haired woman stopped struggling to stare at the gleaming silver, her eyes full of suspicion and fear.

"I think we should put that lot through first," said Grandpa, nodding at the two unconscious men still slumped at the foot of the desk. "At least they won't put up a fight."

Ben took hold of the first man's feet.

"Sounds good to me."

He and Grandpa tossed each one into the city, finally approaching the auburn-haired woman. Rose and Matt stationed themselves on either side to prevent her escape.

"Ready?" said Ben with a grin, glancing at the others.

Matt and Grandpa nodded, their faces set, and Ben removed the spells binding the woman to the spot. He pushed her hard, sending her through the arch before she could steady herself or use magic. Rose fought back a laugh as the woman scrambled to her feet and began beating at the entrance, sending useless spells at the barrier bet-ween the two worlds.

"Let me out of here!"

Grandpa tapped the archway and it pooled into its usual shape, silencing the woman's cries.

'See you later, maybe," laughed Matt.

Ben grinned and turned to the others.

"Let's go and help Alison."

Grandpa tucked the archway into his pocket and followed Ben out into the hall. Rose and Matt took up their weapons once more and ran after them. Rose could hear Mary's voice yelling something indistinct and saw what appeared to be large glass marbles hurtling into the hall towards the blond man, who was forced to put up a shield spell.

"Sounds like Mary's holding her own in there," she chortled, gripping her shelf with both hands.

A look of alarm spread across the man's face as he noticed the group in the hall, and in a heartbeat, Ben sent him to sleep. Another deep, shuddering groan filled Rose's ears and she staggered into the wall as the floor sank several inches on one side, sending everyone reeling.

Cries of pain issued from the room at the end of the hall, followed by more sounds of breaking glass and wood. Memories of the sinking tower in Grandpa's city came flooding back to her.

"Oh great, the house is coming down! Now of all times!"

She flung her arms up over her head, watching the cracks in the ceiling deepen.

"I'm amazed it's held up this long," remarked Grandpa, standing with his back to the wall. Matt took a tentative step forwards, but Grandpa's hands darted out to stop him, his grip tight on Matt's arm.

"No! Don't move!"

He pointed at something above their heads. Rose gasped and pressed herself against the wall. Alison had also used reinforcement spells to keep the roof and ceiling stable, but the damage to this part of the house had been much more substantial. Rose was able to see up into the roof, and patches of pale blue sky were visible through the tiles far above her.

Exposed beams hung suspended above their heads

as though held by invisible supports, ready to come crashing down the moment Alison's spells broke. Bricks and tiles had stopped halfway through the act of tumbling down onto the floorboards. It was an odd sight, and Rose had to blink several times to make sure she was seeing correctly.

The house shuddered more violently and the blond man stirred. Alison appeared in the doorway, her clothes and hair splattered with a blue substance that resembled ink. She glanced up at the roof, releasing several tiles. They struck the man on the head and shoulders, knocking him out.

Pressure rose around the house once more, and just as Grandpa had predicted they would, both Alison's and Ben's reinforcement spells gave out.

"Whoa!" Matt hit the hall beside Rose with a thud. "I think it's time to go!"

Rose caught a glimpse of falling beams before plaster began to rain down on her, obscuring the hall. Screams and yells issued from down hall and Rose struggled to regain her balance, wiping powder out of her eyes.

A heavy beam had fallen on the blond man's legs, breaking them and pinning him to the rapidly sinking floor. Without her abilities, there was no way she could move it. Turning away from this unpleasant sight, Rose covered her nose and mouth with the sleeve of her shirt to avoid breathing in the dust, hoping the others were safe.

The man in black, his clothes now a dusty grey,

appeared in the doorway, backing away from something out of sight. He turned to retreat down the hall and stopped, taking in the damage. His eyes met Rose's briefly before travelling over the rest of the group waiting on the other side of the rubble. Shock filled his face, and a moment later he'd disappeared, leaving his friend trapped in the rubble.

"Coward!" Alison yelled after him, running from the room and fighting her way between the beams as though hoping to find him hiding beneath the mess.

Rose inched towards Grandpa, floorboards shifting underneath her feet. Matt was right. It was time to go.

"We've got to get out of here before the whole upper floor comes down," she said.

Alison nodded once and vanished, reappearing at Rose's side, along with Mum, Dad and Mary. Mary's cheeks were flushed and Dad was clutching a heavy mallet in one hand, which he tossed aside with a thud. Mum was limping but seemed otherwise unhurt, holding the splintered leg of a table out like a spear.

"Who has the archway?" she asked. "There are a couple of people back there that we should put inside before we go, and we can't leave *him* there, either." She jerked her chin at the blond man. "If this place collapses, he could be killed."

"I've got it."

Grandpa removed the gleaming silver invention from his pocket and offered it to Ben, who took it and turned back to the debris-strewn hall.

"I'll help you," said Alison, glancing up at the roof as

the house continued to settle around them. "It'll be quicker."

Using travel spells, she and Ben extracted the trapped man from the wreckage and dragged him into the archway, using magic to splint his legs.

Alison tapped the silver frame and waited until its transformation was complete before picking it up and taking it into the last room. Seconds later Rose heard the sound of bodies being dragged over the floorboards. What remained of the roof was now so low over their heads that Rose was beginning to feel claustrophobic. She closed her eyes for a moment, trying to remain calm, and then opened them to find Matt watching her. He gave her a reassuring grin.

"You OK?"

Rose did her best to grin back as Alison and Ben reappeared beside Grandpa.

"Yeah, I'm good."

Mum looped her arm around Rose's elbow and tugged her back towards the stairs. The rest of the group followed, speaking in hushed voices.

"So it's just that guy in black left now?" Matt asked as they tiptoed down the stairs, looking out for any sign of movement below.

"I think so," replied Rose, her eyes travelling over the deep cracks in the downstairs walls. "Not counting Hunter, of course."

She kept close behind Alison and Ben as they passed the room in which she, Matt and Mary had been held captive, half expecting to find the man in black hiding inside, waiting to attack. But they reached the room full of experiments without incident, and Rose glanced around the doorframe. It was silent and still, the experiments that had survived the Fragmenter puffing smoke and casting their coloured lights on the walls. The group gathered near the front door, glancing around warily.

"Where did he go?" asked Mary, her voice carrying in the silence.

A figure solidified in the doorway and Rose came to an abrupt halt as Lawrence Hunter stepped over the threshold. His eyes locked on Alison and Ben, and a look of surprise flitted across his face, quickly replaced by a broad grin as both Archivists froze.

"I thought you'd turn up sooner rather than later," said Hunter, his grin growing wider.

"I could say the same for you," retorted Alison, her eyes narrowed in dislike.

Hunter laughed. Each party seemed to be waiting for the other to make the first move, and it wasn't until Hunter took another step into the hall that Alison and Ben sprang into action, hurling curses at him.

Hunter conjured up a shield only just in time. The curses buzzed as they made contact, forcing him to stop, braced against the impact. Rose could feel the strength of their spells from where she stood, the hairs on the back of her arms standing up in response to the magic.

Alison and Ben continued their assault, filling the entrance with spells. Hunter's shield held, and he took a step forward, shunting the group backwards as he went. Rose's feet seemed to move of their own accord, stumbling back down the hall towards the experiment room. The others retreated with her, and soon they were bottled up in the doorway.

The door to the boiler room stood ajar behind them, casting a golden strip of light across the floor. Hunter closed his eyes and the screech of twisting metal reached Rose's ears. Amber liquid flooded into the hall as the boiler burst, spewing its contents over the floor. She yelped and backed further into the room of experiments, away from the scorching liquid.

With a wave of his hand, Hunter sent it into the air, flowing like a river over their heads to form a protective barrier around himself. Wrapped in a thick bubble, he released his shield spell and continued down the hall, ignoring the burning liquid still pooling on the floor.

Ben and Alison began aiming spells at the amber wall, which simply absorbed the magic and thickened as it cooled, shrugging off all attempts to break through or move it aside. The amber substance parted for a fraction of a second and a spell shot out from behind it, striking Ben in the chest.

"No!" Alison cried, trying to catch Ben as he fell.

The rest of the group rushed forward to help as Ben's knees hit the floor, his eyes open and staring. Rose gaped at him, stunned, her insides turning to ice. Hunter shunted them all backwards another step towards the basement, while Mum and Dad half-supported, half-dragged Ben along with them. Alison sent a storm of magic in Hunter's direction, her face streaked with tears.

"He's not - he's not dead is he?" stammered Mary,

staring down at Ben with fearful eyes.

She turned to Matt, gripping his arm with white fingers, but Matt could only shake his head, his mouth opening and closing silently. Rose gulped as Hunter forced them back yet another step. She looked at Ben's chest, desperate to see any sign of life, but steam from the shock absorber had obscured most of the room, including Hunter, who continued to make his way towards them.

Rose stopped as her feet met the top step down to the basement. She staggered a little, throwing out an arm to steady herself on the wall. Seeing that they were about to be trapped once again, she threw herself behind a desk crowded with magical equipment before Hunter could push her further down the stairs.

She beckoned to Matt, but he was pushed down the steps with the others, into the flooded basement before he could dive out of the way of Hunter's spell.

It's job done, Hunter flung the shock absorber away from himself, sending it flying in an amber sheet onto the floor and tables, where more steam billowed from the equipment as the gel made contact.

Hunter walked down the basement steps after them, reaching in and plucking Grandpa from their midst, using one last spell to shove the others towards the back wall.

"You're coming with me," Hunter said, holding Grandpa steady as he wobbled on the bottom step. With another wave of his hand, he conjured bars over the entrance to the basement and held out the small bottle of grainy liquid Matt had almost stepped on upstairs.

"Just in case the rest of you try to escape the other way …"

Hunter replaced the spells around the room and tossed the bottle through the bars so that it smashed underneath the window pane. Mum, Dad and Alison recoiled as the grainy liquid began to spread across the wall and around the glass, making escape impossible.

Fear had kept Rose rooted to the spot until this moment, but now anger and worry sent her creeping out from her hiding place, ready to pounce before Hunter could take her grandfather again.

She hurled herself towards Grandpa. He and Hunter disappeared in an instant and Rose's hands met only air. She let out a growl of frustration and whirled around, her eyes darting around the room, but it was no use. She had no way of knowing where Hunter had gone. Running to the hall, she checked all of the rooms on the ground floor, carefully avoiding the pool of shock absorber, and not daring to go upstairs now that the upper level was so unstable. But the rooms were empty.

She rushed to the front door and stared around at the fields. All she saw was the tall grass, rippling in a gentle breeze.

26

Last Hope

Trying hard to keep calm, she ran back to the basement, gripping the bars tightly in both hands. Her parents ran to her, their faces a mixture of hopefulness and distress.

"You got away!"

"Did you see where Hunter took your grandpa?"

Rose shook her head, wishing she had something to tell them.

"There was too much steam in the room to see anything. I'm sorry."

She looked down at her feet as Mum rested her head against the bars in defeat.

"It's not your fault, I'm just glad you're OK," replied Mum, wrapping a hand around Rose's. Rose stood on tiptoe to look over her mother's shoulder. Alison crouched ankle-deep in water beside the sofa where Ben now lay, his eyes still open and staring. He hadn't moved or made a sound since Hunter's spell had struck him. Rose swallowed the lump in her throat.

"Is he going to be all right?"

Alison closed Ben's eyes gently with a finger.

"He's not dead, but I don't know what Hunter did to him. It's not a spell I've seen before."

"It's like he's in a coma or something," remarked

Matt, as he and Mary gathered around Ben.

"We've got to get you all out of there," said Rose, tugging at the bars, but Alison shook her head.

"Those bars aren't made from the normal type of magic that you're used to, the kind that responds to any person's willpower if they're strong enough," she reminded Rose. "These spells only respond to magical commands. So I guess that explains why none of Hunter's friends seem to stay in prison for long," she added with a scowl. "Hunter keeps letting them out."

Rose looked at her parents in confusion and Dad gave her a sad smile.

"Spells like these take more power, but they're also much more permanent. They're used to keep magical people in prison because you can will them away all you like, but they won't budge unless you give the right command in the language of magic."

"You need to have a complete understanding of the language to use the spells," said Alison, sitting on the armrest of the sofa, her shoulders drooping. "And until today I'd only ever met two people who were truly fluent in it."

"Miranda?" said Mary, her eyes widening suddenly.

Alison nodded. "And your grandpa."

"And he wouldn't be able to remove the bars now that he can't do magic," mused Rose.

Matt's expression darkened and he kicked the sofa with a sodden shoe, sending a cascade of freezing water into the air.

"And we can't get to either of them. Rose can't use a

travel spell to wherever Miranda is, and there's no one else around here to ask for help. This place is in the middle of nowhere! Do you have your phone with you?"

Alison dug it out of her pocket and showed Matt the blank screen.

"It won't even start up. There are too many spells blocking it."

"So there's nothing we can do then?" said Mary, tears sparkling in her eyes. "Hunter's going to take our magic and there's nothing we can do about it. We still don't even know where the Fragmenter is."

Mum and Dad hung their heads, lost for words, and Matt seemed to deflate at their reaction. He stared around the room desperately and his hands shook as he fumbled in his pocket for something. Retrieving his Hook, he waded to where his parents stood and placed the invention on the bottom step, activating it with a tap.

"Bring the Fragmenter to us," he told it, giving it an encouraging push up the stairs. The Hook uncurled its body, its head in the air like a dog sniffing for its prey.

"C'mon, you can do it!" Matt urged.

Rose watched the little invention take a few steps forward, only to circle back to Matt's hands. Matt groaned and scooped the Hook back up again.

"It was worth a try," said Rose consolingly.

Alison approached the basement window, which had transformed into a mushy substance that reminded Rose of soggy bread. The grainy liquid had now travelled alarmingly close to where Ben lay, and Alison moved the sofa back several feet before doing something to halt the liquid's progress. She leaned against the table with a sigh.

"I'm going to keep looking for the Fragmenter," Rose declared, pushing away from the bars and her mother's grip. "It's the only way to end all of this."

Her parents' faces were pained as she left them, but they couldn't argue. Dad watched her go in silence. He knew that she was right. Rose gave them one last grim look of determination before marching up the basement steps and through the ruined experiments.

Inspired by Matt and his Hook, she pulled out her Viewer and held it in her hand, thinking about the dark room it had shown her. She hadn't the faintest idea where it could be, but the image was at least a starting point, something for her to work with.

Surely she would be more likely to find the Fragmenter by using her Viewer than by blindly searching the house and grounds for hints of magic?

She could feel the portion of herself bound to the Viewer reaching for her, waiting to do her bidding. Holding it in both hands, she stopped beside the book of magical symbols she'd played with earlier and rotated the Viewer to activate the dark blue eye. She concentrated on the bud, staring into the glass pupil of her invention.

"Where are you?" she murmured as it began to spin.

It gathered speed, unimpeded by the blocking spells that had held it back so many times before. A scene flashed into the pupil. The same scene the Viewer had shown her last time. Now, however, lamps had been lit, illuminating a circular, bricked area.

Rose's heart began to race, the picture flooding into her mind with a sense of urgency, as though the Viewer was in a hurry to answer her question. The Fragmenter was set in the centre of the room, on top of a wooden trunk, and Hunter prowled around the invention while another, smaller figure, stood a little way back.

Frustration rose up inside her again. Where was this room? She pushed the invention for more information and almost at once the image changed. Rose saw Grandpa, on his knees on a concrete floor. His lips were moving, but the picture was silent. He appeared to be arguing with Hunter.

The scene transformed again, this time showing her the window in the small room by the stairs that she, Matt and Mary had been locked in. Nonplussed, Rose walked to the window like a sleepwalker, her attention still on her Viewer.

The three images flashed into the glass pupil once more before the invention deactivated and the pupil went blank. Rose stared out at the grassy fields, unsure what this had to do with the Fragmenter. There were no buildings in sight, and as far as she could tell, there was no hidden extension to the house.

She raked a hand through her hair impatiently, wondering what the Viewer was trying to tell her. What else had happened in that room? Her lips curled into a grin at the memory of Matt's complaints and Jacob's fury. With a chuckle, she stood in front of the window. It had felt so good to laugh.

She was about to return to the experimenting room

and attempt to decipher some of Hunter's handwritten notes when another memory presented itself to her.

She stopped, her mind going back to the first time Jacob and the blond man had brought the Fragmenter inside the house. The defensive and illusion spells around the house had broken. Rose had been standing at the window, looking out at Hunter's gang and laughing at them when she'd caught sight of something dark out in the fields before Jacob replaced the spells. It hadn't looked anything like a building . . .

Tucking the Viewer back into her jeans pocket, she raced to the front door, throwing it open and charging out into the fields. The smell of warm grass filled her nostrils and the long stems whipped at her sides as she ran, doing her best to remember where she'd seen the strange shape. After a minute or so of running, she guessed that she was in roughly the right spot and began to search. The wind had picked up, and she pushed her hair out of her face, staring out over the grass for any sign of a dark mass.

Seeing nothing, she continued to walk in circles, going further out each time until she stumbled upon a small clearing, quite a distance from the house. Curious, her bare feet now covered in dirt, she took a step forward and stubbed her toe on something solid. Muttering an oath under her breath, she hopped on one foot, wondering what she'd walked into.

Moving more carefully this time, she stretched out a hand and felt around in the air until she found something. She jumped back. The moment her fingers had brushed the object, the illusion spells concealing it had disappeared, revealing a brick-lined well at the centre of the clearing.

Only the topmost layer of bricks would be visible from a distance, and Rose couldn't help but admire Hunter's choice of hiding place. Almost as if to prove her suspicions right, Rose stuck her head into the well, sure she could hear voices raised in anger somewhere nearby.

She peered down into the space, wondering how she was going to reach the bottom without magic when she noticed a row of metal rungs embedded in the bricks, leading down into the dark depths.

Placing a foot on the first rung, Rose climbed awkwardly downwards, clinging to the ladder with trembling hands. She climbed deeper until the patch of light above her shrank to the size of a basketball. Finally, she stretched a foot down and found solid ground.

Here the bricks gave way to concrete, and she turned around, peering down the dark tunnel that stretched on behind her. At the end of this tunnel was another patch of light. Two people were gathered around something glowing in the centre of the room, one of them kneeling on the floor. Rose squared her shoulders and began to walk towards them, her feet padding quietly on the concrete.

The voices grew louder as she walked. Both figures were facing the Fragmenter, and Rose continued down the passage unnoticed. Snatches of conversation filtered back to her as she crept along, and her heart beat faster as she approached the room at the end.

"So, are you enjoying your new life without magic?" Hunter asked, looking down at Grandpa with a tight smile. His skin was pale and his face was thinner than usual. He looked as though he hadn't slept in days.

"I never wanted to make the Fragmenter," replied Grandpa, his voice soft and tired. "I never agreed with the government's views. I told them so! There are always other ways! They should never have commissioned such an invention."

Hunter scoffed at this.

"No, they shouldn't have!"

A ringing silence fell as Hunter's eyes bored into Grandpa's, his face full of contempt.

"But you made it anyway. I guess you thought it was OK as long as the invention was being used on someone else."

Grandpa seemed to have no answer for this. He sighed and hung his head, and Hunter approached the green bud. Rose stared around the room as she neared the ring of light cast by the lamps. There was nothing at all down here that could be used as a weapon, but she reminded herself that there was very little she could do to defend herself against someone with magical abilities now anyway, weapon or no.

She came to a stop behind Grandpa, deciding that she should make her presence known. She could hardly remain hidden in the tunnel, after all. As she moved, a breath of air made the nearest lamp gutter and Hunter looked up from the Fragmenter, finally noticing her. He sighed and ran a hand through his already unkempt hair.

"I had a feeling you'd find your way down here at some point," he said in a tone of resignation as Grandpa whipped around in surprise. "There really is no escaping you, is there? And where are Matt and Mary? They're never far behind you."

"They're still in the basement," she replied, returning Grandpa's grin. "I got away before you put the bars over the doorway."

Hunter sighed again and resumed his laps around the bud.

"Of course you did." He fixed his gaze back on the invention. "Well, since you're here, you can sit quietly with your grandpa."

Invisible hands pushed Rose down beside Grandpa and she hit the ground with a huff, the concrete biting into her knees.

"Was this well already here when you took over the house, or did you build it to hide the invention?" she asked, sitting down more comfortably.

Hunter looked over at her in a distracted kind of way.

"Hmm? No, it was already here; I just added this extension. At first, I was going to put the Fragmenter in the basement, but then I realised that it wouldn't be enough. The invention would still react with my experiments and the house's disguises, so I created this reinforced space down here instead and found another use for the basement."

He turned away, his attention back on the bud glowing in the centre of the room.

"Why isn't it working?" Hunter murmured, as though to himself. He looked at Grandpa, who shifted uncomfortably before answering.

"Well, it could be a number of things," he said. "The parameters of the invention won't allow for -"

Hunter rolled his eyes and cut across him.

"Spare me the unnecessary details."

He picked up the Fragmenter and twisted the base anti-clockwise. The invention's casing darkened in colour until it was almost black, and Rose tensed as Hunter placed his fingertips on the glowing shards of glass. The light accumulated there, and as he withdrew his hand, the glow inside the shards followed.

Rose could feel part of that energy reaching out for her, calling to her, but with a rush of energy, the Fragmenter pushed the magic towards Hunter instead. Grandpa stiffened beside Rose as the light continued to seep out of the glass shards, following Hunter's movements before abruptly changing direction and retreating into the glass.

Hunter made a sound of frustration and tried again. The light snapped back into the glass pieces more forcefully, and the bud gave a crackle of energy, flashing its warning. Hunter took a step back, waiting for it to become docile once more.

It settled slowly into a resentful slumber, the casing turning its usual bright green. Grandpa took a deep, shuddering breath and glanced at Rose, his eyes full of desperate worry. An idea struck Rose as Hunter resumed his laps around the room, and she waited for his back to be turned before leaning in close to Grandpa, whispering into his ear.

"Make the bud start the Fragmenting curse! You're connected to it, just like Matt's connected to his Hook. Can you influence it, make it angry so it sees Hunter as a threat?"

Grandpa looked at the invention uncertainly and Rose turned back to the bud, her mind racing. They had to get it to complete its curse. It was the only way to defeat Hunter, their only chance to remove the danger long enough to reclaim their magic. But how could they accomplish this when Hunter was able to deactivate the bud with a single glance?

"Try it!" urged Rose, straightening up as Hunter continued around the room, his gaze flickering in their direction.

Rose smiled to herself, wondering if Hunter was aware of the strange connection between maker and creation, regardless of their abilities, or lack of. She guessed not, or he would never have allowed Grandpa to come anywhere near the Fragmenter …

Hunter stopped pacing and stood with one hand outstretched, this time allowing the magic to come to him. The invention's casing unravelled and changed colour. Rose could feel Hunter beckoning the stored magic towards him wordlessly while Grandpa settled himself more comfortably on the floor, surreptitiously placing a hand palm up on the floor beside him. His posture relaxed and he closed his eyes.

The light gathered at the tips of the glass pieces for a

third time, following Hunter's call. There was another burst of energy from the Fragmenter, pushing the light away from it's rightful owners, and this time it parted from the invention entirely, flowing through the air with a rushing sound.

Horror constricted Rose's throat at the sight. She grasped her grandfather's arm tightly.

"Grandpa!"

Grandpa's eyes flew open and fear clouded his face. The light made its way across the room towards Hunter and he took an impatient step forward, stretching his hand out to meet it.

"No!"

Grandpa gave a mental tug on the Fragmenter and it surged back to life, releasing a protesting wave of energy that caught Hunter off guard, sending him staggering backwards. The light returned to the bud and the air around it blurred in the way that Rose had come to recognise as the invention's defensive spells activating. She repressed the urge to glance over shoulder as the sensation of being watched descended on her.

"What the -"

Hunter threw out an arm to save himself, his eyes wide with astonishment at the bud's extreme and sudden reaction. Currents of energy streamed around them, making the tiny hairs on Rose's arms stand up.

Hunter barely had time to regain his balance before the lamps exploded over their heads, leaving scraps of twisted metal hanging from the walls and plunging the room into semi-darkness. The only source of illumination now was the bud itself, glowing like a beacon in the centre of the room. Rose let her breath out in a rush.

"Good one, Grandpa," she whispered with a grin.

Grandpa's posture didn't relax.

"We're not safe yet," he murmured, so quietly that even Rose beside him could barely make out the words.

Hunter didn't seem to think it wise to use magic to light the room. Leaving the lamps twisted and broken, he approached the bud cautiously. Grandpa closed his eyes and the space seemed to shrink, the darkness closing in on them. Rose shuddered as shadows moved at the edges of her vision, hinting at vaguely human forms that dissolved and changed shape, holding her attention and muddling her mind.

She tore her eyes away to glance at her grandfather. Both he and Hunter were now staring, transfixed by the menacing forms stalking the room. The shadows flickered, and without warning, the Fragmenter's defensive spells bore down on Hunter, the only other source of magic in the room.

Blinking as though coming out of a trance, he hastily conjured up a shield to defend himself. The Fragmenter ripped through his spell like a knife through tissue paper, and Hunter grimaced, struggling to fend off the invention, forced to put up multiple shields to keep it momentarily at bay.

Pressure grew until a low groan escaped Rose's lips. Clutching at her head and chest, she watched the struggle impatiently through watering eyes, feeling like she was being squashed in a vise. She was happy for

Hunter to try fighting the Fragmenter himself for a change, but why wasn't it starting its curse? They needed him unconscious, not just exhausted …

"What can I do to help?" she murmured into Grandpa's ear.

"Stay safe," he replied, concentrating on the invention before him.

Rose sighed and nodded, attempting to keep her gaze from the shadows swirling around her. With another loud crackle of energy, the bud broke its way through the last of Hunter's shields and the two began to fight in earnest, sending sparks into the air as magic collided with magic. Rose shivered, a numb weariness settling over her as the bud finally began its curse.

Hunter's breathing was becoming more laboured as he fought to deactivate the invention, but his spells were not weakening. Rose began to find it increasingly difficult to keep her eyes open, and she yawned deeply, struggling to rouse herself.

The shadows at the edge of her vision closed in as the invention glowed brighter, and the irrational part of Rose's mind took over under the influence of the bud. She shrank back, sure that something terrible would happen if they touched her.

Hunter seemed to be struggling with similar emotions. Both he and Rose flinched as an arm-like shadow reached out towards them, dissolving into nothingness as it drew near. Hunter took a step back, uncertainty on his face. Grandpa, however, remained still.

"What are they?" Rose whispered.

Grandpa shook his head, unconcerned.

"Nothing to worry about," he replied. "Just tricks of the mind. Distractions."

His face was lined with tiredness but his control over the Fragmenter remained steady. "Not long to go now."

His eyes locked onto Hunter's, a hint of a challenge in his voice. Rose nodded, hoping her bones weren't about to break under the strain. The mixture of pain and exhaustion was overwhelming, and it was no surprise to her when Hunter finally sank to his knees, his shoulders drooping. Hope sparked inside Rose, even as deep cracks appeared in the walls, travelling over their heads and down towards the floor.

Grandpa made an almost-imperceptible gesturing motion with his outstretched hand, and the Fragmenter's defensive spells descended on Hunter once again, cutting through the air with a rushing, whispering sound. Fear forced Rose's weary limbs to shuffle backwards, out of the way, and this time she knew that Hunter was not going to be fast enough to conjure a shield.

Resignation washed over Hunter's face as he seemed to realise this himself, and muttering a strange word under his breath, he allowed the energy to wash over him, bathing him in a cloud of brilliant white light that burned itself into Rose's eyes before dissipating, leaving Hunter unharmed.

He got to his feet wearily, deactivating the bud with a wave of his hand, and Grandpa let his own hand close beside him. The hope that had sprung up inside Rose plummeted. The shadows, the exhaustion and the crushing pressure vanished. What had happened? Was it all over?

A trickle of fear ran down her spine. The invention seemed diminished somehow, as though it had lost some important quality. She gulped and whipped around to face Grandpa.

"What happened? Did he find a way to take our magic?" Horror made her voice catch in her throat as another thought occurred to her. "Or destroy it?"

"No," Grandpa said, now shaking with fatigue. "No to both. You can't destroy energy, you can only change it from one form to another. He transformed magical energy into light energy."

Rose blinked, thinking fast. If Hunter had done away with the magic that was attacking him, did that mean the Fragmenter had now lost part of its protection? She began to ask Grandpa if the invention was now powerless, but it was Hunter himself who answered her question.

"It can still defend itself."

Rose lifted an eyebrow, regarding him in silence.

"The Fragmenter has a lot of power, but it can be exhausted. Its defences are powerful but they're not infinite, or the invention would be infinitely powerful, which would violate the rules of invention-making. Right?"

He turned to Grandpa, who sighed and turned away.

Rose's throat went dry. What was to stop Hunter from transforming the rest of the bud's defensive magic? Rose met her grandfather's eyes, conveying her thoughts without words. They needed to end this quickly.

"Try again?" she mouthed, her back to Hunter, who was now wrapping himself in layers of very familiar spells. Grandpa made a sound of contempt.

"I'm not sure that's such a good idea," he warned Hunter.

Hunter raised an eyebrow.

"And why not? Jacob and Adrian told me all about your fake city and the spells you used on that stone safe house. Enough that I think I can recreate them. Perhaps it's time to test them in the real world. According to your grandkids, the spells were very effective at holding the Fragmenter back."

He grinned at Rose as he finished casting spells, and she glared at him, wishing Matt had never told him how they'd finally overcome the invention. Grandpa's expression betrayed a hint of uneasiness as Hunter reached out for the invention again and rotated the base, calling the stored magic to him.

Rose surged to her feet as the casing darkened and light blossomed at the tips of the glass shards once more. Grandpa gave a mental tug on the bud. The invention flashed and sputtered like a broken light bulb, and Rose gave an anguished cry as magic streamed out of the glass towards Hunter. She felt Grandpa pull again, but with no defensive spells to protect it, the Fragmenter could do nothing to fend Hunter off.

Hunter reached out, and in desperation, Rose hurled herself in front of him, pushing his hand out of the way.

"I thought it still had magic!" she yelled, as Hunter

sent her staggering backwards with a spell.

"It does, but it will take time for it to gather the rest of its energy!" Grandpa cried, watching the bud flash brighter and faster in the centre of the room.

Pressure built up in the room once more, constricting Rose's chest until it was difficult to breathe. White spots burst in front of her eyes like she'd just pressed her palms into them.

Light floated into the air around the bud and hung there like a shimmering cloud, waiting. Hunter rushed towards it and Rose collided with him, blocking his path. Hunter cursed as the light seemed to give up, coursing back into the invention.

The energy in the room contracted around them and the Fragmenter flared to life. It raged around Hunter, still powerful, but noticeably weaker than before. Whispering filled the room and the temperature dropped dramatically.

"Oh no, not mind magic again," Rose pleaded, dreading what the bud was going to inflict upon them this time.

Grandpa groaned, his head in his hands. The rustling, whispering sound grew louder until it became a howl, filling Rose's ears as the bud failed to fight Hunter off. Gashes appeared on her face and neck, and she flung her arms up for protection.

Raising her head a fraction, she saw that Grandpa was suffering the same fate. Her eyes then travelled to Hunter. She scowled. He remained unharmed, standing beside the bud with one hand outstretched.

Rose noted with grim satisfaction that, while the safe spells protected him from the physical damage caused by the Fragmenter, they appeared to be entirely useless against the mental effects. His body was free of scratches, but he was grimacing against the pressure just as she and Grandpa were.

Grandpa didn't seem to have noticed this. His eyes were closed in concentration, and he flinched as another gash sliced down his neck. Long scratches gouged the walls and ceiling, as though some enraged, caged animal was fighting for freedom. The cracks in the walls deepened and Rose wondered if the room could withstand the invention after all.

"Yes!" Rose gasped as green roots sprouted around the base of the bud and grew towards the floor, tangling like brambles.

Weakness stole over her and she shuddered, resisting the urge to lie down on the floor and sleep. For a fleeting second Hunter seemed to run out of strength, losing his grip on the spells protecting him. Gashes appeared all over his body and blood splattered the floor before he managed to wrap the spells back around himself, gasping in pain.

Too weak now to hold herself up, Rose collapsed onto the floor as a new sensation crept over her. It was as though her body had stopped responding to her brain. She gave a strangled gasp, and panic bubbled up inside her as she grappled with the sudden loss of her limbs. Grandpa was going all out this time.

He fell forward with one arm flung out weakly to

support himself, his hands shaking as he opened his eyes, staring up at Hunter, who alone remained standing.

He was still, as unable to move as Rose was, but his face was calm and Rose could feel him casting more spells around the bud. Rose was suddenly struck by how odd this scene would look to anyone who stumbled upon them: three people motionless in a bare concrete room, with the invention growing like some alien plant in their midst.

"Almost there," choked out Grandpa in a strangled voice, blood trickling from a deep gouge above his left eye.

His hands twitched as he gave the Fragmenter the mental equivalent of a kick, and the tangle of green roots began to snake their way across the floor towards each of them. The scratching stopped and Rose and Grandpa breathed sighs of relief, bruised and aching all over.

Hunter stood rigid, panting with the effort of maintaining his protective spells, but his eyes were open and alert, watching the roots' progress. Rose lay with one cheek pressed to the concrete. If they could just keep him under control for another minute …

But Rose was closest to the bud, and she panicked as she realised that the roots would find her first. What would happen when they touched her? Would they hurt her, or would she regain her magic?

Fresh hope bloomed inside her and she dug her fingernails into the rough floor, pushing her hand forward an inch, willing to take the risk.

Hunter muttered something inaudible, his words

coming out with difficulty. The roots' growth slowed and the concrete around the Fragmenter softened, creeping up over the roots heading his way before hardening, trapping them.

Grandpa let out a snarl of anger and Rose let slip a swear word she was sure her parents had no idea she knew as she inched towards the root growing ever closer to her. The room was silent except for her ragged breathing when the root finally closed around her wrist.

She flinched as the cold metal touched her skin. The sensation of being watched by someone unseen became so strong that it was overpowering, and she attempted to turn her head, sure that if she did, she would see a shadowy form standing there, staring down at her.

She gulped, unnerved as a low hum of energy buzzed through the root gripping her. Her gaze travelled along it to the Fragmenter itself, and a desperate longing filled her. One of the glass pieces now shone more brightly than the others. Rose was more aware than ever of the missing piece of herself, reaching for her, wanting to be reconnected.

Hunter observed this exchange with a look of deep suspicion and fear. His shoulders drooped with fatigue and sweat beaded on his brow. He looked barely conscious, barely aware that one of the more determined roots had almost fought its way to him.

Almost done now, Rose thought, as the root around her wrist began to burn. Memories of her time in the fake city came back to her in a rush. The Fragmenter had used their fears to keep them incapacitated, and she realised now that this strange loss of control, this feeling of restriction and helplessness, was just another trick, this time aimed at Hunter. It was an odd feeling to be in contact with the invention, but safe from harm. The glowing glass was almost blinding now, and a deep sense of calm had come over her. Everything would be all right in a moment.

The roots were an inch from Hunter's feet when he sent a spell at the invention. It was a desperate attempt at freedom, an instinctive reaction, and just like it had when Mary had performed magic in the tower, the illusion shattered in an instant.

The invention roared to life and Hunter deactivated it hastily, backing out of reach of the roots with a groan of relief. On the opposite side of the room, the root relinquished its grip on Rose's arm. She blinked several times as though coming out of a deep sleep, yearning for the magic she had almost reclaimed. Grandpa watched the green casing of the Fragmenter weave itself back over the glass pieces, their brightness dimming as the bud slumbered.

Defeat crashed into Rose's stomach like a rock. Hunter strode across the room towards them, and tears of exhaustion and bitter disappointment brimmed in Rose's eyes. Getting to her knees, she turned to her grandfather and saw her own emotions reflected on his face. His hands shook as he pushed wispy strands of hair out of his face, looking utterly spent.

Hunter stood before Grandpa, frowning down at him, and Grandpa, sensing danger, held up his hands innocently.

"Don't look at me! You took my magic away, remember?"

Hunter scowled.

"I don't know how you're doing it, but it stops here," he declared, grabbing hold of Grandpa's arm and starting to pull him away towards the base of the well.

Rose scrambled up in an instant. She knew now what she had to do. Bending down, she grasped a knife-like piece of metal from the nearest broken torch in her hand and hesitated for a moment, wondering if she had the nerve to do what needed to be done. She would have to get this just right …

Hunter dragged Grandpa to the base of the ladder and Rose stepped up to the wooden trunk, driving the metal bracket deep through a gap in the Fragmenter's casing, deep into the heart of the bud.

The bud opened in response to the attack, the screech of metal on metal filling the room as Rose twisted the bracket free and retreated from the damaged invention. Hunter whirled around, the anger on his face replaced with horror.

"No!"

His voice thundered down the passage and Rose gave him a grim smile. Horrendous, unnatural amounts of thick green ooze poured out of the bud, dripping down the sides of the trunk and spreading rapidly over the floor.

Hunter turned to Rose, his eyes wide.

"What have you done?!"

Rose met Grandpa's disbelieving gaze and flung her weapon aside with a clang, confident she'd done the right thing. Hunter released Grandpa and rushed to the invention, standing as close as possible without touching the green ooze. Rose shoved him hard, forcing him sideways a step, into a tangle of creeping roots.

Hunter made a sound of annoyance as the roots took hold of his ankle, holding him there. Rose looked down at the spreading pool of green blood. Would it be as harmless to her as the roots now were?

"What happens if we touch this green stuff?" she called to Grandpa.

He shuffled over to where Hunter stood, struggling to free himself. Rose held her breath as Grandpa bent down and placed a hand into the goo. When seconds trickled by and nothing happened, he gave Rose a reassuring smile.

"It's harmless. For us," he amended. "We have no magic anymore." He turned to Hunter, his expression sombre. "Not so good for you, I'm afraid."

Hunter swore and aimed another spell at the roots holding him captive. They retreated slightly but refused to relinquish their grip. He began to work his foot free, but Rose stepped forward again, pushing Hunter until he fell to his knees in the green ooze, allowing more roots to take hold of him.

He surged to his feet at once, but Grandpa shoved him back down. In no time at all, the Fragmenter had begun its curse, and Rose fought to keep Hunter down as weariness crept over her yet again.

"He can't use a travel spell from here, can he?" she asked Grandpa, as the roots wound themselves around Hunter's waist.

Grandpa shook his head.

"No, he only took me as far as the top of the well by magic. You've got to climb to get in or out."

Satisfied that Hunter could not use magic to escape, Rose braced herself on the tangle of roots surrounding the bud as Hunter tried to throw them off. They showed no interest in either Rose or Grandpa now that they had found a victim, and Hunter strained against the roots pinning his arms to his sides. He looked at the bud and the light gathering at the tips of the glass pieces.

"You won't be able to deactivate it now," said Grandpa, leaning wearily against the trunk, ignoring the ooze flowing over him. He let go of Hunter and inspected the damage to the invention.

"She's activated the healing process. It has to protect the energy stored inside it."

"But it can't use a person to heal itself!" snarled Hunter, still fighting to free himself.

"No, but it will take and store the magic of anyone it thinks is a threat to it," replied Rose.

Devastation filled Hunter's face as he realised there was no escape. Rose released him and waded through the growing pool of sludge. She stood beside Grandpa, resting her head on his shoulder as exhaustion finally won. Hunter slumped against the roots holding him, his head lolling.

Grandpa left the pool of green blood and sat with

his back to the wall, patting the ground beside him. Rose smiled and curled up at his side, allowing the Fragmenter's magic to wash over her. Hunter fell against the trunk, unconscious, and Rose felt her eyelids droop, dimly aware of Grandpa wrapping a comforting arm around her before she knew no more.

27

The Fragmenter's End

Rose's eyes opened with a start. She looked to her left, where Grandpa sat beside her. His arm had fallen to the floor and his face was peaceful, almost as though he were asleep. Rose shook him gently, calling his name.

"Grandpa, wake up! We did it!"

There was no response. Rose clambered awkwardly to her feet. Remembering what Mum had told her about keeping warm after being exposed to the Fragmenter's curse, she removed her jacket and did her best to wrap it around her grandfather. When it was secure around his shoulders, she settled herself back under his arm, gazing around the room.

Hunter lay where he had fallen, draped over the wooden chest. The roots had relinquished their grip on him, retreating into the Fragmenter once the healing process had run its course. The invention remained broken, having found no suitable source of magic for its repairs, and Rose peered across Hunter's unconscious form to the glass pieces, seven of which now shone with bright white light.

Soon Grandpa began to stir, and Rose let her breath out in a rush of relief. His eyes opened slowly, and he stared at the scene in front of him for a moment before a look of triumph spread across his face.

"Finally!"

His eyes became anxious as he turned to Rose, and she grinned at him to show that she was fine.

"I guess the upside to having no magic left to lose is that we won't have much of a reaction to the Fragmenting curse," Rose remarked, grateful to have avoided the weakness and nausea she'd experienced last time.

"Hunter won't be so lucky," Grandpa replied.

He got to his feet and approached the Fragmenter, his fingers brushing the glass pieces as he inspected them more closely. Rose stood beside him, looking down at Hunter.

"I guess we should move him out of here before he wakes up."

Grandpa agreed and they each took hold of an arm. Together they dragged him along the tunnel to the base of the well, leaving a trail of green ooze behind them. Rose stopped beside the ladder, looking up at the circle of blue sky above her.

"Er, maybe I should go up on my own first," she said. "I can go back to the basement and borrow Alison's phone. If I take it far enough away from the house I should be able to call Miranda to remove those bars."

She turned to Grandpa to see what he thought of this plan, and he nodded.

"We should restrain Hunter as soon as possible. When he wakes he'll try to reverse the Fragmenting curse unless we stop him."

Rose put a foot on the bottom rung of the ladder and began to climb.

"I'll be quick."

She reached the top of the well and swung a leg over the side, stumbling out onto the grass. She sprinted towards the house, ignoring the long grass stalks whipping her legs and hands, and hurtled over the threshold, sending the front door crashing against the wall.

Darting into the room full of experiments, she raced along the hall and down the steps to the basement, calling out as she ran, "Mum! Dad! We got the bud to take Hunter out for us!"

There was a flurry of movement and Matt, Dad and Alison rushed over. Rose gripped the bars with trembling fingers, suddenly caught between laughter and fear that Hunter would wake up before he could be restrained.

"What!?" gasped Alison. "You did it?"

"You found your grandpa?" Mum asked, standing behind Matt, who looked dumbfounded.

"Awesome!" cried Mary, wriggling in beside her brother.

Rose nodded, beaming at them all. But Dad held a hand up to Rose's cheek, his blue eyes filled with concern.

"What happened? You're covered in scratches!"

"Oh, yeah," she said, glancing down at the cuts on her hands. "That was the invention. Me and Grandpa are both fine, though. I'll be able to explain everything when I get back. But we have to be quick. Hunter's still out cold but he could wake up at any moment and reverse the spell. Grandpa's watching him."

Rose turned back to Alison.

"Can I borrow your phone to call Miranda? She can get you all out of here."

Alison handed the phone over without hesitation.

"Head for the treeline!" she called as Rose raced back up the steps. "The spells give out about there!"

"Run fast, Rose!" Matt yelled, his voice full of urgency.

Rose ran out into the fields, heading downhill towards the river. She turned the phone on as the sound of rushing water grew louder. She stopped at the trees and gave a delighted whoop as the phone booted up. She found Miranda's number and dialled.

Miranda answered on the second ring and Rose explained the situation in a rush. The older woman seemed shocked at the tale and agreed to use a travel spell to meet Rose where she stood. She appeared seconds later and grinned as she caught sight of Rose.

"I knew you could do it!" she cried, pulling her into a quick hug before turning to stare at the house among the fields. "So this is where your family's been all this time?"

She sighed and hurried after Rose, who led the way back to the well.

"Alison and I were so close to this spot, so many times! We were sure something must be nearby, but the disguise and illusion spells kept pushing us off course!"

She looked furious with herself as she followed Rose through the grass.

"How did you even find the well?" she asked, peering out over the seemingly empty fields.

"I caught a glimpse of it when the Fragmenter broke the disguise spells on the grounds," Rose replied, "but I don't think I'd have realised what it was without the Viewer telling me to look there."

Arriving in the clearing, Rose put out a hand, feeling for the bricks. The well reappeared as her hand brushed it, and she and Miranda leaned over the edge, peering down into its depths. Grandpa was there, standing beside Hunter, who was mercifully still unconscious. Rose's nerves settled a little.

"Grandpa! I've got Miranda!"

Grandpa looked up and his posture relaxed.

"You'd better hurry. He's starting to come to."

Rose took a step back, allowing Miranda to break down the spells surrounding the well. A moment later, she'd appeared at Grandpa's side. Bending down, she took hold of both men before using a travel spell back to the surface.

Hunter stirred as they lowered him onto the grass. Miranda hastily conjured a chair and bound him to it with spells. His head rolled back and his brow furrowed as sunlight streamed down into his face, but he remained otherwise still as Miranda checked her spells.

"He's not going anywhere now," she declared with a satisfied smile. "It'll be safe for us to go inside and free the others. Someone should stay with him, though." She jerked her chin in Hunter's direction. "Just in case."

Rose nodded, thinking that this was a good idea.

"I'll stay this time," she offered.

She could see that Grandpa wanted to check on the rest of his family, and she had no fears now of Hunter escaping.

"It'll be OK," she insisted. "He's stuck until we let him go."

Grandpa nodded and headed for the house with Miranda. Rose watched them go, listening to the sounds of the crickets in the grass. She sat on the edge of the well, her chin propped in one hand. It wasn't long before movement caught her eye.

Hunter woke with a start. Rose watched him warily as he sat up, pulling at the spells keeping him in place. He looked down at the chair with a scowl. Closing his eyes, he took a deep breath in and then exhaled. Rose was sure she could see the memories of the bud's attack playing across his face as they returned to him. She struggled with herself for a moment, torn between triumph and pity, but she bit back the urge to gloat. Hunter was facing a lifetime without magic. That would be more than enough punishment all on its own.

Hunter's eyes opened. The colour drained from his face and he began to shiver. Taking another shuddering breath, he glanced around at the fields as though looking for a distraction.

"Where are the others?" he said in a hollow voice.

"Miranda's freeing them from the basement," replied

Rose. "Your friends are inside Grandpa's fake city. Well, everyone except for that guy who wears black, anyway. He disappeared somewhere before we could reach him."

"Adrian?" murmured Hunter, his expression souring. "Of course he did."

Hunter stared across the fields, his gaze distant. Silence descended again and Rose stood up, pacing around the well and wondering if Miranda had managed to remove the bars yet. She glanced over at the house anxiously. The place looked like it could collapse at any second.

"You know, I was impressed with the spells on your Viewer," said Hunter, taking Rose by surprise. "One of them is remarkably similar to a spell of my own."

His eyes met Rose's and she blushed.

"I guess I should thank you for that. If I hadn't seen your Illuminator thing, I'm not sure if I'd have figured out exactly how that spell was supposed to work until it was too late."

Tucking a flying strand of hair out of the way behind an ear, she bit her lip, thinking of her family.

"Matt and Mary would probably hate that I used something of yours, but I figured that it would be childish and stupid to ignore something that could help me just because *you* made it."

Hunter stopped tugging at the binding spells, apparently surprised by her answer. He sighed.

"Well, at least I achieved something," he muttered, as though to himself.

Rose raised an eyebrow, wondering if he was

mocking her, but his expression was sombre and sincere.

"That's all I ever wanted, you know, even as a kid," he said wistfully. "To add to people's knowledge of magic and to create spells that people would use." His face clouded with regret. "If I took it too far …"

"If?" repeated Rose with exasperation. But she shook her head, reminding herself of her decision not to crow. "To be honest, I wasn't sure I'd managed to do the spell properly. I couldn't quite figure out how to make it work the first few times. It's similar to the normal dissolution spell, but different at the same time."

Hunter managed a faint smile.

"If your Viewer could see through all the disguises around this place, you got the spell right. But it'll only work if you leave your mind open to the possibilities, letting the spell be what it needs to be rather than what you think it should be. That's the problem with using the spell only to block or remove magic, when it can do so much more."

Rose considered this in silence, not entirely sure she understood. Some of her uncertainty must have shown on her face.

Hunter sighed again and said, "The only thing that will stop you from mastering the spell is your belief that you can't, or shouldn't. It's the same with invention-making. Sometimes the best inventions are the ones that seem impossible at first."

Rose wasn't sure what to say to this, but she was saved from answering by signs of movement at the front of the house. Shielding her eyes with a hand, she broke into a grin as Matt and Mary charged through the front door, their voices carrying across the fields, laughing and whooping with victory.

Rose glanced briefly at Hunter and then ran to meet them. She arrived at Matt's side, out of breath as Mum, Dad and Alison emerged, looking heartily relieved to be out of the basement. Miranda and Ben appeared seconds later, materialising on the grass, far enough away from the house that Ben would be safe if it collapsed.

"Rose, guess what?" trilled Mary as the adults gathered around him. Rose rolled her eyes but grinned at her sister.

"What?"

"Miranda took out that guy in black!" Mary informed her. "He was waiting for us when Miranda let us out."

"It was great, you should've seen it!" laughed Matt. "By the time she was done with him, he looked like he was made of putty."

Rose blinked, shocked. She looked at Miranda but struggled to imagine her doing anything violent.

"Where is he now, then? Did you put him in the fake city?"

Matt's grin grew wider.

"Of course!"

"Well, I'm glad Miranda caught him," remarked Rose. "You know, in his own way, I think he's worse than Hunter. And he always gave me the creeps."

She pulled a face and Mary laughed. The three of them looked up as Mum called their names, and they turned their backs on the crumbling house. Rose returned Alison's phone with a word of thanks and then joined the adults standing in a huddle, close to where Hunter sat. Listening to her grandfather, she realised they were discussing what had happened inside the well.

Alison magicked the Fragmenter out of the underground room while they talked, and Grandpa held it in his hands, wiping green ooze from the metal casing. Matt and Mary stared at the bud in horror.

"We'll still be able to get our magic back, won't we?" asked Mary in a wavering voice.

Grandpa gave her a reassuring smile.

"Hunter needed the bud intact to transfer the magic to someone it doesn't belong to, but as long as the glass pieces are unbroken it will be able to release our magic to us, and the spells on the Fragmenter are mostly intact. Rose only damaged it enough to trigger the healing process. It'll be able to perform the unification spell. The question is what are we going to do with Hunter's magic?"

Matt gave Grandpa a questioning look.

"What do you mean? We're not giving it back, are we?"

Grandpa weighed the invention in his hands.

"No, I don't think so. He's lost his magic and now he's going to prison. But when we release the magic stored inside the Fragmenter, it will give up all of it, not just ours."

Matt's face flushed with outrage and Grandpa added in a hurry, "But I have a way to fix that."

He twisted the braided base of the invention clockwise and the glass pieces loosened. Plucking a single shining shard from the cluster, he held it out for the others to see.

"What we need to decide is whether to break this and destroy his magic permanently, or to lock it away intact somewhere out of his reach, giving him the possibility of a second chance one day."

"No way!" cried Mary at once, folding her arms across her chest.

But Grandpa's face was grave as he turned the shard over. Rose glanced around at the uneasy expressions on her parents' and Alison's faces. Rose thought about Grandpa's words. Surely everyone deserved a second chance? She knew what she would choose for herself if she were in Hunter's place …

"I guess we'd be as bad as him and his friends if we took someone's magic away forever, even if that person is Hunter," Matt mumbled, glowering in the man's direction.

Alison regarded Hunter for a long moment, doubt etched into her features.

"If he doesn't change his ways, I suppose we can just keep his magic hidden."

Mum and Dad glanced at each other before nodding, and Miranda gave Grandpa a meaningful look.

"I'm sure we could find somewhere to keep the shard safe. There are places in the Archives nobody else knows about. Not even *him*."

She indicated Hunter, slumped in his chair. Grandpa

gave the glass shard to Miranda, looking satisfied.

"Well, that's taken care of. Now all we need to do is call the police and see to Ben. Then we can take our magic back finally."

Rose turned to look at Ben, lying still beside them, and a chill ran down her spine.

"We had no luck finding a magical doctor when I got hurt. If it wasn't for Nate I'd probably have lost the use of my whole arm by now. Maybe we could ask him to look at Ben, too?"

She flexed her fingers instinctively, feeling another rush of gratitude towards Nate and trying not to think about the condition she might be in right now if things had been different.

"I'm sure he'll be happy to help Ben," Alison assured her. "It wouldn't be the first time," she added with a chuckle.

"Nate was the best supervisor the Archives ever had," said Miranda with fierce pride. "His medical knowledge combined with his genuine care for the other Archivists made him popular with everyone, including Ben. And I have to admit, I'd be relieved to have someone with Nate's experience looking after him."

Alison pulled her phone out of her pocket again.

"I'll go and call Nate and the police. Then we can all go home."

She turned and headed for the trees, her curly hair like a tumbleweed in the wind. Rose craned her neck to see across the fields, watching as Alison stopped beside the river. In no time at all, people in blue uniforms appeared at her side, the red emblem on their breasts flashing in the sunlight, identifying them as the magical members of the police.

Alison led them towards the well, where Hunter continued to strain at the spells holding him down. As they approached, however, he seemed to realise that time was up. Falling still, he watched them draw closer.

Rose knew that the loss of his magic must have been hard on him, and she once again fought back feelings of pity as a pair of officers released him from the chair. He scowled but remained silent as they handcuffed him and broke down the spells surrounding the house and grounds. His grey eyes found the invention in Grandpa's hands, and his face filled with longing.

"Why don't they just take him over to the trees, so they can use a travel spell from there?" asked Mary, coming to stand beside Rose as the whole party watched. Rose's lips twitched in amusement.

"They've been waiting to bring him in for a long time," she said. "I'm guessing they're unwilling to risk him escaping into the grass on the way to the treeline. They'd rather break the spells so they can take him away from here."

"Can't say I blame them," remarked Matt with a snort of laughter.

A moment later the trio had disappeared, and Alison approached the remaining officers, the silver archway gleaming in her hand.

"They're going to have their work cut out for them, sorting through everything in the house," said Rose.

"Especially as a lot of the stuff in there has got magic no one's ever seen before."

"Not to mention Hunter's rooms in the Archives," Matt reminded her with a grin.

Miranda approached them while Alison spoke to the police about the archway and its contents.

"I'm going to take Ben to Nate now. I can take you all home, too, if you like," she said. "The police say they'll examine the Fragmenter and get statements from you later. Ben's not the only one who needs to rest and recover." She looked particularly hard at Grandpa. "You've been locked up for more than two months."

Grandpa grimaced.

"It would be wonderful to be back at home. I think I'll have about as much work repairing all the damage to my own house as the police will have to fix up this place here, just so that they can search it."

He gave a rueful laugh and Mum leaned her head on his shoulder.

"We'll fix it, and in the meantime you'll come and stay with us," she said in a tone that made it clear that there would be no arguments.

They all gathered around Miranda, Grandpa holding the remains of the Fragmenter tightly in one hand. Rose took one last look at the lonely house among the fields and the river bubbling in the distance before closing her eyes. She was finally going home.

The ground changed under her feet and Rose found herself standing in the driveway. Matt and Mary laughed delightedly and ran to the front door.

"I'll let you all settle in," said Miranda with a smile. "Call if you need anything."

Grandpa thanked her for her help and she disappeared with a wave.

"Let's get our magic back!" sang Mary, jumping up and down on the doorstep.

"OK, settle down, we're coming," Dad laughed, searching for the spare key hidden behind the lamp. Mary charged inside as soon as the door opened and Grandpa directed everyone into the living room.

"Are you sure this is going to work?" asked Matt, a hint of worry in his voice.

Grandpa placed the Fragmenter on the coffee table and activated it.

"It will work. The glass pieces are undamaged. That's the most important thing."

Grandpa settled himself in an armchair while Mary squeezed herself onto the sofa between Rose and her father.

"Wait, don't we have to rotate the base of the bud to release our magic?" asked Rose, looking at Grandpa. "That's what Hunter did …"

Grandpa shook his head.

"Hunter was making use of the purging function of the invention so that he could release the magic without giving it back to us," he said simply. "It's only supposed to be used if the bud has stripped magic from something that could be harmful to the rest of the magic stored inside it. It's a bit like an emergency release function, but it leaves the user with more control."

"Oh." Rose settled back down, once again impressed by the level of detail Grandpa put into his creations.

"So how do we get the bud to give us our magic back, then?" asked Matt, sitting sandwiched between his mother and Rose.

"All we have to do is activate it and let it do it's thing," replied Grandpa, putting his feet up.

They waited in silence as the casing unravelled, the scratches from Rose's attack illuminated by the bright light that surged out of the glass pieces, surrounding the invention like a halo. In no time at all, she felt herself drifting off to sleep again. Warmth flooded her body as familiar energy coursed through her, and she relaxed, welcoming it back.

Rose ran down the hall as Mum called to her from downstairs. It had been two days since Miranda had taken them all home and Rose was rapidly readjusting to having her abilities back. She used a travel spell downstairs, just to prove to herself that she could, arriving in the living room to find Alison, Ben and Nate gathered around the coffee table alongside her family.

Nate had used his spellmaking skills to heal Ben in record time, and had assured them all that the young man would make a complete recovery. Ben sat in one of the armchairs, wincing slightly whenever he moved and clutching at his side where Hunter had hit him with the mysterious curse. But he seemed to be in good spirits, and his usual grin soon returned as Alison told him the story of how Hunter had been beaten at last.

Mum opened the front door and stood back to let Grandpa and Miranda inside, ushering them into the living room where the rest of the group looked up eagerly.

"How did it go?" said Rose breathlessly. "What did the lawyers and government officials say?"

Grandpa took a seat beside Nate and set the briefcase he'd been carrying on the coffee table. He and Nate had gotten on like old friends from the moment they'd been introduced, ensconcing themselves in the corner for most of the morning before the meeting to discuss various aspects of magic.

Now, however, Grandpa's expression was grave. Flipping the clasps, he opened the case and showed the room a stack of paperwork beside the Fragmenter. It remained broken, Grandpa having refused to repair it, claiming that it should never have been made.

"Well," he said, as Mum conjured a chair for Miranda and Rose perched herself on the armrest of the sofa. "It didn't go quite as we'd hoped. The government has agreed to let me destroy the invention on one condition: that Hunter's magical friends receive the same treatment as Hunter himself. I argued that the Fragmenter posed a serious risk to people's health and safety, like I should have done the last time they approached me, but they didn't seem to take me seriously."

"All five shards containing magic have been transported to the Archives, to be kept in a secure location," said Miranda, her hands fidgeting in her lap.

"We argued again that Hunter's friends should keep their magic, seeing as Hunter is unable to free them now anyway, but we had little say in the matter."

"Hold on," said Ben, peering into the case where the bud lay, now short of five glass pieces. "So it's already been done? They've already had their magic taken from them?"

Grandpa nodded, his expression solemn.

"The officials took the bud down to the holding cells as soon as they were satisfied that it was still functional."

Rose glanced at the stony faces of her family, faintly alarmed at the government's determination to essentially maim four people who were already imprisoned. Hadn't her family's experiences shown the officials just how dangerous the Fragmenter's curse could be?

"But it's so unnecessary!" she cried, eyeing the invention with disapproval. "What if it actually killed one of them? They'd have died for no reason! Like Miranda said, even *with* their abilities they can't break the spells holding them in! They don't know the commands!"

Grandpa sighed and ran a hand through his wispy hair.

"I agree. It is unnecessary. But it was the only way I could get the government to agree to the Fragmenter being destroyed permanently. At the very least, the possibility remains that Hunter and his friends could have their magic returned to them one day. We'll have to content ourselves with that."

There was a tense silence until Grandpa spoke again.

"So the only thing left to do now is to destroy the invention."

Getting to his feet, he lifted the bud out of the case and placed it on the coffee table, regarding it with a mixture of sadness and grim satisfaction.

"Are we all ready?"

He turned to the rest of the group. Everyone murmured and nodded, and Matt leaned forward in his chair.

"Let's get this over with. We've all waited long enough!"

Grandpa shot him a quelling look as he produced the report that documented the invention's construction. He turned to the last page and wrote a few lines in his neat, flowing handwriting.

"I need witnesses to confirm that the Fragmenter has been destroyed," he gestured towards Miranda, Alison, Ben and Nate, "and to complete the documentation." He held up the report in his hand. "In any case," he continued, "I'll be glad to have your help if this goes badly."

Placing the report on the table, he picked up the bud instead, holding it firmly in both hands. The room was still, and Rose leaned forward to watch as he began to demolish the invention.

With a wave of his hand, Grandpa activated the invention and, working quickly, severed the connection between the bud and its defensive magic. The remaining glass pieces cracked with a sharp *snap*. The casing unravelled completely, its movements becoming slower and more clumsy as Grandpa removed the spells that animated it. A bruise-like purple colour spread up from the base of the bud and magic seeped out, dissipating into the room. Finally, at long last, the casing collapsed outwards onto the tabletop, nothing more than twisted pieces of metal.

"Well, that's done," said Grandpa, sweeping the materials up into a pile and vanishing them. "Now we just need to deal with the paperwork."

He signed his name with a flourish at the bottom of the report before turning to the stack of papers. He then passed the lot to Miranda, Alison, Ben and Nate so that they could do the same.

Rose followed the proceedings with relief. It was finally done. She had her family and her magic back, and she was grateful. The rest of the group moved into the dining room for lunch and Rose ran to collect the report she'd begun on the construction of her Viewer.

She'd decided that completing a report would be the most appropriate way to document each step of her work, and she'd spread her work out across the dining room table so that Grandpa could show her how to complete each section.

She'd come clean to her family about using Hunter's dissolution spell on her Viewer, cringing at the outrage on her siblings' faces. Mum, Dad and Grandpa, however, had merely laughed.

"Why on earth would it matter which version of the spell you used?" remarked Grandpa, his eyes full of mirth. "The important thing is that you succeeded in making the invention you set out to make."

"I suppose so," replied Rose, feeling rather foolish for worrying.

"But it's *Hunter's* spell!" Mary cried, looking at the Viewer with disappointment. "On *your* invention!"

Rose rolled her eyes.

"Imagine what might have happened if your sister hadn't used the spell," insisted Mum, as Matt and Mary continued to give their grandfather dubious looks. "It would be silly not to use it when it could be so useful. She might not have found the well in time to stop Hunter from taking our magic. Besides, now that she's mastered one version of the spell, she'll find it much easier to use the standard version."

Mary thought about this in silence for a moment, her lips pressed into a hard line.

"I guess you're right," she admitted. "Maybe it's not so bad after all …"

Rose smiled inwardly as she gathered up the invention and her notes and made her way back to her room with Cocoa at her heels. Matt folded his arms across his chest and gave her a shrewd look as she passed him.

"I suppose you're going to take that apart now and complain that it's not good enough?"

But Rose shook her head, clutching the invention to her chest.

"No, I think I'm going to keep this one," she told him.

Retreating into the quiet of her bedroom, she reached up and placed the Viewer on the shelf above her bed, standing back to admire it. She'd begun to have ideas about the next invention she wanted to make. She hadn't figured out the details, but she was in no hurry to rush the process this time. The answers would come when they were ready, and she was excited to see where they would lead her.

Taking one last satisfied look at the Viewer, she picked up her pencil and sketchbook before heading back downstairs to join her family.

www.ingramcontent.com/pod-product-compliance
Lightning Source LLC
Chambersburg PA
CBHW070838020826
48982CB00022B/1479/J

* 9 7 8 0 6 4 6 7 1 5 8 9 6 *